IN THE BEGINNING...

DOCTOR BRUCE BANNER WAS ONCE A BRILLIANT NUCLEAR PHYSICIST WORKING FOR THE UNITED STATES GOVERNMENT.

DURING A TEST DETONATION OF A GAMMA BOMB HE DESIGNED, HE NOTICED A TEENAGER HAD SNUCK ONTO THE TEST SITE. REALISING THE BOY WOULD BE KILLED, BANNER RUSHED OUT AND PUSHED HIM INTO A PROTECTIVE TRENCH SECONDS BEFORE THE BOMB WAS DETONATED.

Dr. Bruce Banner

UNFORTUNATELY, BRUCE WAS CAUGHT IN THE WAKE OF THE BLAST, AND WAS SUBJECTED TO HIGH LEVELS OF **GAMMA RADIATION**. INSTEAD OF BEING KILLED BY THE BOMB, BRUCE BANNER NOW FINDS HIMSELF TRANSFORMED INTO THE **HULK** WHENEVER HE BECOMES **STRESSED** OR **ANNOYED**.

WAIT! WHAT'S THAT? GOOD LORD. IT'S A BOY!

A TEENAGER! HE'S DRIVING INTO THE TEST AREA!

CURRENTLY BRUCE IS A FUGITIVE, HUNTED BY THE MAN HE USED TO WORK FOR -- GENERAL ROSS, AND HIS HULKBUSTERS -- DESPERATELY TRYING TO FIND A CURE FOR HIS CONDITION! WHILE HIS ALTER-EGO, THE HULK, CONTINUES TO BE AN UNSTOPPABLE ENGINE OF DESTRUCTION...

REMEMBER: DON'T MAKE HIM ANGRY...
YOU WON'T LIKE HIM WHEN HE'S AN**GRY**!

IN THIS ANNUAL...

HULK HISTORY!
LEARN ABOUT THE HULK'S TROUBLED PAST...

£6.99

HULK HISTORY!

MOTHER, WHERE ARE WE GOING?

AWAY, SWEETHEART. FINISH PACKING QUICKLY.

ROBERT BRUCE BANNER HAD A VERY UNHAPPY CHILDHOOD GROWING UP ON AN ARMY BASE, WHERE HIS DAD, BRIAN BANNER, WAS AN ATOMIC SCIENTIST. ALTHOUGH HE WAS DEEPLY LOVED BY HIS MUM, HIS FATHER, WHO WAS AN ALCOHOLIC, GREW JEALOUS OF BRUCE'S RELATIONSHIP WITH HIS MOTHER.

EVENTUALLY, BRIAN MURDERED HIS WIFE, REBECCA, AND WAS PLACED IN A MENTAL HOSPITAL. BRUCE WENT TO LIVE WITH HIS AUNT, WHERE HE WAS AN INTELLIGENT, BUT HIGHLY **WITHDRAWN** AND **UNHAPPY** CHILD.

AS AN ADULT, BANNER THREW HIMSELF INTO HIS WORK AND BECAME A GENIUS IN **NUCLEAR PHYSICS**. HE WENT TO WORK AT A UNITED STATES DEFENCE DEPARTMENT NUCLEAR RESEARCH FACILITY AT DESERT BASE.

ARE YOU OKAY, BABE? YOUR FORE-HEAD'S AWFULLY WARM--

I THINK I HAD A BAD DREAM.

THERE HE WORKED UNDER GENERAL THADDEUS "THUNDERBOLT" ROSS, THE HARD-NOSED COMMANDER OF THE BASE. HE ALSO MET GENERAL ROSS' DAUGHTER, BETTY ROSS, WHO HE INSTANTLY FELL IN LOVE WITH AND LATER MARRIED.

General Ross.

BRUCE'S LIFE WAS GOING WELL, UNTIL THAT FATEFUL DAY WHEN A TEENAGER CALLED **RICK JONES** SNUCK ONTO THE TEST SITE MINUTES BEFORE A GAMMA BOMB WAS TO BE TESTED, AND BRUCE WAS CAUGHT UP IN THE EXPLOSION SAVING HIM...

BECAUSE OF AN UNKNOWN GENETIC FACTOR IN BANNER'S BODY, HE WAS NOT KILLED BY THE GAMMA RADIATION. INSTEAD, THE HULK WAS BORN -- A 7 FOOT GREEN GIANT, FULL OF FURY, AND THE MOST POWERFUL CREATURE TO EVER WALK THE EARTH!

RRAAAARRGH!

THE TIME: NEARLY SIX YEARS AGO. A MORE INNOCENT TIME, PERHAPS...

...BUT NO LESS TUMULTUOUS!

A MENACE TO THIS GREAT COUNTRY WE ALL LOVE AND SERVE, AND QUITE POSSIBLY--THE ENTIRE WORLD!

Stan Lee Presents...

THE RAMPAGING HULK

A Journey Into The Past of The World's Strongest Mortal!

"THE MONSTER OR THE MAN?"

Brought to you by...

GLENN GREENBERG - writer
RICK LEONARDI - penciller
DAN GREEN - inker
TOM SMITH - colorist
BILL OAKLEY - letterer
JAYE GARDNER - editor
BOB HARRAS - editor in chief

FOR THOSE OF YOU WHO DON'T ALREADY KNOW ME, I'M GENERAL THADDEUS ROSS--

--AND I'VE BEEN CHASING DOWN THIS MAN-MONSTER SINCE HE FIRST APPEARED!

7

THOSE OF YOU WHO *DO* KNOW ME KNOW THAT I'M NOT ONE FOR *MELODRAMA*--

"THIS COMMAND CENTER-- CODE NAMED *GAMMA BASE*--WAS FORMED BY THE U.S. GOVERNMENT WITH THE INTENTION OF CAPTURING AND CONTAIN- ING THE CREATURE!

--SO YOU'LL BELIEVE ME WHEN I TELL YOU THAT THE HULK IS ARGUABLY THE MOST POWERFUL--AND *DANGEROUS*-- CREATURE TO EVER WALK THE EARTH!

"OUR GOAL IS TO *STUDY* HIM, SEE WHAT LESSONS CAN BE LEARNED FROM HIS AMAZING *PHYSIOLOGY*--HIS *INVULNERABILITY* AND HIS *HEALING POWER*--"

--AND DETERMINE IF THEY CAN BE APPLIED TO MEDICAL SCIENCE AND TO GIVE OUR ARMED FORCES A NEW *EDGE*.

THAT'S THE *GOAL*. BUT THE TRUTH IS, WE MAY VERY WELL HAVE TO WORK TO *DESTROY* HIM, TO PREVENT ANY MORE OF HIS DESTRUCTIVE *RAMPAGES*!

...MAJOR GLENN TALBOT.

THANK YOU, SIR.

GENERAL ROSS HAS ASKED ME TO EXPLAIN THE HISTORY AND FACTS OF THIS MATTER.

AT THIS TIME, I'LL TURN THE FLOOR OVER TO MY SECOND-IN COMMAND...

WELL, THE STORY OF THE HULK BEGINS WITH ONE OF THIS NATION'S GREATEST *SCIENTISTS*--

"--DOCTOR ROBERT BRUCE BANNER.

"DR. BANNER WAS CAUGHT IN THE BLAST OF THE *GAMMA BOMB* THAT HE HIMSELF HAD CREATED FOR THE U.S. MILITARY..."

"...WHEN, DURING THE FINAL COUNTDOWN OF ITS INITIAL TESTING, HE RAN OUT TO SAVE A TEENAGER NAMED *RICK JONES*, WHO HAD UNWITTINGLY DRIVEN ON TO THE TEST SITE!"

...YOU'RE MY DARKEST IMPULSES, EVERYTHING THAT I'VE ALWAYS TRIED TO BURY AND HIDE FROM THE WORLD!

EVERYTHING I EVER HATED ABOUT MY *FATHER!*

OOF!

HOW--HOW CAN PUNY BANNER BE SO *STRONG?!*

RICK JONES--OUR ONLY FRIEND IN THE *WORLD*--LEFT BECAUSE OF HOW *OUT-OF-CONTROL* YOU'D BECOME!

AND IT'S BECAUSE OF *YOU*--THAT I LOST *BETTY!*

ALL...BECAUSE... OF...YOU!!

BECAUSE OF HULK...?

NO!! RICK AND BETTY WERE HULK'S *FRIENDS*--AND YOU DROVE THEM *AWAY* FROM HULK! *YOU!*

YOU AND YOUR BIG WORDS AND STUPID *MACHINES!*

AWLP!

HULK HATES YOU, BANNER! AND NOW...

...HULK WILL SMASH YOU TO *BITS!*

ELSEWHERE...

RAARGH!

NO WAIT--HE'S STARTING TO LOOK MORE LIKE THE *HULK* NOW!

WHAT IN BLAZES IS GOING *ON* IN THERE?!

23

WH-WHAT IS *HAPPENING* TO ME? HARD TO THINK--TO *CONCENTRATE!* FEEL LIKE MY MIND IS--*SHUTTING DOWN!*

WHAT--IS HAPPENING-- TO HULK? FEEL-- *STRANGE!*

YOU FEEL IT TOO, HUH? BUT WHAT DOES IT *MEAN?*

WAIT A MINUTE! *LOOK* AT US! WE'RE *FADING AWAY! BOTH* OF US!

LISTEN TO ME! I THINK I UNDERSTAND WHAT'S GOING ON HERE!

OUR BODY CAN NO LONGER TAKE THE STRAIN OF BEING STUCK IN MID-TRANS- FORMATION! IT'S GIVING OUT!

IT HAS TO BE ONE OR THE OTHER--YOU OR ME! WE HAVE TO STOP THIS *FIGHTING!* YOU HAVE TO LET ME TAKE *CONTROL--*

--OR WE'LL BOTH *DIE!*

YOU LIE! THIS IS A TRICK TO DESTROY HULK! BUT YOU WON'T FOOL HULK, BANNER!

YOU WON'T TRAP HULK IN *DARKNESS* AGAIN!

HE WON'T COOPERATE! WON'T STOP FIGHTING ME! HAVE TO SUMMON UP EVERY LAST OUNCE OF MY WILL--

--TO CONQUER *HIS!*

I'M *LOSING* HIM!

GOD HELP ME, BUT I CAN'T HELP BUT *WONDER*--WOULD BANNER'S DEATH BRING ME AND BETTY CLOSER *TOGETHER--*

OR JUST DRIVE US COMPLETELY *APART?*

THIS...THIS ISN'T THE WAY I THOUGHT IT WOULD END...

LOOK! HIS CONDITION IS *STABILIZING!* HIS BODY'S FINALLY CHOOSING A *FORM!*

THANK GOD!

UH...

...I DON'T *THINK SO!* EVERYBODY OUT OF THE CELL! *OUT!!*

DAD, WHAT--?

IS THE DOOR SEALED?

TIGHT AS A *DRUM,* SIR!

UH-OH...

WHO LOCKED HULK IN STUPID CELL?!

BANNER PUT UP A GOOD FIGHT...BUT HE ULTIMATELY *LOST.*

HUHN? *ROSS?!* SO *YOU'RE* THE ONE WHO'S TRIED TO CAPTURE HULK!

YOU AND BANNER *TOGETHER!* BUT HULK *CAN'T* BE CAPTURED!

WHUMP

KRAK

--HULK SMASHES!!

HAH! HULK IS FREE!

WHUMP
WHUMP
WHUMP
WHUMP
WHUMP

KRKLLL

WHUMP
KRAK
WHUMP
KRR--
WHUMP

KRAKLE--

FWA-BOOOM!

INSIDE...

...I'LL MOBILIZE THE TROOPS, SIR! WE'LL GO AFTER HIM AT ONCE!

THE KID GLOVES ARE OFF FROM NOW ON, TALBOT! THAT MONSTER HAS TO BE BROUGHT DOWN!

BY ANY MEANS NECESSARY!

WITHIN MINUTES, MAJOR GLENN TALBOT WILL LEAD THE ELITE FORCES OF GAMMA BASE INTO THE DESERT TO SEARCH FOR THE GAMMA-SPAWNED CREATURE.

BUT DEEP DOWN, HE ALREADY KNOWS THAT THIS WILL BE A FUTILE EFFORT...

TAKE COVER!

WE'VE TURNED BACK THE TIME TO SEE IF YOU COULD SAVE DR BRUCE BANNER FROM EVER BEING EXPOSED TO HIGH LEVELS OF GAMMA RADIATION, WHICH TURNED HIM INTO THE HULK...

WAIT! WHAT'S THAT? GOOD LORD... IT'S A BOY!

A TEENAGER! HE'S DRIVING INTO THE TEST AREA!

THE BOMB IS ABOUT TO BE DETONATED, AND BANNER NEEDS TO GET INTO A SAFETY TRENCH FAST! CAN YOU HELP? MEASURE THE PATHS FROM BRUCE TO EACH BUNKER WITH A PIECE OF STRING -- TO FIND THE CLOSEST ONE TO HIM!

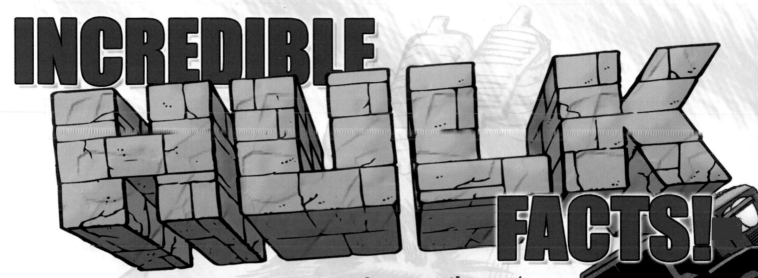

INCREDIBLE HULK FACTS!

When Banner turns into the Hulk, he becomes the most powerful man-monster to walk the earth. However, when he gets really stressed out, he becomes one of the strongest beings in the entire universe!! Read on to find out more...

FULLY LOADED, THE TANKER WEIGHS FORTY TONS.

IT MIGHT AS WELL WEIGH AS MANY OUNCES!

THE INCREDIBLE HULK

Strength: *Superhuman class 100*
Speed: *Enhanced human*
Stamina: *Meta-human*
Durability: *Demi-godlike*
Weakness: *Occasionally changes back to puny Banner!*
Characteristics: *Likes to get angry and smash things!!*

SUPERHUMAN STRENGTH!

THE HULK HAS A SUPERHUMAN CLASS 100 STRENGTH LEVEL, WHICH MEANS HE CAN LIFT MORE THAN 100-TONNES. HOWEVER, BECAUSE HIS STRENGTH INCREASES DURING TIMES OF FEAR, RAGE, OR STRESS, THE HULK HAS ALMOST IMMEASURABLE PHYSICAL POWER!

ONE GIANT LEAP!

HIS SUPER-STRONG LEG MUSCLES ENABLE THE HULK TO LEAP OVER HUGE DISTANCES, AND HE HAS BEEN KNOWN TO COVER THREE MILES IN A SINGLE JUMP!

HEALTHY HULK!

THE HULK ALSO HAS SUPERHUMAN RESISTANCE TO INJURY, PAIN AND DISEASE. HIS SKIN IS CAPABLE OF WITHSTANDING INTENSE HEAT WITHOUT BLISTERING, GREAT COLD WITHOUT FREEZING AND HUGE IMPACTS, LIKE A DIRECT HIT FROM A FIELD ARTILLERY CANNON, WITHOUT DAMAGE! HOWEVER, HE WOULD NOT BE ABLE TO SURVIVE A NEAR HIT FROM A NUCLEAR MISSILE!

DR BRUCE BANNER MAY BE A GENIUS IN NUCLEAR PHYSICS, BUT AS THE HULK HE HAS A MUCH LOWER INTELLIGENCE LEVEL, SIMILAR TO THAT OF A SMALL CHILD!

HULKBUSTERS!

HULK'S TERRIBLE TEMPER TANTRUMS CAUSED HIM TO BE CLASSED AS A MENACE, AND THE U.S. GOVERNMENT SET UP A TASK FORCE CALLED THE HULKBUSTERS, WHOSE PRIMARY OBJECTIVE IS THE CAPTURE, OR DESTRUCTION OF THE HULK.

LED BY GENERAL ROSS, THE MAN BRUCE BANNER USED TO WORK FOR, THE HULKBUSTERS HAVE HAD MANY RUN-INS WITH HULK, BUT HAVE NEVER MANAGED TO DESTROY HIM...BUT HOW CAN YOU DESTROY SOMEONE WHO'S AS STRONG AS A THOUSAND ARMIES?!

BIG BATTLES!

THE HULK HAS HAD SOME MAJOR BATTLES IN HIS TIME, FROM FIGHTING FRIGHTFUL FOES ON FAR AWAY PLANETS, TO TAKING ON ENTIRE ARMIES HERE ON EARTH. WE DECIDED TO ROUNDUP A FEW OF HIS FIERCEST FIGHTS!

HULK VS THE ABOMINATION!

THE ABOMINATION'S STRENGTH LEVEL EXCEEDS THAT OF THE HULK WHEN HE IS IN HIS 'CALM' STATE. THESE TWO HAVE HAD SEVERAL BATTLES AGAINST EACH OTHER, HOWEVER, BECAUSE THE HULK'S STRENGTH INCREASES WITH ANGER, HE NORMALLY COMES OUT ON TOP!

HULK VS JUGGERNAUT

FIGHTS DON'T COME MUCH BIGGER THAN THIS! PERHAPS THE TWO STRONGEST PEOPLE ON EARTH, THE HULK'S INCREASING STRENGTH STILL ISN'T ENOUGH TO HARM THE INVINCIBLE JUGGERNAUT AND THESE TWO NORMALLY END UP FIGHTING TO A STANDSTILL!

THE HULK VS THE THING

DESPITE NOT BEING AS STRONG AS THE HULK, THE THING IS DETERMINED TO PUT ONE OVER ON HIS OLD ENEMY! THEY'VE HAD SEVERAL BATTLES, BUT THE THING IS ALWAYS THE ONE LEFT WITH EGG ON HIS ORANGE FACE!

MARVEL'S STRONGEST!

HULK
THE STRONGEST ONE THERE IS!!

The Hulk may be the strongest creature to ever walk the earth, but how does he compare to Marvel Universe's other BIG HITTERS? We've searched the solar system and beyond to bring you some of the strongest around!

NAMOR THE SUB-MARINER
Strength: *Superhuman class 100*
Speed: *Superhuman*
Stamina: *Godlike*
Durability: *Meta-human*

Namor is the amphibious monarch of the sunken empire, ATLANTIS. Like the Hulk, he has a dislike for humans, who he blames for polluting his home, and used to attack the surface dwellers every opportunity he got! However, more recently, he has teamed up with the AVENGERS on several occasions to defend all humanity!

JUGGERNAUT!
Strength: *Superhuman class 90*
Speed: *Normal*
Stamina: *Immeasurable*
Durability: *Totally indestructible*

When Cain Marko discovered the mystical CRIMSON GEM of CYTTORAK, he was transformed into a human juggernaut! His mystical helmet produces a FORCE SHIELD, which enables him to survive without food, water, or oxygen, and when Cain moves in a certain direction, nothing and no one can stop him -- not even the HULK!

THOR

Strength: *Superhuman class 100*
Speed: *Superhuman*
Stamina: *Godlike*
Durability: *Meta-human*

Thor is the Norse God of THUNDER, and ruler of the legendary ASGARD! Armed with his indestructible enchanted Uru hammer Mjolnir, which enables Thor to fly, control the elements of storms, project mystical energy, and open trans-dimensional portals! One of the greatest superheroes in the universe, Thor also helped form the mighty Avengers!

THE SILVER SURFER

Strength: *Superhuman class 100*
Speed: *Warp Speed*
Stamina: *Godlike*
Durability: *Godlike*

The Silver Surfer used to be a herald for the great Galactus *(see below)*. His skin is made from a metallic silvery material, which makes him totally indestructible! He possesses vast amounts of cosmic power, can fly at warp speed, and can fire beams of energy from his hands with enough destructive force to level a large city!

GALACTUS

Strength: *Immeasurable*
Speed: *Warp Speed*
Stamina: *Meta-human*
Durability: *Godlike*

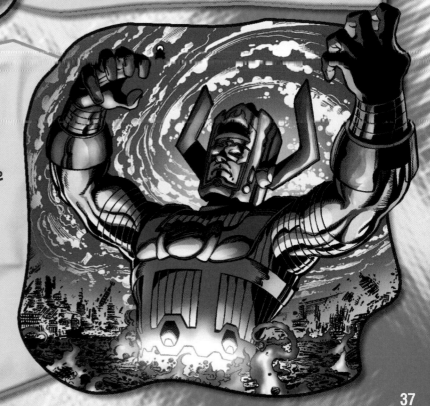

They don't come much bigger, or more powerful than Galactus! Possibly the strongest being in the universe, Galactus possesses cosmic power beyond the abilities of human beings to even measure! He gave the Silver Surfer his incredible powers, so that he could surf the universe to find planets with enough energy for Galactus to consume... yep, that's right -- he eats planets!!

POWER STRUGGLE!

THREE OF MARVEL'S MIGHTIEST SUPERHUMANS ARE COMPETING AGAINST EACH OTHER -- TO FIND OUT WHO IS THE STRONGEST!
FIND OUT WHO WINS BY ADDING UP THE POWER POINTS ON EACH CHARACTER'S PATH!

PRODUCE A HUGE ELECTRICAL STORM! POWER POINTS: 4

STOP A SPEEDING CAR! POWER POINTS: 2

DEFEAT AN ENTIRE ARMY! POWER POINTS: 7

STOP A METEOR HITTING EARTH! POWER POINTS: 7

SURVIVE BEING HIT BY AN INDUSTRIAL DUMPER TRUCK! POWER POINTS: 4

FLATTEN A TANK! POWER POINTS: 4

DEFEAT A FROST GIANT IN ONE BLOW! POWER POINTS: 5

SURVIVE A LASER ATTACK! POWER POINTS: 6

FLATTEN A MOUNTAIN! POWER POINTS: 7

SURVIVE A MASSIVE EXPLOSION! POWER POINTS: 6

LEVEL A LARGE BUILDING! POWER POINTS: 6

SURVIVE AN ARTILLERY ATTACK! POWER POINTS: 5

ANSWER: Thor = 22, Thing = 18, Hulk = 23. Hulk wins! (Well, he couldn't lose in his **own** annual, could he? That would make him really **ANGRY!**)

TOTAL: ☐   TOTAL: ☐   TOTAL: ☐

NO THANKS ARE *NECESSARY*, GENERAL. THE PUBLIC NEEDS TO BE *PROTECTED* FROM THE HULK'S DESTRUCTIVE BEHAVIOR.

AND I'VE LONG BEEN HOPING TO FIND A WAY TO HELP BANNER FINALLY *CURE* HIMSELF--

--AND LIVE OUT THE REST OF HIS LIFE IN *PEACE*.

ME, I'VE BEEN ITCHIN' FOR A *REMATCH* WITH OL' *GREENSKIN* FOR A *WHILE* NOW!

I KNOW HOW YOU *FEEL*, MR. GRIMM.

WHUMP

...CONGRATULATIONS ON YOUR MARRIAGE TO *MAJOR TALBOT*, BETTY. REED AND I WISH YOU BOTH THE VERY *BEST* OF LUCK.

THANK YOU, *SUSAN*. I MUST ADMIT, IT HASN'T BEEN *EASY*...

...WHAT WITH MY HUSBAND SO *ENMESHED* IN HIS *WORK* AND CONSTANTLY PUTTING HIMSELF IN *DANGER*.

STORY OF MY LIFE!

:*sigh*: C'MON, GANG, ENOUGH WITH THE *CHATTER*!

LET'S GET *MOVING* ALREADY!

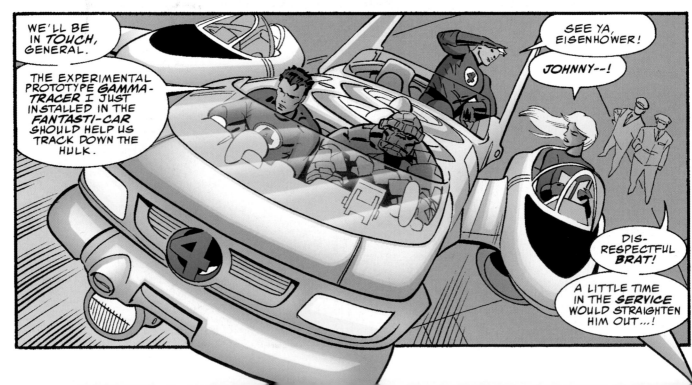

WE'LL BE IN *TOUCH*, GENERAL.

THE EXPERIMENTAL PROTOTYPE *GAMMA-TRACER* I JUST INSTALLED IN THE *FANTASTI-CAR* SHOULD HELP US TRACK DOWN THE HULK.

SEE YA, EISENHOWER!

JOHNNY--!

DIS-RESPECTFUL *BRAT*!

A LITTLE TIME IN THE *SERVICE* WOULD STRAIGHTEN HIM OUT...!

CRYSTAL FALLS, COLORADO.

A SMALL, TRANQUIL TOWN WITH A TIGHT-KNIT *COMMUNITY*...

...AND A MOST UNIQUE *VISITOR*, IN THE FORM OF *DOCTOR ROBERT BRUCE BANNER*.

... MY SITUATION IS LOOKING MORE AND MORE *HOPELESS* WITH EACH PASSING DAY!

I'VE ALWAYS SORT OF THOUGHT OF THE HULK AS A KIND OF *DISEASE*, LIKE *CANCER*--

--SOMETHING THAT COULD BE *CURED*, IF ONLY THE PROPER METHOD FOR *TREATMENT* COULD BE FOUND.

BUT IT SEEMS TO BE A LOT MORE *COMPLICATED* THAN THAT!

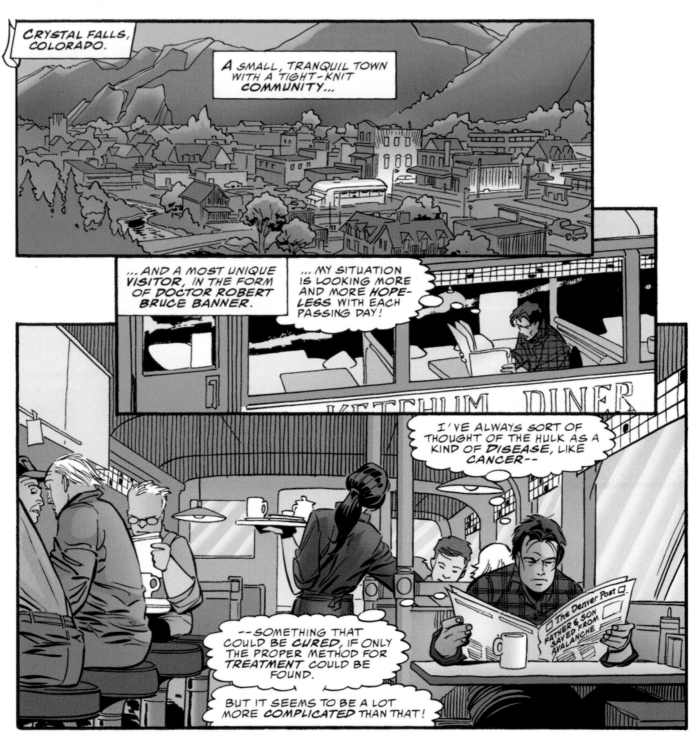

THE *REALIZATION* I CAME TO RECENTLY -- THAT THE HULK SEEMS TO HAVE BECOME A SEPARATE, *INDIVIDUAL* PERSONA, *MORE* THAN JUST MY *DARK SIDE* BROUGHT TO LIFE --

--SUGGESTS THAT HE'S GOING TO BE HARDER TO GET RID OF THAN I EVER *THOUGHT*!

EXCUSE ME, SIR -- ARE YOU READY TO *ORDER* YET?

SOMETHING BESIDES *DECAFFEINATED COFFEE*, THAT IS?

HUH? OH--! SORRY...

41

...I GUESS I SHOULD'VE BEEN READING THE *MENU* INSTEAD OF THE *NEWSPAPER*, HUH?

HMH. Y'KNOW, I'VE LIVED HERE IN CRYSTAL FALLS ALL MY LIFE, THOUGHT I KNEW PRETTY MUCH *EVERYBODY* IN THIS TOWN...

...BUT I'M *SURE* I'VE NEVER SEEN *YOU* BEFORE! ARE YOU *NEW* IN TOWN?

JUST PASSING THROUGH, ACTUALLY.

OH. WELL, YOU WON'T FIND MANY PLACES BETTER THAN *THIS!*

YOU SOUND LIKE THE TOWN'S *PUBLICITY DIRECTOR!*

ALTHOUGH YOU *DO* SEEM VERY SINCERE.

I *AM!* I *LOVE* THIS TOWN. I CAN *EASILY* SEE MYSELF SPENDING THE REST OF MY *LIFE* HERE.

OH, BY THE WAY-- I'M ABBY. *ABBY DAVIS.*

I'M BRUCE. BRUCE... BIXBY.

SO, BRUCE BIXBY, WHERE ARE YOU *HEADED?*

I-I'M NOT *SURE.*

THE SKIES OVER SALT LAKE CITY, UTAH.

...THE GAMMA-TRACER HAS YET TO DETECT THE HULK'S GAMMA RADIATION SIGNATURE.

WHICH MEANS EITHER HE'S NOWHERE IN THE VICINITY, OR HE'S SWITCHED BACK TO *BANNER--*

--IN WHICH CASE THE TRACES OF GAMMA RADIATION WOULD BE MUCH MORE *DIFFICULT* TO DETECT.

Y'KNOW, REED, TH' HULK'S ALWAYS MAKIN' A BIG DEAL 'BOUT HOW HE WANTS TA BE LEFT *ALONE.*

SO IF HE'S STILL IN *HULK* MODE, I FIGGER HE'S PROBABLY LOOKIN' FOR A PLACE THAT'S *SECLUDED.* ISOLATED.

AS FAR AWAY FROM PEOPLE AS HE CAN *GET.*

WE'VE ALREADY COVERED THE *DESERT* AND COME UP WITH *ZIP,* AN' THE CITIES ARE THE *LAST* PLACES WE SHOULD BE LOOKIN'!

COLORADO ISN'T SO FAR AWAY -- WHAT ABOUT THE *ROCKY MOUNTAINS?*

A FELLA COULD CERTAINLY HIDE AWAY *THERE* FOR A WHILE!

AN *EXCELLENT* SUGGESTION, BEN! LET'S CHANGE COURSE AND HEAD OUT THERE!

WHAT DO YOU KNOW-- BEN'S THINKING LIKE THE *HULK!*

HOPE IT DIDN'T TAX YOUR BRAIN *TOO* MUCH, THING!

WHY, YOU LITTLE--!

BEN--!

C'MERE!

BEN!

PAY ATTENTION TO THE SKY AHEAD, WOULD YOU, PLEASE?

HA HA HA

LITTLE MATCH-STICK...

CAN'T TAKE YOU TWO *ANY-WHERE,* CAN WE?

43

...SO I'M WORKING HERE WHILE I'M PUTTING MYSELF THROUGH *GRADUATE SCHOOL.*

Y'SEE, MY FOLKS DIED IN A CAR CRASH BACK WHEN I WAS IN HIGH SCHOOL, SO I'VE BEEN ON MY OWN SINCE THEN.

WHAT ARE YOU STUDY-ING TO BECOME?

I'M HOPING TO BECOME A *TEACHER,* MAYBE AN ENGLISH PROFESSOR.

I FIGURE I'D HAVE TO DO SOME *TRAVELING,* SEE SOME *MORE* OF THE WORLD...

...BUT I'D *ALWAYS COME* BACK TO CRYSTAL FALLS.

WELL... I WORK IN THE *SCIENCES.*

BUT I'M ...BETWEEN POSITIONS RIGHT NOW.

A *SCIENTIST!* I'M *IMPRESSED!*

YOU DON'T SEEM ANYTHING LIKE THE OLD, BORING, STODGY, ABSENT-MINDED SCIENTISTS YOU SEE IN THE MOVIES AND ON TV--

--AND AT MY *SCHOOL,* FOR THAT MATTER!

HEH. THANKS.

CAN'T BELIEVE HOW *COMFORTABLE* I FEEL TALKING TO HER!

I'VE ALWAYS BEEN *SHY* AND *AWKWARD* AROUND WOMEN-- EVEN *BETTY,* AT FIRST!

BUT ABBY IS SO FRIENDLY, SHE MAKES ME FEEL SO MUCH AT EASE...

...AND I CERTAINLY CAN'T IGNORE HOW *PRETTY* SHE IS!

HEY, ABBY--

--WE'VE GOT PLENTY OF *OTHER* CUSTOMERS WAITIN' T' BE SERVED!

BE RIGHT THERE, MR. WARD!

UM, BRUCE, LISTEN... HOW LONG WILL YOU BE STAYING IN TOWN?

I'M NOT REALLY SURE.

I MEAN, I'VE TAKEN A ROOM AT THE *MOTEL* FOR THE NIGHT, BUT...

45

THIS IS SO *EXCITING!* THE FANTASTIC FOUR *AND* THE HULK-- ALL IN THE SAME DAY!

BELIEVE IT OR NOT, THOUGH, BRUCE, CRYSTAL FALLS ISN'T *USUALLY* THIS *BUSY!*

BRUCE...?

HATED TO LEAVE ABBY LIKE THAT! GUESS OUR DINNER DATE IS *CANCELLED!*

CAN'T LET RICHARDS AND HIS TEAM *CATCH* ME--

--THEY'D JUST TURN ME OVER TO GAMMA BASE!

I'D BE A *PRISONER* AGAIN-- LOCKED UP, POKED AND PRODDED, TREATED LIKE A *FREAK!*

ALL I WANT IS TO BE LEFT *ALONE,* TO HAVE A CHANCE TO CURE MYSELF!

WHA-- WHAT'S GOING ON? BEGINNING TO FEEL-- *STRANGE!*

I'M-- CHANGING! BUT WHY?!

MUST BE *ANGRIER*-- AT THE SUDDEN APPEARANCE OF THE FANTASTIC FOUR--

--THAN I REALIZED!

PERHAPS...

...PERHAPS NOT.

EITHER WAY, IT IS A QUESTION FOR ANOTHER TIME.

RAARRGH!

49

COOL BY *ME*, GREEN-SKIN! LET'S GET *BUSY!*

JOHNNY, GET *BACK* HERE! DON'T BE *RECKLESS!*

I HAVE A *PLAN--*

TAKE IT *EASY*, BROTHER-IN-LAW--

--I'VE GOT A NEW *TRICK* I'VE BEEN ITCHIN' TO TRY OUT!

FWOOSH

hunh? CHAINS--MADE OUT OF *FIRE?!*

ARRRGH! FLAMES-- *ANNOY* HULK!

BURN THE INSIDES OF HULK'S *NOSE!*

HULK WILL GET *RID* OF FIRE-CHAINS!

KRUNCH

SPLOOSH

HAH! HULK SHOWED *YOU*, HUMAN TORCH!

HSSSSSSSSS

DON'T KNOW WHY YOU'RE AFTER HULK --AND DON'T *CARE!*

NOW YOU KNOW THAT *NOTHING* CAN STOP THE HULK!

WE'LL JUST *SEE* ABOUT THAT, HANDSOME!

WHOOM

OOF!

SOMETHING'S --PUMMELING HULK--

--BUT HULK CAN'T SEE WHAT IT *IS!*

WHOOM

AND DOWN YOU GO!

ARRGH!

GOOD WORK, SIS!

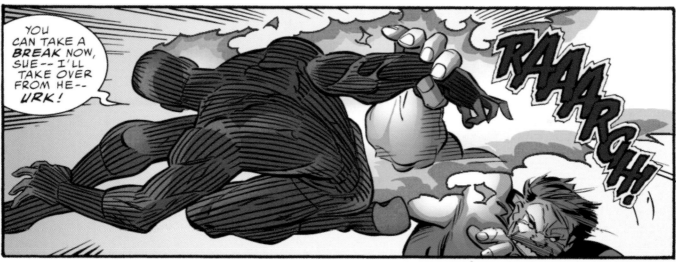

YOU CAN TAKE A *BREAK* NOW, SUE-- I'LL TAKE OVER FROM HE-- *URK!*

RAAARGH!

WHOOSH

JOHNNY!!

PUT HIM *DOWN,* HULK!

HULK WILL PUT TORCH DOWN--

AWLP!

--FAR AWAY FROM *HERE!*

GWILGHH

AWWWGHH!

HAVE TO CATCH HIM IN ONE OF MY FORCE-FIELDS--!

BUT FOR IT TO *WORK*, I HAVE TO PLACE IT ON HIS HEAD--

--AND WITH HIM STRUGGLING *AGAINST* ME LIKE THIS, THAT'S EASIER SAID THAN *DONE!*

RARRGH!

KARAK

WHATEVER THIS STUPID METAL BAND IS--

--YOU WON'T USE IT AGAINST HULK!

AARRGH!

AGONY-- LIKE I'VE NEVER FELT BEFORE!

AND NOW-- HULK WILL TIE YOUR RUBBER BODY INTO *KNOTS!*

LET 'IM GO, STRETCHO --I'LL TAKE CARE OF 'IM NOW!

AFTER ALL--

WHUMP

urk

--IT'S CLOBBERIN' TIME!

≶gasp≶

WHERE'S *BRUCE* IN THE MIDST OF ALL THIS? HE DISAPPEARED SO *ABRUPTLY...*

FOR ALL I KNOW, HE'S ONE OF THE PEOPLE THAT THE FANTASTIC FOUR HAVE ALREADY EVACUATED TO *SAFETY--*

...OR HE COULD BE *INJURED--* LYING UNDER RUBBLE SOMEWHERE, DESPERATE FOR *HELP!*

I KNOW I JUST *MET* THE GUY-- BUT I WANT TO BE SURE HE'S *ALL RIGHT--!*

WHA--?!

RAAARGH!

THWA-KRAKSH!

HUNH?

HRH...DOES HULK...*KNOW* YOU?

≷gulp≷

DON'T WORRY, MISS-- I'VE GOT YOU!

oh--!

PICK ON SOMEONE YOUR OWN SIZE, LETTUCE HEAD!

YOU SHOULD BE SAFE *HERE.*

YOU DON'T UNDERSTAND! I'M *LOOKING* FOR SOMEONE! I HAVE TO MAKE SURE HE'S OKAY!

IF HE HAS HALF A BRAIN, HE'S ALREADY TAKEN SHELTER FAR AWAY FROM *GROUND ZERO!*

BUT LISTEN, WITH THE FANTASTI-CAR *TRASHED* AND ALL, WE COULD BE HERE FOR A WHILE. WHEN THIS IS *OVER,* HOW'D YOU LIKE TO GET TOGETHER FOR *DINNER?*

THANKS, BUT I ALREADY *HAVE* A DATE-- AT LEAST, I *THINK* I DO!

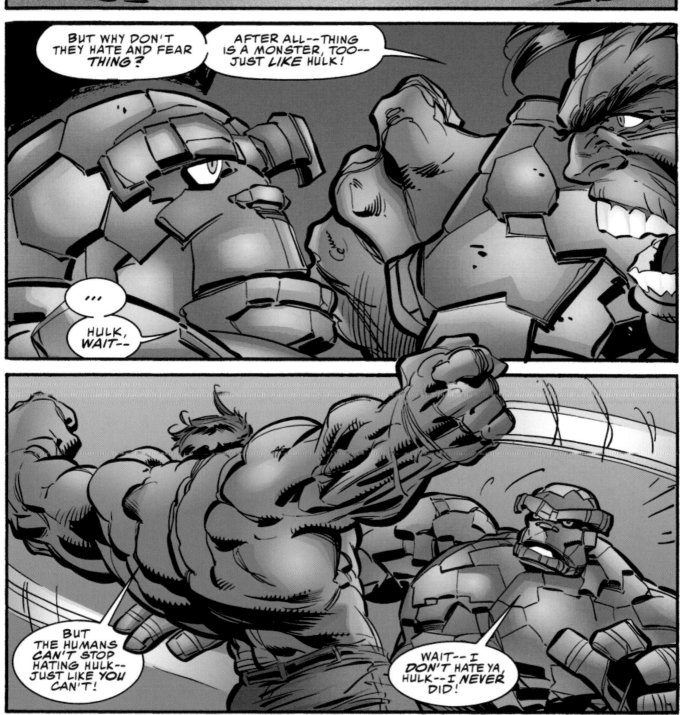

RAAARRGHH!

WHOMP

UNGH!

BEN--!

GET AWAY FROM HULK-- ALL OF YOU!

HULK IS SICK OF HUMANS! SICK OF BEING HUNTED AND HOUNDED!

AND HULK IS SICK OF FANTASTIC FOUR!

HULK WILL FIND A PLACE WHERE THERE IS PEACE--

--WHERE HULK WON'T BE FEARED AND HATED ANYMORE!

IF YOU CAN FIND A PLACE LIKE THAT FOR YOURSELF, GREEN-SKIN...

...MORE POWER TO YA.

SOON AFTER...

I FIGURE REED CAN FIX THIS THING.

AFTER ALL, THE GUY CAN MAKE A RADIO OUT OF BAMBOO AND COCONUTS!

YOU'RE THINKING OF THE PROFESSOR FROM "GILLIGAN'S ISLAND," JOHNNY...

WHAT HAPPENED BACK THERE, BEN? FOR A MOMENT, IT ALMOST LOOKED LIKE YOU WANTED HIM TO GET AWAY.

I CAN'T BELIEVE I'M ADMITTIN' THIS...

...BUT SOMETHIN' JOHNNY SAID EARLIER ACTUALLY HAD SOME TRUTH IN IT.

HEARIN' THE HULK'S SIDE O' THINGS, I ACTUALLY DID GET INTA HIS HEAD, SEE THINGS FROM HIS POINT O' VIEW.

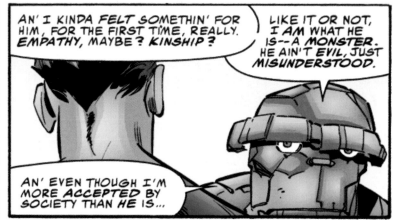

AN' I KINDA FELT SOMETHIN' FOR HIM, FOR THE FIRST TIME, REALLY. EMPATHY, MAYBE? KINSHIP?

LIKE IT OR NOT, I AM WHAT HE IS--A MONSTER. HE AIN'T EVIL, JUST MISUNDERSTOOD.

AN' EVEN THOUGH I'M MORE ACCEPTED BY SOCIETY THAN HE IS...

...IT AIN'T LIKE FOLKS AREN'T STILL GIVIN' ME THE SAME KINDA LOOKS THAT THEY GIVE HIM.

AND I FEEL FOR BRUCE BANNER-- THE MAN WITHIN THE HULK.

HIS TRAGIC FATE COULD EASILY HAVE BEEN MINE...

COME ON, OLD FRIEND...

...LET'S GET SOME COCO-NUTS AND TRY TO REPAIR THE FANTASTI-CAR...

THE END

59

FACT FILE: THE FANTASTIC 4

Whilst on an experimental spaceship, Reed Richards, Sue Richards, Benjamin Grimm and Johnny Storm set out on the first ever attempt at interstellar travel. However, when something went wrong with their spacecraft, they were each exposed to high levels of cosmic radiation.

Their mission was a disaster, but when they returned to earth, they discovered they possessed fantastic new powers!

MISTER FANTASTIC!

Real Name: Reed Richards
Height: 6' 1"
Weight: 180 lbs
Superhuman Abilities: Can transform his body into virtually and shape!
Favourite Saying: None! He's far too sensible!

MISTER FANTASTIC!

REED IS THE FOUNDER AND LEADER OF THE FANTASTIC FOUR. HE HAS A SUPERHUMAN INTELLIGENCE LEVEL, WITH EXTENSIVE KNOWLEDGE OF ALMOST ALL SCIENTIFIC FIELDS. RICHARDS HAS THE ABILITY TO ALTER HIS BODY INTO A HIGHLY MALLEABLE STATE, ALLOWING HIM TO STRETCH, DEFORM, AND REFORM HIMSELF INTO VIRTUALLY ANY SHAPE!

THE THING!

Real Name: Ben Grimm
Height: 6'
Weight: 500 lbs
Superhuman Abilities: Super-human strength, speed, stamina and durability!
Favourite Saying: It's clobbering time!

THE THING!

BEN GRIMM IS REED'S BEST FRIEND. HE WAS A TEST PILOT AND ASTRONAUT WHEN REED WAS BUILDING HIS SPACESHIP, AND BEN OFFERED TO FLY IT. WHEN BEN WAS IRRADIATED, HIS BODY BECAME COVERED IN AN ORANGE, FLEXIBLE, ROCK-LIKE MATERIAL. HE ALSO DISCOVERED HE POSSESSED SUPERHUMAN STRENGTH, STAMINA AND DURABILITY, AND THAT HE COULD GO TOE-TO-TOE WITH SOME OF THE STRONGEST VILLAINS AROUND!

HUMAN TORCH!

Real Name: *Jonny Storm*
Height: *5' 10"*
Weight: *170 lbs*
Superhuman Abilities: Can turn into flame and fly at supersonic speeds!
Favourite Saying: *Flame On!*

HUMAN TORCH!

JOHNNY STORM IS A NATURAL ADVENTURER! WHEN HE HEARD REED WAS PLANNING A TEST FLIGHT, HE INSISTED THAT HE COME ALONG WITH HIS SISTER AND JOIN THE WOULD-BE HISTORY MAKERS! JOHNNY HAS THE ABILITY TO COVER HIS BODY IN A FIERY PLASMA WITHOUT HARMING HIMSELF! HE CAN ALSO UTILISE HIS HEAT ENERGY TO FORM FIERY SHAPES, FLY AT HIGH SPEEDS AND FIRE NOVA FLAME BURSTS!

INVISIBLE WOMAN!

Real Name: *Susan Richards*

Height: *5' 6"*

Weight: *120 lbs*

Superhuman Abilities:

Can make herself completely invisible!

Favourite Saying:
Who wants to play hide and seek?

INVISIBLE WOMAN!

SUE RICHARDS IS MARRIED TO REED, AND STANDS IN FOR HER HUSBAND AS LEADER WHEN HE IS NOT AROUND. SHE HAS THE ABILITY TO MANIPULATE COSMIC ENERGY, MAKING HERSELF AND OTHERS AROUND HER COMPLETELY INVISIBLE. SHE CAN ALSO FORM PROTECTIVE FORCE FIELDS AND CAN TRAVEL THROUGH THE AIR BY PROJECTING COLUMNS OF PSONIC FORCE BENEATH HER!

REED PERSUADED HIS FELLOW FRIENDS THAT THEY SHOULD USE THEIR NEWFOUND SKILLS TO AID HUMANKIND AND PRESERVE THE SECURITY OF EARTH AGAINST SUPERHUMAN THREATS!

OPERATING FROM THEIR HEADQUARTERS IN NEW YORK, THE BAXTOR BUILDING, THE FANTASTIC FOUR HAVE BECOME THE GREATEST BAND OF SUPERHUMAN EXPLORERS EVER AND HAVE DISCOVERED HIDDEN CIVILIZATIONS, SECRET NATIONS, AND HAVE EVEN BROKEN THROUGH DIFFERENT PARALLEL DIMENSIONS!

HULK ON THE RAMPAGE!

AFTER HIS ENCOUNTER WITH THE FANTASTIC FOUR, THE HULK HAS GONE ON A MAD RAMPAGE AROUND THE STATE OF COLORADO! USING HIS GAMMA-TRACER, REED HAS TRACKED THE HULK'S MOVEMENTS. LOOK AT HIS FINDINGS BELOW, AND SEE IF YOU CAN FIND THE HULK'S CURRENT LOCATION.

HULK STARTED AT GRID F7 >> HE LEAPED AN INCREDIBLE 3 SQUARES NORTH AND A FURTHER 2 SQUARES WEST >> NEXT HE JUMPED 3 SQUARES SOUTHWEST, WHERE HE CONTINUED TO FLATTEN A MOUNTAIN BEFORE HEADING EAST 2 SQUARES AND THEN NORTHWEST 3 SQUARES >>

FINALLY THE HULK HEADED NORTHEAST 2 SQUARES WHERE HE STOPPED >> WHAT IS THE HULK'S CURRENT COORDINATES?

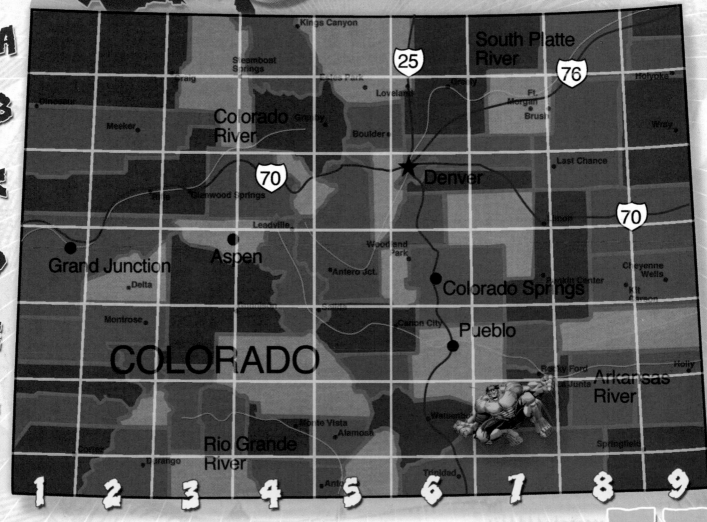

ANSWER: Hulk stops at grid A3.

ENTER COORDINATES:

CACHE Level 2

Child Care and Education

4th Edition

Penny Tassoni

www.heinemann.co.uk

✓ Free online support
✓ Useful weblinks
✓ 24 hour online ordering

01865 888118

Heinemann is an imprint of Pearson Education Limited, a company incorporated in England and Wales, having its registered office at Edinburgh Gate, Harlow, Essex, CM20 2JE. Registered company number: 872828

www.heinemann.co.uk

Heinemann is a registered trademark of Pearson Education Limited

Text © Penny Tassoni 2007

First published 2007

12 11 10 09 08 07

10 9 8 7 6 5 4 3 2 1

British Library Cataloguing in Publication Data is available from the British Library on request.

ISBN 978 0 435987 41 1

Edited by Caroline Low, Virgo Editorial and Susan Ross, Ross Economics and Editorial Services Ltd

Designed by Kamae Design
Original illustrations © Pearson Education Limited 2007
Illustrated by Duncan Mackenzie & Kamae Design
Cover design by Wooden Ark Studio
Picture research by Chrissie Martin
Cover photo/illustration © Masterfile
Printed in the UK by Scotprint

Acknowledgements

Every effort has been made to contact copyright holders of material reproduced in this book. Any omissions will be rectified in subsequent printings if notice is given to the publishers.

Websites

The websites used in this book were correct and up-to-date at the time of publication. It is essential for tutors to preview each website before using it in class so as to ensure that the URL is still accurate, relevant and appropriate. We suggest that tutors bookmark useful websites and consider enabling students to access them through the school/college intranet.

Contents

Unit 1 An introduction to working with children   1

This introductory unit looks at the range of services for children and their families. It also provides some initial information that will help you to get started on your course and in placement.

Unit 2 The developing child   29

This unit will help you to have a good understanding of child development. It will also teach you how to observe children and why this is important when planning for children's learning.

Mandatory units for Certificate and Diploma:

Unit 3 Safe, health and nurturing environments for children   107

This unit looks at the importance of safeguarding children and supporting them in a range of situations including protecting them from abuse. The unit also looks at how you might help children to manage their behaviour.

Unit 4 Children and play   145

This unit looks at how play supports young children's learning and development. In this unit you will learn about how to plan play activities for different ages of children.

Unit 5 Communication and professional skills within child care and education   179

This unit looks at the many communication skills that you will need to acquire in order to be an effective practitioner. The unit also explores how you might learn to reflect on your practice and how you might plan for your future career.

Acknowledgements

Photo acknowledgements

The authors and publisher would like to thank the following individuals and organisations for permission to reproduce photographs:

Alamy/Bananastock p **421**; Alamy/Brand X Pictures p **11**; Alamy/Design Pics Inc. p **121**; Alamy/Gary Roebuck p **287**; Alamy/Jacky Chapman p **266**; Alamy/Jupiter Images/Bananastock p **130, 180, 419**; Alamy/Martin Mayer p **276**; Alamy/Mary Evans Picture Library p **49**; Alamy/Norman Wharton p **236**; Alamy/Peter Griffin p **263**; Alamy/Photofusion Picture Library p **204, 333**; Alamy/Picture Partners p **43, 125**; Art Directors and TRIP/Helene Rogers p **115**; Brand X Pictures p **35 (right), 372 (image 2)**; Corbis p **1, 29**; Corbis/ Rune Hellestad p **119**; Department for Education and Skills p **366**; Dreamstime/Christopher Testi p **145**; Dreamstime/QWASYX p **399**; Eyewire p **97, 307, 376**; Getty Images/Digital Vision p **164, 273**; Getty Images/PhotoDisc p **58, 200, 202, 267**; Getty Images/Photographer's Choice p **293**; iStockPhoto/ Chris Schmidt p **7**; iStockPhoto.com/Iryna Kurhan p **42**; iStockPhoto.com/Lise Gagne p **208**; Jupiter Images/Photos.com p **65, 415**; Pearson Education Ltd/Clark Wiseman p **296**; Pearson Education Ltd/ Debbie Rowe p **409**; Pearson Education Ltd/Gareth Boden p **113, 161, 250, 383**; Pearson Education Ltd/Ian Wedgewood p **51, 192, 220, 359**; Pearson Education Ltd/Jules Selmes p **2, 10, 15, 18, 21, 24, 30, 33, 35 (left), 41, 63, 74, 75, 79, 82, 95, 100, 108, 135, 146, 149, 152, 154 (top 3 images), 156, 174, 182, 190, 195, 218, 223, 231, 234, 239, 242, 248, 252, 278, 282, 295, 300, 304, 306, 314, 316, 320, 330, 337, 341, 344, 351, 360, 368, 372, 380, 385, 388, 400, 406, 413**; Pearson Education Ltd/ Malcolm Harris p **150, 154 (bottom), 167**; Pearson Education Ltd/Studio 8/Clarke Wiseman p **241**; Pearson Education Ltd/Tudor Photography p **17, 32, 107, 179, 207, 225, 311, 378**; Photoedit/Michael Newman p **369**; Photoedit/Myrleen Ferguson Cate p **127, 408**; Reed International Books Australia Pty Ltd/Lindsay Edwards Photography p **157**; Report Digital/Roy Peters p **347**; Science Photo Library/ Lauren Shear p **329, 335**; Science Photo Library/ Maximillian Stock Ltd p **67**

Feature icons: Pearson Education Ltd/Jules Selmes

Every effort has been made to contact copyright holders of material reproduced in this book. Any omissions will be rectified in subsequent printings if notice is given to the publishers.

Author's acknowledgements

As with many writing projects, this book has required a team approach. I would like to begin by thanking Caroline Low of Virgo Editorial for her thoroughness and determination to finish this project at a special time in her life. I am also grateful to the Heinemann team who have carried out a lot of work behind the scenes, especially Beth Howard for her continued support. I would also like to thank Wendy Taylor and Ann Brooks from CACHE as their help has helped me to tailor the book more carefully to the needs of students. I would also like to thank the many tutors and students who provide me with feedback and, reassuringly, encouragement about my writing. I must also thank my mother, Jennifer Enderby, for her excellent proof reading skills. Finally, I must thank the Tassoni Team once more for their continued support.

Dedication

This book is dedicated to Ayşegül, who at 2 years old keeps me on my toes and reminds me how much fun working with children can be. Thank you.

About the author

Penny Tassoni

Penny Tassoni is an education consultant, author and trainer. Penny trained and worked as an early years and primary teacher before lecturing in a FE college on a range of childhood studies courses. Penny has also worked as the UK Education and Training manager of one of the larger day care nursery chains. She has written over twenty books including the bestselling *Planning Play for the Early Years* as well as the previous editions of the *Diploma in Child Care and Education*. She also writes for various early years publications such as *Nursery World* and *Practical Pre-school*. In addition to her writing, Penny works for CACHE as a revisor for their awards. Penny is an experienced trainer and keynote speaker both nationally and internationally.

Introduction

Congratulations on your decision to take a qualification that will enable you to work with children! It is an exciting time to work with children as there are many varied career opportunities that you might in time choose to take. A Level 2 qualification will allow you to work under supervision with children and so gain some valuable experience. You may also use it as a launch pad to furthering your employment prospects by going onto a Level 3 qualification. The skills and knowledge that you are required to show at Level 2 will provide you with the building blocks for this.

About your course and assessment

The CACHE Level 2 course in Child Care and Education is divided into units. There are three pathways to this qualification – Award, Certificate or Diploma – depending on the number of units completed. The chart below shows how many units you will need to take for the course that you are studying.

Mandatory Units	Diploma	Certificate	Award
Unit 1	✓	✓	✓
Unit 2	✓	✓	✓
Unit 3	✓	✓	
Unit 4	✓	✓	
Unit 5	✓	✓	
Unit 6	✓		
Optional Units	✓		
Unit 7	1 optional unit		
Unit 8			
Unit 9			
Unit 10			
Unit 11			

CACHE Level 2 Award in Child Care and Education

To gain the Award you have to complete:

→ *Unit 1: An introduction to working with children*
→ *Unit 2: The developing child*

These are both mandatory units.

Assessment

→ Unit 1: an assignment tests your knowledge and understanding of the unit. This is set by CACHE but will be marked by your tutor.
→ Unit 2: assessment is via a multiple choice question paper (MCQ) which is externally marked. This means that CACHE will mark it directly rather than your tutor.

CACHE Level 2 Certificate in Child Care and Education

To gain the certificate you have to complete Units 1 and 2 plus:

→ *Unit 3: Safe, healthy and nurturing environments for children*
→ *Unit 4: Children and play*
→ *Unit 5: Communication and professional skills within child care and education*

These units are mandatory.

Assessment

You will complete the same assessments as for the Award. In addition:

→ For each of Units 3, 4 and 5, you will have an assignment that CACHE has set. Your tutor marks each assignment.
→ There is also a short answer paper based on a case study that checks your knowledge of Units 3, 4 and 5.

CACHE Level 2 Diploma in Child Care and Education

In order to gain the full Diploma you will need to complete Units 1–5 plus:

→ *Unit 6: The childcare practitioner in the workplace*

These six units are mandatory. Unit 6 is the practical component and this means that you will need to attend placements and show that you are competent in a range of practical skills.

In addition to completing the mandatory units, to gain the full Diploma you will also need to complete *one* of the following optional units:

→ *Unit 7: Working with children from birth to age 5 years*
→ *Unit 8: Play activity for children from birth to age 16 years*
→ *Unit 9: Supporting children with additional needs*
→ *Unit 10: Introduction to children's learning*
→ *Unit 11: Supporting children and families*

Your college will decide the optional unit to be studied. In this book, all of the optional units are covered.

Assessment

You will complete the same assessments as for the Certificate (and Award), but in addition:

→ For Unit 6, to show your practical competency when working with children, you will need to achieve a grade E or above on your Practice Evidence Records and a pass on your Professional Development Profiles. These are checked by your tutor.
→ For the optional unit, you will complete an assignment task that has been set by CACHE. It will be marked by your tutor.
→ To complete the Diploma, you will also have an externally assessed assignment that takes the form of a short answer test. This will check that you can remember and apply the knowledge that you have gained in Mandatory Units 1–6.

Preparing for external assessment

The term 'externally assessed' means that an examiner employed by CACHE will mark your work.

Multiple Choice Questions (assessment for Unit 2)

In this type of exam you are given a question and then four possible answers. You have to choose the best answer and mark it on the sheet.

Multiple Choice Questions (MCQs) need to be read very carefully. You should read through all the possible answers before making your choice. If you think there are two possible answers, go back to the question and read it again. For example, two toys that are suitable for 2-year-olds may be given as possible answers to the question 'The BEST toy to promote a 2-year-old's fine motor development is...' You will need to decide which toy will best develop the child's fine motor movement.

To help you practise your MCQ technique, some sample questions are provided on the Heinemann website. Go to www.heinemann.co.uk/CACHE and enter the password: 4child

Short Answer Paper (assessment for Units 3, 4 and 5)

In this type of exam you are given a case study to read and then a series of questions that link to the case study. You must then write a short answer to each question.

It is important to read the case study through carefully and to think about how best to answer the questions. A good tip is to look at the first word in the question and the number of marks allocated; doing this will help you to judge how best to tackle a question. For example:

→ *Identify ways in which...* Look to see how many marks are allocated. For example, if there are five marks allocated, you would be expected to make five appropriate points.
→ *Discuss/Consider/Analyse ways in which...* These words at the start of a question indicate that you will need to answer using sentences and in depth. Think about whether you can use an example of a theory in your answer.

Short Answer Test

If you are taking the Diploma, towards the end of your course you will sit a short answer test. This test will have a series of questions which you will be required to answer. Most of your answers will only be a few sentences, but will show that you have remembered and understood Mandatory Units 1–6.

It will be important to revise for this test and to practise writing short answers. A good tip is to look at how many marks are available for each answer. Use this information when working out how many points you should make or how in-depth your answer should be. Your tutor should be able to give you further guidance on taking short answer tests and may set you some practice tests.

About this book

This book has been specially written to support you through your CACHE qualification, whether you choose to complete the Award, Certificate or Diploma. All the mandatory and optional units are covered in this book so that you will be in a great position to gain the underpinning knowledge that will be essential for your assessments. The book has been written in a clear and informative way and support and supplement the teaching that you will receive from your tutors. The book has been carefully written to match the delivery guidance of the qualification so should be a good tool to aid your study. There are also many features included in the text, which are explained below.

In each unit you will find a number of learning features, as shown below, which are designed to help you get the most out of your studies.

In the real world – This feature presents a short 'real world' scenario to help you understand why what you are about to learn is important for working with children.

Tips for good practice – This feature contains advice which will help you work towards best practice.

Find out! – This feature provides suggestions for where to find more information on a particular topic.

Case study – These contain scenarios with a 'real world' feel to help you relate what you have learned to practical situations. Case studies are followed by questions of increasing difficulty.

Back to the real world – This feature refers back to the 'real world' scenario from the beginning of the section to help you apply what you have learned.

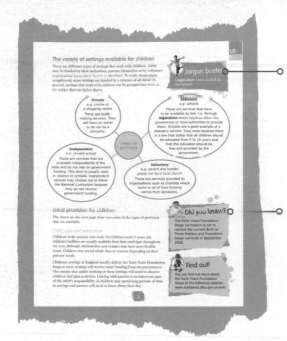

Jargon buster – A concise definition of important concepts and terms is provided when they are first used in a unit.

Did you know? – This feature provides you with interesting facts or statistics.

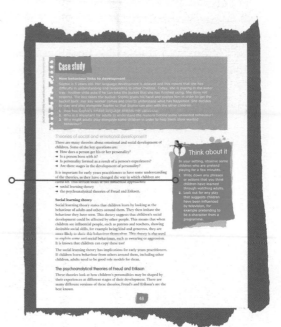

Think about it – This feature contains short questions or activities to provoke thought or discussion.

The features page:

In each unit, you will find two magazine-style spreads called 'The Features Page'. Each one covers a different childcare topic and contains a number of additional learning features to help you in your studies.

My story – Short stories of 'real world' experiences written from the perspective of the childcare practitioners' themselves.

Focus on... – Short articles on important topics relating to childcare.

Ask the expert – A letters page with frequently-asked questions and the expert response.

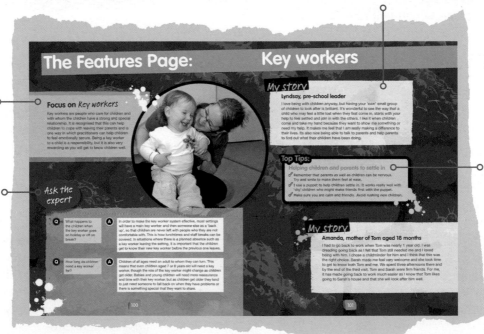

Top tips – A short list of practical tips relating to the topic.

I hope that you enjoy your course and using this book.
Good luck with your studies!

Penny Tassoni

Unit 1

An introduction to working with children

In this unit you will learn:

1. The types of settings and local provision for children

2. How to prepare for placement

3. The responsibilities and limits of your role in placements

4. Children's individual needs and necessity for fairness and inclusive practice

5. Your own preferred learning style and how to develop relevant study skills

Section 1

The types of settings and local provision for children

In the real world

You have just started your course. You think that you would like to work with children but need to gain knowledge and understanding. People sometimes ask if you know what age of child you would like to work with, or where. You are not sure because you do not really know what is available.

By the end of this section you will know about the type of settings where adults work with children and you will also have found out about what is available in your area.

The variety of settings available for children

There are different types of settings that work with children. These may be funded by local authorities, parents themselves or by voluntary organisations (sometimes known as charities). To make things more complicated, some settings are funded by a mixture of all three! In general, settings that work with children can be grouped into four, as the spider diagram below shows.

TYPES OF SETTINGS

Private
e.g. crèche at a shopping centre

These are profit-making services. They will have an owner or be run by a company.

Statutory
e.g. schools

These are services that have to be available by law, i.e. through **legislation** which requires either the government or local authorities to provide them. Schools are a good example of a statutory service. They exist because there is a law that states that all children should be educated from 5 to 16 years and that this education should be free and provided by the government.

Independent
e.g. private school

These are services that are provided independently of the state and do not rely on government funding. This term is usually used in relation to schools. Independent schools may choose not to follow the National Curriculum because they do not receive government funding.

Voluntary
e.g. parent and toddler group run by a local church

These are services provided by organisations such as charities where some or all of their funding comes from donations.

Local provision for children

The charts on the next page show you some of the types of provision that are available.

Child care and education

Childcare helps parents who work. For children under 5 years old, childcare facilities are usually available from 8am until 6pm throughout the year, although childminders and nannies may have more flexible hours. Children may attend whole days or sessions depending on their parents' needs.

Childcare settings in England usually deliver the Early Years Foundation Stage as most settings will receive some funding from the government. This means that adults working in these settings will need to observe children and plan activities. Liaising with parents is an important part of the adult's responsibility as children may spend long periods of time in settings and parents will need to know about their day.

Did you know?

The Early Years Foundation Stage curriculum is set to replace the current Birth to Three Matters and Foundation Stage curricula in September 2008.

Find out!

You can find out more about the Early Years Foundation Stage at the following website: www.standards.dfes.gov.uk/eyfs

✍ **Childcare settings**

Setting	Purpose	Age range
Childminders	Care and education for children in the childminder's home	From birth upwards
Nannies	Care and education for children in the child's home	From birth upwards
Workplace nurseries	Care and education for children in a building where parents work	3–6 months upwards
Day care centres	Care and education for children	3–6 months upwards
Children's Centres, i.e. SureStart centres	Care and education for children. Other services for parents may be available in the building, including health and social services. After-school provision may be available. Training for other professionals may be organised from the centre	3–6 months upwards
Crèches	Sessional care for parents who need a safe place for their child to stay while they are doing something else, for example shopping, at the sports centre, on holiday	Often from 2 years

Out-of-school provision

Out-of-school provision provides a safe environment in which children can play and relax. It also allows parents to work. Adults working in these settings will need to provide play opportunities for children and know how to observe their play needs. In addition, they will need to liaise with parents and schools.

✍ **Out-of-school provision**

Setting	Purpose	Age range
After-school clubs, i.e. extended schools	Care and play provision for children after school ends	5 years upwards
Holiday clubs	Care and play provision for children during holidays	5 years upwards
Educational settings:		
Nursery schools	Pre-school education – likely to be sessional or similar to a school day	2–3 years
Pre-schools	Pre-school education – likely to be sessional or similar to a school day	2–3 years
Infant schools	To provide education. In England, state schools follow the Early Years Foundation Stage and the National Curriculum	5–7 years
Primary schools	To provide education. In England, state schools follow the Early Years Foundation Stage and the National Curriculum	5–11 years

Other settings

There are many other settings and services for parents and their children. These may vary according to where you live.

Other settings

Setting	Purpose	Age range
Parent and toddler groups	These help parents meet each other and allow children to play with a variety of toys and equipment. Some parents and toddler groups also provide support and advice for parent. Parents have overall responsibility for their children. They may be held at a Children's Centre.	0–3 years
Drop-in play sessions	These help parents meet each other and allow children to play with a variety of toys and equipment. Some groups also provide support and advice for parents. They may be held at a Children's Centre or toy library.	0–5 years
Toy library	Places where parents and children can borrow toys and equipment. Many toy libraries also have play sessions.	Birth upwards
Clubs	Many leisure centres and groups provide clubs and activities for babies, children and their families, e.g. baby swim classes, Brownies, Beavers, football, Tumbletots.	Birth upwards

Find out!

Find out about the different types of early years provision available locally. You can do this by:

→ using the local phone book
→ visiting the library (they may have leaflets)
→ looking in the *What's on* section of the local newspaper
→ contacting the local Children's Information Service, which is run by the local authority to help parents find out more about children's services in their area. Your local Children's Information Service is likely to have a website; you may be able to access it via your local authority's website or by trying an Internet search.

Think about it

A new family has arrived in your area. They have a baby aged 6 months and a child who is 4 years old. What children's services would be available for them?

Multi-agency work and professionals and agencies working with children

The term multi-agency work is used to describe the way in which many early years settings work closely with other professionals such as health visitors, speech and language therapists and social workers. This is because it is recognised that children and their families may need a range of support. Some settings such as Children's Centres have been set up with this in mind, and you may find that alongside the nursery there is, for example, a baby clinic or a Job Centre.

As part of this course, you will need to learn how to work with other professionals who may work in different ways with families.

Back to the real world

You should now know that there is a wide range of settings that work with children. You should also be aware of the provision available in your area.

1. Give an example of statutory provision in your local area.
2. Give an example of a setting that works with children under 3 years.
3. For each setting that you have given, explain its purpose and the role of people who work there.

Section 2

How to prepare for placement

In the real world

In the next few days you will be starting in a new placement. You feel anxious about this as it will be your first work placement. You are not sure what to wear or how to make a good first impression.

By the end of this section you will know how to prepare for a work placement, what you should wear and how to make a good start.

Expectations of placements

While placements are happy to have learners, the people who work there will expect you to:

→ attend on placement days
→ be punctual and appropriately dressed
→ be polite and show respect to staff, children and parents
→ bring any work required such as placement diaries
→ provide information about activities and observations that need to be carried out in plenty of time
→ listen, take notes and learn about the setting
→ show enthusiasm and a willingness to learn.

A work placement's priority is to work with children and their families, so while placements are usually happy to help learners, they cannot do this if their work with children will be affected. This means that your placement supervisor may only have limited amounts of time to work with you, so you will need to ensure that you are on time for any meetings and listen carefully to instructions and information.

Appropriate dress and behaviour

Every work placement will have its own code of behaviour, so it is a good idea to phone in advance to find out whether there is anything that you should or should not wear. Most schools will expect a smarter look than in nurseries and not allow you to wear jeans. Below are some general points that you might find useful.

Clothing

Practical, easy-to-wash clothing is always best when working with young children. Most adults working with children have items of clothing that they only wear at work. They know that paint often stains and that their clothing might get messy.

Tips for good practice

Choosing your clothing

→ Check what staff members are wearing and adjust your clothing accordingly.

→ Avoid any large branded T-shirts or sweatshirts or those with messages and slogans.

→ Aim for a smart, casual look.

→ Avoid short skirts and dresses as you will be getting down to interact with children and bending over.

Footwear

In general terms, you should avoid high heels or heavy shoes as these could harm a child if you stepped on them accidentally. Since you will be on your feet most of the day, low comfortable shoes are best, although you will need to check whether you can wear trainers.

Personal hygiene

As well as clothing, it is important that you look clean and tidy. Preventing the spread of infection is vital in all settings working with young children. This means that your hands, nails and skin must be kept clean. If you have long hair, you should consider tying it back. This will not only help you to look tidy, it may also prevent you from getting head lice.

Make-up and jewellery

Working with children is a practical occupation, not glamorous. Your make-up and jewellery should reflect this, otherwise you will not be taken seriously.

Did you know?

Head lice are unpleasant parasites that live in the hair and are easily picked up in placements with children. You should brush and comb your hair thoroughly to help prevent head lice.

Tips for good practice

Wearing the right make-up and jewellery

→ Nails should be kept short and usually unvarnished as you may be expected to help in the preparation and serving of food and drinks. Keep jewellery to the minimum for the same reason.

→ Avoid wearing dangly earrings in case a baby or child accidentally pulls at one and rips your ear lobe!

→ Keep make-up to a minimum – the natural look is best and actually looks more grown up.

Behaviour

The key to a successful placement is to try to fit in. This means that your behaviour should be similar to that of other staff. You should try always to be courteous, patient and thoughtful of others.

Time-keeping

It might seem obvious but one of the most important things you must do on placement is to be there on time and, ideally, a few minutes early. This is an essential point to remember at all stages in your training but also later in your career (see Unit 6, pages 212–13). Being punctual gives a good impression. It shows that you care enough about the course and the placement to get there on time. If you cannot attend your placement, you should always contact both the setting and your college tutor. You will need to have an extremely good reason why you cannot attend. Remember, too, that your college has to show that you have completed the practical training element of the course.

A positive attitude

In order to do well on placement, you will need to show that you have a positive attitude. This means showing your enthusiasm as well as being there on time and wearing appropriate dress. Showing a positive attitude means smiling, listening and genuinely taking an interest in the children and the work of the setting. Learners who have a positive attitude are willing to volunteer for jobs, stay behind a little later if needed and are generally ready to help out.

◁ **You will achieve the most from your placement if you show a positive attitude**

Back to the real world

You should now feel confident that you can make a good impression in the first few days of your placement.

1. Explain why it is important to be punctual.
2. Describe how you might dress to fit in.

Section 3

The responsibilities and limits of your role in placements

In the real world

You are aware that, as a learner, you have various responsibilities. Your tutor has told you that it is also important to be aware of the limitations of your role. You are not sure quite what this means or what you should do about it.

By the end of this section you will understand your responsibilities and the limits of your role as a learner.

The responsibilities and limits of your role

As a learner you have various responsibilities, but there are also limitations on what you can do. It is important that you understand the limits of your role in placement. The guidelines in this section are very general and you will need some further guidance specific to your placement. A good starting point is, of course, to listen to both your tutor and placement supervisor.

Ways in which you are responsible to children

Children see you as an adult, as someone they can trust and not simply a learner. This means that you have responsibilities towards children in the same way that any adult does. Below are some key ways in which you will need to be responsible.

Health and safety

You must follow the setting's health and safety procedures in order to keep children safe. This involves simple things such as closing doors behind you and making sure that you do not bring anything into the setting that could harm children, such as matches or lighters. You should also bear in mind that children will look and copy your actions, so your behaviour must always help children to be safe and play safely. The case study below shows what might happen if you fail to do this.

Case study

Setting a good example

Mark is a learner on placement. He is loved by the children and enjoys their attention. He shows a group of children how he can run on a high wall and jump off at the end. A few hours later, one of the children copies what Mark has done but falls and breaks his arm. When his mother talks to him, he says that he wanted to do the same as Mark.

1. Why is it important to remember that children will copy your actions?
2. What did Mark do that was dangerous?
3. Why is it important to think through your actions when working with children?

Health and safety is covered in more detail in Unit 3, pages 109–20.

Child protection

Sadly, not all adults are safe to be with children. Some adults abuse children, so it is important that you work with children in ways that will help them to be safe and learn about safe behaviour.

Every setting will have a **child protection policy**. You will need to find out whether you must wear a badge, how to sign in and in what situations you may work with children. It is usual for settings to insist that you should never be alone with children – this is important for your own protection, too.

Jargon buster

Child protection policy
Written instructions that inform staff what they should do if they suspect that a child is being abused and how they can prevent abuse from taking place in the setting

You should also be aware of how much physical contact you may give children. Learners often find that children are keen to hug and touch them. While this might be appropriate with young children, it is unlikely to be encouraged with older children. Try to notice the amount of physical contact that other staff use with children as this is likely to be appropriate for the children's age and stage of development.

Managing children's behaviour

Children can often become silly and excited when they are with learners because they see them as being friendly. It is important that you find out about your setting's policy in relation to managing children's behaviour, for example in what type of situations you may intervene and how to do so. You will also need to be aware of your own actions when working with children, since there is a fine balance between playing with children and encouraging them to become silly or stopping them when they are meant to be doing an activity. It will be necessary to look at how experienced staff manage children's behaviour and to notice the 'rules' and conduct that is expected.

Case study

Setting an example for children

Hannah is on placement in a Reception class. The teacher asks her to sit with the children at story time. During story time, Hannah keeps talking to one of the children next to her. She lets the child sit on her knee and tickles her. The child giggles loudly and the other children start to get silly. The teacher becomes cross and eventually asks Hannah to start tidying the art area.

1. Explain why the teacher became cross.
2. Why is Hannah in danger of not following child protection procedures?
3. How should Hannah have behaved?

The Features Page:

Focus on *Starting placement*

Starting placement for the first time can feel very daunting. It is, however, essential as this is the way that you will practise your skills. You can help yourself get off to a flying start on placement if you take time to read up about the setting. Many settings now have their own website, so it is worth doing a little background reading. You can find out what you should wear and the times you will attend from your tutor.

It is essential that you work out how to get to your placement. If you are using public transport, you will need to be familiar with the timings and routes. Being late on placement is a real no-no and makes a very bad impression.

When you arrive, make sure that you introduce yourself clearly. It has been known for learners to be mistaken for supply staff or interviewees. Remember also that first impressions count and that you should try and show that you are enthusiastic – smiling goes a long way!

Q I have started on placement and am finding it really uncomfortable in the staff room. No one really talks to me.

A It can be hard being the newcomer in a setting. The main thing is not to take this personally but to remember that other staff already know each other and probably want to 'catch up' at break times. If you feel uncomfortable about being 'left out', you might like to take a magazine with you or something else to do so that you do not feel isolated. Offering to help by washing up mugs can make you popular so is worth a try. Most learners find that over time staff become more friendly as they get to know you.

Q I am really shy and am worrying about how I will cope on placement.

A Most learners feel a bit nervous before they start on placement. If you are shy, this can make it seem even more daunting. There are many strategies that you can use to overcome your shyness. The first is to focus on the needs of others rather than yourself. Think about how smiling might make it easier for people to greet you. Many shy people also feel especially worried when others ask them questions. A good tactic here is to turn things around so that you initiate some of the questions, such as asking 'How long have you been working here?' or 'Where did you train?' This means that you can show interest in others while not having to worry about what you might be saying. The more effort you make, the easier it can become, and practice definitely makes perfect!

Ask the expert

14

Starting placement

Top Tips:

Getting to your placement on time

✓ Make sure that you have the phone numbers of your placement and your college.

✓ Work out the route you will take to your placement, so that you can be sure to arrive on time.

✓ Ask your placement supervisor about what you should wear.

✓ Remember to look enthusiastic and to smile!

✓ Try and find nice things to say about your placement.

My story

Jayne, nursery nurse

I remember my first placement. It was in a nursery. I was really nervous and was not sure what to do or wear. Our college sent us for an introductory visit and I found that useful because I was given things to read and was shown around. The staff were really kind to me and I tried my best to fit in. I used to make sure that I looked for things to help staff with and ways of joining in. This helped me to build my confidence and learn new skills. A few times I had to ask for advice and help because when you are new and learning, you can't be expected to know everything. Luckily, my placement supervisor was patient and didn't mind.

It is funny to think about my first placement because I now act as a placement supervisor and so understand what it is like for placement supervisors. I like having learners; most of them are really good and try hard, although there are always a couple who turn up late or not at all. If they keep doing that, we tend to have a policy of not letting them stay on with us.

Recognising the limitations of your role

As a learner, there are limits to what you may do. You are not yet qualified so, as you saw earlier, you should never be left alone with a child or group of children. Below are other important limitations.

Talking to parents and carers

While you may greet parents and carers and it is important to be friendly, you must not let them think that you are a member of staff. If they wish to pass on or gain information, make sure that you direct them to a member of staff straight away.

Confidentiality

Everything that you learn as a result of being on placement which is personal or not general knowledge is confidential. This means that you should not talk about children or staff members outside of the setting. You may also find that you will be asked to leave the staff room or meeting if there is confidential information to be discussed. This is normal practice, so do not be offended.

Relationships with staff members

Knowing how to act with staff members can be difficult for some learners. It is important to remember that they are not your tutors, friends or parents. This means that you cannot expect them to help you with your assignments, listen to your moans or clear up after you. Aim to be friendly and remember to be as helpful and thoughtful as possible. Remember, too, that many staff will be friends with each other and at break times may spend time chatting to each other rather than to you. This does not mean that you are not liked, but simply that they want to catch up with each other. It is therefore best if you avoid interrupting conversations.

Back to the real world

You should now feel confident and ready to go into your work placement. You should understand why it is important to be prepared in order to make a good impression.

1. Explain why it is important to make a good impression.
2. Describe four ways in which you might be able to show that you are interested in working with children.
3. Provide two examples of situations when you would need to seek advice and so refer to your placement supervisor.

Section 4

Children's individual needs and necessity for fairness and inclusive practice

In the real world

Your tutor keeps talking about the way in which professionals working with children must meet their individual needs. You have also heard the expression anti-bias practice, but you are not sure what this means.

By the end of this section you will understand why fair and equal practice is important when working with children.

The importance of understanding children's individual needs and your role in meeting those needs

Adults working with children should want the best for them. This means that you will have to to think about each child's individual needs – that is, what each child requires in order to do well and be happy while in the setting. For example, a child who has recently joined the setting will need extra adult attention from their **key worker** in order to settle.

Children's needs can vary enormously. While some needs may be long-term, others are often short-term, such as a child's need for more adult time while settling in. Children may also have several needs, all of which must be taken into account if you are to work well with them. For example, a child with hearing loss who has difficulty settling into a setting may have a passion for toy cars, and this interest could be used to help the child settle.

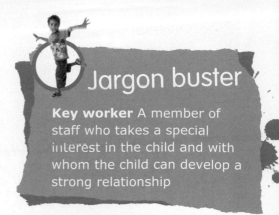

Jargon buster

Key worker A member of staff who takes a special interest in the child and with whom the child can develop a strong relationship

Finding out about children's needs

There are several ways in which you can find out about the individual needs of children.

Observations

By watching children you can sometimes learn more about them and their individual needs. You might spot that a child looks unhappy or worried, or that the child is having some difficulty joining in with other children. From these observations, adults should think about how best to work with the child. (You will learn more about observations in Unit 2, pages 52–7, and Unit 6, pages 219–24.)

Listening to children

Children can sometimes tell you what they enjoy doing and about their worries. Talking to children is an important way of working with them.

Listening to placement supervisors

When you are qualified you will gain a lot of information about children's needs from parents. As a learner this is not appropriate, but your placement supervisor may tell you about some children's needs, for example that a child is allergic to wheat so follows a special diet, or that a child has asthma so you should look out for signs of breathlessness. The information you are given about individual children's needs is confidential, which means that you must not share this information with others.

⇧ **Observing children is a key way in which you will find out about their individual needs**

Meeting children's individual needs

It is important that children's needs are met once they have been identified. You will probably find that your setting adapts activities or puts out specific equipment or toys to meet the needs of individual children. You will also have to think about children's individual needs when you plan activities in a setting, and it is important to think about their interests, too.

The importance of treating children with fairness and equality and how to do this

Anti-bias practice is used when working with children. This means that adults in the setting do everything they can to make sure that all children are treated fairly and equally. The aim is to give every child opportunities to do well.

In UK society, there have traditionally been some children and their families who have not been given the same chances as everyone else. When this happens, it is called **discrimination**. An example of discrimination is a child with a disability being unable to play in the sandpit because the sandpit is in a place that the child cannot access.

Prejudice and discrimination

Discrimination occurs when people are prejudiced. **Prejudice** comes from the idea of pre-judging someone. If you are prejudiced against a person, you already hold negative views about them before you have even met and taken time to get to know that person. (To read more about prejudice and discrimination see Unit 7, pages 282–94.)

Equal treatment does not mean the same treatment

Treating children equally means thinking about each child as an individual and treating them with the same concern and value. As each child is unique, this means, in practical terms, that you will meet their needs differently. For example, a child who needs more attention will get more attention because he or she requires it.

Remember, treating children equally does not always mean that children receive exactly the same amount of help, time or adult attention. To treat children equally you may sometimes provide different activities or adapt equipment.

Jargon buster

Anti-bias practice Steps taken in a setting to ensure that children are treated fairly and with equal respect

Discrimination When a person is treated differently because of their age, gender, ethnic background, culture or disability

Prejudice Making assumptions about a person before you know them

Case study

Children may have different needs

It is snack time in the nursery. Kylie and Zainep are the same age and are sitting at the table. The learner gives them both a clementine. Zainep quickly picks hers up and starts to peel it. She is pleased with herself and chats away happily. Kylie is struggling with hers. She looks frustrated but the learner refuses to help her. She says to Kylie that she must do it herself as it would not be fair on Zainep, who managed to peel it by herself. She says that she must treat them the same.

1. What should the learner have done differently?
2. How might Kylie feel if she is not given some help?
3. Why might you need to treat children differently in order to treat them with equal concern?

The box below describes some ways in which you might show equal concern to children and ensure they can do as well as other children.

Tips for good practice

Ways to show equal concern

→ Adapt activities to meet individual children's needs.

→ Observe and plan activities based on children's individual interests and stage of development.

→ Value and get to know each child.

→ Make sure that no children or their families are 'favourites'.

→ Listen to children and give them attention when they need it.

→ Think about children's behaviour and the help they might need.

 Back to the real world

You should now know some of the ways in which adults working with children try to treat children fairly and the importance of this.

1. Think of two ways in which you would need to work with children so they could be treated equally and fairly.

Section 5

Your own preferred learning style and how to develop relevant study skills

In the real world

You know that you have an assignment to do in order to complete this unit. You are a little anxious about it as this will be the first piece of work you will have done. You have also been told by your tutor that you should keep notes but are not sure how best to do this.

By the end of this section you will know how you learn best and how to study.

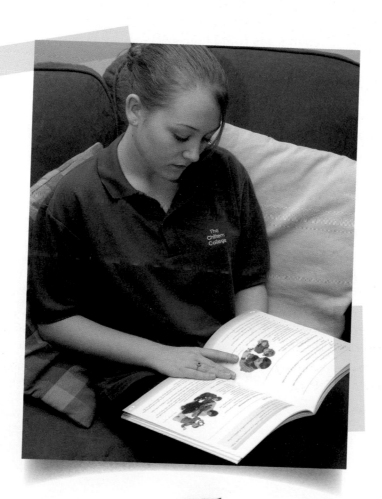

The different learning styles that people use and how to identify your own preferred style

People appear to process information or new bits of learning in different ways, sometimes using a combination of skills. You will need to discover how you learn and study best.

The following three headings are often used when talking about learning styles:

→ *Auditory* – processing by listening, for example you enjoy being told about things

→ *Kinaesthetic* – processing by doing or moving, for example you enjoy practical activities

→ *Visual* – processing by watching, for example you enjoy being shown things or like to remember information by drawing.

While you might recognise that you prefer to take in information using one of the learning styles above, you might also discover that you use all three types depending on the learning situation. Most people find that a practical skill such as being able to display children's work is learned better when someone shows them (visual learning style) or encourages them to practise the skill themselves (kinaesthetic learning style). It is unlikely that anyone would be able to learn how to display children's work from just hearing about it.

Recognising how you process information can help when it comes to revising or learning for tests. For example, if you know that you process information best through listening, you could prepare tapes for yourself; if you learn best by doing, you might physically cut up information on bits of paper and make yourself move them around the room. On the other hand, if you are good at remembering information in 'picture' format, you might use a mapping technique (see opposite page) or display words and diagrams in the area where you study.

Knowing yourself

To discover how you learn and study best, it is important to be honest with yourself and think about how you normally work. Some people work best in the morning, while others perform better in the evening. It is also helpful to think about the effects of pressure on you. Some people work well when under pressure and can juggle more than one assignment or task at a time, while others find that stress causes them to work more slowly or is a distraction.

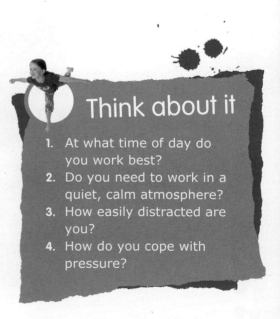

Think about it

1. At what time of day do you work best?
2. Do you need to work in a quiet, calm atmosphere?
3. How easily distracted are you?
4. How do you cope with pressure?

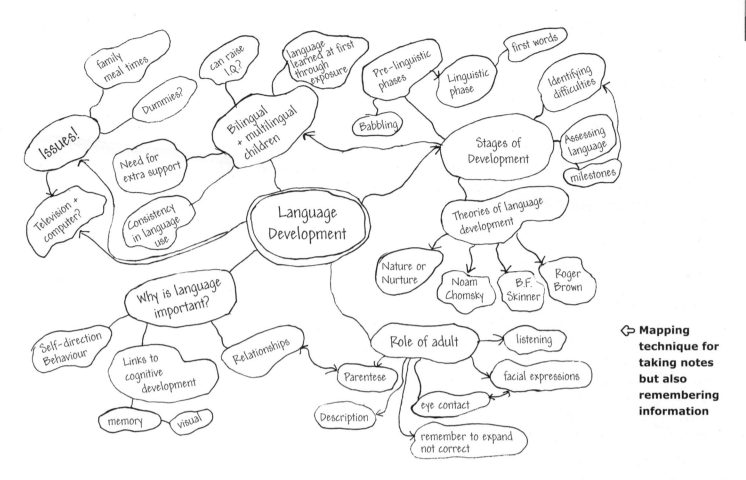

Mapping technique for taking notes but also remembering information

The study skills that will help you to complete your course

By now you should have thought about how you learn best, but you will also need some study skills. On this course you will need to be able to write assignments, prepare for tests and plan activities and observations for when you are in placement. There are many skills that you will need in order to do this.

Using appropriate books for information

You will be expected to read and use books in order to complete your assignments and to find information that will help you while on placement. A good starting point when looking for books is your college or local library. Most colleges have a range of books to support learners, while most local libraries will order books for you if you know the title. In addition, your college tutors should be able to recommend books that will be right for your needs on a course.

Finding your way around a book

Indexes are useful when looking up specific pieces of information (see the index on pages 426–31 of this book), while the contents pages will show you how the book is structured (see pages iii–iv).

Practice makes perfect!

Some books are easier to read than others. If you find reading difficult, begin by reading some text that you find straightforward and then read about the same subject in a book that is more demanding. This way you will already have some idea about the subject area you are studying.

Reading and summarising information

Taking notes is a skill that comes with practice. It is vital that you do not copy out the book itself. This takes too much time and there is a danger that you might be accused of **plagiarism** (using someone else's words) if you use the text you have copied in your assignment.

To avoid copying word for word, try reading a short passage at a time and then asking yourself what it means. Imagine explaining it in your own words to someone else. With the book closed, write down the information you need to remember. Some people do this with bullet points; this should help you to check that you understand the information.

Another tip is to write the title of the book and the page number in your notes. Then, if you realise later that you need more information, you will know which book to go to. This can save you a lot of time. It also means that you can include the book in the bibliography (see page 25).

If you need to quote someone's ideas directly from a book, you should clearly show which book you are referring to (see page 25 on referencing).

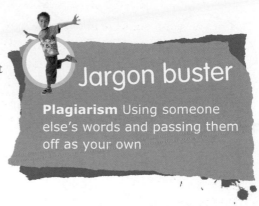

Jargon buster

Plagiarism Using someone else's words and passing them off as your own

Taking notes in class

Taking notes can help you to remember information because you are actively doing something with it. You might like to receive handouts from tutors, but there is a danger that simply reading through the information will not help you to remember what you have learned. You will also need to take notes from books to help with your work.

People take notes in different ways. For example, you might find that the people you sit next to in class write a lot more or a lot less than you do. Some people find it helpful to write nearly everything down, while others number points or draw circles around things. It is important to make sure that you can understand your notes afterwards so that you can use them to help with your assignments or tests. Giving your notes a heading will enable you to remember afterwards what the subject was about.

Giving presentations and sharing information

As part of your course you may be asked to give a presentation or report back to the group about something you have learned or have done. Learning presentation skills will help you later on when you are looking for a job. Talking at interview is rather like giving a presentation, and so practising how to talk to others is a useful skill. A good way of

⇧ **The ability to present information to others is a vital communication skill**

preparing for presentations is to make some simple notes. Think about the knowledge or ideas others in the group need to hear about and then focus on the best way of sharing this information.

Participating in group discussions

Talking about subjects in class can be a good way of learning and absorbing information. For this to work well, everyone in the group should be ready to join in by giving their views and sharing their knowledge. Group members also need to show respect for each other by not talking over other people or laughing if a mistake is made. Groups can fail to learn if they argue or if one or two people dominate the group.

Compiling a bibliography and using references in assignments

Bibliography

To get higher grades on this course, your assignments will need to include a bibliography. This is really easy to do. You simply write a list of the books, websites or magazines that you have used to help you with the assignment. There are many ways of writing a bibliography but the essential information to include for a book is:

➜ title of the book
➜ author's name
➜ publisher
➜ date of publication
➜ edition.

The same information is needed if you use other sources, such as a magazine, although for a website you should write the website address and link and give the date that you used it.

Referencing

As you saw earlier (page 24), you are not allowed to write someone else's words in an assignment and pass them off as your own. This is known as plagiarism, and if you do this you will fail your assignment. You can still use words from books, magazines and other sources as long as you credit them – this is called referencing. There are two types of references: direct and indirect.

Direct reference

An example of a direct reference is given below. Note how it contains an actual quote from a book along with the author's name and the date that the book was published. It is also good practice to include the page number as well. Make sure that you copy out any text accurately.

> While I observed Ayse, I noticed that she enjoyed playing with buttons. I believe she was enjoying the sensory experience. According to Tassoni, 'Children need opportunities to explore the natural and man-made world. For babies and toddlers, this exploration can take the form of sensory play and heuristic play' (Tassoni, 2006, p.163).

Department of Health (2003) *Keeping Children Safe*. London: HMSO

Hucker, K. (2001) *Research Methods in Health, Care and Early Years*. Oxford: Heinemann

Meggitt, C. (2003) *Food Hygiene and Safety*. Oxford: Heinemann

Tassoni, P. (2006) *Diploma in Pre-School Practice*, 2nd edition. Oxford: Heinemann

⇧ **Example of a bibliography**

Indirect reference

Now consider the indirect reference below. An indirect reference refers to what an author has written about rather than using his or her exact words.

Piaget's work has been criticised by others studying children. Margaret Donaldson suggested that children found it hard to do the tasks because of the design of the experiments. She argued that this made it hard for the children to find the right answers (Donaldson, 1978).

Listing references

At the end of your assignment you will need to write out a list of the books or sources that you referenced. This is usually put under the heading 'References'. As with writing a bibliography, you should include the author, book title, publisher and date of publication. In theory, it should be possible for your tutor to read a reference and then, from the information given, go to the book or other source and find the reference. This is why it is important that the date of the book or source is given along with a page number.

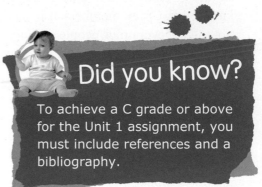

Did you know?

To achieve a C grade or above for the Unit 1 assignment, you must include references and a bibliography.

Writing different documents for assignments

You are required to complete written assignments for this course. Many learners find this daunting, so you will not be alone if you feel anxious about it. The key to coping is firstly to listen carefully to your tutor as the assignment task is given out. Most tutors will give you some ideas as to how you can structure your assignment. You can also look at similar documents; for example, if you have been asked to write a leaflet, look at some leaflets to see how they have been written.

While you will need to write, remember that this is not a writing course and so, providing you have met the grading criteria, it does not matter if you are not absolutely word perfect. You may also find that the more you read, the better your writing will become.

Punctuation, spelling and grammar

Punctuation, spelling and grammar are the tools of writing and so are important. If you have difficulties with writing it is essential to ask for help and not to be embarrassed. Writing is a skill that will be needed in your career and not being able to write may hold you back later. Colleges have many ways of supporting learners who need help with writing skills and it is a good idea to seek help now, while you are a learner and have more time. Help is free and confidential, which means that other learners in your group do not have to know that you are receiving it.

If you are someone who can write, but find punctuation and spelling difficult, you may like to think about learning to touch type so that you can word-process your assignments. This can be useful as the computer can pick up mistakes and help you to correct them.

Time management

Being able to complete an assignment or prepare for an exam requires good time management skills. Some capable learners may find that they do not fulfil their potential because their time management skills are weak.

Planning your time

It is important at the start of any assignment or task to be aware of how much of your time it will take. You may know, for example, that you find reading a little difficult or are someone who has to put ideas down in draft before writing out an assignment. This means that when you are given an assignment, you should work out how much time each part is likely to take you. It is important to be realistic when you do this and to allow for any problems, such as difficulties printing out your work or getting hold of books that you need. It is also worth considering that you might be unwell during this period or that something unexpected may happen. This is why it is usually best to do some work straight away.

The example below shows how a task can be divided into steps and how you might start to consider the possible difficulties in a task.

Example assignment

Sara and her group have been asked to carry out an observation on a child in placement. They have been told to ask permission from their placement supervisor and then choose one child and look at that child's fine motor skills. Once they have completed the observation, they must then consider how they will use books to work out how the child's skills compares to the normative development. Both the observation and their evaluation of the child's physical skills must be presented in writing. The tutor is expecting around three pages of writing.

The task in the example above can be divided into five different steps.
1. Asking the placement supervisor for permission to observe a child
2. Observing the child
3. Writing up the observation
4. Researching normative development
5. Writing up an evaluation

Possible problems might include:
1. The placement supervisor may not be available.
2. It may not be possible to observe the chosen child.
3. There may not be any books available to research normative development.

Possible difficulty with skills could include:
1. Sara's observation skills may need practising.
2. She may find it hard to find the words she needs when writing up the observation.
3. She may find taking notes and choosing the relevant points about normative development difficult.
4. She may find it hard to put her thoughts into words.
5. She may have difficulties with handwriting/typing and/or spelling and punctuation.

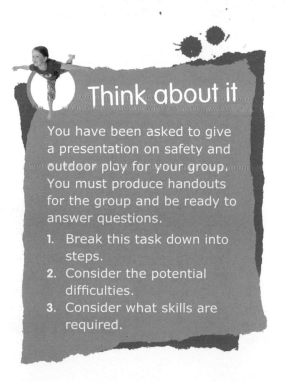

Think about it

You have been asked to give a presentation on safety and outdoor play for your group. You must produce handouts for the group and be ready to answer questions.

1. Break this task down into steps.
2. Consider the potential difficulties.
3. Consider what skills are required.

Revising for tests

Some learners find tests difficult, while others prefer them to assignments. Learners who do well with tests and exams tend to be 'active' revisers. This means that they do not simply pick up a book or their notes and read them but do a variety of things that actively engage their brain when revising. The spider diagram below shows some useful strategies for revising.

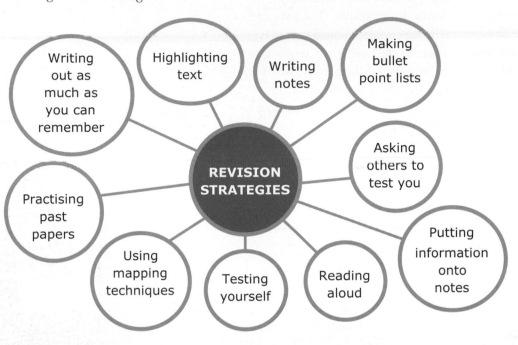

You should now have thought about how you learn. You should also have tried out some different study skills.

1. Explain your preferred learning style. Describe what this means in practice.

2. How should you use a reference in a text?

Getting ready for assessment

Unit 1 is assessed through an introductory task that has been written by the awarding body. If you have worked through all the activities in the 'Back to the real world' features in this unit, you will be ready to successfully complete your assessment.

Unit 2

The developing child

In this unit you will learn:

1. The expected pattern of development

2. The importance of careful observations and how they support development

3. How to identify influences that affect children's development

4. How to use everyday care routines and activities to support development

5. How to support children through transitions in their lives

The expected pattern of development

In the real world

You are working in a nursery where there is also an after-school club for older children. You need to plan some activities for the children but are not really sure what they can do at different ages.

By the end of this section you will know about how children develop and change as they grow.

The physical development of children from birth to 16 years

Whatever early years setting you work in, it is important to understand the ways in which children physically grow and develop. Understanding children's stages of physical development will help you to work out what type of play activities they will enjoy and how you can support their independence skills.

Understanding the difference between growth and development

There is a difference between growth and development. Growth means that children gain in height and weight, whereas development means that they are gaining control of their body. Although most children's growth and development are matched, there are some children who may grow without developing control of their body, because of a disability for example.

Checking that children are growing and developing well is therefore important so that any problems can be detected as early as possible. Most checks are carried out by health visitors, doctors and school nurses, although sometimes it is early years practitioners and parents who notice that children are not developing as they should be. This is why you will need to have some understanding of physical development.

Measuring growth

Children's height and weight are measured and plotted on standard charts. These are called **percentile charts**, although many people call them 'centile' charts. There are separate charts for boys and girls because boys tend to be larger than girls. Health professionals, such as health visitors and doctors, measure children's height and weight then plot these measurements on the percentile chart. As children grow and are measured, a pattern of growth can be seen.

There are two main factors that can affect growth.

➔ The height of parents and other family members usually has a strong influence on the height of children.
➔ The quality and quantity of food that children eat also affects growth patterns. In the UK, diets have improved greatly in the last 60 years and this is why most people today are taller than their great-grandparents!

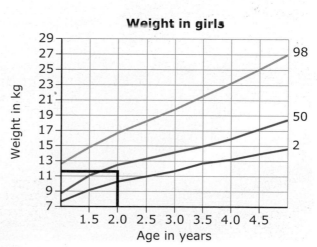

Jargon buster

Percentile chart A chart that is used to plot babies' and children's growth rate

☝ **Percentile chart showing range of growth rates for children**

Height in girls

Height in cm vs Age in years. Curves labelled 98, 50, 2.

Weight in girls

Weight in kg vs Age in years. Curves labelled 98, 50, 2.

Measuring development

To gain complete control of the body, children need to master two different types of movements:

➜ large movements such as walking and running – these are called **gross motor skills**

➜ smaller movements such as turning a page in a book and throwing a ball – these are called **fine motor skills**.

Fine motor skills are split into gross manipulative skills and fine manipulative skills.

➜ Gross manipulative skills use a single limb only but are more controlled than gross motor skills.

➜ Fine manipulative movements are more precise, for example threading beads.

Fine manipulative skills are particularly important in the development of children. These skills allow children to become increasingly independent – by using these movements they are able to play with toys and feed themselves.

In addition to gross and fine motor skills, children need to develop the skills of **coordination** and balance.

➜ Coordination is linked to the way in which the brain is able to pass messages and take in information. Hand–eye coordination, for example, involves using information from the eyes to help the hands do something such as thread a bead on a string.

➜ Balance is also linked to the way in which the brain is able to handle information. Balance is required for mobility.

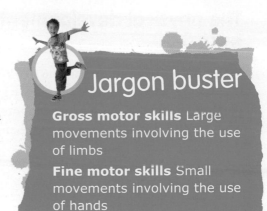

Jargon buster

Gross motor skills Large movements involving the use of limbs

Fine motor skills Small movements involving the use of hands

Jargon buster

Coordination The ability to combine several movements fluently, for example to bend down while holding a brush

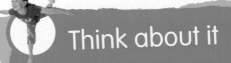

Think about it

Observe two children of different ages playing.

1. Write a list of the physical skills that they are using in order to play.
2. Can you see a difference in their skill level?

◁ **Fine manipulative skills allow children to become increasingly independent**

Principles of physical development

Researchers have observed three principles of physical development in young children, as follows:

1. *Physical development follows a sequence; children do not suddenly jump stages.* For example, babies need to be able to support their head before they can learn to sit up or crawl.

2. *Physical development begins with the control of head movements and continues downwards.* This is particularly true of babies' development and it is thought to be a survival mechanism. Babies need to be able to turn their head to feed. The downwards pattern of development also applies to the process of **ossification**. This is the way in which children's bones, which are soft at first, become harder. This is a long process which does not finish until the teenage years. During this process the bones in the hand harden before the feet.

3. *Development begins with uncontrolled gross movements before becoming precise and refined.* If you look at babies' early movements, you will see that they are able to reach out for an object with the whole arm before they can use their fingers to grasp it.

What is 'normal' development?

Development is harder to measure than growth because it is a gradual process and children gain control of their body at different rates. For example, some children may walk at 9 months whereas others may not walk until they are nearly 2 years old.

The wide variation between children means that it is impossible to say that by a certain age all children will have mastered a movement or skill. It is important to remember this when working with children so that activities or equipment are matched to meet individual children's needs.

Jargon buster

Ossification Hardening of bones

Jargon buster

Milestones The range of skills that children are expected to show at certain points in their childhood

Milestones

To measure children's development, most health professionals look at the skills children have mastered. These skills can be broadly linked to age and are often called **milestones**, the idea being that children have reached a certain point in their development. For example, most children can kick, throw and bounce a ball by the age of 5 years. The chart below shows some aspects of expected physical development for children aged 0–16 years, although it is important to remember that there will be differences between children.

⇧ **Can you identify the principles of physical development in action in this 4-month-old baby?**

♨ **Expected physical development from birth to 16 years**

Age	Fine motor skills	Gross motor skills
3 months	• Watches hands and plays with fingers • Clasps and unclasps hands • Holds a rattle for a moment	• Lifts up head and chest • Waves arms and brings hands together over body
6 months	• Reaches for a toy • Moves a toy from one hand to another • Puts objects into mouth	• Moves arms to indicate that they want to be lifted • Rolls over from back to front
9 months	• Grasps object with index finger and thumb • Deliberately releases objects by dropping them	• Sits unsupported • Likely to be mobile, i.e. crawling or rolling
12 months	• Uses index finger and thumb (pincer grasp) to pick up small objects • Points to something with the index finger	• May stand alone briefly • May walk holding on to furniture (although some children may be walking unaided)
18 months	• Uses a spoon to feed with • Scribbles • Builds a tower of three bricks	• Walks unaided • Climbs up onto a toy • Squats to pick up a toy
2 years	• Draws circles and dots • Uses spoon effectively to feed with	• Runs • Climbs onto furniture • Uses sit-and-ride toys
2½ years	• May have established hand preference • Does simple jigsaw puzzles	• Kicks a large ball • May begin to use a tricycle
3 years	• Turns pages in a book, one by one • Washes and dries hands with help • Holds a crayon and can draw a face	• Steers and pedals a tricycle • Runs forwards and backwards • Throws a large ball
4 years	• Buttons/unbuttons own clothing • Cuts out simple shapes • Draws a person with head, trunk and legs	• Walks on a line • Aims and throws a ball • Hops on one foot
5 years	• Forms letters; writes own name • Colours in pictures • Completes 20-piece jigsaw	• Skips with a rope • Runs quickly and able to avoid obstacles • Throws a large ball to a partner and catches it
6–8 years	• Able to join handwriting • Cuts out shapes accurately • Produces detailed drawings • Ties/unties shoelaces	• Hops, skips and jumps confidently • Balances on a beam • Chases and dodges others • Uses a bicycle and other wheeled toys such as roller skates

Age	Fine motor skills	Gross motor skills
8–12 years	Fine motor skills become more refined allowing for intricate work such as model making, knitting and typing. Less concentration is required allowing children to talk as they use their hands	Increased coordination and perceptual skills. These allow children to concentrate on strategies during games such as football or netball
12–16 years	Hardening of the bones in the hands and wrists completed. This allows for increased strength in hands enabling movements such as twisting lids off jars	Stamina increases as lungs and heart develop. This allows young people to walk for longer distances and to take part in more energetic sports

Growth and maturation

Alongside development, children's bodies grow and mature as they move towards adulthood. Growth and ageing (maturation) are biological processes and tend to follow a pattern – one of the results is a change in body shape and size. A good example of this is the way in which the body lengthens in relation to the head. A baby has a relatively large head in comparison to its overall body length. This changes as children become older, and while the head continues to grow, it does so less rapidly than the trunk, arms and legs.

⇦ **What do you notice if you compare the length of the body in relation to the head for this 12-month-old baby and 14-year-old girl?**

Puberty

From about 10 years old, many girls' bodies show signs that the process of **puberty** has started. For most girls, puberty finishes at around 15 years when their body is biologically ready to conceive and carry a baby. Outward signs that a girl's body is maturing include the development of breasts and widening of the hips. Most girls will begin to menstruate (start their periods) between the ages of 12 and 14 years, although this can vary.

Jargon buster

Puberty Stage of adolescence when sexual development begins and a person becomes capable of sexual reproduction

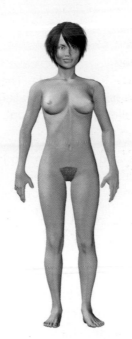

⟵ **During puberty the body's shape changes dramatically**

Did you know?

Puberty for both boys and girls begins with a growth spurt.

For boys, puberty begins at around 12 or 13 years and for most will end at about 17 years, although many boys will continue to grow until they are 18 years old. Outward signs that boys are going through puberty include a sudden growth in height, the voice becoming deeper and facial hair growth. At the end of this process, most boys will be stronger than girls because the ratio of fat to muscles is higher in girls than in boys. On average, boys will also be taller.

The communication and intellectual development of children from birth to 16 years

Learning how to communicate

Learning how to communicate is an essential skill. It helps children get their needs met and make friends and is linked to the ability to think (see below). There are many skills involved in communicating, as shown in the spider diagram, and these are learned gradually.

How communication and language are learned

From the moment a baby is born, he or she will tune into sounds. The baby will quickly start to turn their head in the direction of sounds and soon recognise their main carers' voices. In the first year, they also learn the key skills of communicating, which include eye contact, facial expression and smiling. Gradually, babies start to work out what words mean, and by the age of 9 months many babies are able to understand some key words, such as 'bye bye' or 'drink'.

At the same time as tuning into language, babies are practising their speech. They start by cooing but quickly move on to babbling. From 6 months, even the babbling becomes more complex and increasingly sounds like the language they are hearing. From 12 months, babies start mixing babbling with recognisable words. By 18 months, children often have ten or more words.

Grammar

Speaking and writing requires knowledge of grammar. Words have to be put in the right order to make sense, and children have to know about plurals and past tenses. Fortunately, children seem to learn the grammar of their language fairly naturally if the people they are with speak in sentences.

Tuning in and listening

Babies need to work out the sounds that are used in the language they will be learning. Older children need to be able to listen and make sense of what is being communicated to them.

Vocabulary

Children need to learn the meanings of words and know when and how to use them.

Gestures and body language

As well as words, children need to know what someone is feeling. Body language and gestures are ways of communicating feelings and moods.

SKILLS INVOLVED IN COMMUNICATION AND LANGUAGE

Pronunciation

In a spoken language, children need to be able to create the sounds that they are hearing. Babies begin this process by babbling and practising sounds. Older children often make the occasional mistake as they learn how to say a new word.

Facial expressions

Children need to understand what facial expressions mean. They also have to use them when they communicate.

Pitch and intonation

The sound of your voice is important. Through pitch and intonation, you let everyone know how you are feeling. It also helps other people to stay interested. Through early babbling, babies learn how to modulate their voice.

Taking turns

Good communication is a process which involves listening, thinking and responding. Babies learn how to be responsive if adults play with them and encourage them to babble.

How young children build their language

Once children begin to learn words, they quickly start using them. The amount of babbling decreases and the number of words increases. From 2 years, this is often noticeable, as children literally learn dozens of new words each week. From single words, children start to put two words together; 'Cat-gone' or 'Drink-no' are examples of the way children are able to make mini-sentences. This is known as **telegraphese**. From this point, children soon make whole sentences, and by the age of 3 years

Jargon buster

Telegraphese Children's early speech consisting of two or three words their speech is likely to be understood by someone who does not know them. From 4 years, children are likely to sound fairly fluent, although the odd mispronunciation or mistake will carry on until children are around 7 years old.

⟱ **Language development from birth to 8 years**

Age	Stage	Role of adult
0–6 months	Babies are trying to communicate. They make eye contact and babble. They imitate and repeat sounds.	Good eye contact, running commentary and repetition of phrases, e.g. 'I think you're feeling hungry now, aren't you?' As babies begin to babble, they need praise and recognition that they are trying to communicate.
6–18 months	First words are made. One word may stand for several things. Children begin to point to attract adult's interest. They respond to pictures of animals and familiar objects. By 18 months, most children are using 15 words.	Getting down to the level of the child and making eye contact is important. Children need to feel that they are being understood and listened to. Rhymes, songs and books can be introduced. Children need plenty of adult input and running commentary, e.g. 'It's time for a bath now. You like your bath, don't you?'
18 months – 3 years	During this time children's vocabulary increases quickly. By the age of three, children are putting sentences together and are beginning to use questions. Children enjoy and are able to follow stories and remember rhymes. By 3 years, some children are using 900 words.	Adults need to allow children enough time to think and answer. They must be patient, as children often enjoy repeating questions and asking for stories and rhymes over and over again. You can help children with their pronunciation and grammar by using the same words, but correctly, e.g. 'I felled down' – 'You fell down, did you? Shall I look at your knee?'
3–8 years	By the age of 5 years, most children have a vocabulary of 3000 words and are using complex sentences and questions. By the time children go to school, they can often understand simple jokes and enjoy stories. By 8 years, children can use language in many different ways, e.g. to socialise, to express a need, to recount and predict events.	Adults need to extend children's vocabulary and help them to use language as a way of thinking. One way is to use open questions. This means asking questions where children have to give more than a one-word answer. For example, 'Why did you think the ice melted?' Children need to have time to think and may stammer if they rush to explain something. You need to show them that you are listening by, for example, nodding your head and making eye contact. They may use words that they have heard without understanding their meaning, such as swear words, and you may need to explain that some words are not nice. Stories and rhymes are still needed and enjoyed even when children can read for themselves.

How older children use language

Once children have become fluent users of language, they are soon able to use it to their advantage. They may start to pester adults and argue back, as well as enjoy jokes and even make them up. Once children have mastered spoken language, the next stage is to learn how to read and write. Most children will be ready to do this at around 6 years, although they may sometimes be encouraged to start younger. Learning to read is a skill and relies on children remembering visual signs as well as linking sounds with signs. Writing is linked to reading, so many children need to learn how to read before they can write easily.

Intellectual development

Intellectual development is about how children learn, think and develop ideas. It is an interesting area of development, and is one in which research continues to broaden our knowledge. It is hard to give an accurate picture of children's development, especially as children become older. This is because children's development will be strongly shaped by the following factors.

Experience

Children's experiences will make a difference to their intellectual development. A good example of this is their learning of colours. Some children know their colours by the time they are three, but this is dependent on adults pointing them out and drawing children's attention to them.

Language

Children's level of language seems to affect their intellectual development. This is because we tend to use language when thinking. Some people talk aloud to themselves when they are trying to get themselves organised, and this is an example of language used for thinking. Children with good levels of language often find it easier to problem solve and also think about the consequences of their actions.

Interests

As children get older, their cognitive development becomes linked to the way in which they are taught and their own preferences about subjects. This means that some children at 14 years will be competent mathematicians, while others may find mathematics quite a struggle! The chart below shows some broad aspects of children's development.

 Find out!

Using an MP3 player or a similar recording device, record a child from each of these age groups:

→ 0–2 years   → 2–4 years   → 4–7 years

(Note that you will need permission from your placement supervisor or the children's parents.)

1. How does their speech compare to the expected development for their age?
2. What differences do you notice in the way they talk?

⏣ **Cognitive development in children from birth to 16 years**

Age	Play and learning development
0–6 months	• Watching adults closely • Exploring by using the mouth and by touch • Playing alone with toys such as rattles and baby gyms
6–12 months	• Exploring by using the mouth and by touch • Watching and copying adults • Repeating movements such as dropping a rattle • Enjoying simple games such as peek-a-boo • Exploring toys alone
12–18 months	• Learning through trial and error, e.g. banging two cubes and discovering the sound it makes • Repeating actions that they have enjoyed • Beginning to play with adults and notice other children • Playing and 'talking' alone
18 months – 2 years	• Learning through trial and error • Imitating other children and adults • Exploring things with the mouth • Possibly carrying out repetitive actions, e.g. putting things in and out of boxes or scribbling on several pages • Watching other children but not joining in • Enjoying playing with adults as well as by themselves
2–3 years	• Beginning to show some reasoning skills and asking questions such as 'why' • Starting to concentrate for longer on a play activity that interests them • Recognising shapes and letters • Solving jigsaw puzzles through a mixture of reasoning and trial and error • Playing cooperatively together and taking turns • Playing imaginatively, e.g. playing in the home corner, dressing up
4–6 years	• Showing more understanding and using reason based on their experiences • Starting to use and understand symbols, e.g. writing and reading • Starting to understand simple rules in games • Playing cooperatively, taking turns and enjoying table-top games
6–8 years	• Enjoying using rules and understanding the need for rules • Showing reasoning skills but still using some trial and error learning • Playing in small groups and making up their own games which tend to have rules • Enjoying playing competitive games but not always coping with losing • Tending to play with children of their own sex
8–12 years	• Able to reason and use logic to solve some problems • Showing creativity in writing, drawing and role play • Beginning to use information from one situation and transfer it to another
13–16 years	• Able to read and write confidently • Good at transferring information from one situation to another • May be competent in using abstract information, e.g. chemistry, maths • Questioning sources of information, e.g. parents, books and teachers • Growing awareness of issues such as poverty, pollution and politics

⇧ **Up to 2 years of age, children will find out about objects by putting them in their mouth**

⇧ **By 6 to 8 years of age, children enjoy using and understand the need for rules**

The social, emotional and behavioural development of children from birth to 16 years

Humans seem to be born with the ability to live in groups and to be sociable. This can be seen in babies, as very early on they are able to make eye contact and smile.

Being able to fit in with other people is an important skill which we require in order to have friends, live side by side with strangers and have close relationships with others. For children, this area of development is important too, as they will want to play with other children and have to learn how to share and be with others in group situations, such as in school.

Stages of emotional and social development

There are different stages to the emotional and social development of children and, although ages can be given, the age at which children reach different stages may vary greatly. The speed at which children are able to start playing and cooperating with other children and leaving their primary carer often depends on individual circumstances, for example younger children in the family may learn to play quickly, as there are other children around them. As with other areas of children's development, it is more important to build up a picture of a child's emotional and social development than to concentrate on what is 'normal' at a particular age.

Development from birth to 1 year

Babies learn to play and communicate their needs. They laugh, smile and make eye contact with their primary carers and family. These are important social skills.

Age	Stage of development
1 month	• Watches primary carer's face
3 months	• Smiles and coos • Enjoys being handled and cuddled
6 months	• Laughs and enjoys being played with
8 months	• Fears strangers
9 months	• Plays peek-a-boo • Discriminates between strangers and familiar adults
12 months	• Is affectionate towards family and primary carers • Plays simple games such as pat-a-cake

⇧ **Smiling and making eye contact is an important social skill that babies develop**

Development from 1–2 years

At this age, children learn that they are separate from their primary carers. They recognise and begin to use their name, and begin to explore independently. At about the age of 2 years, they begin to show anger and frustration if their needs are not met immediately. They do not recognise that other people have needs as well. During this year, children start to play alongside other children.

Age	Stage of development
15 months	• Begins to explore environment if familiar adult is close by • Begins to use words to communicate with • Has a stronger feeling of being an individual
18 months	• Language is increasing • Points to objects to show familiar adults • Explores environment and shows some independence but still needs familiar adults
2 years	• Plays near other children (parallel play) • Begins to talk when playing (pretend play) • Imitates adults' actions • Strong emotions, e.g. anger, fear, jealousy and joy, are shown

Development from 2–3 years

This is an important year in children's lives and there is great progress in their social and emotional development. It is often a difficult year for both children and carers, as children come to terms with their independence and strong desires. Tantrums and strong feelings at the start of the year lessen as children gradually develop more language and physical skills. Early years practitioners need to support and reassure children who are starting to leave their primary carers during this year.

There is a wide variation in the way children progress over the year so it is hard to put specific times to these steps. During this year most children will:

→ move out of nappies
→ have a strong sense of identity, including gender and age
→ be happy to leave their primary carer for short periods
→ start taking an interest in other children and play with them
→ show concern for other children, for example telling someone if a baby is crying
→ start to wait for their needs to be met.

Development from 3–4 years

This is a more settled year for children. They grow in confidence as they are able to make friends and play with other children. Their language and physical skills have developed. They show social skills, for example turn taking, sharing and concern for others. Emotionally, children still need reassurance from their immediate carers but are more independent and may play by themselves for longer periods. Strong emotions are still felt and quarrels and temper tantrums occur at times.

During this year most children will:

→ be affectionate towards family, friends and carers
→ want to help and please primary carers and other familiar adults
→ imitate (in play) actions seen, for example putting teddy to bed, feeding dolls
→ share playthings
→ play with other children, mostly pretend play
→ show concern for other people, for example rubbing back of crying baby.

Development from 4–6 years

In some ways, the expression 'I can do' sums up this period of a child's life. Emotionally, most children feel confident and express themselves in terms of their achievements, e.g. 'I got a sticker today' or 'Look at me, I can climb this now'. They may start to use words and actions in imitation of other people. Playing with other children is increasingly important and some children start to make close friendships. At this time, children start to play with members of their own sex, which may link to their understanding of gender roles.

Development from 6–8 years

Children start to gain a sense of fairness and justice, which means they can share equipment and materials more easily. By the age of 7 years, children have started to become more self-aware and can be critical of their efforts, for example they may stop drawing if they are not happy with what they are producing. Children start to be influenced by adults and children who are not family members. Having a friend or group of friends becomes increasingly important to them and is sometimes a source of sadness. Children start to compare themselves to their peers and may need adult reassurance to cope with this.

⇧ **Children aged 2–3 years may reveal a strong sense of identity, including gender, through their preferences for certain toys, activities and clothes**

Development from 8–12 years

During this period, children become more aware of what other people think about them. They begin to compare themselves with others. Children make comments such as 'I can draw a little but not as well as my brother'. Children usually have a group of established friends of the same sex.

Development from 13–16 years

Young people in this age range tend to have strong friendships and form groups. Time spent with friends increases and they are likely to become more independent from their family. This can be a difficult time for young people. They see that their body shape has changed and their role as 'child' is also changing. This raises issues that they need to resolve. The transition from child to adult may not be fully completed until a young person leaves home to become fully independent.

Children's behaviour

Children's behaviour is complex because it is linked to many areas of development. It is also a factor in children's social development, as friendships and being with others requires being able to exercise some control.

Think about it

At what age do you remember having strong friendships?

Language development

Children have strong emotions. They will find it easier to control their emotions when they can explain how they are feeling. Up to the age of 3 years, children have more difficulty in controlling their feelings. Those who have speech and language delay may find it harder to control their behaviour.

Cognitive development

Children's behaviour becomes easier when they can understand the reason behind rules. This is why once children reach the age of 3 or 4 years, it becomes a little easier for them to be cooperative.

FACTORS AFFECTING CHILDREN'S BEHAVIOUR

Social development

Children need to spend time with other children as well as adults. This helps them to learn what behaviour is acceptable. This socialisation also teaches children, as they 'model' from watching adults and other children.

Emotional development

Children need to feel secure, valued and loved. Without this emotional support, they find it hard to show cooperative behaviour. Attention-seeking behaviours can be a sign that a child needs more support.

Physical development

Children find it easier to manage and control their behaviour when they are responsible and independent. Physical skills mean that children can be more self-reliant. This can help them to become less frustrated. In older children, physical growth and the release of hormones play a significant role in their moods and ability to control their feelings.

Section 2

The importance of careful observations and how they support development

In the real world

It is your first day on placement. Your supervisor says that you will be expected to help out with observations of children. You are a little concerned about how to do this.

By the end of the section you will know about some of the key ways in which you might observe children. You will also know how to contribute to other people's observations.

Introduction

As an adult, it is usually easy to see that children are having fun while they are playing. However, if you look more closely you will see that children are often very intense in their play and concentrate on what they are doing. Through play, they are also gaining skills and learning. By looking closely at children, you will be able to choose activities that will promote their learning and development. This means considering how children use materials or play and then working out what their next steps might be. Observations will also help you to learn more about how children are developing and can be used to make sure that children receive extra support where required.

The importance of confidentiality and objectivity when observing children

Confidentiality

An important starting point is to understand that children and their families have a right to confidentiality. When you observe children, you will be finding out more about them, and this is information that you would otherwise not have had before. This information therefore needs to be treated as confidential. You should not discuss what you have observed with anyone other than your tutor or your placement supervisor. When you are employed, it is also good practice to share information with parents as well but, as a learner, your placement supervisor is the person who should be talking directly to parents. If, during the observation, you have some concerns about the child's development or behaviour, these should be passed on to your placement supervisor.

Case study

The importance of objectivity when observing children

Two different people are observing the children today. One is a member of staff and the other is a visiting early years adviser. Mandy is in the group of children. She is 4 years old. The staff find her very uncooperative, as she only does things when she wants to. Today, the children have been told to tidy up, but Mandy carries on playing. The member of staff observes Mandy and is not surprised by her behaviour. She sees it as another example of Mandy being difficult.

The early years adviser does not know Mandy. She watches closely and begins to think about whether Mandy is hearing properly. She mentions this to the member of staff. Over the next few days, the staff watch Mandy with this thought in mind. They start to realise that Mandy is not always hearing instructions. A few days later Mandy's hearing is properly tested and the result shows that she has hearing loss.

1. Which adult was the most objective when observing Mandy?
2. Why did the member of staff fail to notice that Mandy was not hearing well?
3. Explain why it is important not to jump to conclusions when observing children.

Being objective

Observing children involves several skills, one of which is to be objective. This means you must observe children as if you have never seen or known them so as to avoid having set ideas about them and their development. This is essential because you may miss things or not realise their importance if you think that you know a child. The case study above shows the importance of being objective.

A range of techniques for observing children

Experienced early years practitioners observe children continually, as they look for signs that they are enjoying activities, need support or are becoming bored. As well as informally observing children and noticing what they are doing, there are some simple methods you can use to record what you are seeing.

Structured recording – tick charts and checklists

A structured recording involves looking out for particular skills or behaviour that children show. Many settings do this by using checklists or tick charts.

There are many advantages to using checklists and tick charts. They are easy and quick to use and they can be repeated on the same child at a later date to see if the child has gained further skills. This means that progress can be mapped. The main disadvantage of this method is that it is quite narrow, as it focuses the observer on looking only for the skills that are on the checklist or tick chart.

Name of child: ....

Age of child: ....   Observer: ....

Date of observation: ....   Time: ....

Activity	Yes	No	Comments
Puts together three-piece puzzle			
Snips with scissors			
Paints in circular movements			
Holds crayons with fingers, not fists			
Can thread four large beads			
Turns pages in a book, one by one			
Can put on and take off coat			

⇧ **Example of a checklist**

Unstructured recording

An unstructured or free recording is used to 'paint a picture' of a child at the moment when the observation is taking place. The observer is free to choose what information to record, although most observers find that it is helpful to have an idea of what they particularly want to note down about the child, for example their language development or their ability to play with other children. Many settings use either time samples or free description to collect information in this way. Some settings use sticky notes to jot down anything of interest that they see a child do.

14/11/07   14.55pm

Ayse

Turns head when she hears a voice outside. Focuses and then smiles when she sees Charlie.

⇧ **Some settings use sticky notes to jot down anything of interest they observe in a child**

Time sample

A time sample collects information by 'sampling' what a child or group of children is doing at regular intervals. For example, an observer might choose to look at what a child is doing every ten minutes. This means that every ten minutes the observer will note down what the child is doing at that moment.

The main advantage of the time sample is that you can see what a child does over a period of time, say, over two hours. One disadvantage is that the child might show some interesting behaviour or skills outside of the 'sample' time which would not be captured.

⇩ **An unstructured time sample; recordings have been made at 15-minute intervals**

Time	Activity	Social group	Comments
11.00	Snack time	Whole group	Anna is sitting with her legs swinging on a chair. She is eating an apple. She is holding it in her left hand and she is smiling. She puts up her hand when a member of staff asks who wants a biscuit.
11.15	Outdoor play; climbing frame	Anna and Ben	Anna is on the top bar of the climbing frame. She is smiling at Ben. She calls 'Come up here!'
11.30	Taking coats off	Anna, Ben and Manjeet	Anna unzips her coat and pulls out one arm. She swings around and the coat swings with her. She laughs and looks at Manjeet.

Free descriptions (also known as narrative records)

A free description or narrative record allows the observer to note down what a child is doing for a short period of time. It can provide a 'snapshot' of a child and is a little like filming them. The main problem with free descriptions is that most observers cannot keep up the recording for a long period of time; usually two or three minutes is the maximum. Free descriptions also require the observer to be good at writing while watching and so most learners find they need to practise a few times.

Carrying out observations

Before you can carry out an observation on a child, you must seek either the supervisor's permission or the parents' permission. Most supervisors and parents will want to know what you will be observing and must be allowed to look at what you have written. This means that you should be particularly careful to record only what you have seen and not what you are thinking. Most observers find that if they are using an unstructured method, it is helpful to have an aim, for example 'To observe a child's hand–eye coordination', as this gives them a focus for the observation.

How to share your observations with colleagues to promote development

There may be times when you will be asked to observe a child so that a fuller picture of the child's development or needs can be made. An example of this might be in a nursery when you are asked to look out for whether or not a child can now write their name alone or can pour a drink without spilling it.

It is exciting to be asked to observe children, but it is also a responsibility. A good starting point is to be clear about what you need to observe. It is always best to ask if you are not totally sure. It is also essential when sharing observations that your observation is careful and accurate, as the case study below shows. You must also find out how you should record the observation. In some cases, you might be adding notes to existing observations or using a tick chart. If you are worried about your handwriting or spelling, it is best to mention this at the start.

Sharing observations

Observations are only useful if they are used in some way. Sometimes they are used to provide information to parents or to help a child's **key worker** build up a picture of them. Observations can also be used when activities are being planned so that you can be sure that there are activities available that will meet the needs of every child in the setting.

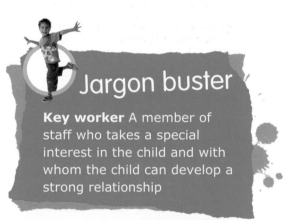

Jargon buster

Key worker A member of staff who takes a special interest in the child and with whom the child can develop a strong relationship

Case study

An inaccurate observation

The nursery staff are completing a tick chart on Metin's physical skills. They have seen that he can do several things, but they are wondering if he can now put on his coat unaided. Lisa, a learner, has been asked if she can observe Metin over the next few days to see whether or not he can do this. Lisa likes Metin and even though he needs a little help, she decides to put a tick next to his name to say that he can put on his own coat. A few days later, Metin asks another member of staff for help with his coat. The member of staff tells him that he is now a big boy and that he should be able to do it by himself. Metin looks worried.

1. Why do you think that Lisa decided to tick that Metin could put his coat on by himself?
2. Why was this not helpful for Metin and the other staff?
3. Explain why it is important to be accurate when carrying out observations.

There are many different people with whom you may share observations on a child depending on where you are working and your level of experience. The spider diagram below shows ways in which you might share your observations.

Colleagues

Other people working directly with the child will be interested to find out more about them. Observations are usually put into a child's folder and from time to time a report is written up about the child.

Tutors

Observations are a good way of learning about child development. Your tutor may ask you to carry out an observation in order to see how well you are learning techniques. To avoid breaching a child's right to confidentiality, you should change the child's name or use 'child A'.

PEOPLE WITH WHOM YOU MIGHT SHARE YOUR OBSERVATIONS

Other professionals

Sometimes other professionals will ask you to observe a child so that you can find out more about him or her. For example, a speech therapist may be interested to find out how often a child talks to other children, while a physiotherapist might need to know about a child's play interests.

Parents

Parents have a right to see observations that have been carried out on their child. If you were the child's key worker, you would share this information with them. As a learner, however, your contact with parents is likely to be limited.

Before sharing an observation

Before you share an observation, it is important that you check through what you have written or recorded. Make sure that your writing is legible and that everything you have written makes sense. It is best to do this as soon as possible after the observation, while it is fresh in your memory. It is important to think about how the observation sounds, especially if a parent will be reading it. The best observations are clear and factual and are not negative about children.

Tips for good practice

Observations

→ Get permission before starting to observe.

→ Think about what you would like to learn about the child and then choose the best method.

→ Ask experienced members of staff about the recording techniques that they use.

→ Find out how old the child is and write this down in years and months.

→ Always write down the date and the time of the observation.

→ Write up an observation neatly soon afterwards so that you can read it easily.

Back to the real world

You should now know about some of the observation techniques and why early years practitioners observe children's development.

1. Give an example of a structured method of recording.

2. List one advantage of using a narrative record.

3. Why is it important to be accurate when recording?

Section 3

How to identify influences that affect children's development

In the real world

In your work placement you notice that the development of children of the same age can vary. You wonder why this is and ask your placement supervisor. He says that there are many reasons and influences.

By the end of this section you will understand some of the key influences that might affect a child's development.

The factors that contribute to development

The child's background

For many years, people have discussed the factors that contribute to children's development. This is known as the nature versus nurture debate. Some people believe that children's development will be influenced by the qualities and character they are born with; others that it is what happens to them once they are born that will shape their development. Most people feel that it is a combination of what the child is born with and what happens to them that influences their development. Since no child will have exactly the same upbringing and background, this is one reason why children need to be treated as individuals and seen as special. Below are some general factors that influence children's development.

Inherited influences

We know that things such as eye and skin colour as well as height are inherited. Some medical conditions and disabilities can also be inherited. These can affect a child's development. It is a matter of debate whether such things as personality or intelligence are inherited.

Siblings

The number of siblings and the age difference between them can affect children's development. Siblings can help children to learn to socialise, but sometimes they can be a source of conflict in children's lives.

Structure of the family

Children can live in a variety of family types. Some families may be small while others might be large. The style of parenting can also vary enormously, with some parents being more relaxed than others.

Immediate and wider environment

Children's emotional and social development can be affected by events that happen in their lives. They may have to cope with moving country, home, or learning a new language. Some children have to deal with losing a parent through separation or through death. Other children may have to learn to live in a new family if they are being adopted or fostered.

Health and welfare

You will work with some children who have health problems. Understanding what the child needs and how their medical condition affects them is important. The spider diagram below shows some of the ways in which a medical condition may affect a child's development. Note that some medical conditions may hardly impact on the child at all. This means that it is essential to find out about each individual child rather than to jump to conclusions.

Physical limitations

Some medical conditions mean that certain physical activities may not be possible. This may mean that a child needs an activity adapted to suit their needs. It may also mean that certain skills are harder to develop.

Tiredness

Some medical conditions can make children tired. This may mean that they have less energy to play and to concentrate. Tiredness can also make children irritable, so they may find it harder to control their behaviour.

HOW A MEDICAL CONDITION MAY AFFECT A CHILD

Absence

Some children will need to spend more time at home, in hospital or have frequent medical appointments. This may mean that they are absent from the setting, which can affect a child's ability to make friends. Children may also miss out on certain learning activities. In schools there is a danger that children may fall behind.

Confidence

Children like to feel the same as others; living with a medical condition may make a child feel different. This can cause children to lose confidence, although adults should try to find ways of helping children to feel independent.

In addition to health, children also have basic needs that will contribute to their welfare. They will, for example, need to be cared for emotionally as well as physically. Diet and sleep are good examples of this.

➔ *Diet.* What a child is given to eat can affect their development. Children need a balanced diet in order that they grow and remain healthy.

➔ *Sleep* is important for children's development. Sleep seems to keep people healthy and is linked to growth in children. It is also important for intellectual development, as the brain appears to need sleep. Memory and concentration are affected by a lack of sleep.

Case study

A good start in life

Janine is 2 years old. Her parents are keen that she should have a good start in life. They spend plenty of time talking to her and involving her in daily activities, such as laying the table and shopping. They also know that it is important that she should eat well and they have read the latest guidance from the Food Standards Agency. Janine also has a good bedtime routine and she sleeps well each night, in addition to having a nap in the afternoon. Janine's parents take her on outings to the park and to the swimming pool. At Janine's latest check, the health visitor commented on how well she was doing.

1. How might Janine's diet and sleep be contributing to her development?
2. In what other ways is Janine having a good start?

Immediate and wider environment

Experiences seem to play an important part in children's lives. This is why most settings will work quite hard to give children varied play opportunities and activities and may also take them on outings. Some children will be lucky to be in environments that are more stimulating than others.

Think about it

Read over the following list of amenities that some children will have access to and which may provide stimulation for children.

- → Library with computers
- → Playground
- → Playing field
- → Community hall
- → Garden
- → Museums and art galleries
- → Theatre
- → Swimming pool
- → Leisure centre
- → Clubs, e.g. football, chess,
- → Woodland

Choose three amenities and consider what children will learn or gain from each of them.

Cultural influences

There are many different ways of bringing up children. Each family will have their own style and beliefs. This can affect children's development. A child whose family believes that children should play outdoors for most of the time is more likely to be physically active and may be more physically coordinated. In the same way, a child whose family is interested in cooking and encourages children to help in the kitchen may be more skilled with their fine motor movements. In some families, children are encouraged to talk, while in others they may be encouraged to read more. Perfect families do not exist! Most families in their own way will be important in developing their children.

Social and economic influences

There is plenty of research to show that children whose families are on low incomes may find it harder to achieve their potential. Understanding why this should be so is complex. Below are some general points about children and low income.

Health and diet

Families on a low income may find it harder to buy food that is nutritious. This, in turn, may affect children's overall health. Children may also be living in poor housing conditions, for example in homes that may be damp or badly heated. Again, this can affect children's health.

Education

Children in low-income areas may not have access to well-equipped schools and expectations of their abilities may be low. This can lead to a lack of achievement.

Toys, equipment and experiences

Children on low incomes may not have the same access to toys, equipment and stimulating experiences, for example holidays or outings, as children from better-off families. Parents may not have the money to pay for clubs, sports centre activities, and so on. Transport can also be a problem as it may cost too much to go to places such as a library or there may not be a bus available. Research shows that in children's early years, being stimulated by new things is important to brain development.

Family pressures

Parents who are on low incomes are more likely to suffer from stress. This can affect parents' emotions and their ability to cope with their children. Being a parent requires high levels of emotional energy and some parents may not always feel that they can manage.

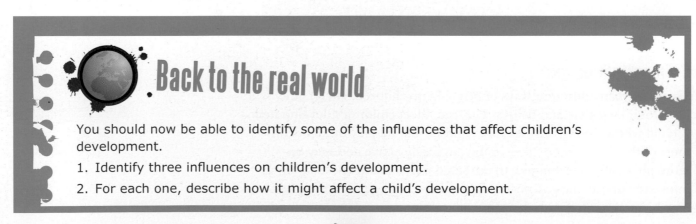

Back to the real world

You should now be able to identify some of the influences that affect children's development.

1. Identify three influences on children's development.
2. For each one, describe how it might affect a child's development.

How to use everyday care routines and activities to support development

In the real world

You are working in the toddler room at a nursery. Your placement supervisor has said that you must be organised so that the children's needs are met and so that each child follows his or her own routine. You are not sure what is meant by this.

By the end of this section you will understand the importance of meeting children's care needs and ways in which you might do this.

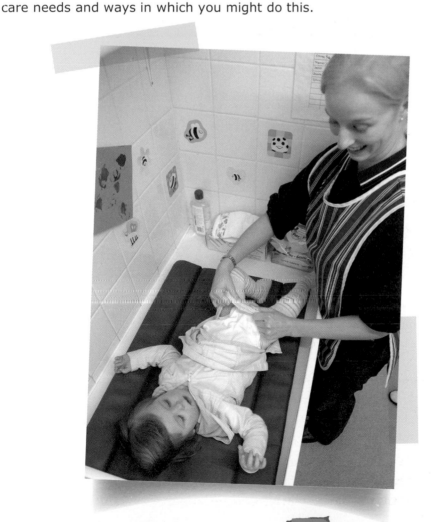

The care needs of individual children

Adults working with children need to look for ways to promote their development. You will look at how to do this through play and activities in Unit 8, pages 295–328. This section explores how some basic needs can be met through routines and daily care activities.

A good starting point is to identify the type of care needs that children have. These will not only vary according to their age and stage of development but also according to their parents' preferences. This means that it is essential to talk to parents and carers to find out how best to meet their needs. The spider diagram below shows some basic care needs; later in this section you will look at how care needs can be met in children of different ages.

The importance of supporting the health and welfare of the child

In each of the four home countries, there are National Standards which are designed to ensure that children are looked after properly. This has led to the belief that children's needs come first and that routines and care activities should be individualised. In the past, children often had to 'fit in' with the routine of the organisation, but now it is recognised that children's care needs should be more personalised. Normally, it is the child's key worker who is responsible for making sure that the child's needs are met. The key worker will also liaise with parents and carers to ensure that information is exchanged and that the routine is working.

If you work with babies and toddlers, you will find that routines often have to be adapted as the child's needs change, for example their nap times may alter. In addition, there will be times when a child needs extra support. They may, for example, have slept badly or be particularly hungry while going through a growth spurt. Some children may also need medication or particular skincare as a result of a medical condition.

Sleep and rest

Why children need sleep

Newborn babies spend most of their time asleep, while young children need considerably more sleep than adults. Sleep is essential for the human body, which uses the time to rest muscles, repair cells and refresh itself. Children also need sleep because at this time the body releases a hormone that helps them to grow. Sleep is needed by the brain, although scientists are unsure why this is the case. Lack of sleep can affect mood, memory and the ability to concentrate.

⇧ **Adequate sleep is essential to children's overall health and development**

Recognising when children are tired

You will need to learn to recognise when children are tired and require sleep or rest. Some children need more sleep than others of the same age, so first you must find out about a child's routine and sleep habits.

Common signs that children are tired include:
→ rubbing eyes
→ twiddling hair
→ sucking thumb
→ needing comforter
→ lacking interest in what is going on around them
→ mood changes, e.g. tearfulness, uncooperativeness
→ dark rings around eyes.

How to help children sleep

Most young children have a sleep routine, although these vary enormously from child to child. This may mean that a 3-year-old has a nap after lunch for an hour or a child of 18 months has a short nap in the morning and another before tea. The wishes of parents and carers are always important in establishing a sleep routine. Some may prefer their child to have a sleep in the late afternoon so that they can spend some time with them after work, while others may find that a late afternoon nap can mean that they cannot get their child to sleep at night. Finding out about children's sleeping habits by working with parents and carers will help you to meet children's needs. You will need to know:
→ when they go to bed or have a daytime nap
→ how long they tend to sleep for
→ if they have a comfort object
→ if they are used to having a light on or the door wide open.

When children are being cared for in large settings, they may at first find it difficult to get to sleep. They may not be used to the environment and be unused to sleeping in a room with other children. In some settings, adults stay next to the child until they have fallen asleep and carry on doing this until the child is used to the new routine.

Some children do not need a nap in the day but do need to rest. Activities for resting children may include listening to story tapes, doing jigsaws, reading a book or playing a quiet board game.

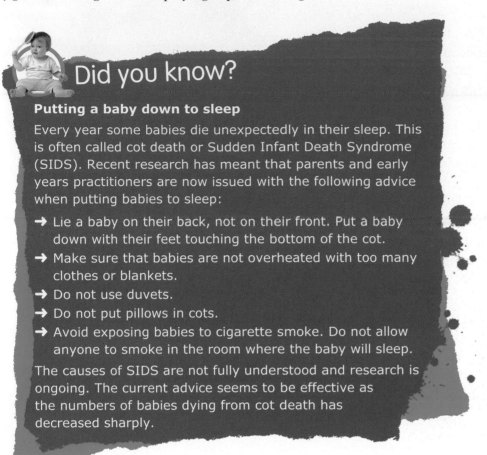

Did you know?

Putting a baby down to sleep

Every year some babies die unexpectedly in their sleep. This is often called cot death or Sudden Infant Death Syndrome (SIDS). Recent research has meant that parents and early years practitioners are now issued with the following advice when putting babies to sleep:

→ Lie a baby on their back, not on their front. Put a baby down with their feet touching the bottom of the cot.

→ Make sure that babies are not overheated with too many clothes or blankets.

→ Do not use duvets.

→ Do not put pillows in cots.

→ Avoid exposing babies to cigarette smoke. Do not allow anyone to smoke in the room where the baby will sleep.

The causes of SIDS are not fully understood and research is ongoing. The current advice seems to be effective as the numbers of babies dying from cot death has decreased sharply.

Food and drink

Food and water are essential for life. The food that children eat is especially important, as it helps them to grow and gives them energy so that they can develop. Studies show that the food you eat in childhood can make a difference to your health when you are older. Mealtimes are also opportunities for children to enjoy being together and learn about other cultures, as well as developing healthy eating patterns.

Nutrients

In order to grow and develop, children's bodies need **nutrients**. The body needs several different nutrients to stay healthy. These are:

→ carbohydrates
→ fats
→ proteins
→ vitamins
→ minerals.

Jargon buster

Nutrients Substances in foods that help humans to grow and stay healthy

To gain all the nutrients that the body needs, humans have to eat a range of foods. This is what is meant by a balanced diet. At different times in your life, your body needs differing amounts of nutrients. For example, extra nutrients will be needed by children for growth, adolescents during growth spurts and women when they are breastfeeding.

⇩ **The proportion of different foods that should be eaten in a balanced diet**

One of the main differences between the diets of children and adults is the energy content. For their size, children need more energy than adults. This means that children up to the age of 5 years should be given full-fat milk and dairy products, as they need more calories.

⇩ **Some groups of foods are particularly good for children**

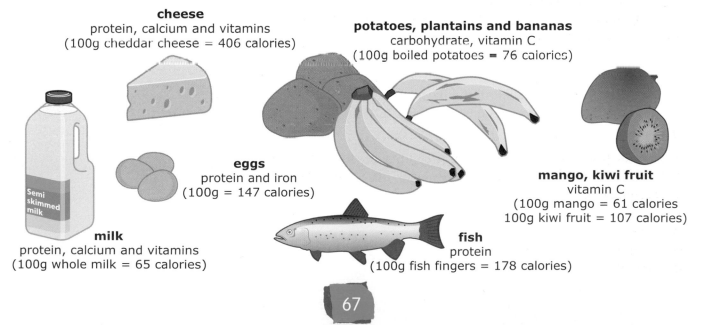

cheese
protein, calcium and vitamins
(100g cheddar cheese = 406 calories)

potatoes, plantains and bananas
carbohydrate, vitamin C
(100g boiled potatoes = 76 calories)

eggs
protein and iron
(100g = 147 calories)

mango, kiwi fruit
vitamin C
(100g mango = 61 calories
100g kiwi fruit = 107 calories)

milk
protein, calcium and vitamins
(100g whole milk = 65 calories)

fish
protein
(100g fish fingers = 178 calories)

67

The following chart shows the nutrients in common foods and why the body needs these nutrients.

⬧ **Nutrients in common foods**

Nutrient	Benefits to the body	Examples of foods
Carbohydrate	Gives energy	Bread, pasta, flour, potatoes, yams, bananas, plaintains and vegetables, sweet potatoes
Protein	Helps the body to grow and repair cells. In children protein is linked to growth.	Meat, eggs, fish, milk and dairy products, soya, *wheat, corn, oats, pulses, beans and peas* (the proteins shown in italics need eating with other foods to work well, e.g. beans on toast)
Fat	Gives energy and helps the body to absorb vitamins A and D	Butter, margarine, vegetable oil, as well as hidden fats in meat, fish and dairy products
Vitamin A	Good for eyes and eyesight	Carrots, milk, apricots, fatty fish, margarine
Vitamin B (there are a number of vitamins in the vitamin B group)	Good for nervous system. Helps release energy from other foods.	Bread, meat, yeast, pasta, flour, rice, noodles
Vitamin C	Good for skin and gums	Oranges, lemons, grapefruit, blackcurrants, potatoes, kiwi fruit
Vitamin E	Has many essential uses in the body including the protection of cells	Vegetable oils, green leafy vegetables, milk, nuts, wheatgerm
Vitamin K	Helps blood to clot	Present in most vegetables
Vitamin D	Good for teeth and bones	Milk, margarine, cheese, yoghurts and other dairy products
Iron	Helps the body to carry oxygen	Red meat, broccoli, spinach, plain chocolate, egg yolk
Calcium and phosphorus	Good for teeth and bones	Milk, cheese, butter, yoghurts and other dairy products
Fluoride	Good for teeth and bones	Water (where added), sea fish

Nutritional values of foods

The energy that food gives is measured in kilo calories or kilojoules. Most wrapped foods have labels that show how many kilo calories or kilojoules they contain. Some food labels also give a breakdown of the main nutrients.

The chart below shows how much energy children are likely to need per day at different ages. It is interesting to note that boys need more energy than girls.

⇩ **Energy requirements (in kilo calories) of boys and girls at different ages**

Age	Boys' energy requirement (kilo calories)	Girls' energy requirement (kilo calories)
0–3 months	545	515
4–6 months	690	645
7–9 months	820	765
10–12 months	920	865
1–3 years	1230	1165
4–6 years	1715	1545
7–10 years	1970	1740

Planning a balanced diet for children

To plan a balanced diet, it is important to look at what children eat over a few days. A balanced diet needs to be varied so that different foods are used. The chart below shows a sample menu for four days. Notice that a range of different foods has been used.

⇩ **A balanced diet**

Time	Day 1	Day 2	Day 3	Day 4
Breakfast	Milk Cereal with banana Toast	Milk Porridge Apple	Milk Yoghurt Toast	Orange juice Cereal Toast
Mid-morning	Diluted apple juice Fruit scone	Lassi (yoghurt drink) Banana	Diluted orange juice Rice crackers	Milk Cheese straws
Lunch	Pitta bread filled with tuna and sweetcorn Fresh mango Water	Macaroni cheese Broccoli Fresh fruit salad Water	Cheese and spinach Rice salad Blackcurrant mousse Water	Trinidad stew (made with plantains) Sweet potatoes Yoghurt and banana Water
Mid-afternoon	Diluted fruit juice Cheese and biscuit	Hot chocolate Dried fruit mix (raisins, apricots)	Milk shake Home-made biscuit	Diluted fruit juice Raw carrot sticks
Tea	Three-bean sausage stew Bread rolls Pancakes Milk	Cold chicken pieces Rice salad Strawberry mousse Milk	Jacket potato with a choice of fillings Stewed apple and yoghurt Milk	Home-made pizza Salad Home-made ice-cream Milk

Providing drinks for children

Drinks are just as important as food in keeping the body healthy. Children who do not drink enough are likely to become dehydrated. This can be serious, as the body needs water to do many things, including control temperature.

Drinks need to be offered several times during the day, particularly if it is hot. The best drinks for children are considered to be water and milk. Water is good because it is pure and quenches children's thirst, while milk contains many nutrients including calcium and protein. Sugary and sweet drinks not only cause dental decay but can also spoil children's appetites.

Foods to avoid giving to children

→ *Nuts* are not recommended for children under 5 years, because although nutritious there is a danger of children choking on them and some children may have a violent allergic reaction, particularly to peanuts. If children are known to be allergic to nuts, adults have to be extremely careful when buying shop-made products, such as biscuits, where nuts may be a hidden ingredient.

→ *Sugary foods and drinks.* Although sugar does provide energy, it can also cause dental decay. Sweets and sugary drinks fill children up without giving them any other nutrients. It also means that children develop a taste for sweet things and may dislike other more nutritious foods.

→ *Undiluted fruit juices.* Fruit juices can be good for children, but they need to be diluted with water because otherwise the acid in them can cause tooth decay.

→ *High-fibre foods such as bran.* Although adults need fibre in their diets, children do not need as much. Fibre fills up the stomach, which means that there is less space for foods that can give children the energy they need.

→ *Salt.* Children do not need extra salt in their diet and it can affect their kidneys. Eating salty foods such as crisps can mean that they develop a taste for salt. As there is a link between salt and high blood pressure in adults, it is better that children do not crave salty foods.

→ *Uncooked eggs.* The advice is that children should not eat uncooked or partly cooked eggs because they may contain salmonella bacteria which causes food poisoning. Examples of foods which should not be offered include home-made mayonnaise and boiled eggs with runny yolks.

How much food should children be given?

The best guide as to how much food to give a child is the child him or herself! Some children may eat a lot at one meal and less at another. Following a child's appetite is often the best way to decide how much food to give, providing the food that is offered is nutritious and varied. Appetite is often a guide to children's needs. Children tend to eat more just before a growth spurt and less if they are feeling poorly.

Should children be offered snacks?

Three meals a day suits adults very well, but children can get hungry between meals. This is because children's stomachs are smaller, and providing a snack for them can give them the extra energy that they need.

→ *Good snacks* help keep children going without spoiling their appetite and are nutritious, for example slices of apples, oranges, bananas, dried fruit, a slice of bread or savoury biscuit with a drink of diluted fruit juice or a glass of milk.

➜ *Poor snacks* fill children up with sugar or fat that stops them from being hungry at the next meal and do not provide many nutrients, for example sweets, crisps, biscuits and sugary drinks.

What happens if a diet does not contain enough nutrients?

Eating a diet that meets the body's requirements is important for everyone. The right balance of nutrients can help the body fight infection and prevent diseases. Food also gives the energy you need to enjoy life!

Children who are not eating enough or who are not eating a balanced diet can:

➜ lack energy
➜ fail to gain in height or weight
➜ have less resistance to infection, for example colds, sore throats
➜ be less alert mentally (studies have shown that diet affects cognitive development).

Calcium and vitamin D in children's diets

Calcium is taken in by the body only when there is vitamin D. Where children do not have enough calcium and vitamin D in their diets, there is a risk of stunted growth, because calcium is needed to make strong bones and teeth. Children who do not have enough vitamin D may develop a disease called rickets. Milk, cheese and other dairy products are good sources of calcium and vitamin D.

Common food allergies

Some children and adults are allergic to certain types of foods. This means that you should always check with parents or carers if there are any foods or drinks that children should not be given. It is also important to check the ingredient labels of food as many ingredients, such as nuts, may be included even though they are not a major ingredient.

Common food allergies include:

➜ nuts
➜ milk and dairy products
➜ seafood such as prawns
➜ strawberries.

Allergic reactions can vary from rashes and migraines to more serious difficulties where children are unable to breathe.

Medical conditions

Some children may also have specific medical conditions which will mean that they have special requirements.

Diabetes

In this medical condition the pancreas finds it difficult to regulate the sugar levels in the body. Most diabetics avoid sugar in their diets but need to take regular snacks. If you are caring for a child with this condition, it is essential to find out more information from parents or carers and you might have to record how much food a child has eaten.

Coeliac disease

Children with this condition are not able to eat foods with gluten in them. Gluten is commonly found in cereals such as wheat, oats, barley and rye. As many products are made with wheat flour, for example ordinary bread or biscuits, it is extremely important to check that foods are suitable.

Diets associated with different cultures and beliefs

For thousands of years, food has played a major part in people's lives and in their cultures. Food has been used to celebrate festivals and life events, for example marriage, birth and even death. Recognising the significance of food and how it is eaten is important so that you can meet all children's needs by respecting their culture and beliefs. Knowing which foods are not permitted and checking with parents or carers about children's dietary needs is essential if parents and children are to feel that their values are respected.

Below is a chart that shows the main dietary customs of the major world beliefs where certain foods are restricted or forbidden. The word 'some' used in the chart means that some members of these groups may eat these products.

↧ **Main dietary customs of major world beliefs**

Food	Islam	Judaism	Sikhism	Hinduism (mainly vegetarian)	Rastafarianism (mainly vegetarian although take milk products)	Seventh-Day Adventist Church
Lamb	Halal	Kosher	Yes	Some	Some	Some
Pork	No	No	Rarely	Rarely	No	No
Beef	Halal	Kosher	No	No	Some	Some
Chicken	Halal	Kosher	Some	Some	Some	Some
Cheese	Some	Not with meat	Some	Some	Some	Most
Milk/ yoghurt	Not with rennet	Not with meat	Yes	Not with rennet	Yes	Most
Eggs	Yes	No blood spots	Yes	Some	Yes	Most
Fish	Halal	With fins and scales	Some	With fins and scales	Yes	Some
Shellfish	Halal	No	Some	Some	No	No

Food	Islam	Judaism	Sikhism	Hinduism (mainly vegetarian)	Rastafarianism (mainly vegetarian although take milk products)	Seventh-Day Adventist Church
Cocoa/tea/coffee	Yes	Yes	Yes	Yes	Yes	No
Fast periods	Ramadan	Yom Kippur				

Halal and kosher meat

Jews and Muslims will eat meat only if it has been killed in a certain way. This is what is meant by kosher and halal. Meat that has been killed in this way is bought at specialist butchers.

Vegetarians and vegans

Some families for cultural or religious reasons choose not to eat meat. It is important to find out whether the parents wish their child to have a vegetarian diet or a vegan diet and find out how best this can be provided.

Vegetarians do not eat meat or fish, but will eat products that come from animals such as milk and eggs. Vegans do not eat any food that comes from animals or fish.

Preparing and storing foods

A good level of hygiene is essential when preparing food, especially for babies and young children. The main rules are quite simple. There is more information about food hygiene in Unit 7 (pages 244–5).

Preparing food and feeding babies aged 0–1 year

If you ever care for babies, you may need to prepare feeds for them. This is a major responsibility as feeding equipment needs to be sterilised and feeds have to be made up correctly.

Nutritional needs

In the first year of life, most babies treble their birth weight. This means that they need to feed well to allow this growth to take place. In the first six months, babies gain all the nutrients they need from either formula or breast milk. After six months, babies need other sources of food, especially those that contain iron.

The choice of whether to breastfeed or bottle-feed lies with the mother. Some mothers start by breastfeeding and then decide to use a bottle. It is important that mothers are not made to feel guilty about their choice, as babies thrive on both types of feeding. The process of starting solid foods is called **weaning**, although milk still remains an important part of a baby's diet.

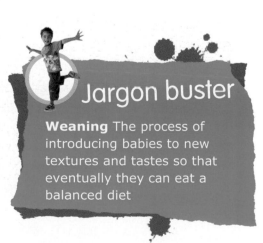

Jargon buster

Weaning The process of introducing babies to new textures and tastes so that eventually they can eat a balanced diet

Breastfeeding

Breast milk is recognised as being the best type of milk for babies – after all, it was designed for human babies! The milk contains not just the nutrients that are needed to promote growth but also the antibodies from the mother which help fight against infections. Breast milk also changes according to the needs of the baby. In the first few days, the milk is thin and yellow – this is called colostrum and is particularly good for babies, as it contains antibodies. After the third day, the milk changes and is lighter in colour.

For women who cannot always be with their baby but who wish to breastfeed, it is possible to 'express' milk (squeeze it out of the breast) and put it into a bottle or freeze it.

The advantages of breastfeeding include the following:
→ It provides antibodies.
→ There is close contact between mother and baby that makes it a pleasant experience for both.
→ Feeding is instant because there is no waiting for bottles to cool and no sterilisation to be done.
→ It is also free, which may be important for families on low incomes but who do not qualify for state benefits.
→ It helps the womb to contract more quickly.

Bottle feeding

Some parents decide to bottle feed using formula milk. There are many reasons why a woman may decide to bottle feed. She may feel that she cannot cope if she has had a multiple birth (for example, twins or triplets) or she may wish to return to work. In some cases, doctors advise some women not to breastfeed, for example if a woman is on strong medication, some of the drugs will be passed on to the baby through the milk. The main advantage of bottle feeding is that anyone can take over from the mother, although where possible it should be the same people feeding the baby. The disadvantages of bottle feeding are that all items need sterilising and great care must be taken in making up feeds.

Types of milk

Bottle-fed babies are given formula milk. This comes in several forms, derived from cow's milk, goat's milk or soya beans. Ordinary cow's milk cannot be given to babies until they are at least 6 months old, although the current advice is that it should not be given as a main milk drink until babies are 1 year old.

As there are different types of formula milk, parents or carers must be asked which type of milk should be used, as sometimes there may be religious or cultural preferences. For example, some babies have milk made from soya because they are allergic to other types of milk or because their parents are vegans.

Did you know?

To produce enough milk for a baby, it is important that the mother eats well and drinks plenty of fluid. It is estimated that milk production in breastfeeding mothers uses an additional 500 kilo calories per day (*Source:* British Nutrition Foundation).

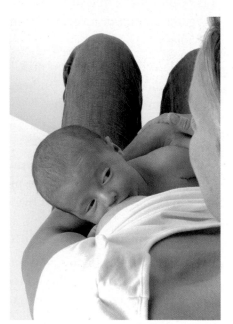

⇧ **There are many benefits to both mother and child of breastfeeding**

Feeding a baby safely

Early years practitioners have to be organised if they are caring for babies. Babies who are crying with hunger want to be fed immediately! It is important that feeds are ready for them. This means keeping an eye on the time and getting feeds ready beforehand. Most settings make up several bottles as part of the daily routine.

Bottles that have been made up in advance need time to heat up or reach room temperature. Bottles that are made just before a feed need time to cool down.

Never use a microwave to heat up bottles. There is a risk of scalding a baby's mouth because the milk can be unevenly heated and have 'heat spots'.

By about 4 months old, babies try to hold their bottle. You should still support the bottle to make sure that no air is taken in while they are feeding.

Tips for good practice

Feeding babies

→ Never leave a baby propped up with a bottle – they may choke or drown.

→ Always wash your hands thoroughly before preparing or giving a feed.

→ Always use sterilised equipment.

→ Always check the temperature of the feed.

Find out!

Ask your supervisor if you can prepare a feed and/or bottle feed a baby.

1. Write down how you did this task.
2. What did you learn from doing it?

Making up bottle feeds

Making up feeds is a major responsibility, as they must be made up accurately and hygienically. It is essential that the manufacturer's instructions are followed.

→ Putting too much powder in a feed can mean that babies develop problems with their kidneys.

→ Putting too little powder in a feed can mean that babies lose weight or show poor weight gain and become constipated and distressed.

The amount of milk that babies need depends on their weight not their age. New-born babies need less milk than older, heavier babies. They will usually need several small feeds, for example eight feeds in 24 hours. It is extremely important that babies are offered the correct amount of milk for their weight. Always check with parents or carers and supervisors to make sure that you understand how much milk should be offered at a time, as this can vary from baby to baby.

⇧ **If you work with babies as an early years practitioner, you will be responsible for their bottle feeds**

⏱ **Stages of weaning**

Stage	Age	Preparation	Types of food
1	6 months	Puréc or liquidise food so that it is easy to swallow.	*Introduce tastes one at a time:* • Baby rice • Vegetable purées (potato, yam, carrot) • Fruit purées (plantain, banana, apple, pear, etc.) *Once spoon feeding is established introduce:* • Vegetable and meat or fish purées • Yoghurt • A wider range of vegetables
2	6–9 months	Mash foods so that they are slightly thicker, but still easy to swallow.	• Fish, meat, poultry and a wide range of vegetables and fruit. • Anything that can be mashed. Babies can join in family meals, if the food is mashed for them. • *Highchairs can be used, but babies must not be left alone in them.*
3	9+ months	Introduce foods that can be eaten with fingers as well as with a spoon.	• Give babies foods that they can handle, e.g. pitta bread, chapattis, fish fingers, pieces of banana, etc. • *Stay near the baby in case of choking.*

Stage 1 weaning (puréed food)

Starting weaning requires patience, as the baby needs to learn how to take food off a spoon and what to do with the food! If parents or carers have asked you to start this process, it is best if you choose a time when the baby is not too hungry or tired. After a nap and part way through a milk-feed is often a good time. A sterilised plastic spoon and bowl is needed along with a bib or cloth to wipe the baby's mouth.

Baby rice is often given as a first food as it is not dissimilar in taste to milk, although different types of cereals can be used as a first food. A small quantity – enough for three to four teaspoons – should be mixed with formula or breast milk. The spoon is put gently on to the baby's lips. At first, babies tend to suck the food off. Many babies spit out the food initially, as they are not used to the texture. Over a period of a few days, babies gradually learn to take from the spoon.

Once the baby is used to the spoon, new tastes can gradually be added, although it is a good idea to introduce new foods one at a time. This means that if a baby is allergic to any food, it is easier to identify.

As babies take more and more solid food, they will need less milk, although it should remain an important part of their diet until they are at least 2 years old. From now on, babies must be offered drinks so that they do not dehydrate. Cooled boiled water is considered to be the best, and babies can be introduced to the use of beakers.

The amount of solid food taken depends on each baby. Some babies take a tablespoon at a time, others may take only a teaspoonful. It is important to make sure that the baby is not hungry.

Stage 2 weaning (mashed foods)

During this stage, babies are learning to chew a little before swallowing. Food can be mashed rather than puréed. At this stage, babies also begin to want to feed themselves and show this by trying to hold the spoon. It is important that you encourage babies to feed themselves and you can do this by praising them and letting them have a spoon of their own. From around 6 months, most babies are sitting in highchairs and can be at the table with other children or their families. Harnesses need to be used and babies must not be left alone in a highchair. Babies will be dropping a milk feed but will still need a drink. Cooled boiled water is considered to be the best drink.

Stage 3 weaning (developing independence)

Babies are now starting to feed themselves and can chew their foods. Finger foods such as bread, toast and bananas are eaten independently. This is also a messy stage, as babies are using their senses to explore their food. They may squeeze food and drop it and many times they may take it towards their mouths, only to miss!

Encouraging babies to feed themselves is important, as it helps them to become independent. It also encourages their physical development, as it helps them to control their hand movements. A good supply of flannels, bibs and cloths are needed though!

Advice about foods

As an early years practitioner, you need to listen carefully to any health advice about foods and change your practices accordingly. Present guidelines about weaning and food for babies are shown in the Tips for good practice box below.

⬅ Babies can make quite a mess when eating finger foods, but it is important to encourage babies to feed themselves

Tips for good practice

Present guidelines about weaning and food for babies

→ Weaning should not start until 6 months.

→ Sugar and salt should not be added to foods.

→ Uncooked or soft-boiled eggs should not be given to babies or young children.

→ No wheat products should be given until babies are over 6 months.

→ Liver should not be given to babies and young children.

→ Cow's milk should not be given before 6 months and preferably not until after the first year.

→ Unpasteurised cheeses should not be given to babies.

Reasons why babies might have difficulties in feeding

If you are concerned about how a baby is feeding, you must immediately tell the parents or carers if you are in a home environment or the supervisor if you are in a group setting.

Common difficulties include:

→ Babies being sick in large quantities during or after the feed. This can mean that too much air is being swallowed and the baby needs to be winded more often. It can also be a sign of illness.

→ Babies crying but not taking the bottle. This can happen because the teat is blocked or the milk is flowing too slowly. It can also be a sign of colic (stomachache) or a baby not being able to suck.

→ Babies with colds may find it hard to suck as their noses are blocked up or running. This might mean that they need to take longer to feed.

There are many other reasons why babies may have difficulties, but your role is always to seek help.

Food allergies and special diets

Some babies may be put on a special diet if they have food allergies.

→ *Gluten-free diet.* Babies who have coeliac disease must avoid gluten. This is commonly found in bread, biscuits, cakes, pastry, breakfast cereals and other foods made with wheat and other cereals such as rye.

→ *Dairy-free diet.* Babies who have allergies such as eczema and milk intolerance need to avoid dairy products such as cheese, milk and butter. Products made from soya beans are often given instead, including soya milk.

Always find out from parents what foods should be avoided. In large settings, check with your supervisor if you are unsure about a baby's diet.

Did you know?

You can learn more about weaning, allergies and other issues concerning food by contacting a local health visitor, family practice or health promotion unit.

When feeding babies, it is good practice to keep a record of the time a feed is given and how much milk is taken. This allows parents and other carers to make sure that the baby is getting enough food. Parents should always be told when their baby has refused feeds or meals or has not taken as much milk or food as normal. This can be a sign that the baby is feeling unwell. If you have any concerns over the way babies are feeding, it is important they are passed on to the parents or the supervisor, depending on your workplace.

How to promote and maintain good hygiene and hygiene routines

Infections

Young children pick up infections easily so it is very important that early years settings are as hygienic as possible (as children get older, they develop more resistance to infection). Hygiene is about keeping things clean. In most environments, there will be small micro-organisms such as bacteria and viruses, which are sometimes referred to as germs. These can cause illness if they enter the body. The diagram below shows the three ways that bacteria and viruses can enter the body.

⏷ **How infections may enter the body**

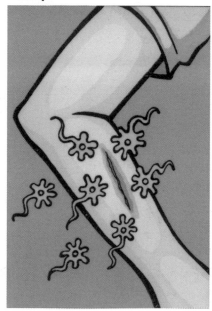

When infections are passed on to others, this is called **cross-infection**. Where children are being cared for in large groups, there is always a danger of cross-infection, as children share equipment and are in close contact with each other. Colds, food poisoning and gastroenteritis can all spread through cross-infection.

Ways of minimising cross-infection

There are some simple measures that you can take to prevent cross-infection, although it is impossible to provide a completely sterile environment.

Jargon buster

Cross-infection The process by which micro-organisms such as viruses and bacteria are spread and infect others

Handwashing

Bacteria are often spread on hands. Children share toys and put things in their mouths which often means that infection can be spread. It is, therefore, important that you make sure that children wash their hands:

→ before snacks, meals and drinks
→ after using the toilet
→ after playing outside or touching animals
→ after using substances such as water, paint or dough where bacteria may be present on the hands.

As you are in contact with many children and may also be responsible for preparing and serving food, it is essential that you wash your hands frequently, for example after helping children to blow their nose!

To prevent cross-infection, it is important that bacteria are not spread on towels or other items that children touch. In some settings paper towels are used to make sure that no cross-infection can take place. Other settings have flannels and towels that are named and used only by these children. Paper tissues are also better than handkerchiefs because they can be thrown away, whereas a handkerchief may still have bacteria on it from the last time it was used.

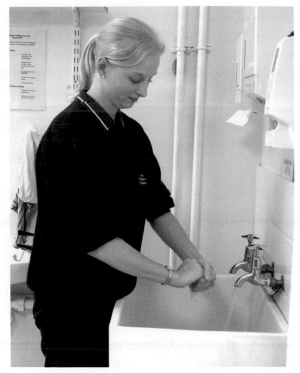

⇧ **In your work with children, you will need to know how to wash your hands thoroughly and do so frequently throughout the day**

Sterilising equipment

Babies and children under 2 years are particularly vulnerable to infection and so great care must be taken when preparing food or drinks for these children. If babies are in day care settings, sterilisation procedures must be carried out for longer than in a home environment, probably until 12 to 15 months. This means that bowls, cutlery and beakers all need to be sterilised before they are given to children. You will need to follow the manufacturers' guidelines on sterilisation procedures. Unfinished foods should be thrown away as bacteria from spoons will grow on the food even if it is kept in the fridge.

Bathing and washing children

Bathing and washing children is occasionally part of an early years practitioner's responsibility, for example if children are being cared for at home. This may include looking after children's hair, skin and teeth. If you have this responsibility, it is important for you to discuss children's needs with their parents or carers, especially if children have skin conditions – such as eczema – or if the religion of the family means that certain practices relating to bathing or hair care need to be followed.

Looking after children's hair

In recent years, there has been an increase in outbreaks of head lice in pre-school settings and in schools. Head lice are parasites that live close to the scalp. They are sometimes known as nits, as this is the name given to the eggs that they lay. Regular combing with a fine-toothed comb can prevent and kill head lice. The comb pulls the live lice out and damages the eggs.

Brushing and combing hair

If you are responsible for washing and combing hair, you need to follow parents' or carers' wishes, for example some children may have braids or dreadlocks that should not be brushed or African-Caribbean children may need oil rubbed into their hair.

Tips for good practice

Brushing and combing hair

➜ Comb or brush hair twice a day.

➜ Check for headlice or nits (the eggs).

➜ If hair is tangled, start with a wide-toothed comb and then use a brush.

To make it more enjoyable:

➜ Give toddlers a doll of their own to brush.

➜ Encourage older children to brush their own hair.

➜ Let children look in the mirror while you are brushing.

Washing children's hair

Young children may need to have their hair washed several times in a week, depending on their activities! This is likely to be a care activity that is done at home, unless you are caring for a young baby in a nursery. Many young children get food and play materials such as dough in their hair as they tend to touch their heads with dirty hands. Older children may need their hair washing only once or twice a week unless they have been particularly active in their play and are sweaty. Most children have their hair washed as part of their shower or bathtime and you should discuss with parents or carers any fears or particular needs that children have. Many parents also like to use conditioners on children's hair as it makes it easier to comb.

Some younger children find hair-washing distressing, as they do not like getting water on their face.

Caring for children's skin

Good skin care is important for everyone. Skin plays a vital role in a person's overall health and maintaining it in good condition means keeping it clean and dry and, at certain times, moisturised. Protecting skin from the sun is also vital, which means that you must be aware of the need to use high-factor sunscreen products on children as well as keeping them covered or out of the sun in the summer. Remember, though, that you can only apply sunscreen products if you have been given permission to do so by parents or carers.

As children have different types of skin and many children may have skin conditions, it is essential for early years practitioners to find out from parents how they should look after children's skin; for example, a child with severe eczema may not be able to use soap on their hands or face and children with dry skin may need moisturisers or oils.

Handwashing

Developing good handwashing routines with children is important to prevent infections and stop germs spreading. It also gets them into the habit for when they are older.

Tips for good practice

Hand washing

→ Keep children's nails short.

→ Ensure children wash hands after going to the toilet, after playing outside and after touching animals.

→ Ensure children wash hands before eating or drinking.

→ Use a nail brush if there is dirt under the nails.

→ Dry hands thoroughly – each child should have their own towel.

Washing the face and body

Bath or shower time is usually a source of great pleasure for children and is often part of a bedtime routine at home. If you are employed in a child's home, it may become your responsibility, although many parents enjoy this part of the day with their children. It is essential to remember never to leave children unattended in a bath or bathroom, as young children can easily drown or be scalded by hot water.

The bottom and genital areas of children need to be washed every day, although older children should be encouraged to wash themselves in these parts. Each child should have their own towel and flannel to prevent the spread of any infection. After a bath or shower, it is important that skin is thoroughly dried to prevent soreness. Younger children have folds of skin under their arms and neck that need to be patted dry.

Although many children have a bath or shower before going to bed, they will still need to have their hands and face washed in the morning and younger children will need to have their faces and hands washed after meals.

Caring for children's teeth

A good diet with foods rich in calcium and vitamins can help children form healthy teeth. Sugar is often the main cause of dental decay. Dentists recommend that if sugary foods are given, they should be eaten at the end of a meal and that teeth should be cleaned afterwards. Regular visits to the dentist can help children get used to someone looking at and probing their teeth.

Tips for good practice

Looking after children's teeth
➡ Brush teeth with a small-headed toothbrush after meals.
➡ Brush teeth in a circular motion.
➡ Avoid sugary drinks and sweets between meals.
➡ Use toothpaste with fluoride to strengthen teeth.

Bathing babies

The skin is a protective layer that acts as a barrier to infection as well as helping to control our temperature. This means that to keep babies healthy, their skin needs to be cared for. Bathing and changing babies is therefore an important task.

Choosing washing equipment and toiletries

The skin-cleaning routine will depend on the parents' or carers' wishes and should respect cultural traditions. For example, many Muslims bathe under running water, which will mean that a baby bath might not be suitable. You should always find out how parents want their child cared for. This extends to toiletries, as some babies may need lotions or other skin products for skin conditions such as eczema or because their parents prefer particular products. If you are left to choose toiletries, you should check that they are mild and suitable for babies. This means that it is a good idea to look for products designed specifically for babies.

Making bathtime fun for babies

As well as being important in the routine of caring for babies, bathtime is often great fun for them. Most babies love being in the bath and gain many benefits from playing in the water. They learn from the **sensory experience** of touching the water and also developing muscles while kicking and splashing around!

You need to allow the baby plenty of time to explore the water. As babies get older, you can provide some simple toys for them to grasp and use. Some babies are afraid of water, so you may have to reassure them by talking or singing to them.

Jargon buster

Sensory experience
Pleasure gained from the feelings (sensations) experienced when touching objects

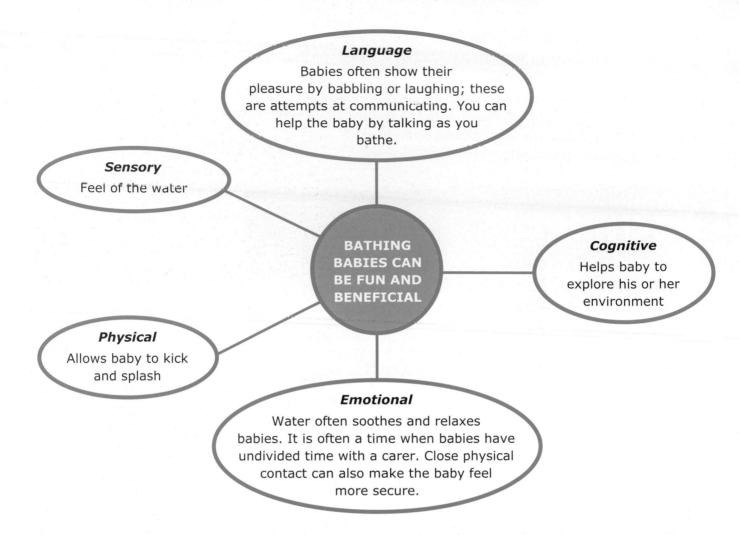

Language
Babies often show their pleasure by babbling or laughing; these are attempts at communicating. You can help the baby by talking as you bathe.

Sensory
Feel of the water

BATHING BABIES CAN BE FUN AND BENEFICIAL

Cognitive
Helps baby to explore his or her environment

Physical
Allows baby to kick and splash

Emotional
Water often soothes and relaxes babies. It is often a time when babies have undivided time with a carer. Close physical contact can also make the baby feel more secure.

Ensuring that bathtime is safe

Although bathtimes can be fun, they can also be dangerous. Every year some babies drown or are scalded at bathtime. The following safety advice must always be followed when bathing babies and young children.

Tips for good practice

Keeping bathtime safe

→ Never leave babies or young children alone near or in water.

→ Always check the temperature of water. It should be around 38°C – warm, but never hot.

→ Make sure that any toys for the bath are suitable for the age of the baby.

Preparing to bath a baby

Good preparation and organisation are essential when bathing a baby. Everything should be laid out before starting to undress the baby. The room needs to be warm (20°C) as babies chill quickly. You also need to check that you are not wearing anything that might scratch baby's skin such as a watch or jewellery. An apron is often useful, as babies tend to splash!

✋ Checklist of items required when bathing a baby. (The optional skin products should be used only after checking with parents or carers as babies may have skin allergies.)

Essential checklist	Optional checklist
• Clean nappy • Clean clothes, including vest • Cotton wool or baby wipes • Bag or bucket for waste materials such as dirty nappy and wipes • Towels • Shampoo	• Thermometer to check temperature of water • Barrier cream to prevent nappy rash • Soap • Bubble bath • Talcum powder

As babies get older, they are able to sit up in the bath and you can wash their hair by gently pouring water over their head.

Bathing a baby

Once you have prepared all the equipment and filled the baby bath with warm water, you should be ready to start. You will then need to bath the baby, following the steps below.

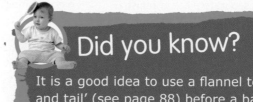

Did you know?

It is a good idea to use a flannel to 'top and tail' (see page 88) before a baby gets into the bath, so that if the child drinks any of the water it is likely to be clean.

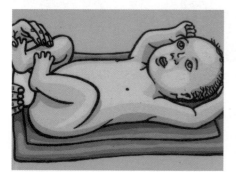

1. Put the baby on a flat surface, undress him/her and take off the nappy. Clean the nappy area.

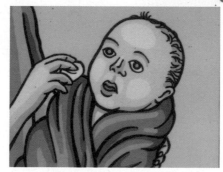

2. Wrap the baby gently but securely in a towel, so that the arms are tucked in. Wash the face with moist cotton wool.

3. Hold the baby over the bath and wash the head and hair.

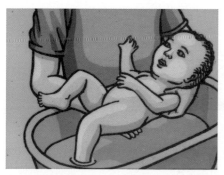

4. Take off the towel. Holding the baby securely under the head and round the arm, lift him/her into the water.

5. Use your spare hand to wash the baby.

6. Lift the baby out of the bath, supporting under the bottom, and quickly wrap him/her in a warm towel.

⬆ Step-by-step guide to bathing a baby

Care of skin, hair and teeth

Topping and tailing

This expression means washing and drying baby's face and bottom! The idea is to keep babies clean and fresh instead of or between baths.

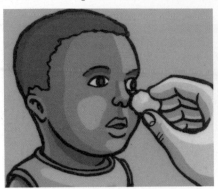

1. Take off outer clothing. Wash each eye with a separate piece of moist cotton wool. Use warm water.

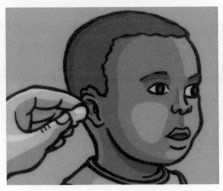

2. Wash each ear gently with a clean piece of moist cotton wool.

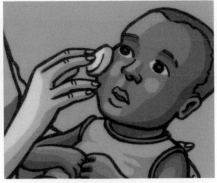

3. Wash the rest of the face and finally the mouth.

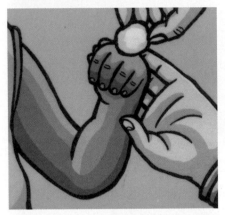

4. Wash the baby's hands.

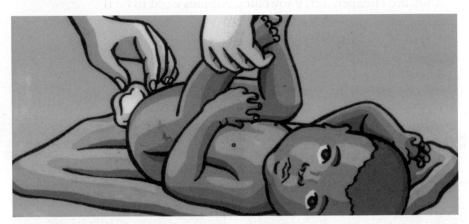

5. Take off the nappy and wash and clean the nappy area in the usual way.

⇧ **How to top and tail a baby**

Hair

Some babies are born with no hair, while others have masses of it! Caring for babies' hair is relatively simple. It needs to be gently brushed with a soft brush or a wide-toothed comb and washed as part of the bathing routine. Where babies' hair is styled – some African-Caribbean babies may have small plaits, for example – it is important to ask parents what they would like you to do when brushing or washing it.

Teeth

At around 6 months, babies start getting their first teeth. It is important that these are cared for, as they help guide the more permanent teeth into position. Gentle brushing with a small-headed, soft-bristle brush should start once the first teeth appear. Sugary drinks and foods need to be avoided to prevent dental decay. Fruit juices and sugary drinks in bottles are not recommended.

Changing babies' nappies

One of the less pleasant aspects of caring for babies and young children is nappy changing. It is, nonetheless, an absolutely essential part of the job. Frequently changing nappies prevents the skin in this area from becoming sore and prevents infections. Never leave a baby in a dirty or wet nappy.

Parents and carers choose between types of nappies for many reasons and there are advantages and disadvantages to both types. Some parents may use both.

Types of nappies

→ *Disposable.* There is a large choice of disposable nappies. At present, 80 per cent of parents use disposable nappies. Disposable nappies come in different sizes according to the weight of babies and children. Some brands also sell separate types for boys and girls. Cheaper nappies are made of wood pulp and the more expensive 'Ultra' nappies contain granules that turn into gel when the nappy becomes wet.

→ *Terry towelling.* Some parents prefer to use terry-towelling nappies because they feel they are more environmentally friendly or because they are cheaper. Terry-towelling nappies need to be thoroughly disinfected and rinsed through. To avoid this, some parents use laundry services that deliver clean folded nappies and take away the soiled ones. In the last few years, different types of terry-towelling nappies have become available, including shaped nappies with Velcro fastenings.

Find out!

1. Using catalogues, shops and the Internet, find out about the range of nappies available and their costs.
2. Design a questionnaire to find out which types of nappies parents prefer and why they chose them.
3. Ask at least five parents to answer your questionnaire and present the information as a simple word-processed report.

Safety when changing nappies

To change nappies quickly and safely, you must be well prepared and have everything that you need to hand. Babies must never be left alone as they could put their hands into a dirty nappy or roll off a surface. Some early years practitioners prefer to change nappies on the floor to prevent any possible accidents.

To avoid chills, babies should be changed in warm rooms – about 20°C – that are free from draughts.

If you are using disposable nappies, you should check whether the size of nappy is correct for the weight of the baby. Many disposable nappies are made differently for boys and girls, which means you should check that you are putting on the correct nappy. Nappies made for boys tend to have more padding and absorbency at the front!

Below is a simple guide to changing nappies. Nothing beats practice or being shown by a supervisor.

Guide to changing nappies

Checklist of items required	Changing a nappy
• Changing mat • Disposable gloves • Clean nappies • Nappy pin and plastic pants if using terry-towelling nappies • Cotton wool or wipes • Bucket or bag to dispose of soiled nappies and waste products • Spare clothing • Barrier cream (to prevent nappy rash)	1 Wash your hands; put on disposable gloves. 2 Undress the baby as needed and lie on mat. 3 Undo nappy – if removing a terry-towelling nappy, close pin and put somewhere safe. 4 Gently lift up baby's legs by ankles. 5 Wipe off faeces using cotton wool or baby wipes. 6 Remove soiled nappy and waste materials. 7 Thoroughly clean the genital area. 8 Make sure that the skin in the nappy area is dry. 9 Put on clean nappy.

Tips for good practice

Nappy changing

→ Always wipe girls from front to back to avoid infection.
→ Do not pull foreskin back on baby boys.
→ Always wash hands before and after changing nappies.
→ Wipe down changing mat using disinfectant.

Talk to babies during the nappy-changing process so that they feel reassured. It is also a good idea to give them rattles or simple toys to distract them as they get older. As boys often urinate during the nappy change, it is sensible to wear an apron to avoid the fountain!

Nappy rash

Nappy rash is common in babies. It is sore and painful and so early years practitioners must do everything they can to prevent babies from developing it.

Reasons why nappy rash may occur and how to prevent it

Reasons for nappy rash	How to prevent nappy rash
• Reaction to washing powder or bath product • Diarrhoea • Poor nappy-changing technique • Nappies left on for too long • Teething (although some doctors disagree with this)	• Change nappy frequently • Make sure that skin in the nappy area is dry before putting on new nappy • Leave nappy off for a few minutes each day • Use barrier cream to stop urine and faeces directly touching the skin

Bowel and bladder actions

Young babies can produce interesting bowel movements or stools in their nappies! As they get older, colours often vary according to what they have been eating. Regular bowel movements show that the digestive system is working well and can be very frequent in young babies. This is quite normal.

There is a difference between the stools of breastfed and bottle-fed babies.

➜ *Breastfed babies* – orange, yellow mustard, often watery
➜ *Bottle-fed babies* – pale brown, solid and smelly (not unpleasant smell)

You need to note any significant changes of bowel action, such as a baby not passing any stools in the day or stools becoming hard. Any changes in the colour, frequency or softness of stools must be reported immediately to supervisors or parents as it may be a sign of an infection or illness. It is important to be sure that babies are passing urine frequently, as this means that the kidneys are working properly. If you think that babies are not passing enough urine, you must pass on this information to supervisors or parents.

When to seek help

➜ Any sign of blood
➜ Small green stool over a period of days (may indicate underfeeding)
➜ Stools are very watery and have unpleasant smell
➜ Baby cries when passing a motion.

Unusual skin conditions and reactions

As well as looking out for signs of unusual bladder or bowel movements, you should also check the skin for unusual rashes or marks. Blotches can mean that the baby's skin is reacting in some way – for example to a change of toiletry – while tiny spots might indicate the onset of eczema. It is important to pass on any concerns immediately to either the parent, if you are at home, or your supervisor, so that medical help can be sought.

Cultural differences in toileting

It is extremely important to understand that many families will have a range of views on how their children should be cared for. Some families prefer their babies to be washed under running water or not at certain times of the day, while other families might have strong feelings about certain baby products such as nappies. Not all cultures and countries use nappies. For example, some families choose to put their babies on a pot before and after feeds. This encourages babies to empty their bowels as a reflex. Towels may be put under the babies at other times. If you work with a family where this is the case, you must respect this decision, although in large settings, babies need to wear nappies to avoid cross-infection.

Think about it

Ask three parents about the way in which they wash their baby.

1. How do they wash their baby? (Use a baby bath? A shower?)
2. Which toiletries do they use?
3. What time of day do they wash their baby?

Dressing babies

Clothing and footwear

Babies grow very quickly. In addition, they often need several changes of clothing in a day. This is one area where parents or carers can save money by buying items second hand. By law, all garments have to show washing instructions and fabric content. Most baby clothes are made with cotton as this fabric is easy to care for and does not irritate the skin. It is important to check that clothes still fit the baby, as they grow very quickly in the first few months. Clothes that are too small can cause pressure marks, while clothes that are too large can prevent the baby from being able to move.

It is important to find out from parents or carers if they have any particular preferences about the clothes their babies wear. Some parents tend to keep a few clothes for special occasions or have particular 'favourites' that they like to see their children in.

Tips for good practice

Choosing clothes

→ Are they easy to put on? Small babies may need to be changed several times in the day because of being sick or because a nappy leaked. Older babies who are crawling may not want to lie still while having their nappies changed, which means that clothes must be easy to put on and remove.

→ Do they allow for growth and movement? This is especially important when babies start to crawl. Dresses are harder to crawl in than dungarees!

→ Are they easy to wash? Most baby clothes can be machine-washed. Manufacturers' washing instructions should always be followed.

Young babies do not need shoes until they start walking. Babies' feet can be kept warm using socks or padders. Any footwear must be checked for size and should not restrict the feet. Babies' feet can be damaged by socks and other items of clothing that are too small, so it is a good idea to check the amount of foot space in bodysuits.

Washing babies' clothes

It is important that babies' clothes are regularly washed to prevent the spread of bacteria and also for them to be comfortable. Very few babies will make an outfit last a day and so this means that there is always a lot of washing to be done. A good starting point when washing babies' clothes is to always read the manufacturers' washing instructions, which are normally sewn into the back of a garment or into a side seam. You should also separate white garments from coloured ones to prevent any dye from colouring the white garments.

Babies' clothes need to be washed with a gentle detergent as their skin is sensitive. Non-biological detergent is suggested and all items need rinsing thoroughly. Babies with eczema may need special detergents that are particularly gentle. Some garments may need to be hand washed and it is advisable to wear household gloves to protect your own hands. You should always make sure that clothes are thoroughly dried and aired before putting them on a baby so that they do not cause the skin to chap, or chill the baby.

How to safeguard children to keep them safe and healthy

Accidents and illness can affect babies and children's development. This means that a major role for anyone working with children is to understand how best to prevent children from having accidents and how to prevent the spread of infections. This is a significant area and is covered in Unit 3 (see pages 108–120). You will need to read the relevant pages in Unit 3 in order to complete your learning for this unit.

The importance of routines for everyday care in supporting children's development

A routine provides a predictable pattern to a session or day. The body tends to like routines, for example you probably get hungry at certain times of the day and tired at others. Routines for children are particularly important as they help children to feel secure. They also prevent children from becoming overtired, hungry or bored.

Did you know?

In the past, routines for children were rigid and care was timed! Today, people still think it is important to have a routine, but at the same time to have a little flexibility within it.

Planning routines to meet individual needs within a range of provision

Regardless of the setting in which you work, children's needs have to be met and a routine devised that will allow for this to happen. In order to plan a routine, it is important to begin by identifying children's needs. This information can be gained by talking to parents or carers, but also by observing the child. A good starting point when planning a routine is to work out when children will need feeding and also when they will need to sleep. Other things such as bathtime, going out and playing can then be slotted in.

You will need to be realistic in timings. Young children can sometimes be slow eaters, while some toddlers tend to wake up feeling groggy after a nap and may need a slow start. By observing children of different ages, you can start to get a feel of how long things take and what works best at different times of the day.

Reviewing a routine

Children can sometimes show you through their behaviour that a routine is not working for them. A child whose behaviour is difficult may be hungry or tired, while a group of children who are not concentrating on a story might be showing that story time is at the wrong point in the day. It is therefore important to look at each part of a routine and consider whether it is working. Even so, routines that work well for one child might not work so well for another child even if the children are the same age.

A good routine should feel relaxed and enjoyable for the adults, too! A sign that part of a routine is not working well is if an adult feels very rushed or stressed as the case study below shows.

Case study

Finding the right routine

Since Tiny Tots nursery had opened, it was the tradition for the children to go outdoors straight after snack time. The children waited for everyone to finish and then they all put on their coats to go outside. This always felt very rushed and the children's behaviour was not easy to manage.

A new manager looked at what was happening and talked to the staff about the reasons behind this routine. Everyone agreed that the situation was not ideal. As a team, they decided to split the children into smaller groups with a member of staff taking responsibility for a group. This would stagger snack time and mean that children would go out in smaller groups when they were ready. It also meant that children had more individual attention. The new routine worked extremely well. The children spent less time waiting and staff found that snack and outdoor time was much less stressful.

1. Why is it important to review routines?
2. How might children's behaviour help you to work out whether a routine is effective?
3. Why is it important to create routines that meet individual as well as group needs?

 Back to the real world

You should now understand the importance of meeting children's care needs and how these can support children's development.

1. List three care needs that all children have.

2. Explain why each one is important.

Section 5

How to support children through transitions in their lives

In the real world

One of the children in your placement setting is moving to a new nursery. The staff are working out how best to help the child cope with this change. They talk about 'transition' but you are not sure what this means.

By the end of this section you will be able to identify some of the transitions that children will make and how you might support children through them.

Recognising the importance of a secure base for children's development

Do you remember your first day at a new school, college or job? Can you remember feeling nervous and worrying about how you would cope? Most probably there is a young child feeling the same way at this very moment – perhaps tossing and turning in bed or holding tightly onto a parent's hand! At different points in children's lives, they will need to cope with changes.

A good starting point when looking at the effects of change and separation is to consider the reason why children miss their parents or primary carers so strongly. This is why it is useful to look at attachment theory.

Attachment theory

Attachment theory looks at the needs of children to have a strong stable relationship with their **primary carers** – that is, their mother, father or the main person looking after them. It is increasingly accepted that the attachment children have with their primary carers and their ability to relate to others are linked. The theory is that only when children have a secure relationship with their primary carer can they go on to develop wider relationships. It is now accepted that babies and young children can form several close relationships or attachments and that it is only when their primary carer is not available and no substitute attachment is formed that emotional harm can be done. This means that babies and young children can be cared for successfully by people other than their primary carer. However, it is important that these other carers build a stable relationship with the child.

Bowlby's theory of attachment

John Bowlby (1907–90) is the best-known theorist on children's need to be with their primary carers. There are three aspects to his theory of attachment:

➜ Children who have been separated from their parents are more likely to suffer from psychological problems later in life.
➜ Attachment is an instinct in babies. They must form an attachment by the time they are 12 months old.
➜ Babies' and young children's fear of strangers is instinctive. In nature, animals will follow only their mother, which prevents them being attacked by other animals.

The effects of separation on the child

For most children, separating from their primary carers is a big step. It is important that you understand how children are likely to react to this separation.

Research carried out on the separation of children from their primary carers suggests that there is a pattern to their anxiety. This is often referred to as **separation distress**. There seems to be three stages to this process, with particular signs of anxiety:

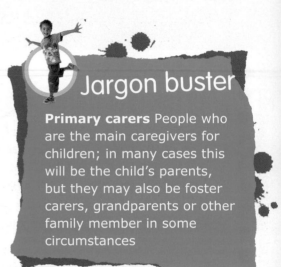

Jargon buster

Primary carers People who are the main caregivers for children; in many cases this will be the child's parents, but they may also be foster carers, grandparents or other family member in some circumstances

Jargon buster

Separation distress Signs that children show when they are upset because their primary carers are not present

1. Protest – anger, crying loudly, frustration
2. Despair – listless, quiet, not participating in activities
3. Detachment – withdrawn, plays by self, does not interact with adults or other children.

Children will go through all three stages only if the care they are receiving is inadequate and if they are not quickly reunited with their primary carer. Children who have reached the detachment stage seem to have 'separated' from their primary carer and are no longer interested in the carer or others around them.

Age and separation

→ Babies under 6 months are unlikely to show any signs of distress, as they will not have formed a strong attachment with their primary carer.

→ Children aged 1–3 years are more likely to show signs of distress when leaving their primary carer.

→ Older children who have had experience of the primary carer leaving and then returning are more likely to cope with short periods of separation.

Helping children who are showing signs of distress

It is important for you to be able to identify signs of distress in children. Ideally, children should always be left with people with whom they have built up an attachment. This is not always possible and so many early years practitioners will see children who are in the first stage of the distress syndrome. Signs will include withdrawal, anger, crying and clinginess. In this situation, it is vital not to ignore them, as they will then feel abandoned! Wherever possible, children should be allowed their comforter, as this can help them to feel more secure.

The importance of a secure base

A strong attachment acts as a secure base. It means that children always know that someone is there for them. Parents usually act as this secure base, although other people in children's lives can also help them. When children come to a setting, it is important that they are provided with a secure base. This is usually done through the key worker system. A key worker is a person who gets to know a child well and develops a special relationship with them. The aim of the key worker is not to replace the parent, but to be an additional person who the child can go to when their parent is not available. A key worker also needs to have good relationships with parents.

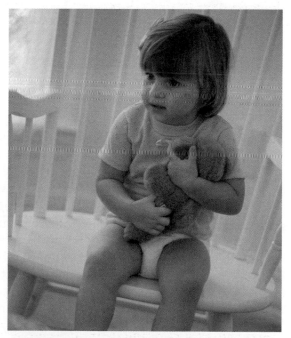

⇧ **Many children have comfort objects that help them feel secure**

Comfort objects

Many children have comfort objects that they need to make them feel secure. They are never a substitute for a child being allocated a key worker but can help children to make a transition. It is surprising what children get attached to – you may find that some children have scraps of blankets, teddies or even cushions!

In the past, children were not encouraged to have such objects, but now it is known that they can help children enormously for the following reasons:

→ they are a link with home
→ children associate them with being happy or secure
→ they can help children to relax and therefore get to sleep more easily.

Patience

Some children need more time in order to feel at ease. It is important that these children get plenty of the key worker's time and support and that the key worker is patient with them.

Reliable

Key workers must be on time and reliable. Children will be counting on their key worker, especially when they first come into the setting and do not know anyone else.

Communication

Key workers should work closely with parents. This means that good communication skills are essential and they will need to listen carefully to information that parents provide.

SKILLS REQUIRED TO BE AN EFFECTIVE KEY WORKER

Observant

Key workers need to observe their children carefully. They need to learn about what the child enjoys doing and get to know what certain gestures or facial expressions mean.

Friendly

Key workers need to show children that they are friendly. This involves smiling and talking in a kind and friendly voice.

Show affection

The key worker should have a special relationship with a child. This means that the child should feel cared for and liked. Showing affection means smiling, and for younger children it also involves some physical contact such as holding hands. It is important that physical contact is appropriate for the age of the child. A baby needs to be cuddled, but this is not appropriate with an older child. Physical affection needs to be offered to children, but if they are not interested in holding a hand, the key worker should never insist.

It is considered good practice to talk to parents about when children might need their comforters and to make sure that children have access to them. This can help children to settle down more quickly if they are changing environments.

The role of the key worker

In order to be a good key worker, you need many skills and qualities. It is important to remember that a child will be relying on you for their emotional security. The spider diagram opposite looks at the skills you need to develop to be an effective key worker.

The changes experienced by children

There will be many times in children's lives when they will have to cope with changes. Changes can be divided into two categories:
→ changes that involve the child moving setting or changing carer
→ other changes that may affect the child's lifestyle.

Change of setting

Children might be moving on to school, leaving the area or changing childminder or nanny. Supporting children through a change can help them to feel more secure and settle in more quickly. It is important to work with parents when preparing children so that we can reinforce anything they have said to the children as well as pass on any concerns that children may have mentioned to us. The table below shows some of the transitions that a child might make.

⇕ **Changes experienced by children**

School	Moving to a new school is always a challenge for children. For some children, they may also move area and not know anyone there. Even when children are in a school, they may have to move class at the end of the year and get used to a new teacher
Nursery/ pre-school	Children may move nursery or start for the first time in a nursery. For some children, this may be the first time that they have left their parents, childminder or nanny. In some pre-schools and nurseries, children change rooms as they get older. This may mean getting to know a new member of staff.
Nanny/ childminder	Nannies and childminders may play an important role in children's lives. A change of nanny or going to a new childminder may be difficult for a child.
Crèche	Some children may attend a crèche from time to time, e.g. in a shopping centre or while on a family holiday. Children may not know the staff or other children.
Holiday club	Some parents will send their children to a holiday club so that they can continue to work during the school holidays. Children may not know other children or staff.
After-school club	Many school-aged children also attend an after-school club. These may be near their school or at their school. Children going for the first time may not know what to expect and may not know the staff.

The Features Page:

Focus on *Key workers*

Key workers are people who care for children and with whom the children have a strong and special relationship. It is recognised that this can help children to cope with leaving their parents and is one way in which practitioners can help children to feel emotionally secure. Being a key worker to a child is a responsibility, but it is also very rewarding as you will get to know children well.

Ask the expert

Q What happens to the children when the key worker goes on holiday or off on break?

A In order to make the key worker system effective, most settings will have a main key worker and then someone else as a 'back up', so that children are never left with people who they are not comfortable with. This is how lunchtimes and staff breaks can be covered. In situations where there is a planned absence such as a key worker leaving the setting, it is important that the children get to know their new key worker before the previous one leaves.

Q How long do children need a key worker for?

A Children of all ages need an adult to whom they can turn. This means that even children aged 7 or 8 years old will need a key worker, though the role of the key worker might change as children get older. Babies and young children will need more reassurance and time with their key worker, but as children get older they tend to just need someone to fall back on when they have problems or there is something special that they want to share.

Key workers

Lyndsay, pre-school leader

I love being with children anyway, but having your 'own' small group of children to look after is brilliant. It's wonderful to see the way that a child who may feel a little lost when they first come in, starts with your help to feel settled and join in with the others. I like it when children come and take my hand because they want to show me something or need my help. It makes me feel that I am really making a difference to their lives. Its also nice being able to talk to parents and help parents to find out what their children have been doing.

Top Tips:

Helping children and parents to settle in

✓ Remember that parents as well as children can be nervous. Try and smile to make them feel at ease.

✓ I use a puppet to help children settle in. It works really well with 'shy' children who might make friends first with the puppet.

✓ Make sure you are calm and friendly. Avoid rushing new children.

My story

Amanda, mother of Tom aged 18 months

I had to go back to work when Tom was nearly 1 year old. I was dreading going back as I felt that Tom still needed me and I loved being with him. I chose a childminder for him and I think that this was the right choice. Sarah made me feel very welcome and she took time to get to know both Tom and me. We spent three afternoons there and by the end of the third visit, Tom and Sarah were firm friends. For me, it has made going back to work much easier as I know that Tom likes going to Sarah's house and that she will look after him well.

Understanding how children might feel

Children are likely to have many concerns about a change of setting, as shown in the spider diagram below.

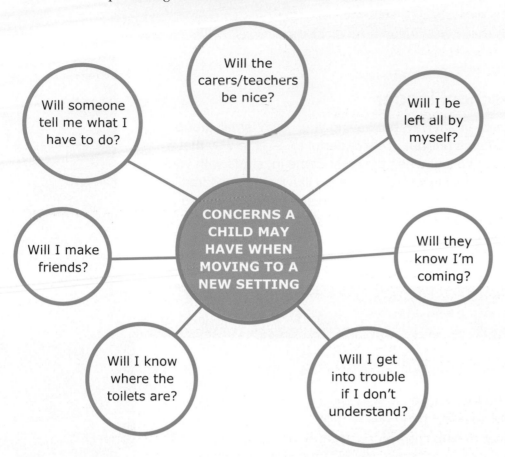

Other changes that may affect children

As well as making transitions between carers or settings, many children will also have to cope with other changes to their lives. These may include bereavement, separation of parents or moving house or country. Some children will also have to cope with the arrival of a sibling or becoming part of a new family if their parents change partners. These types of changes are likely to make an impact on children's feelings of security and emotional development.

How to support children through changes to provide consistency and reassurance

Ways to prepare children for change

These include:

➜ reading books on topics like starting school, going to hospital and starting playgroup
➜ arranging a visit to the new early years setting
➜ involving children in any preparations, e.g. packing a bag, buying items of clothing
➜ encouraging children to ask questions and taking these seriously.

Settling-in children

As well as preparing children to move somewhere else, it is also important that you quickly help children to settle into their new environment. In the past, children were abruptly separated from their primary carers – they were taken from their parents' arms crying and no period for adjustment was allowed. The work of John Bowlby and other people has shown early years practitioners that children need time to settle in.

Most early years settings now have a 'settling-in' policy which is designed to help children adjust to the new environment. A typical settling-in procedure is described in the flow chart below. The length of time between each stage depends on how well children are coping with the separation.

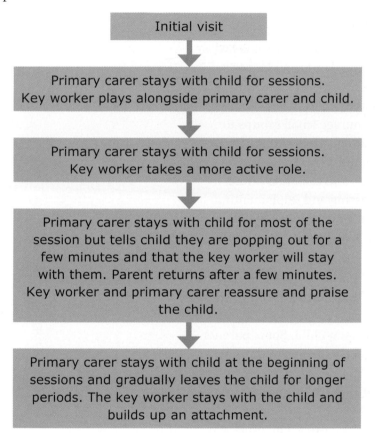

⇦ **Procedure for settling children in to a new setting**

Sometimes the needs of the parents will mean that the normal settling policy cannot be used. For example, if a parent is taken ill suddenly and child care has to be quickly arranged or a child is taken into local authority care and Social Services becomes responsible for placing the child. Sometimes parents may not be able to spend time settling children in because they are unable to take the time off work. In these types of circumstances, you need to be flexible and work with the parent or whoever has parental responsibility to find ways of settling children in.

Helping children to feel they belong

There are a number of things we can do to help children feel they belong. We can label their coat pegs or drawers so they know that some space in a setting is especially for them. Settings can also have displays that show children's photographs, names and how old they are. Young children can have their own beakers and mugs, whereas older children could have special tasks to do which will make them feel important, for example tidying the book corner or giving out pencils.

Home corners can also be used to encourage children to feel that they belong. This is especially important for children who come from homes where the culture and language are different from those of other children in the setting. This means that they should see things that look familiar to them. If you are unsure about what you need to put in the home corner, you could ask the parents for help. They might be able to show you the cooking utensils that they use at home or bring in some fabric or books that are more familiar to the child.

Preparing children and adults in the setting

One of the ways in which you can help new children to settle in is by involving other children and adults in the setting. For example, you might think about activities that will help the 'new' child break into existing friendship groups. You could ask another child to be a 'friend' to the new child, or provide activities that encourage small groups to work together, such as cooking activities or bulb planting. Adults in the setting also need to be prepared for the new child. You might pass on information that is relevant to the child's needs and ask other adults to be aware of the new child when they are preparing and implementing activities. This type of communication should mean that, when new children come into the setting, they feel they are expected.

Supporting parents

It is easy to forget that parents may also have some strong feelings when leaving their children, including the following:

→ Guilt because they are no longer caring for their child. Some parents may have had to return to work through need rather than through choice.

→ Loss because they are so used to caring for their child that it seems strange not to have them there all the time.

→ Anxiety that the child may prefer the key worker to them, especially when children are spending more time with early years practitioners than with the parents.

To help parents with these feelings, you must be able to reassure them that although you are caring for their child, they remain the most important people in the child's life. You will also need to ensure that your communications with parents helps them to give you information about their children but also that they can find out about their children.

Possible effects on children and young people of multiple changes

For children to feel confident, they need to feel secure. This security often comes from routines and familiarity and, with very young children, it comes from having the same people around them. This means that when young children are not with their parents or people they are familiar with, they quickly begin to feel insecure and even frightened. Gradually, as children become older, they begin to be able to cope more easily with being separated from their main carers, providing that their early experiences of separation have been well managed.

When children have had many changes of carer or setting in their lives, they can find it harder to settle in and make new friends and relationships. They may have learned that getting too attached and close to someone results in feeling upset, as either this person leaves or they leave them. This means that if you know that a child has already had many changes in their lives, you will need to be very settled and calm in the way that you work with them. You must also expect that it might take them longer to settle in or show you any affection. You can help children by explaining any changes to them and also by keeping in contact with them from time to time, although you would need permission to do this from their parents or primary carers. Some children whose lives have been very disrupted may also need specialist support and help.

Supporting children with other changes

Where children are coping with changes such as bereavement, loss or making adjustments such as the arrival of a new sibling, it is essential that you think about how to make them feel secure. Their key worker may spend more time with such children to give them opportunities to talk about how they are feeling or just to make them feel secure. A key worker may also look for opportunities to help children express their feelings about what is happening. Some children may choose to act out their feelings using role-play, while others may choose to paint or draw. It is important when helping children cope with changes that you acknowledge how they are feeling. This may mean that instead of trying to 'cheer up' a child, you begin by listening to or trying to understand what a child is feeling.

Back to the real world

You should now be able to identify some of the changes that children will make and understand how these might affect children. You should also be able to suggest ways in which children might be supported.

1. List three changes that children might make.

2. For each one, suggest ways in which the child might be helped.

3. Why is it important for adults to understand how children might be feeling?

Getting ready for assessment

Unit 2 is externally assessed through a multiple choice question paper. It is a good idea to prepare for this assessment by practising answering multiple choice questions on this unit. You can do this by visiting the website www.heinemann.co.uk/cache and typing in the password 4child. The website provides two example question papers (each containing 25 questions) for the CACHE Level 2 qualification in Child Care and Education. You will get instant feedback after answering each question. If you answer a question incorrectly the feedback will tell you which pages of this textbook to read to learn more about that topic.

Unit 3

Safe, healthy and nurturing environments for children

In this unit you will learn:

1. How to prepare and maintain a safe environment and follow relevant policies and procedures

2. How to implement working practices that safeguard children and the adults that work with them

3. The role of the practitioner in working with children to manage conflict

How to prepare and maintain a safe environment and follow relevant policies and procedures

In the real world

It's your first day on work placement at a nursery. You have been asked to come in at 10 o'clock after the children have been settled. You are surprised to find that the door of the nursery is locked. You ring the doorbell and someone answers. You are then asked to sign in and are given a badge. The manager shows you around. As you reach the baby room, you are asked to take off your shoes. The manager explains that this is to prevent infection but also to avoid accidents.

By the end of this section you will know why health and safety is important when working with young children and your role in this.

In the interests of

NURSERY SECURITY

VISITORS & DELIVERIES
Please ring the doorbell and wait for a member of staff to welcome you.

PARENTS
Please ensure that you do not let anyone who is not personally known to you into the nursery and also ensure that the door is firmly shut behind you at all times.

Thankyou

The policies and procedures that support and maintain a safe environment for children

Every setting, including childminders, needs to have a range of policies as a requirement for registration.

In this section you will look at health and safety and the requirements that are in place for settings. Your placement setting will have a health and safety policy which will outline how they aim to comply with health and safety legislation. As part of their health and safety policy, there will also be procedures for staff to follow. Procedures are important as they provide detailed information for staff about what they should do in practice. You may, for example, find that there is a procedure that staff have to follow if a child is due to go home with someone other than their usual carer.

Find out!

Look at the following situations and find out the procedure in your setting for dealing with them.

1. A visitor comes to the setting
2. A parent asks if another parent could pick up their child at the end of the session
3. A parent whose child has chicken pox wants their child to attend the session

Health and safety legislation in the country in which you live

Keeping children healthy and safe is an important part of your work with children. Parents need to know that their children will be properly supervised and kept safe. To ensure children's and your own safety, there are many pieces of **legislation** in place. Some legislation such as the Health and Safety at Work Act relates to all workplaces including restaurants, shops and factories, but others are specific to children.

Health and Safety at Work Act 1974

This Act was designed to protect employees, so many of its provisions apply to workplaces in which there are five or more members of staff. The Act gives duties to both **employees** and employers.

Duties of employees

The Act is clear that employees must follow the setting's health and safety procedures and use the health and safety equipment provided. This means that if disposable aprons are provided you must wear them, or if you have been told how to lift a toddler safely you must follow the advice.

Jargon buster

Legislation Laws passed by Parliament

Jargon buster

Employee Someone who is in paid work

The Act also says that employees should not put others at risk by their actions and that you have a duty to report anything that you recognise as a potential health and safety issue.

Duties of employers

The Act places significant duties on employers. Employers have a duty of care towards their employees and must take every reasonable step to consider their health and safety and to minimise risks. This means providing adequate training and protection and carrying out risk assessments. They must also enforce health and safety procedures. Under this Act, settings with five or more employees must have a health and safety policy that explains how risks are to be minimised. Most settings appoint a senior member of staff to be responsible for health and safety.

Case study

Unsafe working practices

Jamie is working in a day care nursery. He loves his work but is inclined sometimes to take a few short cuts. Today he changes a child's nappy without wearing an apron and disposable gloves. The gloves and aprons are provided by the nursery to prevent staff from picking up any infections. He says that they are too fiddly to put on quickly and that he shouldn't be made to put them on. He says that he doesn't mind running the risk of an infection and that it's his health. His manager says that this is a serious issue and that as a manager he has to insist that Jamie wears the apron and gloves.

1. Explain how Jamie is breaking the law by not wearing the gloves and aprons.
2. Explain why, by law, the manager has to take this matter seriously.

Regulations under the Health and Safety at Work Act 1974

As part of the Act, there are many regulations that settings have to follow. These are often updated and it is one reason why settings usually appoint someone to be in charge of health and safety. Below is a chart that shows some of the regulations that are in place.

Significant regulations under the Health and Safety at Work Act 1974

Regulation title	Description
Control of Substances Hazardous to Health Regulations (COSHH) 2004	These Regulations look at the storage and use of chemicals and other hazardous materials. In early years settings, this might include cleaning products and the disposal of nappies. The Regulations require settings to assess the risks and then write a procedure for managing the risks, for example locking bleach in a cupboard and providing gloves.
Reporting of Injuries, Diseases and Dangerous Occurrences (RIDDOR) 1995	Workplaces must provide an accident report book for their employees (the 1989 Children Act requires an accident book for noting down injuries to children). Any injuries to an employee that mean that he or she cannot work for three or more days must be reported to the Health and Safety Executive.

Regulation title	Description
Fire Precautions (Workplace) Regulations 1997	Workplaces have to show how they would evacuate the building and carry out practices. Signs showing what to do in the event of a fire must be placed in every room. (Note that the 1989 Children Act also requires settings to have an evacuation procedure.)
Health and Safety (First Aid) Regulations 1981	Every workplace must have a first aid box and appoint at least one trained first aider to be responsible in the event of an accident. The contents of the first aid box are left to the discretion of the workplace. (Note that the 1989 Children Act requires that any medication given to children is recorded.)

National Standards

For each of the four countries in the United Kingdom, there are standards that providers of childcare must meet. These are known as the National Standards and childcare providers are inspected to check that the standards are being met. It is important that you find out about the National Standards for the country in which you will be working.

National Standards in England

Since September 2001, the Early Years directorate at Ofsted has taken on this inspection role. The inspection takes place each year and providers are currently inspected against the set of National Standards, of which there are 14. The Standards cover all aspects of children's care, including safety, food and drink, and child protection. Below is a chart showing the National Standards, which includes an Ofsted descriptor of each standard.

☞ **The National Standards**

National Standard	Title	Descriptor
Standard 1	Suitable Person	Adults providing day care, looking after or having unsupervised access to children, are suitable to do so.
Standard 2	Organisation	The registered person meets required adult to child ratios, ensures that training and qualification requirements are met, and organises space and resources to meet the children's needs effectively.
Standard 3	Care, Learning and Play	The registered person meets children's individual needs and promotes their welfare. The registered person plans and provides activities and play opportunities to develop children's emotional, physical, social and intellectual capabilities.
Standard 4	Physical Environment	The premises are safe, secure and suitable for their purpose. They provide adequate space in an appropriate location, are welcoming to children and offer access to the necessary facilities for a range of activities in order to promote children's development.
Standard 5	Equipment	Furniture, equipment and toys are provided which are appropriate for their purpose and help to create an accessible and stimulating environment. They are of suitable design and condition, are well-maintained and conform to safety standards.

National Standard	Title	Descriptor
Standard 6	Safety	The registered person takes positive steps to promote safety within the setting and on outings and ensures proper precautions are taken to prevent accidents.
Standard 7	Health	The registered person promotes the good health of children, takes positive steps to prevent the spread of infection and adopts appropriate measures when children are ill.
Standard 8	Food and Drink	Children are provided with regular drinks and food in adequate quantities for their needs. Food and drink is properly prepared, nutritious and complies with dietary and religious requirements.
Standard 9	Equal Opportunities	The registered person and staff actively promote equality of opportunity and anti-discriminatory practice for all children.
Standard 10	Special Needs	The registered person is aware that some children may have special needs and is proactive in ensuring that appropriate action can be taken when such a child is identified or admitted to the provision. Steps are taken to promote the welfare and development of the child within the setting in partnership with the parents and other relevant parties.
Standard 11	Behaviour	Adults caring for children in the provision are able to manage a wide range of children's behaviour in a way that promotes their welfare and development.
Standard 12	Working in Partnership with Parents and Carers	The registered person and staff work in partnership with parents to meet the needs of the children, both individually and as a group. Information is shared.
Standard 13	Child Protection	The registered person complies with local child protection procedures approved by the Area Child Protection Committee and ensures that all adults working and looking after children in the provision are able to put the procedures into practice.
Standard 14	Documentation	Records, policies and procedures that are required for the efficient and safe management of the provision and to promote the welfare, care and learning of children are maintained. Records about individual children are shared with the child's parents and carers.

How to follow relevant policies and procedures

You will find that each setting in which you work has a health and safety **policy**. The policy outlines how the setting intends to comply with legislation and keep the children safe. As part of the policy there should also be procedures. These are more detailed pieces of information that tell staff and other adults working with children what they should do in different situations, for example if there was a fire alarm or if a child had an accident. It is essential, even when you are a learner, to find out about some of the basic health and safety procedures in your setting, especially emergency ones when every second can count.

Jargon buster

Policy A written document that outlines how a setting intends to work

As a staff member it is important to follow the policy and procedures in your setting as this will be seen as part of your work. Not following the policy and procedures can mean that you may lose your job as you might be putting children at risk.

Emergency procedures

As an early years practitioner you must know what to do in the event of a fire or other emergency. Most early years settings have procedures to deal with the majority of emergencies. It is important that everyone working in a setting knows where all the exit points are and what their role is in an emergency. It is usual for settings to have fire notices as well as fire practices to make sure that staff are able to evacuate a building quickly. Where children are being cared for in their home, it is still important to make sure that there is more than one exit available in the event of a fire.

What to do during an alarm or practice

As part of the fire regulations, all workplaces must carry out fire practices regularly. These are important as they give adults the chance to check that the procedures work well.

There are three parts to most emergency procedures:
1. Make sure that everyone leaves the building rapidly and calmly.
2. Group children, adults and staff together in a safe zone.
3. Use a register to check that everyone is present.

Remaining calm is one of the most important things that adults can do when faced with any sort of emergency. Fire alarms are designed to be loud, but to a young child they can be terrifying. You need to reassure children and explain clearly what is happening and what they need to do. A register of children's names is needed to check that all the children are out of the building and each setting will have someone who is responsible for this.

Emergency contacts

Emergency numbers or contacts are essential for all settings. Children may become ill or have an accident and if this happens, their parents or carers should be contacted. Such information is often stored in a central place – in large work settings this might be an office, but where children are being cared for at home it might be placed by the telephone or in another agreed place.

Making sure that children are safe at the end of sessions

The end of a day or a session can be a very busy time and every early years setting will have a procedure to make sure that children are collected safely. In some settings parents or carers come indoors to collect children, while in others children wait outside to be collected. Most settings ask parents to let them know in advance if a different person is collecting a child. It is always better to check with a supervisor

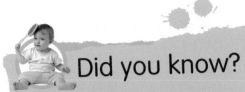

Did you know?

U3
1

⇧ **It is vital that you know where fire exits are and what to do in the event of a fire**

if you are unsure of the arrangements, as in some cases children's parents may not be living together and one parent may not have access to a child.

Informing parents

All accidents, major or minor, need to be reported to parents. Sometimes a minor injury may be more serious than it looks. This is often the case with bumps to the head where children may complain of feeling unwell after a few hours.

Many settings will tell parents about minor injuries when the child is collected. When parents are not able to collect their children, most settings send a slip home with the following details:
➔ what happened and at what time
➔ the treatment that was given
➔ who gave the treatment.

If children have a major injury, parents and carers need to be contacted at once. It is important that they know exactly what is happening to their child. For example, if the child is going to hospital they need to know which one. Parents and carers also need to know who is with their child and, if possible, they should be involved in making decisions about the treatment. For example, they may prefer the child to be taken to the family doctor.

Parents are likely to be upset when they hear their child is injured and you can help by showing that the emergency is being handled calmly. There may be ways in which you can help further, for example by offering to make sure that an older child is collected from school.

The importance of risk assessments and how to identify risks in the setting

The term **risk assessment** is used to describe a process by which any potential dangers to children are identified. Risk assessments help adults to become aware of what they might need to do in order to keep children safe. Risk assessments may also help adults to realise that some activities, areas or equipment might not be suitable for the children they are working with.

In every setting there will be someone who has particular responsibility for health and safety. As part of their work they will carry out risk assessments, although as you have seen earlier it is everyone's responsibility to keep children safe and identify possible dangers. Risk assessments are not just for the children's benefit; some risk assessments look at possible dangers for staff.

Jargon buster

Risk assessment A way of noticing and recording dangers and making suggestions as to how they can be reduced

Activity/ Resources/Area	Risks to be assessed	Strategies for managing risk
Steps leading to entrance	Danger of falls especially when wet; danger of children pushing each other when playing on steps	• Install a grab rail • Supervise children • Restrict numbers on steps
Tricycle area	Danger of falls/ collisions between children	• Create one-way system so that children do not cycle towards each other • Create a designated area for tricycles • Provide cycle helmets
Climbing frame	Danger of falls	• Check that climbing frame is not damp • Make sure that children are wearing shoes rather than Wellington boots • Adult member of staff to stay next to the frame • Low fence around the frame to prevent the toddlers from gaining access • Bark chippings around to soften landings

What happens when a risk is identified?

It is impossible to create an environment totally free from risk. This means that as part of the risk assessment, ways to reduce the risk are considered, for example changing a child's nappy can lead to infection. The risk of infection can be minimised by wearing disposable gloves and washing hands afterwards. The table above shows how other risks might be reduced.

Risk assessments have to be reviewed

It is important that risk assessments are reviewed from time to time. Circumstances change, so a risk assessment that was accurate might no longer be so. A good example of this is equipment – a piece of equipment that was considered to be suitable and safe for 4-year-olds might pose a danger if younger children are put into the room.

Risk assessment and activity plans

It is important to think about health and safety when planning activities for children of all ages. It can be a good idea when writing activity plans to include a section that outlines the possible risks and how they are to be managed. Thinking about health and safety needs to happen even if you have done an activity before or are following an activity from a book. Changes in the age of children, the place in which you carry out the activity or the needs of children can all mean that a 'safe' activity can become a dangerous one.

Sometimes it is worth trying out an activity yourself to work out what the potential difficulties may be. As you are doing the activity, try and remember that children may not always be as skilful or as patient.

Many toys are unsuitable for children under 3 years because of the risk of choking on small parts; such toys should be clearly marked to indicate this

Think about whether there is a danger that they may become bored or frustrated. Boredom and frustration can both mean that a child's behaviour may become an issue. The table below gives some examples of areas of potential risk.

⚓ **Assessing potential risks associated with children**

Choking	• Are toys and materials age-appropriate for children? • Are there any children with particular needs who might put things in their mouth?
Poisoning	• Could any materials be poisonous if swallowed?
Falling	• Is there any danger of a child falling or slipping? • Are there any steps or places where children might climb?
Electrocution	• Are any electrical appliances being used?
Cuts	• Are knives, scissors or any other sharp objects being used?
Infection	• Will children be sharing materials and equipment? • Are children playing outdoors?
Drowning	• Is water involved in this activity?
Burns	• Will children be near any source of heat, e.g. a cooker or heater?

Managing risk

Once health and safety issues have been raised, you will need to think about whether the activity is still suitable or whether it is possible to manage the risks. The spider diagram below gives examples of ways in which risks can be managed.

WAYS IN WHICH RISKS CAN BE MANAGED

Change the group size
Working with pairs or individual children might allow for better supervision

Supervision
Close supervision can sometimes prevent accidents

Change the location
Sometimes moving an activity to a different area can make it safer

Change the size of objects or pieces of equipment
It is sometimes possible to carry out a similar activity but substitute with different equipment

Check the location
Sometimes checks can be made beforehand to prevent accidents, e.g. picking up litter, wiping surfaces

Case study

The importance of risk assessing activities

Bekir is making banana-smelling dough as an activity with the toddler group. He has done this activity before, although the children were slightly older. He has prepared all the ingredients and is looking forward to making the dough with the children. The recipe is easy to make but does not keep for long because there is no salt in it. He is surprised when after the dough is made the children keep trying to eat it. In the end, he has to take the dough away and find something else to do with the children. He is quite surprised. A member of staff tells him that this is because there is no salt and that this age group will often try to eat a little dough.

1. Why is it important to risk assess activities?
2. Suggest ways in which Bekir can alter this activity to make it safe.

Safe working practices

While you might hope that everyone who has contact with children and young people is safe, this is not always the case. To help keep children safe, there are a number of measures that are considered to be essential when working in settings.

Visitors

It is essential that all visitors report to reception and are signed in and out. This is also important for fire safety. Visitors should be given a badge that has their role printed on it. This is to avoid any confusion by parents or members of staff. Visitors should also not be left alone with any child and should be escorted around the building. This means that if you find a visitor who is looking 'lost' you should ask them who they are and help them find the correct person. Any suspicious behaviour should be reported immediately.

There are also safe working practices for staff, and most settings have clear guidelines about how staff should work with children and young people. This is to avoid situations where a practitioner might be accused of abuse or where a child might learn habits that allow others to abuse them more easily.

Overleaf are some examples of safe working practices that you need to remember while you are a learner and later on when you are working with children.

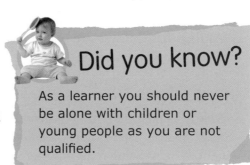

Did you know?

As a learner you should never be alone with children or young people as you are not qualified.

Tips for good practice

Safe working practices

→ Do not pass on personal details such as your phone number or e-mail address to children or young people.

→ Do not contact children or young people that you are working without outside of the setting unless you have been given permission to do so by your supervisor and with the knowledge of their parents.

→ Do not tell children secrets or encourage the use of them, even in fun.

→ Make sure that other staff always know where you are and what you are doing.

→ Make sure that you are not alone with a child in a closed room.

→ When helping a child with toileting or after an 'accident', make their privacy a priority. They may, for example, be able to have the door shut but not locked and be able to wash themselves.

→ Do not physically restrain children.

→ Do not take any photos of children without prior permission.

How to maintain and promote the personal safety of children

As an early years practitioner, you have a role in keeping children safe from abuse (see above and pages 121–6). You also have a role in ensuring that children are safe in other situations, such as when out walking, crossing roads or in cars.

Road safety

As early as possible, children need to be made aware of the danger of traffic. This in itself is not sufficient protection for young children, who ought to be wearing reins or other such restraints until you are sure they will not stray into the road or be tempted to run away, for example because they have seen a cat on the other side of the road. It is useful if toddlers get used to wearing reins as early as possible so that it becomes part of the routine of going outdoors. Reins also allow children some freedom, as they can move a little more independently of the adult.

As children get older they should be dressed in light coloured and reflective clothing if they are walking when it is dark. This means they can be seen more easily by motorists. It is also important to teach them how to look before they cross roads and how to use devices such as pelican and zebra crossings. You must also make sure that you are acting as a good role model. This means waiting until the 'green man' shows before crossing and walking rather than running across the

Did you know?

When young children are holding an adult's hand, their arms are over their head. This is extremely tiring for young children and perhaps one reason why toddlers try to break free.

road. Road safety experts suggest that children will not be competent to cross roads independently until they are much older and are able to judge the speed of traffic accurately.

Car safety

Children also need to be transported safely when in a car. The latest legislation is clear that all children under 14 years must wear restraints, such as car seats or seat belt adjusters, and that drivers can be prosecuted if children are not properly restrained. For very young children this means that they should be in a properly fitted car seat; older children may need a booster cushion or a seat belt adjuster.

Where children sit can also make a difference if there is an accident. While babies under 9 months can sit in the front of the car facing rearward, other children should travel in the back seat as this is the safest place. If babies are placed in their car seat in the front, it is essential, though, to check that any air bags have been turned off.

It is important that you do not give food or drink to young children while in a car. If they choke it can be hard to get them out quickly.

⇧ **It is vital to ensure that children are correctly protected for their age during a car journey**

Cycling, skateboarding and roller skating

Head injuries are a cause of some fatalities in children. Cycling, skateboarding or roller skating can be great fun, but also cause children to fall. This means that you must get children used to wearing cycle helmets even on tricycles and encourage them to wear protective items such as knee pads. Cycle helmets should be a good fit and comfortable for children.

How to work safely outside the setting and how to plan safe outings and trips

Children of all ages enjoy going on outings and even a small outing such as posting a letter can provide learning opportunities. The amount of preparation depends on the scale of the outing. In large settings an outing that requires transport should be planned at least two months ahead of the date. Insurance and parental permission as well as considering supervision arrangements will all take time to plan.

The secret of an enjoyable outing is to choose somewhere which is not too tiring for either the children or the adults. There should be plenty to see and do at the children's level. The only way to really find out what a place is like and make sure it is safe is to do an advance visit.

If children are being cared for at home or by a childminder, parents still need to give their consent to outings. Most parents and early years practitioners may have an arrangement that some types of outings are not discussed in advance, for example walking to the local park or shops, but that early years practitioners ask in advance if they wish to take the children for longer trips.

Find out!

Find out your setting's policy on how many adults are needed to take children on outings.

Think about it

Why is it important to make sure that outings are not too expensive for families?

The spider diagram below lists some of the things you will need to consider when planning an outing.

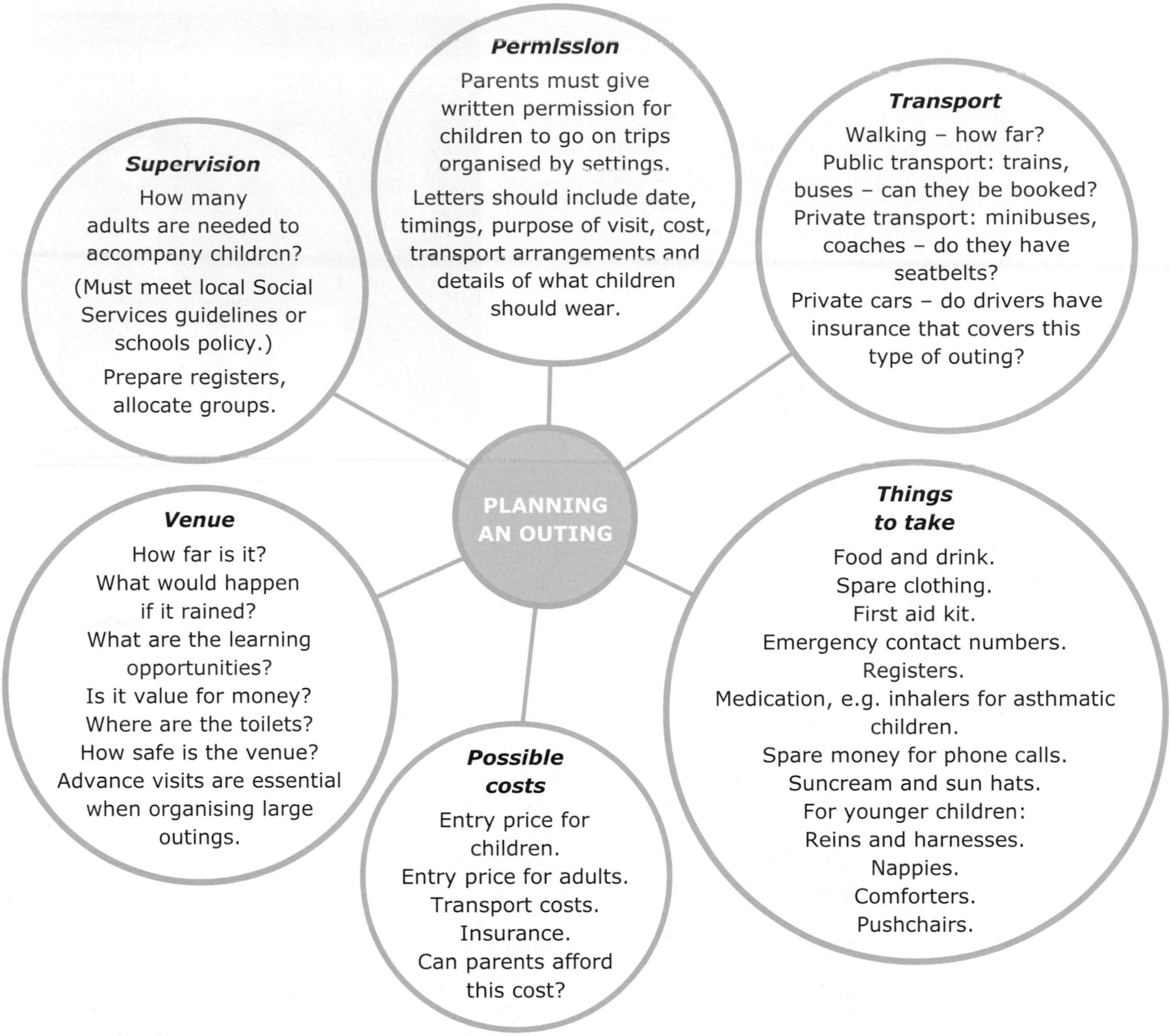

Permission

Parents must give written permission for children to go on trips organised by settings.

Letters should include date, timings, purpose of visit, cost, transport arrangements and details of what children should wear.

Supervision

How many adults are needed to accompany children?

(Must meet local Social Services guidelines or schools policy.)

Prepare registers, allocate groups.

Transport

Walking – how far?
Public transport: trains, buses – can they be booked?
Private transport: minibuses, coaches – do they have seatbelts?
Private cars – do drivers have insurance that covers this type of outing?

PLANNING AN OUTING

Venue

How far is it?
What would happen if it rained?
What are the learning opportunities?
Is it value for money?
Where are the toilets?
How safe is the venue?
Advance visits are essential when organising large outings.

Things to take

Food and drink.
Spare clothing.
First aid kit.
Emergency contact numbers.
Registers.
Medication, e.g. inhalers for asthmatic children.
Spare money for phone calls.
Suncream and sun hats.
For younger children:
Reins and harnesses.
Nappies.
Comforters.
Pushchairs.

Possible costs

Entry price for children.
Entry price for adults.
Transport costs.
Insurance.
Can parents afford this cost?

 Back to the real world

You are now working in a nursery. A visitor comes to the door to visit the baby room. You ask if they can sign in. She looks puzzled. You also explain that visitors must take off their shoes when going into the baby room.

1. Can you now explain why visitors have to sign in?

2. Can you also describe what a risk assessment is?

Section 2

How to implement working practices that safeguard children and the adults that work with them

In the real world

One of the children in your work placement has come to you and shown you a bruise and a graze on her knee. She seems very proud of these marks. You are not sure whether these marks might be a sign of abuse. You are wondering whether you should tell somebody.

By the end of this section you will know more about protecting children and what you should do if you have concerns.

Child protection procedures followed by practitioners across a range of settings

As much as you would like to think that all the children you care for are happy and safe, it is a fact that some children are abused. This means that children may not be treated in a safe and proper manner, for example being burned by cigarettes or left to get their own food. Abuse can take place in children's homes or even in early years settings, and can be by relatives or friends of the family as well as by acquaintances and strangers. It is hard for most people to understand, but parents who abuse their children often still love them and children may find it hard to tell someone that they are being abused. This section looks at ways in which you might be able to identify suspected abuse and the early years practitioner's role in protecting children from abuse.

Policies and procedures of the work setting

The Children Act (1989) makes it clear that adults caring for children have to put a child's welfare first. This means that if you are concerned about a child, you need to pass on this concern. Although you must put the child first, you also need to be sure that you are not jumping to any conclusions.

Every setting that cares for children will have a procedure to follow if abuse is suspected. These policies will have been drawn up so that they follow the guidance in your local area. This guidance is given by the Local Safeguarding Children Board, which is also known as LSCB. Each LSCB is made up of professionals from different areas, e.g. police, social services, health services. The aim is that everyone involved with children can work together to protect children and investigate situations when abuse is suspected. You will need to find out what you should do if a child says something to you or if you notice marks or other signs that worry you. In most procedures, concerns about children are passed on to a supervisor or a manager. It is then their responsibility to decide what type of action should happen next, for example the supervisor may decide to contact the child protection team or Social Services in the area.

If you are caring for children in their own home by, for example, babysitting, you can contact either the NSPCC or Social Services, both of which have a 24-hour helpline. Remember, though, that the Level 2 qualification you are currently studying means that you should be working under supervision.

Confidentiality

Confidentiality is always important, but in cases where child abuse is suspected it is essential. Any written notes need to be passed on to a supervisor and stored away, and any conversation or information that you have heard must be kept confidential. Passing on information which is confidential to adults who are not directly involved could harm the very children who need protecting.

Find out!

Who should you talk to if you have concerns about a child in your work placement?

The importance of awareness and identification of children who may be at risk

Everyone working with children must be aware of the signs of child abuse and be ready to report their concerns. Young children rely on adults to help and support them. They may not be in a position where they either recognise that they are being abused or have the confidence to talk about it. This means that you need to be vigilant and thoughtful if a child says something to you or you notice any physical signs.

Recognising the signs and symptoms of abuse

To protect children from abuse, you must be able to recognise its signs and symptoms.

Abuse is often grouped into four categories:
→ physical
→ emotional
→ sexual
→ neglect.

Children may suffer from more than one of these.

Physical abuse

Although the law currently allows parents to use 'reasonable chastisement', for example a slap on the hand, it is not legal for anyone to bite, burn, shake or in any other way injure a child. This is physical abuse.

Signs that children are being physically abused could include:
→ aggressiveness towards other children
→ reluctance or difficulty in explaining how they received bruises or injuries
→ unwillingness to change for swimming or games.

When children come into the early years setting with a bump or a bruise, you should always ask in a friendly way how the accident happened. Most children are keen to explain exactly how they hurt themselves and are delighted to show off the plaster or the mark. There may be cause for concern if a child becomes tearful or does not want to talk about what has happened.

Did you know?

Organisations such as the NSPCC are campaigning to make smacking by parents against the law.

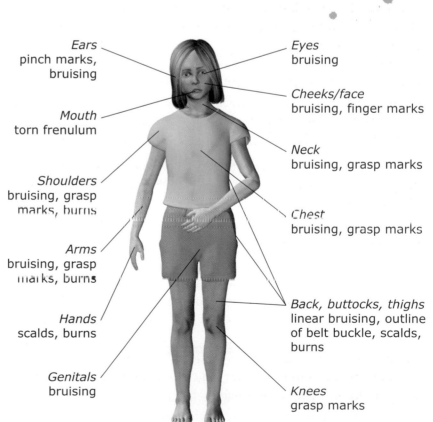

Ears
pinch marks, bruising

Eyes
bruising

Cheeks/face
bruising, finger marks

Mouth
torn frenulum

Neck
bruising, grasp marks

Shoulders
bruising, grasp marks, burns

Chest
bruising, grasp marks

Arms
bruising, grasp marks, burns

Hands
scalds, burns

Back, buttocks, thighs
linear bruising, outline of belt buckle, scalds, burns

Genitals
bruising

Knees
grasp marks

⇨ **Usual position of injuries in cases of child abuse**

Emotional abuse

Children need unconditional love and can be emotionally harmed by taunts, threats and being made to feel guilty. Parents who abuse their children emotionally are likely to be insecure and need reassurance that their child loves them. This form of abuse has been recognised only in the past few years.

It is often hard to be sure if children's behaviour is linked to emotional abuse but signs include:
→ low self-esteem and confidence
→ attention seeking and clinginess
→ telling lies
→ stammering or stuttering
→ tantrums at an age that is not usual, that is beyond 5 years
→ tearfulness.

Sexual abuse

The media has played a strong role in increasing recognition of the fact that some children are sexually abused. Most sexual abuse is carried out by someone that the child knows and trusts. Sexual abuse is any action that gives an adult sexual satisfaction and can include kissing and fondling through to rape. Most cases that come to the public's attention involve men abusing children, although it is not uncommon for women to abuse as well. Many children are told that what they are experiencing is normal or that it is just a secret. This can make children unsure about whether they should tell someone.

Physical signs of sexual abuse may include:
→ wetting or soiling themselves
→ pain on urinating
→ bedwetting
→ bruises and unexplained scratches or marks
→ loss of appetite
→ itchiness of genital areas.

Sometimes it is the behaviour of children that leads early years practitioners to suspect sexual abuse. Most children are interested in their body, but children who are being abused have more knowledge than is usual for their age. This knowledge may be reflected in their drawings and in their play as well as in their behaviour towards adults.

Other behavioural signs may include:
→ regression, for example wanting to be fed or wear nappies
→ withdrawn and solitary behaviour
→ low self-esteem and confidence towards adults.

Did you know?

Most sexual abuse is committed on children by adults that they know.

Neglect

Neglect is the term used when children's needs are not being met, for example they may not be adequately clothed, fed or washed. There are sometimes cases where children are left in their cots while their parents are out. Sometimes children are neglected because their parents are not coping with the responsibility of having children or are having problems of their own. Sometimes children are neglected because their parents do not understand their needs, for example they may not know how important it is to talk to a baby or that children need to be stimulated.

Signs of neglect include:

→ often hungry
→ dirty or badly-fitting clothes
→ tiredness (this is sometimes due to lack of food as well as sleep)
→ poor personal hygiene – dirty hair, skin and bad breath
→ constant colds or infections such as sore throats
→ underweight and not thriving
→ late in arriving to sessions and many unexplained absences
→ bumps and bruises from accidents (due to a lack of safety awareness and supervision).

Case study

A cause for concern?

Cheung is frequently late in the mornings. He often seems untidy and has been known to take other children's snacks at break time. Today he comes in with his older brother. Cheung has a bruise on his forehead. You ask him if it still hurts and how he did it. He looks at his older brother who says that he fell out of the window.

1. Why would you have some concerns about Cheung?
2. What would you do next?
3. Why is it important that your concerns about Cheung are dealt with?

What to do if a child tells you that he or she is being abused

Sometimes children tell early years practitioners that they are being abused. This may happen during an ordinary conversation or a child may say that he or she wants to tell you something. It is important that adults know how to handle this situation as children need to feel that they are believed and that they are not doing anything wrong.

⇨ **If a child tells you about abuse they are experiencing, it is important that you know how to respond to the child and the correct procedures for reporting the abuse**

Tips for good practice

Helping abused children

→ Reassure the child that you believe him or her and want to help.

→ Listen carefully to what the child is saying. You will need to write it down afterwards.

→ Do not ask the child questions. Where a criminal act has taken place, the police may find it hard to prosecute if there is any doubt that a child has been influenced by what an adult has said to him or her.

→ Do not promise the child that you can keep what they say a secret. This is unfair on the child because you are not able to do so. Say to the child that you need to talk to other people so they can help.

→ Reassure the child that he or she is not to blame for what has happened to them.

→ Report what has been said to a supervisor immediately and write down the times and what was said in as much detail as possible. You will also need to write down any incident that led to the **disclosure**.

Jargon buster

Disclosure When a child says something that directly or indirectly helps the practitioner to know that there may be some abuse

Back to the real world

Read the scenario described on page 121 again. You should now know whether grazes on knees are an indicator of child abuse.

1. Can you now explain whether this is an accidental or non-accidental injury?

2. Can you also describe indicators of physical abuse?

3. Do you know what you should do if you have concerns about a child?

Section 3

The role of the practitioner in working with children to manage conflict

In the real world

It is 4 o'clock in the afternoon. Some of the children are beginning to get tired and hungry. You notice that one of the 2-year-olds has just snatched a toy from another toddler. You are not sure what you should do next.

By the end of this section you will know how to deal with this behaviour and why it has happened.

Introduction

In the first years of their life, children have a lot to learn. They become mobile, learn physical skills and start to communicate. At the same time, children have to learn behaviour that is acceptable to the society they live in. This is a gradual learning process because babies are not born with self-control and consideration for others. It is also an essential process because acceptance by others is linked to behaviour.

An important part of your role as an early years practitioner will be promoting what is, in your society, seen as desirable behaviour.

Expectations

Expectations of behaviour vary between countries and change over time. For example, 30 years ago it was considered rude to eat in the street, whereas today people often eat burgers or crisps while walking along. There are also cultural variations, for example in some cultures food is eaten with the fingers while in others this is considered bad manners.

A good starting point when thinking about promoting children's behaviour is to consider your own expectations of behaviour. People have different opinions about what is acceptable behaviour in children. Most of your ideas about what is and is not acceptable come from your own experiences and culture.

As views on behaviour can vary, you need to understand the expectations in the early years setting where you work. Many group settings have policies relating to behaviour but if you are looking after children in a home environment you should talk to the parents about the types of behaviour they consider acceptable. There will be many differences in expected behaviour between group settings and the home environment. For example, some children at home may be allowed to leave the table as soon as they have finished eating, whereas in a busy nursery, staff may not be free to supervise children in another room, so the children would have to wait until everyone had finished the meal.

Think about it

1. What are your views on what is and is not acceptable behaviour?
2. Can you identify where your ideas come from?

What is good behaviour?

Learning to respect other people is the key to good behaviour in society. To do this, children need to learn some self-control, as good behaviour stems from thinking of others and their needs as well as their own. This means that children need to be able to share, take turns, listen to others and be courteous and helpful.

Learning desirable behaviour is a gradual process for children. Being able to share and think of other people cannot happen until children have some communication and cognitive skills. Children also find it hard to share and play well with other children until they are able to control their feelings.

The causes and effects of positive and negative behaviour

One of the ways in which you can support children is to understand the reasons behind their behaviours. You know that children are more likely to show positive or 'wanted' behaviour when they are happy, stimulated and their physical needs have been met. You also know that relationships are important in this. Children always respond well to adults who spend time listening, playing and showing them that they are valued.

In situations where children are not getting their needs met, you are more likely to find negative behaviours. A good example of this is attention-seeking behaviours. These are generally linked to children needing a lot more time from adults. When this time is given positively, children tend to reduce the amount of negative behaviours that were previously gaining them a similar amount (or more) attention.

The spider diagram below shows ways in which positive behaviour can be supported. You will see that some of the ways are reflected later in the section on behaviour management strategies.

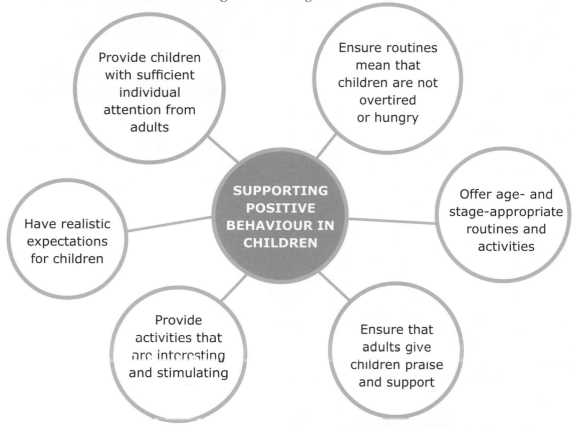

The situations which children may find difficult

As well as some of the general causes of negative behaviour, there are some more specific factors. It is important for early years practitioners to recognise these factors so that expectations of behaviour and ways of managing behaviour are appropriate for the particular circumstances of the children.

How changes in children's lives can affect their behaviour

Children tend to react to such changes in different ways depending on their age and their understanding of the situation. In some situations, such as when a new baby arrives, children need reassurance that they are still loved. In other situations, for example when there is a change of carer, children may try to test out the boundaries and see whether the limits are still the same. The flow chart below shows how changes in children's lives can affect their behaviour.

Separation and divorce of parents (on current trends, 40 per cent of marriages will end in divorce)
New baby in family
Death or illness of family member
Moving house
Changing class or school
Having a new carer, e.g. nanny
Child abuse

→

Attention seeking
Clingy behaviour
Aggression
Temper tantrums
Comfort habits such as thumb-sucking
Withdrawn, quiet behaviour
Regression, e.g. babyish speech, not wanting to feed themselves

Children with particular needs

When children's development is delayed in one or more areas, they may find it harder to meet some of the goals for behaviour (see the chart linking children's behaviour and stages of development in Unit 2, pages 45–7). Some children may not have the cognitive or language skills necessary to show social skills such as sharing and turn-taking.

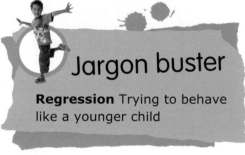

Jargon buster

Regression Trying to behave like a younger child

⇦ **How would you deal with aggressive behaviour in a child?**

Sometimes children with particular needs are aggressive, for example they may bite, throw toys or hit others. Aggressive behaviour is often linked to frustration, as children either cannot express their needs or are dependent on others to meet these needs. This means that early years practitioners need to get to know the children they work with well and supervise them carefully. By doing this, early years practitioners can often prevent inappropriate behaviour.

Behaviour linked to the ages and stages of development

Having realistic expectations of what children can achieve is important when working with children. Such expectations are usually linked to children's age or stage of development. This means that you must adapt your own way of working with children accordingly. It is therefore helpful if you understand what children of different ages can manage, so that you are able to judge what level of behaviour is appropriate for the children you work with; for example children under 3 years of age find it difficult to share toys without adult help. Expecting too much of children can mean that they fail and therefore come to believe they are not 'good'. In the same way, if expectations are too low children will not develop appropriate behaviour.

The chart in Unit 2, pages 45–7, outlines the behaviour of children in relation to their development; it also shows the role of the adult in promoting such behaviour. It will be necessary for you to revisit this chart in order to complete your learning for this unit. However, as with any developmental chart, it must be seen as a guide only because children vary enormously in their development.

Think about it

Look at the examples below and consider whether these types of behaviour are usual for the ages of the children described.

1. A 4-year-old pushes another child down the slide.
2. A 5-year-old has a temper tantrum because she wants the red crayon and another child has it.
3. A 2-year-old snatches a biscuit from another child.
4. A 3-year-old refuses to help tidy up.
5. A 3-year-old cannot sit still and listen to a short story.
6. An 8-year-old takes another child's toy home deliberately.

Find out!

Ask your supervisor if you can observe a child in your workplace.

1. Record the age of the child.
2. Make notes about the behaviour you see.
3. How does this child's behaviour compare to the chart on pages 45–7?

Recognise the ages and stages of social and emotional development and the implications for behaviour

You have seen that children's stage of development can significantly affect their behaviour. This is particularly true in terms of children's social and emotional development.

In general terms, many children under 3 years old find it hard to share and cooperate with other children of the same age, especially for long periods. This means that adults working with children under 3 years or with children at the same stage of development must make sure that the activities and play environment provided for them takes this into account. A good environment for a child under the age of 3 years allows the child to play independently or alongside other children with occasional opportunities for cooperative play. It is also important that children under 3 years rely heavily on adults for attention and as playmates. This can create some headaches in terms of behaviour, as children may show signs of jealousy if they see that 'their' adult is spending time with another child. Hence adults will often have to 'juggle' the needs of two children at the same time, as the case study below shows.

Case study

Toddlers needing to play alongside each other

Mollie is the key worker to Harry and Niamh. They are both 2 years old. At the moment, Harry is making dough 'cakes' and Mollie has to pretend to eat them. While Harry is making the dough 'cakes', Mollie is also helping Niamh with a sticky collage. Both children need her attention but are focused on their own play.

1. Why are Harry and Niamh not playing together?
2. Why is it important that Mollie meets both of their needs at the same time?
3. What would happen if Mollie were to give her attention to only one of the children?

The role of the practitioner in managing children's behaviour

In order to promote positive behaviour with children and deal with unwanted behaviour, it is useful to understand how children learn how to behave.

How children learn behaviour

In Unit 2 you looked at how children learn (see pages 36–50). Some of the theories about how children learn can also explain how they learn to behave. By understanding the theories you can help children to manage their behaviour more effectively.

Social learning theory

Social learning theory suggests that children copy the behaviour of adults and later of other children. This theory is widely accepted and is extremely important in understanding children's behaviour. It means that children learn desirable and undesirable behaviour from watching adults. For example, children who hear adults swearing may try out swear words, while children who see an adult open a door for another adult may copy this behaviour.

⇩ **Social learning theory stresses the importance of being a good role model for children**

Linking theory with practice

→ You can teach children about desirable behaviour through your actions. For example, if children hear you saying please and thank you, they are likely to copy this. Children can learn how to be thoughtful by seeing you act in a kind, caring way towards other children, staff and parents.

→ If children see adults who have an aggressive manner, they think this is acceptable behaviour. This means that you should not shout at children as they will learn that being aggressive is a good way to get what you want. In order to help children settle their disputes you need to show them how adults cooperate with each other.

Think about it

Have you ever seen children copying an action that they have seen adults do, for example pretending to have a cigarette or a cup of tea?

Case study

Setting a bad example

Mandy is tired. She did not get to bed very early so is not feeling on top form. She goes into work and instead of working well with the children starts to tell them to go away. After a little while, you notice that some of the children are starting to tell each other to 'go away'.

1. Why have the children learned this behaviour?
2. Why is it important that adults think about their own words and actions?
3. How can you help the children to behave differently?

The Features Page:

Focus on *Biting*

Biting is a common problem among young children, especially between 15 months and 3 years. Some toddlers only bite a couple of times, but for others it becomes a real habit. As the children are so young, it is not worth spending long on explanations – a sharp 'no' often works better.

Always try and work out why the toddler is biting. If it is out of frustration, this means that you will need to provide different activities or more materials. Look out, too, for toddlers who bite in order to get adults' attention. They may look at you first before biting. This means that you will need to give them more attention at other times, but closely supervise them in the meantime. It's also worth remembering that biting is a very sensory activity. Providing more sensory materials such as dough, cold cooked spaghetti and trays of rice or pasta will divert young children's interest on to other sensory experiences.

Top Tips:
Behaviour

✓ Watch out for hunger and tiredness – these are linked with unwanted behaviour.

✓ Praise and smile loads; children are better with adults that they like.

✓ Don't let children hang about – children who are playing keep out of trouble.

✓ Distract toddlers rather than confront them, otherwise you risk a tantrum.

✓ Get older children to set their own boundaries – they tend to keep to their own rules.

Crossword

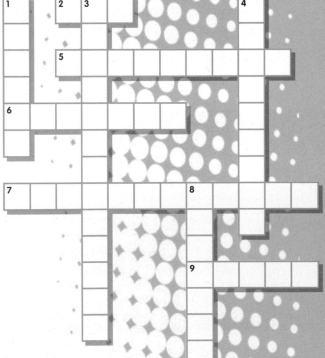

Clues Across
2 Children's behaviour is linked to this. (3)
5 Older children are more able to … (9)
6 Children under 3 years generally find this difficult. (7)
7 Check that yours are realistic when responding to children's behaviour. (12)
9 Children often feel this way when their behaviour becomes disruptive. (5)

Clues Down
1 You will need to give this so that children learn what behaviour is expected of them. (6)
3 To help children develop positive behaviour, you must always be … (4, 4, 5)
4 Too little may result in children showing unwanted behaviour. (9)
8 Common among 2–3-year-olds when tired or frustrated. (7)

Behaviour

Gemma, nursery nurse

One of the things that I have learned since I started is to praise children more. I didn't realise it but I think that I used to always be nagging or getting cross with them. This meant that the children would often refuse to come and do an activity with me. One morning, my manager had a quiet word with me. She asked me to keep a count of every time I said something nice and praised the children. At first my piece of paper was blank, but then I really began to look out for things to praise children for. It made such a difference. For the first time, children began to come up to me and show me things. Since then, my relationships with the children have really changed and I am now no longer the grump of the nursery!

Q ▸ I have started a placement in a pre-school. The staff and children are really nice and I love being there. The only thing is that staff do not make the 2-year-olds tidy up or, if they do, they turn it into a game. I think they are being too easy on them. It's also unfair on the older children who do help.

A ▸ Managing children's behaviour is about working out what are realistic and fair expectations. Two-year-olds do things at their own time and pace, so hurrying them along or pushing them into things, unless strictly necessary, will only result in tears and tantrums. Happily this is a developmental stage and by the age of 3 years, most children have moved on. This is perhaps why you see that the older children are more cooperative. The lack of battles and upsets is perhaps why you enjoy your work in the setting. So relax and enjoy these 2-year-olds with their funny ways.

Q ▸ There are three children in our nursery who keeping running around when they first come in. If you ask them to sit down, they refuse and carry on playing chase.

A ▸ It sounds as if these children are having fun. This means that you will need to do something with them that will be just as fun. Perhaps you can play chase with them in the garden or set up an obstacle course. You might also like to think about what to put out for these children that they will be interested in. How about a 'monster cave' made from a sheet over a table with books about monsters and toy dinosaurs inside?

Ask the expert

Behaviourist theory

This suggests that behaviour is repeated if children get some type of reward. Psychologists call rewards positive reinforcement. These can be in the form of enjoyment, praise, money or food but they can also be in the form of attention. Getting the attention of adults is often important for children. A child who receives praise from an adult while helping another child to pick up toys is more likely to repeat this behaviour. Unfortunately, children also show undesirable behaviour to get adults' attention. If they are successful in gaining the attention they will repeat the behaviour.

Linking theory with practice

➜ Using 'rewards' to help children show desirable behaviour is extremely effective. One of the strongest rewards is praise and encouragement. This means that in your day-to-day practice you should praise children often, making it clear why you are praising them. For example, saying 'Well done, that is kind of you to share the dough' is better than simply saying 'Well done.'

➜ You can also prevent undesirable behaviour from becoming a habit by not giving attention for it. For example, a toddler might squeal at a high pitch; if the squeal attracts attention then it is more likely to be repeated.

➜ Consistency is important. If children learn that sometimes they can get adult attention or other 'rewards' for inappropriate behaviour, it is still worth their while to behave in this way as there is a possibility that they will get what they want. On the other hand, if children never get the attention or reward, they will learn that there is no point in showing this behaviour.

Good Dragon Star Chart

1. When you do a good thing, your teacher or parent will let you colour in a spot on the dragon.

2. When you have coloured all his spots in, you will be given a present.

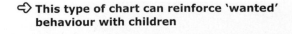 **This type of chart can reinforce 'wanted' behaviour with children**

Self-fulfilling prophecy theory

This suggests that the way adults think about children will influence how the children behave. An adult who believes a child is 'good' will influence the behaviour of that child and the child is likely to show 'appropriate' behaviour. On the other hand, if an adult believes a child is 'naughty and difficult' the child is more likely to behave that way.

Linking theory with practice

→ The self-fulfilling prophecy theory means that in your day-to-day practice you should be extremely positive towards children. Children who feel they can meet your expectations are more likely to show appropriate behaviour. This needs to be shown in your comments and body language. Smiling and praise are good ways of showing children that you value them.

→ When you need to discipline children, you should make it clear that it is their actions that you are unhappy about, not them. Words such as 'naughty' do not help children to believe they can be 'good'.

→ You should also not judge children before you get to know them as this can influence the way you think about them. This is why stereotyping families and labelling children can be so damaging. It can mean that adults are looking for problems when they should be making children feel positive about themselves.

Setting goals and boundaries

You have seen ways in which children can learn behaviour. In terms of strategies, it is important for children to understand what is expected of them. Adults can do this by setting goals and boundaries for them.

→ *Goals* are targets for behaviour, for example saying 'please' when something is wanted. Early years practitioners can show that this is a goal by reminding children to say please and then praising them.

→ *Boundaries* are limits on behaviour. These are often simple rules that children know must not be broken. Boundaries must be clearly set so that children understand what they can and cannot do. For example, an adult might say, 'You may play in the sand but you must not throw it.' Most boundaries are there to protect children, for example doors should never be slammed because someone might get hurt. As children get older and have language, it is essential to involve them in setting boundaries. This works well because children are more likely to keep to the boundaries if they understand their purpose and have had some part in setting them.

Ways of setting goals and boundaries include:

→ telling children – in a positive way – what is expected of them before they begin an activity, for example 'When you have finished feeding the guinea pig, you will need to wash your hands'

→ writing rules down, for example 'No more than four children at the water tray'

→ reminding children, for example 'What must you do when you have finished your paintings?'

Policies in the workplace

Boundary and goal setting works best when everyone involved with the children is in agreement. This is because children are quick to discover any differences in expectations, for example 'Mrs James said I can...!' It is important for children to see that boundaries and goals do not change from day to day. The expectations of adults need to be consistent so that children do not feel they must keep testing them.

It is for this reason that most workplaces have a policy on managing children's behaviour. Most policies outline the strategies to be adopted by members of staff and give direction as to what a staff member should do if a child becomes disruptive. This can vary from setting to setting depending on the age of the children, although physical punishment and restraints must never be used and are often expressly forbidden in policy documents.

A range of strategies practitioners use to manage conflict

There are many strategies that adults use in order to manage children's behaviour and to prevent conflict; the main strategies are described below.

Good supervision

This is an essential tool in promoting children's behaviour. Incidents are more likely to occur when children are unsupervised or bored with activities. For example, a child throwing sand might encourage other children to start doing the same, unless an adult intervenes.

Eye contact and facial expression

These are good ways of clearly showing that behaviour is not appropriate. Eye contact needs to be held with the child. Use praise once the act has stopped.

Saying 'No!'

This one word can be effective, providing it is not over used. Children must also learn that 'no' means 'no' – if they have heard the word and then been able to carry on with their behaviour, it will have no value. Use praise once the act has stopped and explain why the behaviour was unacceptable.

Explaining the consequences of actions

Explaining the consequences of actions helps children to understand why they must not carry on with their behaviour and what will happen if they do. For example, children who are throwing balls at a window must be told that the window might break and if they carry on the balls will be taken away from them. It is important that if a sanction has been threatened it is carried out. Do not impose sanctions that you cannot justify or carry out.

Removal of equipment

This is a final measure and may be used when children are putting themselves or others in danger, for example if a child is hitting another child with a bat. Children should be told why the equipment is being removed and when they are likely to be able to use it again.

Time out

This is often used with older children who are not coping with a situation. The idea is that children are given some time to calm down before returning to the situation. This technique can work quite well, although it should not be used as a punishment – once children feel they are 'naughty' and excluded, they are less likely to show appropriate behaviour. Remember that children with good self-esteem are more likely to show desirable behaviour.

Case study

Managing conflict

Akim and George are 4 years old and are playing with the sand. George starts tipping it over the side and on to the floor. Akim starts to copy him, but also throws it in the air. The adult walks over to them and asks them to stop it, explaining that sand can get in eyes and be painful. A moment later the children start throwing the sand again.

1. Why is it important for the adult to intervene again?
2. How should the adult intervene this time?

Specific types of unwanted behaviour

There are some specific types of behaviour that early years practitioners may need to deal with. If children are showing behaviour that is of concern, for example self-destructive behaviour such as head-banging, you should always talk to your supervisor (or the child's parents or carers if you are working in a home environment).

Challenging racism, sexism and other forms of discrimination

To be able to challenge any form of discrimination, you first need to be able to recognise that it is happening. Discrimination can be direct or indirect. An example of direct discrimination is when children may stop playing with another child because he is black. Indirect discrimination means that it is hidden. This type of discrimination is harder to detect but is just as damaging. For example, a Muslim child in a nursery might be encouraged to make Easter cards but never to celebrate festivals from her own religion.

Type of behaviour	Description and possible reasons for behaviour	How to respond
Attention seeking	Many children show attention-seeking behaviour at times. It can be a sign of insecurity or in some cases mean that children have become used to having a lot of adult attention. There are many ways in which children show this type of behaviour, including answering back, making noises and challenging instructions.	• It is often best to ignore attention-seeking behaviour unless it is dangerous, as by challenging it you may be teaching children that they can get attention this way. • Plenty of praise when children are showing appropriate behaviour can teach them the right way to get your attention.
Destructive	Some children may show aggressive behaviour towards their surroundings and towards others. This can be a sign of frustration or unhappiness, but it is important that children are not allowed to become out of control as this is very frightening for them and teaches them that there are no limits on their behaviour.	• You should stay calm when dealing with children who are aggressive. It is important that they can see that you are in control of the situation. • Talk quietly but firmly to the child. It is often best to take the child to a quiet place where they can calm down. (If you are in a large setting you may need to ask another member of staff for help.) • Once the child has calmed down, it is important to find out what has upset them and to make sure that they understand that their behaviour is unacceptable.
Name calling, swearing and other offensive remarks	Children who call names and make offensive remarks are often repeating comments that they have heard. Remarks such as 'fatty' or 'stupid' need to be challenged but in such a way that children are not blamed for what they have said.	• You should ask children where they have heard the remark. • Explain that what they have said is hurtful and why. • Tell children that these comments are not to be made in the setting.

Direct discrimination – challenging remarks

Children who make remarks that are offensive may well be echoing remarks they have heard or saying something that they do not realise is offensive, such as: 'I don't like Shina's hair' or 'Jack's stupid, he can't write his name yet.'

It is important that you do not ignore offensive remarks. Depending on what is said and how old the child is, you can do the following:
→ Ask the children what they mean and where they heard it.
→ Tell the children that what they have said is not appropriate.
→ Explain why it is not appropriate and that it may be hurtful.
→ Correct any information that is misleading, e.g. 'Black people are hard to tell apart'.

- → Support the other child or children by letting them know that you care about them.
- → Consider whether the workplace is sending out discriminatory messages.
- → Look at resources and activities to make children more aware of the different groups of people in society.

Direct discrimination – challenging bullying

Bullying is never a bit of harmless fun. All types of bullying are harmful, from teasing to acts of violence. Children who are being bullied are being discriminated against and they have the right to be protected. This message is gradually becoming understood by early years professionals. A few years ago, children who were bullied were often left to struggle on by themselves. Their cries for help were often met with responses such as 'you need to stand up for yourself' or 'you need to fight your own battles'.

As an early years practitioner, you have a duty to protect and help children who are being bullied. If you suspect that a child is being bullied, you should talk to your supervisor so that strategies such as closer supervision can be developed to prevent further bullying.

Did you know?

Information about resources and strategies to prevent bullying can be obtained from Kidscape (www. kidscape.org.uk).

Why physical punishment is never used by early years practitioners

Until fairly recently, physical punishment was considered an effective way of disciplining children. Today, attitudes have changed and so has the law. Schools and early years practitioners must not use physical punishments, for example smacking or hitting, as a way of disciplining children.

Although parents are still legally allowed to smack their children, it is not an effective method in the long term for four main reasons:

1. Children learn that in some situations you are allowed to hit people.
2. Children do not learn how to manage conflict and feelings of anger.
3. Children are less likely to tell the truth if they think they may be smacked.
4. Smacking does not teach children why what they have done is wrong.

There is also a danger of serious injury to children, as adults often smack when they are angry and can therefore misjudge their strength. Smacking also creates a negative atmosphere and the key to good behaviour is to create a positive environment where children are guided towards appropriate behaviour.

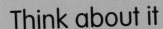

Think about it

You are looking after two children aged 3 and 5 years. One day you mention to their mother that they have had a squabble over a toy, but that you helped them to resolve it and take turns. The mother says that next time you should give each child a smack and take the toy away.

➔ In pairs, work out a role play showing how you would handle this situation.

Working in partnership with parents

It is important to work with parents when managing children's behaviour. In some cases there might be particular reasons why a child is showing unwanted behaviour, such as a change in circumstances at home or feeling unwell. By working with parents you can exchange information and sometimes agree on a particular strategy for managing unwanted behaviour. This is important because children benefit from a consistent approach. As a learner, talking to parents about behaviour will not be your direct responsibility, but this may become your responsibility once you are qualified.

Tips for good practice

Promoting positive behaviour

➔ Be a good role model for children at all times. This means being courteous and calm, and letting children see you sharing and taking your turn.

➔ Praise and encourage children when they show desirable behaviour.

➔ Remember that giving attention to children showing undesirable behaviour may lead them to repeat it.

➔ Make sure that children feel you believe in them.

➔ Do not make any negative remarks in the presence of children.

➔ Make sure that activities and play opportunities are stimulating and fun.

➔ Give clear instructions so that children understand what they can and cannot do.

➔ Make sure that your expectations of children's behaviour are appropriate for their age and stage of development.

Back to the real world

You should now know about children's behaviour. Revisit the scenario on page 127 then answer the questions below.

1. Can you explain whether the child's behaviour is typical for their age?
2. Can you describe what factors are affecting their behaviour?
3. Do you know what you should do next?

Getting ready for assessment

In order to prepare for your assessment, you may like to see if you can complete the following tasks:

1. List four common procedures used in an early years setting to maintain a safe physical environment for children.

   When you have done this, choose two of the procedures that you have listed and explain why they are used and how they may be carried out.

2. List four common procedures used in an early years setting to safeguard and protect children from potential abuse.

   When you have done this, choose two of the procedures that you have listed and explain why they are used and how they may be carried out.

3. Explain how risk assessments are used in early years settings.

4. Explain why early years settings have a behaviour policy.

5. Describe the causes and effects of positive and negative behaviour.

6. Describe how children can be helped to manage their own behaviour.

Unit 4

Children and play

In this unit you will learn:

1. The importance of play and activities and how these link to development

2. The stages of play

3. The types of play and appropriate activities for learning and how to provide them

The importance of play and activities and how these link to development

In the real world

You are working in a pre-school. You overhear one of the parents complaining that their child enjoys the pre-school but is not learning much just by playing. You are unsure how to respond to this. She says that young children should be taught rather than left to play.

By the end of this section you will understand the importance of play in children's learning.

Introduction

In Unit 2 you saw that children's cognitive development is a process (see pages 36–40). You also know that this process is not an automatic one. Babies, children and young people seem to need not only interaction but also stimulation and challenges. This is why early years settings work hard to plan activities and give children opportunities for play. Play is a fantastic way to help children's overall development, as the diagram below shows.

THE BENEFITS OF PLAY

Physical benefits
Children learn many physical skills. For example, fine manipulative skills are learned through playing with small equipment, whereas balance, coordination and gross motor movements are developed through vigorous physical play.

Cognitive benefits
Children learn about the world around them through exploring and touching materials. For example, they may gain an understanding of colour through painting and an understanding of volume and capacity by pouring water into different-sized containers.

Language benefits
Play allows children to learn communication skills in a natural way. For example, when children play pretend games they often use words and phrases that they do not understand but wish to try out.

Emotional benefits
Play has been shown to help children with emotional development by developing their confidence and making them feel good about themselves. Pretend play also allows children to explore roles safely and act out their feelings.

Social benefits
There are many types of play activity where children can learn to be with others. They may work cooperatively using construction toys or they may simply play alongside other children, using pretend play to explore relationships. Social skills such as turn taking, sharing and listening to others can be learned through play.

Cultural benefits
Children can learn about the world around them through play. Their play often reflects the cultural backdrop. Studies have shown that children in different countries play in different ways, reflecting the values of their society. In this country, there are many cultures living side by side and play can be used as a medium for children not only to identify with their family's culture but also to learn about other cultures.

Behavioural benefits
If play is challenging and enjoyable, children are likely to concentrate and develop self-reliance. Think of how much more you learn when you are enjoying yourself! Boredom and frustration are often factors in poor behaviour. This means that you must make sure that play activities are interesting and varied.

How children become involved in their play and activities

You can observe children when they are involved in their play and activities. The first thing you may notice is that they are able to concentrate for long periods, surprisingly even babies. They may also persevere and keep trying to do something even if at first they are not successful.

When you see children and young people engaged in their play, it is useful to consider what is attracting them so much. In some cases, it may be the fun that they are having with other children; in others you may notice that the materials, toys and equipment are particularly interesting them.

It is important to recognise when children are not involved in play and activities. You will notice that they are easily distracted, using the materials in a destructive and dangerous way or are getting frustrated, and you will need to ask yourself why the materials, equipment or activity is not working for the child. If you can get into the habit of doing this, it may help you plan more successfully.

The theories of play that help practitioners to understand its importance

Why do children play?

There are many theories of why babies, children and even adults enjoy play. It is thought that play may help us to learn new skills but also that we seem instinctively ready for play. Play for its own sake also seems to be important. It allows children to feel free, be creative and also enjoy sensations. As children get older, we also see that play is a way in which they can socialise. For young people and adults, play can be a release from the pressures of life and a way of relaxing. This might be the reason why some adults enjoy physical sports or computer games.

Like adults, children have preferences about what they enjoy doing. This means that some children may always want to play with the sand, while others love playing in the home corner. Some children also enjoy playing alone even when they have the social skills to play with others. This means that you might see a child who enjoys being quiet and taking the time to play in 'their' own way one day, joining in with others on another day. Perhaps, play for children can be a way of helping them to relax and respond to their feelings.

Introduction to the theories of play

Today, play is accepted and encouraged – every town has a toyshop and children's organisations campaign for play to be seen as a basic right of every child. Society's attitude towards play has changed enormously since the 1800s, when children were considered little adults and play a waste of time. This has happened gradually, with many people contributing towards today's view of play. Of these, the work of Frederich Froebel and Maria Montessori is still influencing the way that settings plan for children's play and activities.

Frederich Froebel (1782–1852)

Frederich Froebel was one of the first people to believe that children need to learn from doing and playing rather than being taught. This approach is often called '**child-centred learning**'. In 1837, Froebel set up a kindergarten, which means 'children's garden' in German. The kindergarten was for children aged 3–7 years. Pretend play, both indoors and outdoors, was encouraged, as Froebel felt that children learned about the world from exploring materials such as wood and feathers. He also encouraged learning through rhymes and songs. At the time, his ideas were thought to be very unusual, but after his death the idea of kindergartens became popular.

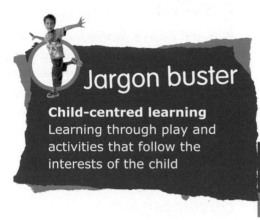

Jargon buster

Child-centred learning
Learning through play and activities that follow the interests of the child

U4
1

⇦ **Froebel believed that children could learn from play, both indoors and outdoors**

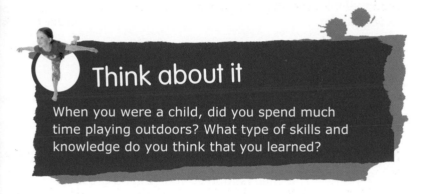

Think about it

When you were a child, did you spend much time playing outdoors? What type of skills and knowledge do you think that you learned?

Maria Montessori (1870–1952)

Maria Montessori worked with poor children in Rome in the 1900s. Her approach was different from Froebel's in many ways. She did not believe that pretend play was particularly useful and felt that children benefited more when play was structured and challenging. However, like Froebel, she believed that children learn by doing. Montessori developed equipment that allowed children to experience different concepts such as shape, size and order. She also believed that furniture, equipment and materials should be child-sized. Like Froebel, she thought that children could learn from being outdoors, so she created a miniature garden where children could do adult activities such as gardening and hanging out washing but with their own tools and equipment.

Montessori considered that children's early years were so important that learning could not be left to chance. The idea of structuring play and using it as way to help children learn has become an accepted part of early years practice. Today, Montessori's ideas and the equipment she designed are still popular and there are many Montessori method nurseries.

The importance of play in supporting all aspects of development

One way to support children's development is to provide a range of toys and equipment at different ages. Later in this unit you will look at different types of play (see pages 157–70). The chart below shows how children's play needs change and how you might support this development.

⇧ **Montessori developed equipment that allowed children to experience different concepts such as shape, size and order through their play**

⇩ **The play needs of children and equipment enjoyed by different ages**

Age	Play needs of children	Indoor equipment and material	Outdoor equipment and materials
1–2 years	The child is mobile and gaining gross motor and fine manipulative skills. The child needs plenty of opportunities to strengthen their muscles and develop coordination.	• Push-and-pull toys • Toys that make music • Dolls • Trolleys • Building bricks • Posting toys	• Paddling pool • Baby swing • Small slide
2–3 years	Children are starting to notice and play with other children. Their language is increasing and much of their play is pretend play. They are gaining confidence in physical movements and enjoy playing outside. Children of this age can be easily frustrated and have a short concentration span – less than 10 minutes – so they need opportunities to be independent in their play and a range of activities. There should be plenty of equipment as children find it difficult to share with each other.	• Dressing-up clothes • Home corner equipment, e.g. tea sets, prams, cooking utensils, pretend telephones • Building blocks • Toy cars and garages • Dolls and cuddly toys • Dough • Paint • Jigsaw puzzles • Musical instruments	• Paddling pool • Sand and water tray • Slide • Climbing frame • Swings • Sit-and-ride toys • Tricycles

Age	Play needs of children	Indoor equipment and material	Outdoor equipment and materials
3–4 years	Children are starting to cooperate with each other and enjoy playing together. Most of their play is pretend play. Pieces of dough become cakes; tricycles become cars! Children enjoy physical activity, gaining confidence in being able to use large equipment, e.g. climbing frames. They are also developing fine manipulative skills and beginning to represent their world in picture form.	• 'Small world' play, e.g. Playmobil, Duplo figures • Dressing-up clothes • Home corner • Dough and other malleable materials • Water and sand • Construction toys such as train tracks, building bricks • Jigsaw puzzles	• Climbing frame • Slide • Paddling pool • Tricycles • Bicycles with stabilisers • Balls and bean bags
4–6 years	Children are more interested in creating things, e.g. making a cake, drawing cards and planting seeds. They enjoy being with other children, although they may play in pairs. Children are beginning to express themselves through painting and drawing as well as through play. They are enjoying using their physical skills in games and are confident when running and climbing.	• Materials for junk modelling • Cooking activities • Dough and other malleable materials • Jigsaws • Home corner • Construction toys • 'Small world' play • Simple board games	• Mini gardening tools • Skipping ropes • Hoops • Climbing frame • Slide • Tricycles • Different-sized balls
6–8 years	Children are confident and can play well with other children. They are starting to have particular play friends and are able to share ideas about their play. Games that involve rules are played and rules are added and changed as necessary! Most children enjoy physical activity and play organised games. Sometimes this age can be very competitive. Children are also keen on making things – either of their own design or by following instructions.	• Creative materials, e.g. junk modelling, crayons, pieces of card and paper • Board games • Jigsaw puzzles • Complex construction toys • Books • Collections, e.g. stamps, stickers	• Balls • Hoops • Bicycles • Roller-skates • Skipping ropes • Climbing frames • Slides • Swings

U4
1

 Back to the real world

You should now have an understanding of why play and practical activities are important for children's development.

1. Work out what you might say to a parent who does not understand why children need to play.

2. Give examples of the way in which children's play changes as they get older.

In the real world

You are working in a school. You notice that most children are able to play well together but are surprised to overhear children making up rules to games. You observe that the way children play in the school is very different to the way that they play in a nursery.

By the end of this section you will know about the stages of play in children's development and how this links to their cognitive development.

The stages of play

Piaget's stages of play

While some theories of play look at how best to provide play, Piaget's theory considers how children of different ages play. Unit 10 covers Piaget's theory of cognitive development (see pages 371–2); here you will look at how Piaget developed a theory of play based on his observations of the way in which children play. He noticed that play changes as children's thinking develops.

Piaget (1896–1980) put forward a theory that children passed through three stages of play. He suggested that each stage built on the knowledge and experience of the one before and it was through play that children gained an understanding of their world. Piaget's ideas are widely accepted and this has meant that pre-school settings and schools use play as a way of helping children to learn. Like Froebel, Piaget felt that children would need to have experience of different materials, equipment and activities so that they could form their own ideas.

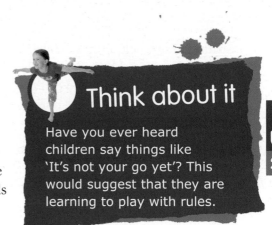

Think about it

Have you ever heard children say things like 'It's not your go yet'? This would suggest that they are learning to play with rules.

U4
2

⬇ **Piaget's stages of play**

Age	Type of play	Common features of this stage
0–2 years	Practice or mastery	Children are concentrating on controlling their body. Play allows them to explore their body, e.g. a baby might put their foot in their mouth. Children are exploring their environment and are keen to see how they can affect it. A child might drop a toy over the edge of the cot or bang a toy against another. A major feature of this stage is that children will keep repeating actions.
2–7 years	Symbolic play	Children are using language as a means of communicating and this is reflected in their play. Children are learning to use symbols in their play. This means that a child might use a stick to stand for a magic wand or an empty plate might have a pretend meal on it.
7–11 years	Play with rules	Children are developing an understanding of games and rules. They play with board games and devise their own games. They are becoming more logical.

Understanding that everyone plays, whatever their age

Some practitioners believe that everyone plays, regardless of their age. The idea behind this is that people are in some way primed to keep playing, although adults tend gradually to use more organised forms of play such as computer games, card games or crossword puzzles. These games often challenge the player mentally and so provide mental stimulation. With babies and young children, there seems to be a link between play and stimulation. Children who are not being sufficiently challenged by an activity or their play often show this through their behaviours.

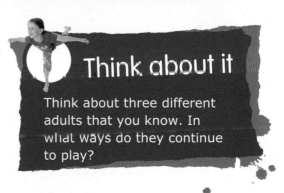

Think about it

Think about three different adults that you know. In what ways do they continue to play?

Many adults enjoy being with children as it gives them an opportunity to play again. It is said that many parents often buy toys and games for their children so they too can have some fun!

Stages of play – key terms

As well as Piaget's stages of play, children's social development may be considered in terms of the way that they are able to play.

Stages of social play

Learning to play with other children is a gradual process. As children grow and develop, they become able to play together, although there are times when children who can play cooperatively will choose to play alone, for example if they are doing a jigsaw or practising a physical skill such as using stilts.

The way children play together can be divided into four stages, as described below.

1. *Solitary play* – Until the age of about 2 years, children usually play alone. They explore equipment and their environment but seek reassurance from adults and enjoy games directed by adults such as peek-a-boo.

2. *Parallel play* – From about 2 years, children seem to be more aware of each other, although they may not communicate or try to play together. Parallel play is children playing alongside each other. Children may play side-by-side in a sandpit, each one playing intently in their own way.

3. *Associative play* – From the age of about 3 years, children look to see what other children are doing and may copy them. Children may stand at the edge of older children's games.

4. *Cooperative play* – By about the age of $3\frac{1}{2}$ years, most children are able to play cooperatively. This means that they actively play together. They talk and decide about their play. You may hear children say things like 'Let's be lions'. By the age of 7 years, most children are able to play games with rules and if you ask them what they are doing, they are very sure of what the game is about.

Observing play

You will find it useful to observe children as they play. It will help you to see what their play needs are and also where they are developmentally. Some children may need support or encouragement in order that they can play with others. Language development is particularly important here. A child who does not speak the same language as other children or who has a language delay may find it harder to play cooperatively.

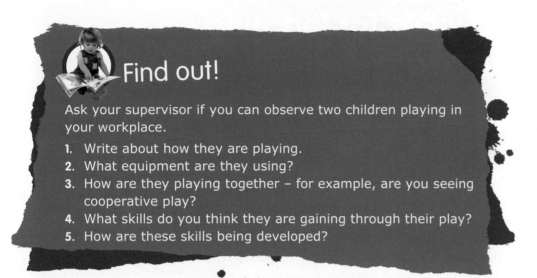

Find out!

Ask your supervisor if you can observe two children playing in your workplace.

1. Write about how they are playing.
2. What equipment are they using?
3. How are they playing together – for example, are you seeing cooperative play?
4. What skills do you think they are gaining through their play?
5. How are these skills being developed?

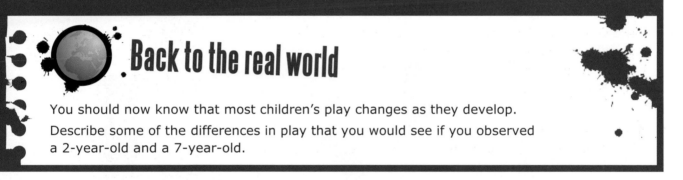

Back to the real world

You should now know that most children's play changes as they develop.

Describe some of the differences in play that you would see if you observed a 2-year-old and a 7-year-old.

Section 3

The types of play and appropriate activities for learning and how to provide them

In the real world

You have been asked to set out some materials for imaginative play. You are not exactly sure what this means. Your manager tells you that this type of play is very important for children's development. She says that it is to be an adult-initiated activity because paper and pads are to be left out to encourage early writing.

By the end of this section you will know about different types of play and how they can benefit children. You will also understand that activities and play can be structured differently.

The areas and types of play

Most early years practitioners plan for children to play in different ways because this allows children to use and develop several skills. For example, playing on a climbing frame develops gross motor skills and a sense of balance whereas playing in the home corner is more likely to encourage language.

Play is sometimes divided into different types. The labels for these types of play may vary. In this section you will look at the following types of play:

→ Creative play
→ Pretend play
→ Physical play
→ Manipulative play
→ Discovery play.

As an early years practitioner you need to understand the benefits of each type of play and know how to provide for it. This section looks in detail at how these types of play can benefit children of different ages.

Creative play

Creative play allows children to express themselves using materials rather than words. It helps them to discover properties of materials as well as giving them the opportunity to use language and develop fine physical skills.

Adults can help children by providing a range of materials and by encouraging children to experiment with them (see the chart below). You will need to make sure that the emphasis is on enjoying the process and discovering the materials rather than on producing an end product.

⇦ **Creative play allows children to express themselves using materials rather than words**

👆 **Materials for creative play**

Material	Benefits	Provision
Sand and water	• *Physical development.* Hand–eye coordination and fine manipulative skills are developed through using the equipment, e.g. pouring with jugs. • *Cognitive development.* Properties of the material are explored through touching them, e.g. water is runny, sand does not pour when wet. • *Language opportunities.* Children tend to chat as they are playing. • *Emotional benefit.* Builds confidence – sand and water are activities with no right or wrong way. Helps release tension and aggression. • *Social skills.* Children take turns with equipment and can play in different social groupings or by themselves.	• *Indoors.* Purpose-built trays are often used. Water can be played with in a sink and sand can be put into a baby bath. • *Outdoors.* Sand pit, paddling pool. • *Safety.* Make sure that these activities are closely supervised. There is a risk of drowning or sand being thrown into children's eyes. Outdoor sandpits need covering after use to prevent access by animals. Inside, keep floors clear as both sand and water can make them slippery. • *Equipment for sand play.* Bottles, jugs, scoops, animals, toy cars, sieves, spades. • *Equipment for water play.* Funnels, bottles, jugs, items that float and sink, boats, beakers, sponges.
Dough, clay, plasticine, etc.	• *Physical development.* Fine manipulative skills and hand–eye coordination, through rolling, cutting and pounding. • *Cognitive development.* Learn about elasticity of these materials and experience making different shapes and forms. • *Language opportunities.* Children enjoy talking about what they are doing. They may use some objects in pretend play. • *Emotional benefits.* Releases aggression, makes children feel in control, no wrong or right way to play. • *Social skills.* Children take turns with equipment although probably choose to play individually.	• Table and protective covering. • *Safety.* Dough needs to be changed frequently. Enough salt must be added to prevent children from eating it. • *Materials.* Dough – it is often important to make up different types, e.g. stretchy dough, cooked dough, smelly dough; Plasticine, clay, other modelling materials. • *Tools.* Rolling pins, cutters, scissors, boards, plates, modelling tools.

Material	Benefits	Provision
Junk modelling and collage	• *Physical development.* Fine manipulative and gross manipulative skills and hand–eye coordination through cutting, sticking and holding. • *Cognitive development.* Helps develop spatial awareness – size, shape and proportion. • *Language opportunities.* Develops vocabulary if unusual materials are made available. • *Emotional benefits.* Gives children sense of satisfaction and ownership when they have finished. Enjoyment through handling and problem solving. • *Social skills.* Turn taking and sharing of materials and equipment. Develops independence and self-reliance through completing their own project.	• Table with protective covering. • *Safety.* Make sure that small items cannot be swallowed by younger children. Do not leave scissors lying around. • *Materials.* A wide range is needed so children can make choices and develop their own ideas, e.g. different-sized boxes, glue, sticky tape, paper, cardboard, foil, plastic lids, lace, pasta, sawdust, newspaper, magazine, fabrics, bottle tops, sweet wrappers, sequins, etc. • *Equipment.* Scissors, aprons.
Paint and drawing	• *Physical development.* Fine manipulative skills and hand–eye coordination through making marks and scribbles. • *Cognitive benefits.* Putting marks on paper helps children to learn about communicating by using signs. This is the first step towards reading. • *Language opportunities.* Children tend to talk as they draw and paint. It is part of their thought process. • *Emotional benefits.* Children can express themselves visually, e.g. they can paint angry pictures. They also enjoy seeing their work displayed, which gives them confidence and a sense of achievement. • *Social skills.* Children learn to take turns and share.	• Painting easel, table, wall covered with Polythene. • *Materials.* Different types of paints, e.g. powder, acrylic, poster, and ready-mixed; chalks, pastels, felt tips, charcoal, different coloured paper, card. • *Equipment.* Different types of brushes for painting, rollers, items for printing, sponges.

Stages of development

By observing children's stage of development, you can see what types of equipment and materials they may benefit from. For example, a child who is beginning to model shapes with dough may be ready to start with clay which could then be painted.

Looking at children's pictures of people is also interesting as it can show not only their stage of fine manipulative development but also their understanding of themselves.

♦ **The development of children's creative (fine manipulative) skills**

Stage	Drawing of people	Dough
One	Scribbling with to and fro movements	Banging and pounding
Two	Circular movements made	Rolling and starting to form shapes
Three	Large head with arms and legs. Children know what they are drawing	Rolling and cutting out shapes easily; using tools
Four	Head, trunk, legs and arms as well	Beginning to make other simple features, e.g. eyelashes, and 3D models

Pretend play

Pretend play is where children talk to toys or objects and make up games using characters. It is also known as imaginative play. Children act out what they see and feel using words. As children get older and they are able to cooperate, they take on roles, for example 'You're the mummy and I'm the baby and the baby's being naughty!'

When children are playing in this way, it can be called role play or drama and imaginative play. This type of play helps children to develop language and communication skills as well as enabling them to act out situations. Children learn to socialise through this type of play and it has emotional benefits as children can act out their fears and fantasies.

Items which children may use for pretend play are shown in the spider diagram below.

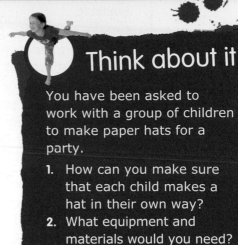

Think about it

You have been asked to work with a group of children to make paper hats for a party.

1. How can you make sure that each child makes a hat in their own way?
2. What equipment and materials would you need?

From about the age of 18 months, children start to pretend in their play. A doll might be picked up and cuddled or put into bed as if it were a real baby. Pretend play can take many different forms depending on the stage of children and their play needs.

Different forms of pretend play include:

➡ *Role play* – children take on a role in their play, for example a fire fighter, a baby
➡ *Socio-dramatic* – groups of children play cooperatively together taking on different roles

- *Domestic play* – children act out activities that they see happening at home, for example ironing, telling off a doll or mumbling about making the tea!
- *Imaginative play* – children act out things that they have experienced, such as going shopping or swimming, and adapt them to suit their play needs
- *Fantasy play* – children pretend that they are doing something that they may have seen or heard about, for example have a baby or going on an aeroplane
- *Superhero play* – children try to take on the characteristics of a current television idol, for example pretending to be a footballer or a detective

⇧ **Pretend play can help children to develop language and communication skills**

Children also enjoy using equipment such as 'small world' toys, dolls and cuddly toys to pretend to play with. They might set out farm animals and make noises for each of the animals or, with a set of play-people, they might give each one a name and a character.

Setting up pretend play areas

It is possible to set up pretend play areas in most early years settings. In a home environment, children may play under a table or behind a sofa, whereas in larger early years settings there will be purpose-built home corners. Pretend play can also take place outdoors and children enjoy using tents as well as finding areas in gardens where they can hide away.

Children often prefer to be able to keep their play private as it is their own world, although you must always make sure that you can see and hear what they are doing.

Equipment for pretend play areas

Equipment does not have to be shop bought. Cardboard boxes can be turned into cars, televisions and cupboards. A good range of materials allows children to extend their play, although too much equipment out at one time might overwhelm them. Where possible, equipment should be varied from week to week, so that children's play does not become too repetitive. As children gain a sense of their cultural identity through play, it is important that all children's home backgrounds are reflected in the choice of items.

Dressing-up clothes
- Clothes that reflect other cultures, for example, saris, tunics
- Uniforms and clothing that help children be in role, for example bus driver
- Hats, shoes, glasses and other accessories, for example bags and suitcases (belts are not recommended)
- A plastic-coated mirror for children to look at themselves adds to their play

Find out!

Ask your supervisor if you can observe and listen to children playing in a 'pretend way'. Briefly describe their activity and write down how you think their play is helping their language development.

Props for domestic play

→ Plates, dishes, cutlery, chopsticks, spoons, cooking utensils (including those from other cultures, for example woks)
→ Telephone
→ Bedding, towels
→ Child-sized furniture, for example cookers, beds, tables and chairs
→ Prams, pushchairs, cots and dolls
→ Shop tills, shopping baskets, paper bags, toy money and notes
→ Pretend first aid kit
→ Dolls of both genders and different skin colours
→ Cuddly toys

Case study

The benefits of role play

Ayse is 2½ years old. Today she is playing in a house that her childminder has constructed in the living room. The 'house' is really a sheet draped across two chairs. She tells the childminder that teddy is crying. The childminder asks Ayse whether teddy might be hungry. Ayse says 'yes' and so the childminder gives Ayse a bowl of uncooked pasta and a metal spoon so that Ayse can feed teddy. Ayse smiles and puts teddy on her knee. She talks to teddy as she is feeding him. When some of the uncooked pasta drops onto the floor, she carefully picks it up. She then takes teddy out of the house before telling teddy that he must go to sleep now. She wraps teddy up in a blanket and puts him carefully on the floor in the 'house'. She then picks him up and rocks him.

1. How is this type of play helping Ayse to develop her language?
2. What other skills is Ayse learning?
3. Why is it important that the childminder is ready to join in and support this type of play?

Pretend play and the early years curriculum

Pretend play fits well into an overall curriculum plan, as you can change the pretend area to match the theme. For example, a nursery working to a theme of 'people who help us' might turn the pretend area into a hospital. The aim is to encourage children to explore the theme of hospitals and use the equipment in a different way. Adults can either play alongside children, for example pretending to be a doctor, or they can increase understanding by inviting visitors into the setting or by reading a story that fits in with the theme.

Providing varied themes in this way can increase children's vocabulary while at the same time extending their play. Children may also enjoy making props to fit the theme, for example making dough cakes for a bakery. Ideas for themes could include hospitals, vets' practices, bakers, post offices, cafes.

Intervening in children's pretend play

There are three situations when you will need to intervene in children's pretend play:

1. *To ensure safety.* You must intervene if play is likely to become dangerous, for example children are becoming over-excited or aggressive.
2. *To support or extend play.* You may decide to intervene when children's play seems repetitive or running out of ideas. You might offer to play alongside them or add more equipment.
3. *To challenge racist or other offensive remarks.* You must always challenge these, even if children are saying them as part of their role. Such situations need to be handled sensitively.

Physical play

In Unit 2, you looked at why physical exercise is important in developing children's bodies and maintaining their health and at the safety aspects of providing physical activity. In this section you will look at how children play when exercising and consider which equipment can best support children's physical play.

Children enjoy running around playing chase, throwing, catching and climbing. Physical play helps children to develop muscles, stamina and coordination of their movements. It can help children to develop an awareness of space and give them confidence. You may hear children say: 'Look at me, I can jump!'

Think abo

A local playgroup has been given £200. You have been asked to draw up a list of possible equipment that they could buy. The playgroup is particularly interested in buying equipment that would encourage pretend play.

→ Write out a list for them and include some reasons for your choices. Where possible include prices. (This activity can be done in pairs or small groups.)

U4
3

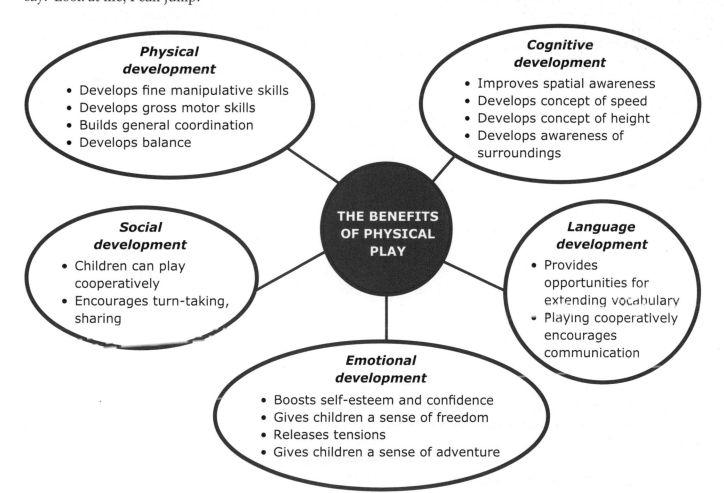

Physical development
- Develops fine manipulative skills
- Develops gross motor skills
- Builds general coordination
- Develops balance

Cognitive development
- Improves spatial awareness
- Develops concept of speed
- Develops concept of height
- Develops awareness of surroundings

Social development
- Children can play cooperatively
- Encourages turn-taking, sharing

THE BENEFITS OF PHYSICAL PLAY

Language development
- Provides opportunities for extending vocabulary
- Playing cooperatively encourages communication

Emotional development
- Boosts self-esteem and confidence
- Gives children a sense of freedom
- Releases tensions
- Gives children a sense of adventure

Physical play with large equipment

Most early years settings are able to provide some large equipment for children to work with. In home environments where there may not be enough space or resources, children can be taken to a local playground where there may be a range of equipment. Equipment can often be adapted for children with special needs. For example, harnesses can be added to swings and grippers can be attached to bars of climbing frames. Specialist equipment is also available, such as tricycles that are strengthened for larger children who cannot use a bicycle.

The chart below shows types of large equipment for physical play and the play potential for children.

⇧ **Children are able to develop many skills through using large equipment**

⇩ **Equipment for physical play**

Type of equipment	Play and developmental potential	Age range
Trampolines	Children enjoy bouncing and this allows them to develop their sense of balance while giving them a sense of achievement. Jumping and bouncing strengthens leg muscles and builds stamina.	3–8 years Some trampolines have handles, which means that children from 3 years can use them safely.
Seesaws and rockers	Children enjoy working in pairs and take pleasure in the experience of moving from side to side. Balance and coordination skills are improved.	Rockers can be suitable for children of 18 months. Seesaws are generally for children aged 3–8 years.
Play tunnels	Play tunnels can be used in many ways. Children can use them as places to hide as part of a game. They can also be used as part of an obstacle course and can often link into other pieces of equipment such as tents. Play tunnels can develop coordination between the arms and legs and general agility.	2–6 years Younger children may become frightened in a tunnel and older children may get stuck.
Slides	Slides help children learn to climb and build up confidence in balancing. Children enjoy the sense of achievement from completing the movement. They enjoy the sense of risk-taking and challenge as they climb.	18 months–8 years+ Different heights of slide are available ranging from two steps upwards.
Swings	Swings give children much pleasure, as they enjoy the rhythmic movements. As they learn to coordinate their movements, they build up strength in the legs and upper body as well as their ability to balance.	9 months–8 years Baby swings are available which prevent children from falling out.
Climbing frames	Coordination and balance are developed through climbing. Leg and arm muscles are strengthened and children enjoy the challenge and the feeling of adventure. Climbing frames can be used as part of a game, e.g. it becomes a house or ship. Cooperative play is often seen when older children are using climbing frames.	3–8 years+ There are a variety of styles of climbing frame.

Type of equipment	Play and developmental potential	Age range
Ropes and rope ladders	Children enjoy learning to climb up ladders. This helps their sense of balance and coordination. They enjoy the challenge of this activity. Ropes can be used to swing on, which strengthens arm muscles. Ropes can be used as part of children's games.	From about 4 years
Sit-and-ride toys, tricycles, bicycles and go-karts	These are versatile and popular with children. Children can make moving around part of their games and can play cooperatively together. Many skills are developed, including the ability to judge speed, steer and pedal. Leg muscles are strengthened and general coordination is developed.	1–8 years+ The range of equipment means that very young children can enjoy feeling mobile.

Helping children to practise physical skills

There are some physical skills, for example throwing and catching, pedalling and balancing, that need practice. To help children gain these skills, adults can structure play activities which are fun yet concentrate on areas that need developing without making children feel frustrated. Bringing out equipment or thinking of activities that children have not used before helps them to come to an activity feeling confident. For example, ideas for helping children to throw and catch might include using different-sized balls, beanbags, Frisbees and airballs. Children can be asked to throw beanbags into hoops or see how far they can throw an airball.

Did you know?

In many playground areas, large pieces of equipment such as slides and climbing frames are joined together to form a single unit. This allows more children to play together and allows children to make physical play into more of a game.

Find out!

1. Make a list of any large equipment in the setting where you are working. Observe how children use this equipment.
2. Are there any pieces of equipment that seem to be particularly popular? How do children use these pieces of equipment?

Stereotyping in physical play

By the age of 3 years, most children are aware of their gender and by the age of 5 years, most children are tending to play with members of their own sex. As physical play is critical to children's overall development, it is essential that although children may choose to play according to gender, their play is not limited by this. As an early years practitioner you can help by being a good role model and make sure that you encourage all children to participate in activities. This means that if children seem to avoid choosing equipment, you could structure an activity that includes that skill. For example, an early years practitioner working with 6-year-olds noticed that the boys were

Think about it

Think of three activities that would encourage a group of 5-year-olds to practise their throwing and catching skills.

not picking up the skipping ropes and that the girls were not using the footballs. She organised an obstacle race that included skipping and dribbling a football.

Find out!

Ask your supervisor if you can supervise and support physical play.

1. Write down how you encouraged all the children to use the equipment.
2. Write down how you made sure that the children played safely.
3. What physical skills did the children develop through their play?
4. What did you learn from doing this activity?

Manipulative play

Manipulative play can also be called construction play. Most manipulative play encourages children to build or fit equipment together. Examples of manipulative play include jigsaw puzzles, interlocking shapes and train sets that fit together. Children gain much satisfaction from this type of play as they are able to see the end product. Self-esteem is also boosted as many types of equipment do not have a right or wrong way of using them, for example Duplo

Physical development
- Develops hand–eye coordination
- Develops fine manipulative skills
- Develops gross motor skills

Cognitive development
- Helps children to think logically
- Develops sorting skills
- Helps children develop a sense of shape
- Develops spatial awareness

THE BENEFITS OF MANIPULATIVE PLAY

Social development
- Can provide opportunities for children to work individually, in pairs or in groups

Language development
- Possibility of introducing new vocabulary
- Developing language skills through playing cooperatively

Emotional development
- Gives children a sense of achievement
- Allows children to set their own goals

Planning

Good quality
and activities
become bore

There are sev
play. As part
which case yo

Stage/age c

How old are t
important as
frustrated if t

Interests of c

What do the c
successful wh
You can learn
For example,
playing a nam

Learning inte

What do child
a curriculum.
in Wales the c
about what sk
activity or typ

Resources

What materia
and resources
for children. Y
age-appropria
do not become

Location

Where will the
require a lot of
place is import

Role of the a

What will the
about whether
for themselves
to do.

bricks can be made into a tower or can be used to make a wall. Through manipulative play, children are also able to develop their fine manipulative skills as well as their gross motor movements. Children might turn and twist small pieces to fit together, which encourages their fine skills, or with larger equipment, such as foam blocks, they might use their whole body for lifting and carrying.

Equipment used in manipulative play

There are many types of equipment to encourage manipulative play. Not all equipment needs to be commercially manufactured. Jigsaw puzzles can be made out of cardboard and older children can make their own by doing a drawing, sticking it down and then cutting up the pieces. In the same way, children can have a lot of fun moving cardboard boxes around.

⇧ **There are many types of equipment to encourage manipulative play**

⇩ **Equipment used in manipulative play**

Name and description	Benefits	Age range
Shape sorters	These early toys help young children to recognise shapes as well as encouraging them to use their hands and problem-solving skills. Young children may need adult help if they are not to become frustrated. These activities help children's confidence and they gain a sense of achievement.	12 months–3 years
Duplo – brightly coloured plastic blocks that fit together; animals and people are also available	Encourages pretend play and allows children to use their fine manipulative skills. Muscles in the hand are also strengthened and hand–eye coordination is developed. There is no right or wrong way to use this equipment, which means that children gain confidence.	18 months–5 years
Lego – small bricks that fasten together. There is a large range of parts available which means that children can make many things, e.g. cars, houses, gardens	The small parts mean that children's fine manipulative skills and hand–eye coordination are developed. There is huge scope for children to make intricate models with this equipment.	From 5 years (The small parts in some of these kits could be dangerous for younger children)
Jigsaw puzzles – a variety of puzzles are available, including tray puzzles where children can slot in shapes, floor puzzles for group play and small-piece puzzles	Jigsaw puzzles help children's spatial awareness and develop fine manipulative skills. Problem-solving skills are also developed along with matching skills. Floor puzzles allow pairs of children to work and play cooperatively together. A range of tactile puzzles is available for children with sensory impairments.	15 months–adulthood

As well as
encourage
Sometime
cars, dino
types. Alv
group you

Discover

Discovery
years. The
→ treasu
→ heurist

Treasure
This play
idea is tha
objects are
what to ta
not to inte
for babies
and explo
Babies ca
good idea

Heuristic
This type
from treas
objects tha
materials,
these are t
seeing wha
enjoy putt
water bott
basket pla
children to

⟱ **Example**

Treasur
- Pineap
- Leathe
- Metal s
- Woode
- Tea str
- Corks
- Shells
- Ball of
- Natura

The Features Page:

Focus on *Outdoor play*

For years, early years settings have been planning for indoor play. Now it is recognised that playing and learning outdoors is beneficial for children, especially as many children today do not get opportunities for physical exercise. This means that you are likely to find that many settings will plan activities for the outdoors. Some settings also have a 'free flow' system. This means that children can go outdoors at any time rather than just in specified times.

Ask the expert

Q Should children go out if it is raining?

A In some countries, children go out in all weathers. In the United Kingdom, individual settings will have different policies. Ideally, it is good for children to be out as much as possible and if they are properly dressed, they can go out if it is drizzly or even raining. Rain can also be used as a learning opportunity – for example, children can see how much rain falls within 10 minutes; they can also try using umbrellas and making a shelter. It is, however, unadvisable for children to be out in a thunderstorm.

Q Our setting has little shade. Is it safe for children to play out in the summer?

A There is clear advice about keeping children out of the sun in the summer. This needs to be followed and so children need to play in shaded areas. Some settings are starting to put up canopies for shade, but you can make your own. Think about how you might attach sheets or tarpaulin to fences, walls or across trees in order to create shade.

Outdoor play

My story

Ben, nursery nurse

We plan play and activities for both the outdoors and the indoors. Some people don't like being outdoors with children, but I see what children can gain from being outdoors and so I really enjoy it. Some of the children that we work with don't have gardens or places where they can play safely outdoors, so it is really important that they get the chance here. Every day, I try and plan an activity which will be a bit of a surprise for the children. Sometimes I hide things so that children get excited as they find them. I once hid a suitcase, a map and some binoculars. The children decided that they would be explorers. For the rest of the morning they made a base camp and pretended to discover things.

Top Tips:

Planning activities for outdoor play

- ✓ Look carefully to see what children enjoy doing. Use these ideas to base some activities and play opportunities on.
- ✓ Be ready to add extra props or materials into a play activity, particularly with young children.
- ✓ If you are short of space, do some tidying up discreetly while children are playing so that the floor or space doesn't get too cluttered. It also makes it easier at the end of the session.

My story

Louisa aged 7 years

I like it when adults leave you to play on your own, especially when there are things to do. I like playing mums and dads with my friends. We play under a table in the playground. It's our house. I don't like it when adults keep on asking what you are doing. I don't like it when you have to go inside and then have to put everything away. It spoils it.

Providing a balance of play and activities

Planning is essential if children's needs are to be met. Without some level of planning, it would be difficult to provide equipment, materials and supervision to enable children to enjoy playing but also learning.

Deciding on the role of the adult is important when planning activities and play. The key question is how much the adult should influence what is happening. The term **structured play** describes activities where the adult has planned how children are to play. The degree in which an activity may be structured can vary enormously. The card game snap, for example, is very structured. There are rules to follow and for the game to work everyone must play accordingly.

Adult-directed activities

Adult-directed activities, where the adult is leading the activity or play, work well where there is a specific piece of knowledge or skill that children need to learn such as how to play a board game. It is important though that the activities are interesting and right for every child's developmental level, otherwise there is a danger that children will grow bored.

Adult-initiated activities

Adult-initiated activities are those where adults provide the materials and equipment so that children can learn from using them. For example, putting out dough with scissors is likely to encourage children to cut the dough and so develop their cutting skills through play.

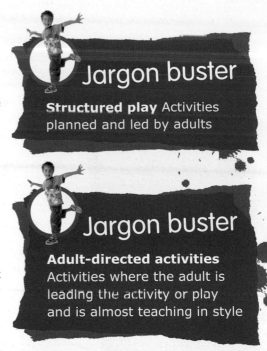

Jargon buster

Structured play Activities planned and led by adults

Jargon buster

Adult-directed activities Activities where the adult is leading the activity or play and is almost teaching in style

Jargon buster

Adult-initiated activities Play and activities that have been planned by adults but not led by them

Case study

Chris has put ice cubes into the tray of water this morning. He thought that the children would not only enjoy seeing how the ice melts but also how the ice floats. With the ice, he put out some boats. The children are excited when they see the ice. Chris watches them and notices how they start to push the ice cubes down into the water only to find that the ice keeps bobbing up. The children also put the ice cubes into the boats. The children talk as they are doing the activity. One of them comments that the ice cubes are getting smaller. They ask Chris if they can have some more ice. Chris mentions that the ice disappears because it is melting. He notices later on that some of the children start to use the word 'melt' as they are talking.

1. What did the children learn from this activity?
2. Is this an example of an adult-directed activity or an adult-initiated activity?
3. Why will children have a good memory of this activity?

Child-initiated activities

These are activities where children choose what to play with and how to play. This type of play is sometimes called 'free play' or 'spontaneous play' by some settings. **Child-initiated activities** work well because children tend to do things that they enjoy. This means that they are able to concentrate for longer periods.

It is usual and helpful for most settings involved in education, such as pre-schools, nurseries and schools, to balance their planning so that there is a mixture of adult-directed, adult-initiated and child-initiated activities.

Jargon buster

Child-initiated activities
Play and activities that children organise for themselves

U4
3

Case study

Gerri wants to help a group of 4-year-olds recognise their names. She decides to hide their names in the outdoor area. She tells the children that she has hidden their names and asks them to go outdoors and have a look. The children are very excited and enjoy this activity.

Later in the day, two of the children ask if they can play the game by themselves. Gerri gives them the cards and watches as the children have fun. She notes how they change the rules and decide among themselves where the name cards can be hidden and who can look first.

1. Explain why the first game was an adult-directed activity.
2. What makes the second game a child-initiated activity?
3. What have the children gained by playing the game by themselves?

How to encourage exploration and investigation through play

You have seen that children need opportunities to learn from practical experiences. By finding ways of supporting rather than simply teaching children, you can help them to learn about their environment. They can also learn concepts, for example exploration and investigation link to science and form an aspect of learning in the Early Years Foundation Stage curriculum.

Find out!

Find out about how your setting plans activities for children. Give examples of child-initiated activities.

Providing interesting materials

You have seen that children enjoy playing with new materials in discovery play. One of the ways in which you can encourage exploration and investigation is to put out collections of interesting objects for children to explore. This is similar to the treasure basket and heuristic play with babies and toddlers that we saw earlier, but on a larger scale. It is, of course, important to check that any materials are safe.

Scrap stores

In some areas, you will find interesting materials by visiting the local scrap store. Scrap stores sell offcuts of materials from businesses and factories such as paper, card and other interesting items like metal springs, cartons and fabrics. Many pre-schools and schools pay a membership fee to a scrap store and then staff can select whatever they want.

Section 1

How to develop effective communication skills to work with children and adults in a variety of settings

In the real world

It is your second week in a placement. One of the children appears to be quite upset. You are not sure what you should do or say to help them. You decide to ask another adult to talk to the child, but you feel bad about this.

By the end of this section you will know how to communicate well with children and how to listen to them. You will also know how to communicate with young people and adults.

How to interact with and respond to children and adults in a range of settings to support a multi-agency approach

Many of the settings in which you will work or be on placement will liaise with other professionals or be part of a larger service. This means that you will need the skills to work not just with children, their parents and colleagues, but also with other professionals.

A key component of your success when working with children and their families will be your ability to communicate and interact well. Childcare is a career where communication skills count. This section looks at some of the skills that are needed to interact well. Fortunately the skills of good communication are transferable, so that once you have learned them you can use them in any setting and in any situation.

A good starting point is to be respectful and polite and to consider the needs and feelings of the people you are with. This can be daunting, especially if you are talking and listening to people who are older or more experienced than you, but it is a skill that can be learned. The spider diagram below outlines some of skills you will need so as to communicate well.

Developing listening skills and recognising children's need for attention

Many people think that good listening just means being quiet at the right moments! This is not the case. Good listening means paying attention, thinking about what is being said and responding in ways

Think about it

Ask a few people who know you how well they think you communicate with people who are unfamiliar to you.

181

that encourages others to feel that they can talk more. Listening well is sometimes known as **active listening**. It is a skill that you can learn but also need to practise.

Proximity

In order to encourage others to listen to you, it is important to think about their comfort. As part of this, you must think about how physically close you should be to them. This is known as **proximity**. Sitting or standing too close to someone as they are talking can make them feel uncomfortable but being too far apart can make them feel as if you are distant and don't care. Adults often show that they are uncomfortable by either leaning forward if someone is too far away or by moving back if someone is too close. This means that you always need to observe and think about whether you are too close to or too far away from others.

Children and proximity

Young children often need you to be close to them when they are trying to talk to you. Some young children may even try, if they like you, to snuggle close in order that they can be sure of your attention. With young children, it is also important to get down to their height. This may mean sitting on the floor or crouching down beside them. Standing over a child means that there will be too much distance between the adult and the child.

Comfort

It is easier to talk to people when you feel relaxed and comfortable. This means that you must think about the environment and the way that you use it. Standing while talking gives the impression that the conversation is only going to last a short time. This is why it is usually better to sit down when communicating. It is also important to find a place that is not too busy so that you are unlikely to be interrupted. If you sit down to talk, it is useful to think about the position of the seating. People tend to find sitting opposite another person more intimidating than being slightly to the side of them.

Paying attention

In order to keep talking, the child or adult must feel that they are being properly listened to. This means that you must not interrupt the other person or jump in and change the topic of conversation. There are other ways to show that you are paying attention:
➜ eye contact
➜ facial expression and nodding
➜ asking interested questions.
These are more subtle and you may like to practise them.

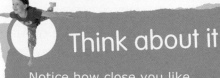

Jargon buster

Active listening The skill of listening carefully and encouraging others to talk

Proximity The amount of space between two people as they communicate

Think about it

Notice how close you like to stand when you talk to someone you don't know. Is there any difference in space when you are talking to a friend?

⇧ **With young children, it is important to get down to their height when listening to them**

Eye contact

In social situations, you can show a child or adult that you are listening by looking at them. This does not mean staring at them but turning your head towards them and looking at their faces and occasionally at their eyes.

Facial expression and nodding

Your face can tell someone that you are finding them interesting. You need to show through your face that you are listening. This means smiling, sometimes frowning but mainly showing some reaction to what has been said using your face. You can also show that you are listening by nodding and using short words or phrases that encourage the speaker such as 'Really', 'Oh dear' or 'That sounds nice'.

Asking interested questions

You can also show that you are keen to listen by asking further questions which show you are genuinely interested. Your questions should not change the topic but encourage the speaker to say more. This is particularly helpful with young children who may need help in order for you to understand them or to sequence events, for example 'What happened next? Did Mummy go with you?'

The non-verbal communication of children and how to interpret this

The term **non-verbal communication** refers to any communication other than speech. It is usually taken to mean body language and gestures but could also be writing.

Body language

Body language refers to the movements and gestures that can be seen while you are communicating. Some people believe that these movements may often be even more important than the words. Body language is a powerful tool in communication and so it is important that you are aware of your body language as you communicate.

Open gestures

The way that a person stands and uses their arms can indicate whether or not they are 'open' and friendly, or hostile. A good example of an open gesture is the way that someone might stand in a relaxed way with their arms at their sides. They may use their arms to help them to talk. On the other hand, an example of a closed gesture would be where someone stands with their arms crossed across their body and looks slightly away. Similarly, sitting in a tight way with crossed legs and crossed arms is a closed gesture, while a more relaxed position will send out better signals.

Think about it

If you had something important on your mind, who would you talk to? What skills does this person have?

U5
1

Jargon buster

Non-verbal communication
Communication through body language, facial expression, gestures, signs and writing

183

Think about it

Look at the diagram below, showing two different types of body language. Discuss which is more effective when working with children, stating the reasons why.

Facial expressions

You have seen that active listening requires that your face should show interest. In terms of non-verbal communication, a person's face is equally important. One of the main things that you can do with your face is to smile when you meet and greet children and adults. Smiling makes you appear to be friendly and open. While this might seem obvious, many people forget to smile when they are feeling nervous or afraid. This sends out a message to other people that they are not interested or that they dislike someone. This makes other people, in turn, less likely to smile, and so the cycle carries on.

Young children and facial expressions

Learning language is a process. Young children rely on an adult's body language and non-verbal communication to understand what is going on. They also listen to the tone of an adult's voice to help them. This means that your facial expressions and the tone of your voice must be expressive. If you watch a parent or an experienced and popular member of staff working with children, you might notice how expressive they are.

Tips for good practice

Non-verbal communication

→ Smiling is a positive signal and shows friendliness.

→ Make sure you smile even when you are feeling nervous.

→ Avoid crossing your arms and using closed gestures.

Think about it

Have you ever heard someone say that they are sorry when you can tell by their face and body language that they are not?

Writing

As part of your work with children and other adults, you will probably have to communicate some information by writing. This is not easy for everyone, but it is a useful form of communication. Written information has a major advantage as it can avoid confusion. It can also be kept and looked at later. This means that most settings will, for example, send a letter home with term dates so that parents and carers will remember them. The chart below shows some examples of writing that you may need to practise.

⏣ **Written information in an early years setting**

Form of writing	What to consider
Observations on children	They may be passed on in the future and read by other professionals as well as the parent. It is essential that these are accurate and fair. Check that spelling is correct and that handwriting is legible.
Letters for parents	Information must be clear. Spelling, punctuation and grammar must be accurate. Consider word-processing them.
Displays	Spelling must be accurate. Use templates to help with large lettering. Draw thin pencil lines to help writing remain straight. Ask a colleague to check.
Notices	Information must be accurate. Wording must be friendly but to the point. Think about word-processing them and ask a colleague to check.
Cards and notes	Tone can be friendly but not too familiar. Handwriting needs to be legible and spelling accurate. This style of writing can be a little more personal.
Reports	These need to be accurate, well-presented and carefully worded. They may be passed on in the future and read by other professionals as well as the parent. Consider writing in draft before getting them checked.

Tone of writing

Different types of writing require different tones. A note on a birthday card will sound different to the comment on an official report card. One way in which you can work out the tone required is to look at a similar piece of writing. In general, it is important that letters and notes sound friendly but not over familiar. You must be accurate in what you say and use correct spelling and punctuation. Many settings now use computers and this can help you with spelling and punctuation, although a

Tips for good practice

Getting your writing right

→ Ask a colleague to look at your writing.

→ Read someone else's writing so that you can learn from their style and layout.

→ If you have difficulties with spelling and punctuation, tell the colleague checking your writing.

→ Use a dictionary or the spell checker on a computer.

→ Read through what you have written.

→ Make sure that information is accurate.

→ Check that the tone seems right.

→ Write things out in draft first and ask a colleague to check it.

computer will not necessarily pick up every mistake. This is why it is useful to ask someone else to read things through.

Using sensitive questioning and encouraging children to express themselves in their own time

You have seen that it is important to be an active listener when communicating. You might also need to help children to communicate. Young children's language skills are developing, so they can find it helpful if adults guide and support them when they are talking. This needs to happen very sensitively so that children who are able to convey their message do not become frustrated by your interventions. One way in which you can support children when they are trying to talk is to help them find the words. This can be done by commentary or by careful questioning. It is important to observe children as you are doing

Practitioner:	I heard that you had a birthday party yesterday!
Kylie:	Yup, it was in my house. I am three now, not two.
Practitioner:	Did you have a birthday cake or something nice to eat?
Kylie:	There were candles on my cake. Lots of candles!
Practitioner:	That sounds fun. Did you have to blow them all out?
Kylie:	I went... (makes sounds of blowing)
Practitioner:	Goodness, you needed a lot of puff to do that. Were you tired then or did you have some games?
Kylie:	We played games and I won some sweets, but Jamie wanted to eat them. But they were mine!

this as their facial expressions may show whether or not you are helping them. The conversation above shows how a practitioner is helping 3-year-old Kylie to talk about her birthday party.

Giving children time to think

As well as supporting children by asking them questions, it is also important that you give them sufficient time to formulate their thoughts. This is especially important for very young children, who often need adults to be patient rather than to rush them when speaking. Once again, if you observe the child's face, you will see whether they are still taking time to think or whether they need more support. Try to prevent other children from interrupting if a child needs this extra time, as this can lead to some children losing confidence in their speaking abilities.

The importance of an objective and non-judgemental approach when communicating with children

One of the skills of a good communicator is to show **empathy**. This means trying to understand another person's point of view rather than judging their actions and thoughts – or, in other words, taking an objective and non-judgemental approach. This is particularly needed in delicate and sensitive situations. Where speakers feel that they are being listened to and understood, it helps them to feel that they can

Think about it

Have you ever been in a situation when another person interrupts you? How did this make you feel?

Jargon buster   U5

Empathy Putting yourself in someone else's place in order to understand how they feel about something

Case study

A non-judgemental approach

Sisi is 4 years old. Her mother has come into the setting to apologise because Sisi has been taking toys home from the nursery. Sisi looks upset. Her key worker Gail has told Sisi's mother not to worry and that she will talk to Sisi. Later that morning, Gail finds Sisi and sits with her. She asks Sisi if she likes coming to the nursery and gently asks her whether she knows that taking toys home is not a good idea. Sisi is at first reluctant to talk, but as Gail does not seem cross, the story starts to come out. Sisi says that she likes playing in the home corner at nursery and with her teddies and dolls at home. At nursery, she likes playing games with a tea-set, but at home she doesn't have the same things. She was therefore trying to keep playing in the same way at home. Gail explains that nursery toys have to stay in the nursery, even though that can be hard sometimes.

1. Why was it important that Gail waited for Sisi to settle down before talking to her?
2. Explain how Gail showed that she was non-judgemental.
3. Why might Gail's approach be more effective than just focusing on the behaviour?

share more information. This is a skill to learn and you might begin by thinking of people you have met whom you really feel you could talk to. Working in this way is particularly important when communicating with children, as the case study below shows.

How to communicate with other professionals in a multi-agency approach

Depending on your role, you may find that you need to communicate with other professionals. This is important as, increasingly, early years practitioners work alongside other professionals in a multi-agency approach.

As with working with parents, it is important to be friendly but adopt a professional manner. You may, for example, be asked for information and the other person may be short of time and so will need you to be efficient. If you are not sure about what the other person is asking you, it is better to say so and then refer them on to someone else.

It can be helpful to understand the other person's role – it is acceptable to ask another professional what they do if you are not sure. Understanding their role will mean that you will have a better idea of what is required.

Look at the section on the importance of confidentiality below. It is essential that you understand this as a concept and apply it to your professional relationships.

The importance of confidentiality and sharing information in line with procedures

Confidentiality is about protecting children's and adults' rights to privacy. If you are good at communicating you might find that adults and children tell you things that are personal and important to them. They may expect that you will keep this information to yourself.

A good rule when thinking about confidentiality is to assume that everything that someone tells you is not to be repeated to other people unless you have their permission. The only exception to this is when you feel that the information is so important that a child might be put at risk. In such cases, you will still need to remember that the information is confidential and only tell your supervisor.

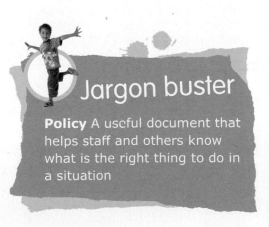

Jargon buster

Policy A useful document that helps staff and others know what is the right thing to do in a situation

Tips for good practice

Keeping things confidential

→ Regard all information learned about children and staff in the workplace as confidential.

→ Read and check that you understand your workplace's policy on confidentiality.

→ If you are unsure whether you may repeat something, ask your supervisor.

→ Think before you speak. Most breaches of confidentiality happen because of thoughtlessness.

→ Never make a promise to keep something confidential if the information will affect the well-being of the child. Your first duty is always the children's welfare.

U5

1

Find out!

1. Ask your placement supervisor about the setting's policy on confidentiality.
2. Is there any information that you would not be allowed to talk about to your friends?

Case study

Breaking confidentiality

Mattie's mum is keen to find out about her new work placement in a school. She knows a couple of parents whose children go there. She asks Mattie about one of the children. Mattie tells her that this child is not reading as well as the others. When Mattie's mum next sees this child's mum, she repeats what Mattie has said about the reading.

1. Why did Mattie breach confidentiality?
2. How would the teacher feel about Mattie working again in the classroom?
3. How might parents feel if their children are being talked about?

Back to the real world

You should now know how to approach a child who is upset.

1. Describe the non-verbal communication skills that you are likely to use.

2. Explain why it is important to listen as well as to talk.

Section 2

How to use your developing knowledge and skills to improve your practice and set appropriate targets to develop professionally

In the real world

You have a meeting with your supervisor at placement. She is very pleased with how you are doing but says that there are some areas of your work that need to improve. She is positive and says that if you are able to develop these, she may be able to offer you some work when you finish your course.

By the end of this section you will understand the process of how to develop professionally.

Introduction

All practitioners working with children and young people are expected to keep up to date and to develop their practice. They are also expected to think about areas of their work in which they can improve. The term used to describe this process is professional development. As part of their professional development, practitioners may attend training, organise study or think about other ways of working. As a learner, you need to know how to develop your own practice. This will help you achieve on your course and make you a better practitioner when you come to work with children.

How to use feedback to identify areas of your practice that need development

Feedback is the term used to describe comments that are made to you by others. It is important to listen to feedback carefully as it should help you identify where you might need to put in more work or change what you are doing.

Jargon buster

Feedback Information about your strengths and weaknesses given to you by others

U5
2

Learning to use feedback

Everyone likes to hear that they are doing well and that they are perfect! While hopefully your feedback will contain positives, good feedback is also likely to contain some suggestions and some identification of weaknesses. It is important that you listen carefully to all parts of feedback. You will need to see feedback as something that will help you succeed rather than something that is designed to criticise you. This can be hard to do but is essential if you are to develop a professional attitude.

Building on the positives

It is important to listen to the positives within feedback. These are aspects of your practice that you need to maintain or build on. A supervisor might say that you are excellent at communicating with children or that you are reliable and punctual. Being aware of your strengths means that you can develop these further, for example by asking if you can take on more responsibility.

Improving weaknesses

Feedback is also likely to highlight areas that you need to improve. It is easy to become defensive, argue or deny that you have any difficulties. The problem with this approach is that the weaknesses that others perceive will not go away! It is therefore better to ask for specific examples of where these weaknesses have been noticed and ask for suggestions as to how they might be handled differently. This is important as you will be able to improve your weaknesses more easily if you have a clear idea in your mind about what needs to change.

Written feedback

It is useful if feedback is written down or you make some notes. This can avoid confusion and afterwards help you to think more carefully about what has been said. You may also find it helpful to summarise what you think has been said to you while the person giving feedback is present. This can be done by writing it down or just talking through it.

As a learner, you will receive feedback from several sources, including those described below.

Tutors

Your course tutors will probably give you feedback about your study skills, writing and your attendance and attitude on the course. It is important to remember that feedback from your tutors will help you gain your qualification as they are experienced at making sure that learners pass.

Tutors visiting placements

It is likely that tutors will visit you when you are on placements. These tutors often receive feedback from staff members who may not always feel comfortable giving you feedback directly. Tutors may also watch you work and will be able to give you direct feedback about your performance. If you know that a tutor is coming at a certain time, it is advisable to be doing something with children so that you can be observed working. This way, you will get feedback about your practice with children.

Supervisors on placements

Your placement supervisor should give you some feedback as to how you are doing. This can be in the form of a 'chat' or even a proper interview. A placement supervisor will have an up-to-date understanding of what a practitioner needs to be able to do. They will also have worked with other learners and should be aware of your needs.

Other members of staff on placements

Team members may provide you with some feedback. This may come in the form of advice or just occasional comments. Try to listen carefully to these, as team members will have more experience than you. Newly qualified practitioners will have been through the process of gaining a qualification recently and may also have some useful tips.

⇩ **Feedback from team members who have more experience than you can be especially helpful to your progress**

Children

It is easy to overlook them, but some of the best feedback about your performance could come from children themselves. They may, for example, concentrate well and show great interest in the activities that you have planned, or show through their behaviour that the activities were unsuitable. Children may also show you how well you are communicating with them. If they find you responsive, they may come to find you so that they can talk and play.

How to keep a placement diary and reflect on your practice in relation to Practice Evidence Records

Your course tutors might ask you to complete a placement diary. Placement diaries take many forms but are particularly useful if they require learners to do some evaluation. You may, for example, write down what you have been doing on placement and then note your own feelings and learning gained from your time there. This can help you to work out the additional skills you need and which activities and experiences you should practise further. You may find it useful to see how far you have progressed during the time that you have been on the course. Looking back at previous activities, ideas and comments will help you to realise the range of your skills.

Practice Evidence Records

In order for you to finish your course, you need to show that you have become competent in many areas of practice. The Practice Evidence Records (PERS) that you have been given are an important part of this course. You should look after them carefully and spend time reading them. They are to be signed by your placement supervisor or tutor when you are able to show that you have certain skills and competencies. You cannot complete your course unless they have been filled in so it is important for you to show them to your placement supervisor during your placement. Choosing a good time to show them to your placement supervisor is important as they will take time for your placement supervisor to complete.

Evaluating activities

You have seen that it can be helpful to write a short evaluation after you have tried out an activity or play idea with children. It is also possible to evaluate without writing anything down, as the most important thing is to think about what you have done and what you can learn from this. The checklist below shows some of the types of questions that you could use to think about activities.

Tips for good practice

Key questions when evaluating activities

→ Did most children appear to be engaged and interested in the activity?

→ Can you identify the ingredients that helped children to be interested, for example the activity was sensory and children were active?

→ Were children encouraged to take control and be active during the activity?

→ How much input from you was needed?

→ Why was this input needed?

→ How did you encourage children to be active in their play and learning?

→ What did the children learn from the activity?

→ Was this learning planned or spontaneous?

→ How could this learning be built upon?

→ What did individual children gain from the activity?

→ What was your role in helping children to learn?

→ What types of resources were used?

→ Were there sufficient resources?

→ Which resources attracted children's attention?

→ What further resources could have been used?

→ What were the limitations of this activity?

→ How could these limitations be addressed?

How to access support to make improvements to your practice

While many people may provide you with feedback, some will also be able to provide you with advice and support. This is why it is important not to become too defensive or negative when receiving feedback.

Tutorials

Most learners have a personal tutor who is aware of individual learners' performance and achievement. Personal tutors can be very helpful to talk to when you have decided which areas of your performance you want to improve. It is useful to make an appointment to see a tutor. This means that the tutor is more likely to have enough time to talk to you and, if necessary, to find out information.

Placement supervisor and staff

When it comes to performance with children, it can be useful to talk to your placement supervisor or a member of staff who is experienced. As with personal tutors, they may be busy and it is best to find out if there is a good time to talk to them. This may mean waiting until after your placement hours have finished or coming in at the end of the shift. It is also important to show that you value their help, as their main role is to work with children rather than to help learners.

Resources

It is possible for you to improve your practice independently. There are plenty of books that give suggestions and ideas for planning play and activities with young children. There are also specific books that deal with aspects of practice such as behaviour, special needs and the curriculum. Magazines, books and other resources can usually be borrowed from college libraries but also with permission from settings.

⇧ **You will be able to gain ideas for improving your practice by reading books and other resources**

The effect of your own background, life history and experiences on your practice

The way that you have been brought up, the type of schools that you went to and the settings you have seen as a learner will all affect your practice, with children. In some cases, this is positive as you will have acquired skills and knowledge that are appropriate. In other cases, what you have seen and experienced may no longer be considered good practice, or it might be that it is fine within a family, but not correct professionally. A good example of this is hygiene standards. Within a family, most parents do not wear disposable gloves to change nappies, but in a professional situation it is essential to do so. In the same way, activities that you might have done and enjoyed at home might not pass risk assessments in a professional setting.

The way that you are inclined to manage children's behaviour can be linked to your own experiences. Again, it is important to realise that this is so and that professional approaches might be different. This means that you need to be aware of what is good practice within the setting you are working with and the age group and needs of the children. In a school, children might be expected to line up before going outdoors, but lining up in a toddler room is not appropriate.

To find out what is good practice, you can observe more experienced staff, ask direct questions or read and research more.

Case study

Eat up!

Rebecca is working as a learner in the nursery. It is meal time and one of the children tells her that he is full up. Rebecca sees that there is still food on his plate and asks him to finish it. Rebecca does this because as a child her parents always made her eat all the food on her plate. Rebecca thinks that this is the right way to handle meal times.

1. How is Rebecca's background affecting her practice?
2. Why is it important to check that your own experiences are in line with good practice?
3. Find out about good practice in relation to children finishing their meals.

How to set appropriate targets to develop yourself as a professional in a multi-agency context

We have seen that professional development is part of being a practitioner. As a learner, you will find that your practice will develop as you study and attend placement. It is important though to learn how to set yourself targets to improve your knowledge and practice.

SMART targets

As part of your professional development, you will need to set yourself targets. This can help you to feel motivated. It is important that any targets you set yourself can be easily met. To help you meet your targets, you might like to use a system known as SMART targets. SMART targets is a term used by many professionals. A SMART target makes you think carefully about the type of target that you are setting yourself. SMART stands for:

→ **S**pecific
→ **M**easureable
→ **A**chieveable
→ **R**ealistic
→ **T**ime.

The idea is that any targets you set yourself should be carefully thought out so that you can realistically achieve them. This often involves focusing on one area of development and being clear about what you want to happen. The aim is to gradually improve your performance. If there are several areas that you need to work on, this might mean deciding on the most urgent or the one that you can achieve the most simply or quickly. The case study below shows how a learner was able to set herself some SMART targets.

Case study

Making an action plan

Amanda was worried about her handwriting and spelling. Her placement supervisor had fed back to her a couple of times that she had made spelling errors when writing on the children's work. Her tutors had said that her handwriting was difficult to read. Amanda was at first a little defensive. She felt that it wasn't her fault that she hadn't been taught how to spell or do handwriting, but after a little time she realised that it would be to her benefit to work on these skills. She decided to get some help and turned first to her personal tutor. Together they constructed an action plan. They began by working out what Amanda could do first. Amanda's first target is below.

Target	Action	Date to be achieved	Reviewed
1. Get support for spelling	Make an appointment with learning support service	14/06/07	Achieved 10/06/07

1. Explain why it is important for targets to have a timescale.
2. Why is it important for targets to be specific and realistic?
3. How do you think Amanda felt when she met this first target?

The importance of setting short-, medium- and long-term targets for personal and professional development

You have seen that there are many sources of support and feedback. You should use these in order to help you decide what you might focus on first. You might also discuss your targets with your tutor; when you are qualified you might discuss professional targets with your line manager.

Short-, medium- and long-term targets

In developing an action plan, it is worth identifying what you would like to achieve in the long term as well as what you need to achieve quickly. Targets can therefore be short, medium and long term. You might, for example, have as a long-term target the wish to become a manager at a nursery. It may take you some time to achieve this target as you will need experience, further qualifications and high levels of skills. Long-term targets can be motivating and provide you with a sense of direction. It is important, though, to be able to break down long-term targets into smaller ones that are SMART. This is a skill and is one reason why it is worth action planning with a tutor or manager.

Developing basic skills

The term 'basic skills' is used to describe skills such as reading, writing, spelling, numeracy and IT that employers look for in their employees. Every learner needs to have these skills when trying to achieve a course.

Think about it

1. What specific target could you set yourself for a week's time?
2. What specific target could you set yourself for a year's time?
3. What would you like to be doing in four years time?

Some learners believe all that is required is to be good at working with children, but today in most jobs this is not sufficient. Practitioners have to be able to complete records, use a computer and manage budgets.

If you feel that there are some skills that you need to improve, this is a good time in your life to work on them. Most colleges have specialist tutors to help learners develop their skills and this support is free. Many adults also find that as they get older, they are embarrassed to seek support and find it hard to make the time when they are working.

Taking an assessment

If you are not sure whether you need support with your skills, you can ask your tutor or take an online assessment that is organised by the government. This is confidential and will also make suggestions as to where you can go to get further support. It is important not to see assessments as tests that you can fail because, in reality, what they do is help professionals to work out what type of support you need.

Find out!

Visit the website www.dfes.gov. uk/readwriteplus to find out how you can get support with basic skills.

How to review, update and amend targets for professional skills

Action plans should be regularly reviewed and updated if they are to work well. When you are drawing up a plan, you will need to set a review date. This can help you to focus your energies and to realise the progress that you are making. It is helpful to review your plans with someone else. This might be your tutor or, if you are employed, your manager. During a review meeting, you should consider what you have achieved so far and what you need to do next. Most people find that reviews with others help them to remain committed and motivated. This is important if you know that you have a significant amount of work to do over a period of time.

Amending a plan or target

In some cases, you might realise that your plan needs to be changed. It could be that you have not given yourself a realistic target or time scale. If you realise that your plan needs to be amended, you should do it as soon as possible. This means that you will not waste time waiting for the review date to come. In some cases, you might realise after working on one target that you need to do something else first; for example, you might be trying to improve your activities with children but then see that you first need to develop your communication skills. This might mean that a new target is required and the plan has to be amended.

Case study

Amending plans

Samantha had decided with her tutor to focus first on her writing skills. Some of her targets relied on her being able to join a support group. When Samantha asked about joining a course, she was told that the group was full and she would have to wait four weeks for the next course. Samantha decided to amend her plan so that she could work on another area of development. She contacted her tutor and arranged a review meeting even though the review date was scheduled for later in the term. Together they looked at other targets that Samantha could focus on.

1. Why was it important for Samantha to amend her plan?
2. Why did Samantha need to bring forward the review date?

 Back to the real world

You should now know why feedback is important and how to use feedback to improve your practice.

1. Explain which areas of practice you might need to develop.
2. Give yourself three realistic targets for this improvement.

Section 3

How to investigate employment opportunities and routes of progression

In the real world

You have nearly finished your course. You have to decide whether you will continue to study or look for a job, but are not sure where to begin. This is an important decision and you know that you need some information to make a proper decision.

By the end of this section you will know where to gain more information so that you can decide.

Local and national organisations in the voluntary, private and public sector that provide employment

From time to time, there may be conferences or exhibitions where employers will be present. These are usually advertised either in the local press or more often in professional magazines and newspapers such as *Nursery World* or the *Times Educational Supplement* (TES). In some cases, this will involve travelling and therefore some expense, so it is important to find out beforehand who will be there and what advice or information will be available. Information about exhibitions and conferences can be found on the Internet – yet another reason why it is useful to master the skill of carrying out an Internet search.

Some colleges invite employers to meet learners towards the end of the course. It is important if you are meeting employers to think about what questions to ask, for example whether they have a training programme or what experience they are looking for.

In Unit 1, you looked at the range of settings that care for children (see pages 3–5). It will be worth referring to this in order to consider what options are available to you locally.

Research

It is important that you play an active part in your own future! This means spending time undertaking Internet searches, looking in newspapers or making direct enquiries. You may be interested in going to university, for example, so will need to know what qualifications are required. Knowing what is needed means that you can choose the right course. Similarly, if you are aware of the jobs that are available in your local area, you will know what types of skills and qualifications are required. The spider diagram below shows how you might find out about employment opportunities in your area.

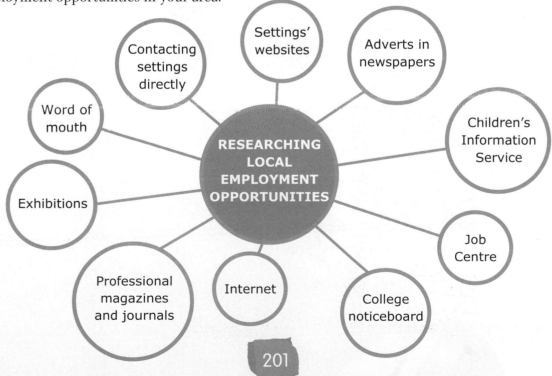

The Features Page:

Focus on *Professional development*

Once you have your qualification and have gained a job, the next step is to start thinking ahead about your career. There are many opportunities within the early years sector, but how can you get your career off to a flying start?

Personal development plans

Personal development plans have become very trendy lately, and there are many advantages of drawing one up.

- Firstly, you are taking responsibility for your own career and development. This is important because, while some employers are good at helping staff build on their skills, they are likely to be limited by their own needs and interests. For example, a setting that does not work with babies is less likely to send a staff member on a training course about heuristic play than a setting that has a dedicated baby and toddler room.

- Having your own plan also means that you can set your own timescales and goals. Taking responsibility for your own training and development is likely to motivate you more than simply being told what you need to do next.

- Finally, a personal development plan can help you to think through what type of work you might like to do in the future and so prevent you from becoming 'stuck' and demoralised in a few years time.

Top Tips:

Start thinking ahead...

✓ What would you like to be doing in three or five years time?

✓ What is preventing you from doing it now?

✓ What skills, knowledge or experience could you build now to help you towards this?

✓ Who might be able to provide you with advice or support?

Professional development

Q I have been told by my placement supervisor that I need to improve my skills with parents. The trouble is that as a learner, I am not allowed to have much contact with them. So how am I meant to improve my skills?

A When you are starting out in a career, it is often the case that you are told that you need more experience or skills, but at the same time you might not be given the opportunities to help you. A good starting point is to begin by asking your placement supervisor about which aspects of your performance with parents needs attention. Pick a quiet moment to have a word or make an appointment. Once you have identified the skills you need to work on, think about how best you might acquire them. A good way of learning new skills is watching and listening to others. You may find that your placement supervisor will let you watch as another member of staff talks to a parent. By spending some time watching or 'shadowing' another member of staff, you might then be able to ask your supervisor if, under supervision, you can have an opportunity to work with parents.

Q I really want to work with babies as a nanny, but at the moment I work in a toddler room of a day care nursery. What should I do?

A A good starting point would be to draw up a personal development plan. Begin by researching the skills, experience and qualifications needed to work with babies. Use this as the starting point for your personal development plan. You would be advised to study for a Level 3 qualification, as nannies should have this in order to care for babies and children unsupervised. It will also be worth talking to your manager about your wish to work with babies. Most managers find that staff work better when they are doing something they enjoy, so your manager might let you spend some time in the baby room.

Ask the expert

My story

Manjeet, nursery nurse

I have been working in a nursery for nearly two years. At the start of my career, I just wanted to get a job working with children. Now I am starting to think ahead as I can see that there are many interesting jobs working in childcare. At the moment, I am studying for my Level 3 qualification part-time. In our nursery, we have a staff appraisal system. Twice a year you meet with the manager to look at your performance and progress in your job. You also talk about what you could do in the future. At the end of the meeting, an action plan is drawn up. Last year, I told my manager that I was interested in working with children with special needs. She has arranged for me to go on some training and is allowing me time off to study, although in return I have agreed that I will spend at least another two years at the nursery.

When I first left college with my Level 2 qualification, I thought that I wouldn't need to do any more training. Since I have been employed, I can see that if you want to get on in your career, you have to keep on learning.

How to find out about career progression

Careers advisors

Child care and education is a developing sector with many job opportunities, and it is important to know about the different possibilities within the sector. You have seen that it is possible to carry out research independently via the Internet, but it may also be worth making an appointment with a careers advisor. Career advice is generally free if you are learner and many colleges have their own careers advisors. You could also visit a Job Centre and ask where to get career advice. If you are under 20 years old, you can contact your local Connexions team. The Connexions team provide support and advice on a range of topics including housing and careers.

Employer links

Many employers have links with colleges and training providers. This means that your tutors may be able to help you find some employment or they may have a system of putting up job opportunities on noticeboards. It is also important to be proactive and try talking directly to settings where you would like to work. Employers also use a local service known as the Children's Information Service. This is run by local authorities to help parents find out about childcare in their area, but most also have information about job opportunities.

⇧ **It is worth speaking to a careers advisor about your future career options**

Find out!

What careers advice is available in your local area?

The range of professional development

Even when you are working, it is important to continue to develop your knowledge and skill base. This is because policies, curricula and approaches to working with children change over time. This is best done through professional development. There are several ways in which you might continue your development.

Find out!

Find the phone number or website address of your local Children's Information Service.

Inset days

Some employers will organise training so that all staff members can focus on a topic and learn together. Inset training is useful and usually focuses on the practical needs of the setting. A staff team may together look at how best to manage children's behaviour or how to encourage and develop children's writing.

Local authority training courses

Many local authorities offer a training programme to settings that are providing care and education. This usually consists of short courses, typically lasting a day or so. Some courses are free, but others have to be paid for by the setting. The training programme is normally sent to the setting rather than to the individuals who work there. This means that you will need to find out what is on offer and ask permission to go. Most training takes place during the working day and this might mean that your employer will limit the number of staff who can attend or the number of days they can spend away. Many employers will also choose which courses they feel will benefit their setting or staff member.

Reading magazines and books

An important way of keeping up to date is to read. Most settings subscribe to professional magazines and journals which can help you to gain ideas and keep you updated.

Shadow visits

The term shadowing is used where a member of staff learns by watching another member of staff or visits another setting. This can be an extremely good way of learning about how they work and plan or relate to children. Shadowing works well if you are able to ask questions to find out more about the way in which the individual or setting works.

Case study

Learning through shadowing

Andrew is working in a nursery. He wants to learn more about how to plan activities that will promote mathematical development as this is an area he finds difficult. His manager has arranged for him to go to another nursery. He is introduced to Jenny, who shows him around. He spends the morning looking at the way in which she works with the children and then asks if he can see how she plans. Jenny is happy to show him because he is interested and she likes his enthusiasm. Afterwards, Andrew tries out one or two ideas that he saw in the other nursery. He also adapts his way of planning and generally feels much more motivated.

1. What has Andrew learned from his 'shadow' visit?
2. Why might it be easier to take in information by visiting another setting?
3. Why was it important for Andrew to try out some ideas quickly after the visit?

 Back to the real world

You should now know what sources of information are available in your area.

1. Give three sources of information about jobs and career opportunities.
2. Explain why professional development is important.

Getting ready for assessment

At the time that this book was written, you need to produce a portfolio of evidence to demonstrate your communication and professional skills. Reflective accounts are a good source of evidence for your portfolio. A reflective account is a description of something that you have done with some analysis of your strengths and weaknesses, and suggestions as to how you could improve your performance.

Choose TWO of the following areas:

→ Confidentiality

→ Awareness of children's development

→ Understanding of children's behaviour

→ Effective communication

For each of the areas you have chosen, you may like to see if you can complete the following tasks:

1. Describe a recent incident or event where you demonstrated good professional practice, and explain why. For example, 'I remembered to make eye contact with the parent and this is an important communication skill.'

2. Explain how you might improve your practice further in the future and what steps you can take to make this improvement. For example, 'I think that I am becoming more confident with parents but my next area for development is to try writing on the notice board for parents. In order to do this, I have decided to ask a member of staff to show me how it is done and to check my writing afterwards.'

Unit 6

The childcare practitioner in the workplace

In this unit you will learn:

1. The professional standards of the practitioner

2. How to observe development across a minimum of two of the following age ranges:
   - birth to 3 years
   - 3 to 7 years
   - 7 to 12 years
   - 12 to 16 years

3. How to carry out planned play and activities

4. How to use effective communication skills and contribute to positive relationships

Section 1

The professional standards of the practitioner

You have nearly completed your course and are being interviewed for a job as nursery assistant. As part of the interview you are asked about what it means to be a professional working with children. You are also asked to give examples of how you might show professionalism. You are not sure what the interviewer is looking for.

By the end of this section you will know what it means to work as a professional and the skills required.

The professional standards required in all settings of the children's workforce

In order to make the step towards being a professional, you will need to understand what this means. A professional is someone who is competent, qualified and focused on their work. They have professional standards which they maintain. They take satisfaction in the work they have done and while praise is welcomed, they do not expect or look for it. A professional does not watch the clock or cut corners in order to get home early or on time. A professional understands that sometimes extra time has to be spent in order for the work to be completed. This might mean, for example, that a nursery manager will see a parent after the nursery has officially closed if it is important to do so or a nursery assistant will wait with a child until the parents come because otherwise the child will become upset. As part of being a professional, both the nursery manager and the nursery assistant will not show that they mind being late home.

Another aspect of being a professional is the ability to prevent your personal life from creeping into your work. This means that even if you are worried about a friend or have had an argument, it does not show in your work or behaviour. This is extremely important as children cannot be expected to understand why someone is cheerful one day but gloomy the next.

Case study

Unprofessional behaviour

Mark has had a row with his girlfriend and they have not made up. He stayed up late last night expecting to hear from her. This morning on his way to work, he sent her a text. In the nursery, he keeps disappearing to one side to check if his girlfriend has texted him. The other member of staff in the room feels that Mark is not pulling his weight this morning and that his mood is affecting the children. One of the children stands next to him as he is looking at his phone. The child asks whether he can see the phone. Mark snaps back that it is none of his business.

1. How is Mark's unprofessional behaviour affecting the children?
2. How is his behaviour affecting his relationship with his colleague?
3. Explain why Mark is not acting as a professional.

The professional standards required of the practitioner when applying learning to practice in the workplace

As a learner you may sometimes find that there is a difference between what you have been taught and the practice that you see in your workplace. This can mean that it can be hard to apply your learning to the workplace without upsetting or appearing to criticise others. Your tutor may, for example, explain that paper towels are the most effective way of preventing cross-infection when washing hands, but you may find that a placement setting is using an ordinary towel in order to keep down costs.

It is important that while you are a learner, you show respect for your placement supervisor, and if you wish to change a practice then you ask your supervisor if you might do so. Once you are qualified and working in a workplace, it will be easier to try out new ideas, but again, it is essential to think about your colleague's feelings. The case study below shows how a member of staff has applied their learning to the workplace sensitively.

Case study

Applying learning to the workplace

Sandra is working in a day nursery. She is studying for a qualification at the local college. As part of her course, she has read about the importance of sleep and naps for young children. This has made her realise that the toddlers in the day nursery might not be getting the opportunity to nap. She decides to photocopy the article and asks her manager if she can talk about sleep and its importance at the next staff meeting. In the meantime, she asks her manager if she can try out one or two ideas. At the staff meeting, she outlines her thoughts and her ideas. As a result of the meeting, it is decided to create a proper space for the toddlers to have a nap in.

1. Why did Sandra talk to her manager first?
2. Explain the importance of Sandra discussing her ideas at a staff meeting.
3. Why is it important to think about colleagues' feelings when changing practice?

The value of interpersonal skills when working with children

The term **interpersonal skills** describes the way that people relate to each other. These skills are essential when working with children, as a significant part of the work is about relationships and communicating effectively. Children need to feel safe and secure with you, and they will feel this if you have good interpersonal skills. Parents must also have confidence in you if they are to leave their children with you and to share information. Again, the extent to which they feel confident will depend partly on your interpersonal skills. You will also require good interpersonal skills in order to work with other professionals and colleagues within the team.

The spider diagram below shows some key interpersonal skills. As you can see from the diagram, **verbal** and **non-verbal** communication skills are as important as empathy. You will be looking at verbal and non-verbal communication skills later in this section and the importance of empathy in Section 4.

Jargon buster

Interpersonal skills The ability to get on with people

Verbal communication skills Communication that takes place using talk

Non-verbal communication skills Communication that takes place through body language, facial expression and gesture

The ability to negotiate and be assertive

You will need to be able to negotiate and put across your point of view positively. One way to learn how to do this is to watch and listen to others who are good at it. You may find that they listen to other's points of view before clearly and calmly saying what they think in a way that is still respectful of others.

Respectfulness and thoughtfulness

It is important to show respect and thoughtfulness when working with others. For example, you might need to talk to a colleague but see that they are busy. You should wait a few minutes before interrupting them. If it is urgent, apologise for the interruption by saying something like: 'I'm really sorry to interrupt you, but Michael's mother is on the phone and it seems fairly urgent.'

How to work in a team

Most early years and educational settings have managers and team leaders but rely on people working together as teams. A team is a group of people who are working together towards the same goal or aim. The team members might not do the same jobs or have the same responsibilities, but by working together they can achieve the aims of the setting. Most employers are looking not only for excellent child care practice but also the ability to be a good team member.

As teams are made up of people and every person is different, it is possible you will not share the opinions or attitudes of the other members in your team. It is important to remember that everyone has different strengths and weaknesses and this makes for a balanced team. In business circles it is sometimes thought that having a team that always agrees can be bad – if team members have different views, this leads to debate and, through the process of debate, the team thinks through what they are doing.

Your role in working with other team members is to establish good working relationships. This is not the same as being friends, although many people do find friends at work. Building a good working relationship involves being able to listen to and respect other people's points of view. It also means putting aside any personal feelings that you may have and putting the children first.

Tips for good practice

How to be a good team member

→ Make sure that you carry out your duties well.

→ Be cheerful.

→ Be considerate of other people in your team.

→ Do not gossip.

→ Contribute to team meetings.

→ Follow instructions carefully.

→ Understand that your supervisor or team leader is the first person you should be talking to if you have any problems.

→ Acknowledge other people's ideas and support.

Think about it

Caitlin and Sarah work as nursery assistants in the same nursery. Caitlin finds out that Sarah is going out with her former boyfriend and she suspects that this boyfriend may have dumped her so that he could go out with Sarah.

Caitlin and Sarah have been asked to work together to produce a list of equipment for the outdoor play area. Caitlin does not feel that she can work with Sarah.

→ In pairs, discuss how Caitlin should handle this situation.

The importance of self-management

A good starting point to becoming a professional is to think about the way that you organise yourself. To be taken seriously as a professional, you need to begin with the basics – punctuality and timekeeping, personal hygiene and dress, and commitment.

Punctuality and time-keeping

In Unit 1, you looked briefly at the importance of time-keeping and punctuality (see page 9). As a professional, being on time and good time-keeping are essential. Below are some reasons why good time-keeping matters.

Commitment

Punctuality shows people that you care about your work and that you are interested. If parents or professionals are kept waiting for you to arrive at an appointment, they may wonder if you are really interested in your work.

Respect and politeness

Being on time is courteous and shows respect for other people. It means that other people do not have to waste their time waiting for you to arrive. Keeping people waiting for you is rude.

Builds confidence

Being on time and having good time-keeping skills shows that you are not only committed but also organised. This creates a good impression and helps others begin to believe that you can take on responsibility. Parents who are leaving their children with you need to feel confident that you are professional

Prevents disruption

Being late means that jobs might not get done and so disrupts the smooth running of sessions. Children, too, quickly get used to seeing you and start to count on you being there. They may become distressed if you are not there when you have said that you will be.

Personal hygiene and dress

As a professional, the way you look matters. Parents and potential employers will notice details such as untidy hair, dirty clothing or too much jewellery. In Unit 1, you looked at how to dress for placement and you will need to re-read pages 8–9 in addition to this section.

The aim is to look smart but at the same time wear practical clothing that shows you are able to work directly with children. Your personal hygiene should be excellent, and your appearance fresh and clean. This means making sure that clothes do not have stains on them and that your hair and skin look well cared for. This is important as parents are not likely to feel happy handing over their baby to someone who looks as if they might pass on an infection!

⚓ **Parents are not likely to feel happy handing over their baby to someone who looks as if they might pass on an infection!**

Commitment

Showing commitment when you first start working is often about doing things to the best of your ability and being ready to do extra. As a junior member of staff, it may mean taking on some jobs that no one else wants to do and doing them cheerfully, such as tidying the stock cupboard or volunteering to get the tea. Commitment means showing that you really want to work and be in the job, and it is often the details that show this to others.

How to use your initiative

Using your initiative means doing something without being told to do it. You might, for example, see that a coat has fallen on the floor and pick it up without being asked. Taking the initiative shows that you have commitment and also shows that you are thinking about what is best for everyone in the setting rather than just doing your job.

Taking the initiative within the limits of your role

It is important to look for ways in which you can use your initiative, although at the same time you should be aware of the limits of your role. As a learner, this means that you should not give information to parents or answer a phone, for example. If you are not sure whether it is appropriate for you to do something, always ask a member of staff. You could say, something like: 'Brett needs feeding. I have picked him up, as he was crying, but I was wondering if you would like me to feed him.' This means that you are showing that you are ready to take the initiative but are aware of the limits of your role.

Case study

Showing initiative

Frankie is supervising the children in the play area. She sees a child fall down, but as the child is not one of the children that she is responsible for she does not go over to the child. The other person supervising thinks that Frankie is lazy and that she couldn't be bothered to help. She does not say anything to Frankie but afterwards tells the manager.

1. What should have Frankie done?
2. Why is it important to do more than just your job when working as a professional?
3. What impression has Frankie given to her colleagues?

Verbal and non-verbal communication skills and how to communicate with children and adults

Verbal and non-verbal communication skills are central to building relationships so are essential for an early years professional. You will need to make sure that you understand the skills involved in non-verbal and verbal communications and practise them during your placement.

These skills are particularly important when you are applying for jobs and during interviews. In Unit 5, you looked in depth at verbal and non-verbal communication skills and you will need to re-read pages 181–8 in order to complete your learning for this unit.

The importance of effective communication skills in the workplace

Being able to communicate well can make a significant difference to your career and how well you fit into a team. It is important, therefore, that you think about how you communicate with other adults. For more information on communication, you should re-read pages 181–8 in Unit 5.

How to provide a positive role model and interact positively with children

Being a positive role model for children

In Unit 2, you looked at how children learn and saw that one powerful way is by copying the behaviour of adults. The term **role model** is used to describe the adult that the child is likely to copy. As a professional working with children, there is no doubt that you will be a role model for them. Children are likely to copy your habits and style of talking and interacting with others. Research shows that role models should behave in positive ways so that children can then adopt these. This means that you will need to think carefully about what messages you are giving children through your body language, facial expression and spoken language.

Jargon buster U6 1

Role model Someone whom children may copy

Think about it

1. What type of qualities should children learn from adults?
2. Think about the ways in which children will learn these qualities from you.

How to interact positively with children

Your interactions with children should be positive ones. Children will learn to talk and act with warmth and respect towards others if the adults around them treat them with warmth and respect. This means that you will need to think about how you work with children. How positive a role model are you?

Think about it

Use the checklist below to think about whether your interactions with children are positive.

→ Is your tone of voice warm towards children?

→ Do you smile when you are talking to children?

→ How often do you smile at the children?

→ Do you get down to the children's level when you are interacting?

→ Do you make eye contact with children?

→ Do you show that you are interested in what they are trying to say?

→ Do you listen properly and show that you are listening?

→ How long do you spend talking and listening to individual children at a time?

Find out!

Find out how good you are at interacting with children.

1. Tape yourself using an MP3 player or a Dictaphone and see whether your voice is warm and attractive.

2. Time the length of your interactions with children. Do they last several minutes or several seconds?

The importance of an inclusive approach to practice when working with children

In Unit 1, you saw that all children had the right to be treated fairly and with equal concern (see page 19). In practice, as a professional this means treating children as individuals and thinking hard about how best to work with them.

An inclusive approach to working with children means that you are able to meet and understand the needs of each child. Every child needs some individual time and attention, and no child should become a favourite within a setting. An inclusive approach involves thinking about the way in which each child feels valued and has a feeling of belonging. You will need to make sure that your interactions with every child are positive and that you consciously think about each child to make sure that they are not left out.

The examples below show how children may have different needs and interests:

→ Shintaro is 8 months old. He needs a great deal of encouragement to smile and his key worker spends a lot of time making him feel secure.

→ Hannah is 4 years old. She likes playing in the home corner and loves it when an adult comes into the home corner to take a role.

→ Jack is 3 years old. He has a speech difficulty and finds it hard to express himself. His key worker makes sure that he is not interrupted by other children and encourages him to take his time.

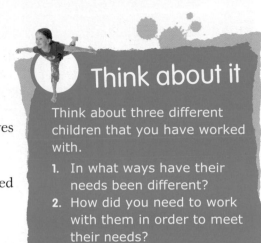

Think about it

Think about three different children that you have worked with.

1. In what ways have their needs been different?
2. How did you need to work with them in order to meet their needs?

Back to the real world

You should now understand what it takes to be a professional practitioner and be able to show that you have the skills to do so.

1. Give an example of how you have used your interpersonal skills.

2. Describe your self-management skills.

3. Give two examples of how you have used your initiative.

4. Give an example of a non-verbal communication skill.

U6
1

How to observe development across a minimum of two age ranges

In the real world

Your tutor has said that you must carry out some observations on children while you are in your placement. You are not sure how to do this, although you have been taught some techniques. Your tutor has also said that you will need to show you can use the observations to promote children's development.

By the end of this section you will know how to record observations and how to use an observation to think about activities for a child.

Methods used to observe children across different age ranges and in a range of settings

In Unit 2 you looked at some techniques for observing children. In order to complete this unit, you will need to re-read pages 52–7.

How to observe children sensitively

Before observing a child, you must obtain the permission of your placement supervisor. You will need to plan your observations so that you do not cause inconvenience to other members of staff.

Observing children is a skill. The first point to remember is that children's behaviour can change when they know that they are being watched. This means that it is sometimes helpful to observe children without them knowing or to be aware that being watched might affect their performance. You should also be alert to the best times to observe children. A child who is tired may not concentrate as well as usual, while a child who is excited about their birthday may have their mind on other things! It is therefore a good idea to observe a child several times and, if possible, on different days.

The importance of maintaining confidentiality and recording and storing information

Maintaining confidentiality

Since the observations that you carry out in placement are required in order to pass this unit, you will need to take them out of the setting to be marked by your tutor. This raises issues of confidentiality. You must make sure that you do not breach the child's confidentiality. The first step is to ensure you have permission to observe the child and the second is to make sure that nothing you write will allow someone else to identify the child. This means that instead of using the child's name in the observation, you might substitute another name or simply refer to the child as Child A. You should also make sure that you put the child's age in years and months and do not use a date of birth. Be careful not to choose a child who has such individual needs that they might be recognised. Finally, it is best to avoid using photographic observations as these can be used to identify children. Your tutor will give you some further guidance about protecting children's confidentiality.

The Features Page:

Focus on
Observing children

An interesting part of working with children is to carry out observations on them. Observing children can help learners understand the link between the theory that they have been studying in the classroom and what children actually do in real life. If you know that you will be in the same placement for a few weeks, you might like to ask your supervisor if you can carry out some observations on a child, so that you can see how the child is making progress.

My story

Liz, pre-school assistant

I love carrying out observations on children. Some of my colleagues think I am mad, but I get really excited. Observing children is different to just being with them. When you set out to observe a child, you start to think about what they can now do and you notice some really fascinating things. Recently, I carried out an observation on one of my key children, Ben. He is new in my group and I always thought that he was quite a shy boy. After watching him playing outdoors for fifteen minutes, I changed my view of him. He is quite boisterous and clearly a bit of a clown when he thinks he is playing alone with some of his friends. It made me realise that Ben's energetic side comes out when he is playing outdoors.

Observing children

Ask the expert

Q I have been told by my college tutor that we must carry out observations. I am not sure which child I should choose or when I am meant to carry them out. Help!

A While you will have to carry out observations as part of your course, your first port of call has to be your placement supervisor. This is essential because otherwise you might get yourself into a lot of trouble as children cannot be observed without their parents' consent and your placement supervisor will know whether this is given. Arrange a time to see your placement supervisor and go with a list of observations that you would like to carry out. Your placement supervisor will let you know whether the observations you have chosen will be possible. Ask your supervisor about which children you should observe and when it might be convenient for you to carry out the observations. Once you have agreed upon this, it is essential that you then carry them out as agreed. It can be frustrating for supervisors to discover that a learner has not completed their observations when they have tried to help out.

Q I want to find out more about a child who does not seem to talk much during a session, but I am not sure about which method I should use?

A When you are trying to discover more about a child's development, it is useful to observe the child in more than one situation and using more than one method. With a child who does not speak very much, first it would be useful to find out how much they talk during a whole session. To gain this information it would probably be best to carry out an event sample. This is the observation method where you would only do a recording if you were to see the child speak. It would give you an idea of how many times the child talks, to whom and for how long. Once you have carried out this observation method, your next step would be to look at the speech itself. Use the event sample to work out when the child seems to talk and then make sure that you are near the child with an MP3 player or other recording device so that you can record the child talking. If this is not possible, aim to be close enough so that you can write down as much of the speech as possible. You can then use this recording to look at whether the child has a speech delay.

Did you know?

→ Using observations to learn about children and to plan activities for them is a legal requirement for those settings in England working with Early Years Foundation Stage.

→ Practising carrying out observations and thinking about what type of activities and play a child would benefit from will help you later in your career.

Case study

Look at this extract from an observation.

> **Time:** 14.30 pm
>
> **Date:** 24/05/07
>
> **Age of child:** 2 years 3 months
>
> **Context:** Playing in the rice tray, nursery room
>
> Child A is picking up a spoon in her left hand and is scooping the rice into a pot that she is holding with her right hand. She is smiling and saying 'one', 'two', 'three' in time with the scoops. The pot is full. She puts both hands around it and pours it out. Some of the rice is on the table. Child A tries and then picks it up. She uses her left hand each time. She then puts her hand flat on the table and makes a waving motion to push some of the rice onto the floor. She takes more rice in her left hand from the tray and drops it onto the table. She uses her left hand to make circular movements and laughs as the rice drops onto the floor. Child B comes and squats down. Child B picks up some rice. Child A looks at her and then copies the action using her left hand and a pincer grasp.

1. Decide whether Child A is showing expected development.
2. Think about the activities you might plan to help Child A based on her interests and needs.
3. Why is it important to plan activities using observations?

Back to the real world

You should now have practised carrying out observations. You should know how to maintain children's confidentiality when writing observations. You should also have seen how it is possible to learn about the child's needs and interests from observations.

1. Give an example of an observation technique that you have used.

2. Explain why you used it and what advantages it had.

3. How did you use this observation to help the child?

Section 3

How to carry out planned play and activities

In the real world

You have been asked by your placement supervisor to plan two activities for next week. She says that she would like to see them written down so that she can discuss them with you. You are not sure why you need to plan activities as you thought that it was possible just to put toys out. Your supervisor has said that you will need to carry out the activity.

By the end of this section you will know why it is important to plan activities and how to write an activity plan.

The importance of effective planning for play and activities

Play is a major way in which children learn and also relax. In settings working with young children, play and activities are planned to support children's development and learning. If you are working in England, the Early Years Foundation Stage requires that activities based on observations and children's needs are planned. It also stresses the importance of play. The spider diagram below shows some of the benefits of planning play and activities.

Organisation

When children are in groups, it is important that play is planned. Children have different interests and needs and these should be catered for. Planning will help you to check in advance that every child will have something available that they will enjoy. This is particularly important for children who spend long periods of time in sessions and for many weeks a year. If the same things are put out day after day, children can become bored.

Supports areas of development

Play can also be planned to help particular areas of development. Playing outdoors using tricycles and climbing frames can support children's physical development. By planning carefully, the right equipment, toys and activities can be prepared, ready for children.

THE BENEFITS OF PLANNING PLAY AND ACTIVITIES

Supports children's learning

Children can learn through play. By playing, they can explore materials and ideas and learn skills. When play is planned, it is more likely to be varied. With every different play opportunity, children gain a new set of skills, ideas and concepts.

Behaviour

Planning activities and play has an effect on children's behaviour. Children who are bored or frustrated because their play interests and needs are not being met will show unwanted behaviour, while children who are enjoying themselves are likely to find it easier to show appropriate behaviour.

Meeting individual children's needs and interests

Children have a variety of needs. They may, for example, need extra support to manage an activity or would benefit from a particular type of play. Children also have their own interests. If you plan each session and think about the types of activities and play opportunities available, children's individual needs and interests can be met.

How to plan play and activities

As part of this unit you will need to plan for play and activities while on placement. You must show that the play and activities are safe and that they will appeal to children. The first step is always to find out as much as possible about the children that you are going to work with. Observations will enable you to find out about their stage of development and interests. Planning using children's interests as a starting point means that children are more likely to take part in an activity.

Writing down plans

There are many different ways in which activities can be recorded. Most settings will have a weekly or daily planner that shows the activities that are planned for each session. As a learner, you are likely to produce plans that are more detailed. This is because you are learning how to go through the planning process and writing out each stage will show that you have thought carefully about the activity. Such plans are often called detailed plans or **activity plans**. A good test of a plan is to see if someone else can follow it!

Your tutor may help you with the style of planning, but you will also need to think about the information listed in the table below. You will need to write all of this in your plan.

Jargon buster

Activity plans Plans that give details about how an activity is to be carried out and the purpose behind the activity

U6
3

⬇ **Factors to consider when writing an activity plan**

Factor	Description
Title of the activity	This will give your placement supervisor and tutor an idea of what you are intending to do.
Aim and purpose of activity	You will need to consider what the child/children will gain from the activity. If you are using a curriculum, you might also show which elements of the curriculum the activity covers.
Age of the children	What age group is the activity intended for? You should have checked that the activity is appropriate for the age or stage of development of the child/children.
Group size	How many children can you work with at any one time? If the activity requires a group such as a board game, you should say how many children must be interested in it.
What resources and equipment will you need?	Don't forget aprons and other items such as paper and pens. This is important so that your placement supervisor knows what you will require to carry out the activity.
Implementation	What will the children be doing in this activity? Think about how you will start the activity and encourage children to be interested in it. What will your role be: will you act as a helper and be there to encourage and support children or is it an adult-directed activity where you will need to show children what to do? (See Unit 4, pages 157–70, for different types of activities.)
Health and safety considerations	What will you need to do and consider to keep the children safe? Examples include providing aprons to keep children clean, making sure that children have washed their hands and supervising the use of scissors.
Adaptations	How do you intend to adapt the activity to ensure it meets children's different needs? This is important when you are planning a group activity, as children may be at different stages of development or have individual needs.

Tips for good practice

Planning activities

→ Observe children or ask your supervisor about their needs and stages of development.

→ Look at tables of development in childcare publications to find out more about children's development.

→ Find out whether play activities need to link into a particular theme, e.g. some settings might plan activities around the theme of 'seasons' or 'growing'.

→ Find out about the resources in your setting – your activity might end in disaster if you rely on a certain piece of equipment that isn't available.

→ Work out how children will benefit from your activity.

→ Write a list of resources or equipment required.

→ Consider how much time you have available to carry out the activity and how much time you will need to prepare for it.

→ Consider trying out your idea first, for example if the activity involves making a new recipe, try it out to find out how long it takes and the potential health and safety hazards.

→ Work out your own role during the activity. Will you be there to support the children during their play or will you have to show them how to use the resources and equipment?

→ Ask your supervisor or tutor to comment on your ideas, as they have had plenty of experience.

How to work with colleagues to plan play and activities

It is extremely important that you work with colleagues when planning play and activities to ensure a coordinated approach and to avoid situations where two members of staff require the same resources or intend to work with the same child at the same time. As a learner, it is essential that you liaise with your placement supervisor so that your plan can be checked and a 'slot' of time made available for you to carry out the activity.

You must not be absent on the day, and if you are supplying any essential materials, remember to bring them with you.

Contributing to and sharing plans

You have seen that it is important for learners to work with colleagues to plan play and activities. As a practitioner, you are likely to do this with others and to draw up a long-term or medium-term plan. (A medium-term plan might last for a month or a term.) It will include the type of activities that are to be planned and the learning outcomes. In settings using the Early Years Foundation Stage in England, you must show how activities will promote children's development and progress towards the Early Learning Goals (see Unit 10, pages 361–3).

Many settings therefore plan activities as a team. You will be expected to contribute ideas, so you must know how children will benefit from the different activities. As you become more experienced, you will have further ideas for activities. As a learner you may find it helpful to make a note of the activities in different settings and try to take part in them. This will give you an idea of the types of materials and resources required and how to encourage children to become involved.

Setting out and clearing away play and activities that encourage children's development

One of the most important things that you will need to learn in your placement setting is how play and activities are organised. You will be expected to help set out and clear away equipment, toys and activities which will enable you to become part of the team. The way settings do this will depend on their style and the age of the children. Some settings put out a minimum of toys and materials so that children become responsible for taking out what they need. Other settings will have a more planned approach and may have a list that shows staff members what is to be put out and where each day.

As with setting out play and activities, there are different approaches to clearing away, although most settings will encourage children to help and to take on some responsibility. Even so, some of the clearing away will require more strength and skill than children may have. While a 3-year-old may help to wipe down the painting easel, for example, an adult will have to return later to wash it properly. It is important that tables that will be used afterwards for snacks and meals are always thoroughly cleaned, so while children may start the process, adults will need to finish it.

You will also need to find out if there are 'set' times for clearing away in your setting and how children are encouraged to be part of this process. In many settings, children are also expected to tidy away some things during the session and again, you will need to observe how staff members remind and encourage children to do this.

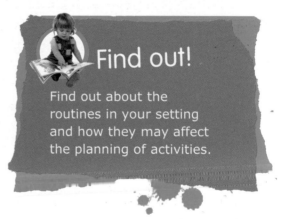

Find out!

Find out about the routines in your setting and how they may affect the planning of activities.

Encouraging children's development

Once play activities are finished, they have to be tidied away. It is good practice for children to help clear away as this encourages them to become independent and self-reliant. Some settings spend time talking to children about the type of play activities that they have been involved in and consider clearing away an important part of the play process. You will therefore need to allow plenty of time to do this.

Below are some suggested tidying activities that adults and children can do together:
→ put away completed jigsaw puzzles and games
→ fold or hang up dressing-up clothes

Tips for good practice

Setting out activities

Space and layout:

→ Is there enough room for children to move safely between activities?

→ Are the fire exits clear?

→ Are activities that need water near a sink?

Equipment:

→ Is the equipment suitable for the age of the children?

→ Is the equipment clean?

→ Has the equipment been checked for safety?

→ Have broken or incomplete toys been removed?

→ Is there enough equipment for the number of children playing?

→ Can children reach the equipment so that they can be independent in their play?

Preparation:

→ Allow plenty of time.

→ Will children need aprons?

→ Do tables need protecting?

→ Are there cloths to hand for wiping up spills?

→ Is there a dustpan and brush ready to sweep up sand?

→ Is there enough paper out for painting and drawing?

→ Is there space to dry paintings?

→ Does the room or outdoor setting look pleasant?

→ Do the activities look inviting and appealing, e.g. fresh paint, dressing-up clothes laid out, books displayed in the quiet corner?

→ put clay and dough into airtight containers

→ put away 'small world' toys into correct boxes, e.g. Duplo animals

→ hang paintings to dry.

How to encourage children to participate and immerse themselves in activities

Play and activities should be fun for children. This means that you should encourage them to participate rather than 'force' them to join in. If children do not seem interested in an activity or playing, it is important to ask yourself whether you have chosen the right activity. Children generally do not need too much encouragement if the activity or play looks appealing and fun.

Ways to encourage children to participate

Start off the activity yourself

Children are often interested in what adults are doing. Sitting down and starting off an activity is a good way to encourage children to participate. You may find that once one child has come to see what you are doing, others will follow.

Play alongside children

Some children will join an activity if they see that an adult is playing. This works particularly well for role play and for games outdoors. It is important once play has been established to consider if you are still needed. Children require their own time and space in order to play.

Show children the activity

It can be helpful to show and tell children about an activity. If, for example, you are blowing bubbles, going over to a group of children and showing them a bubble is likely to make them interested.

Encourage children to participate in setting up an activity

Some children, especially as they become older, enjoy helping to set up an activity. You could ask a child or a group of children if they would like to choose the materials to put out and encourage them to be involved.

⇧ **To encourage children to participate in an activity, you will sometimes need to join in**

Case study

Getting children involved

Activity 1

Jan has decided to make a den with a group of children. The children are already happily playing in the sand. She tells the children that they have to come with her. Once they are ready, Jan tells them exactly what they must and must not do. One of the children tries to return to the sand tray, but Jan insists that they come back to the den. The children stand around looking miserable as Jan does most of the construction of the den.

Activity 2

Caira has decided that the children might like to make a den. Over lunch she talks to a group of children and asks them if they would be interested. She tells them about the materials and fabrics that are available and asks them what things they would use if they were making a den. The children are interested and after lunch they look at what is available. They help to choose the items including a large cardboard box. The children are excited and are able to work out by themselves where to put the den. Caira praises the children and encourages them to do nearly all of the building themselves. Afterwards, she asks the children if they would like to have snack time in the den.

1. Which approach is the most successful?
2. Why did this approach work?
3. In which activity did the children learn the most?

How to provide a safe and hygienic environment for play

In Unit 3 you looked at the importance of providing a safe and hygienic environment for play. You will look at this topic again in Unit 7. To complete this unit, you will need to read Unit 3, pages 109–20, and Unit 7, pages 243–5.

Providing a safe and hygienic environment for play means making sure that you have checked the play area before play starts and continue to monitor it while children are using it. From time to time, you will have to tidy up toys and materials that children might drop or play with on the floor and clean up spills. This is important to avoid falls and to prevent infection.

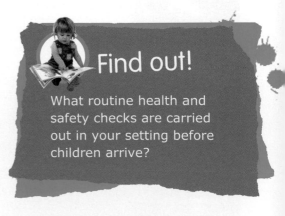

Find out!

What routine health and safety checks are carried out in your setting before children arrive?

In order to provide a safe and hygienic environment, you will first need to find out what your placement does and how the staff routinely work. For example, some settings sieve through the sand at the end of each session to make sure that there is no debris, while others do this occasionally. The setting's hygiene measures will depend on the age of the children and how many children are using the equipment.

You will also need to consider health and safety when planning activities such as cooking. Children should wash their hands and wear aprons, while you will need to ensure that any ingredients have been properly stored and are washed if necessary.

 **Back to the real world**

You should now understand why it is important to plan activities and be able to write out an activity plan. You should also know how you might encourage children to take part in an activity.

1. Give an example of an activity plan that you have written.

2. Describe how you have encouraged children to join in an activity.

3. Explain ways in which you have made sure that children are safe while they are playing.

How to use effective communication skills and contribute to positive relationships

In the real world

You are starting in a new placement and will be working in the toddler room. You are anxious about how you will fit in and whether you will be able to work with this age range.

By the end of this section you will know how to build positive relationships with children and why this is so important.

Introduction

Effective communications skills are important when working with children and their families. You will need to be able to communicate well in order to build a relationship with them. In Unit 5 you looked in depth at the communication skills you will require. To complete this unit, you will therefore need to re-read pages 181–8.

As you saw in Unit 5, communication can be divided into verbal and non-verbal communication. Talk is just one part of being able to communicate. The ability to control and think about your body language and to read other people's body language is also important. You can also communicate through writing, for example via memos, home books and letters, and you will have to demonstrate that you have developed such skills in your work. Below are some questions to help you reflect on the development of these skills.

Think about it

1. Give an example of how you have recognised anxiety in a child. Explain how you reassured the child.
2. Give an example of how you have used written communication. Explain what you had to think about as you were writing.
3. Give an example of how you have listened to a child. Explain how you showed the child that you were listening.
4. Give an example of how you reported back to a member of staff. Explain how you made sure that your message was clear.
5. Give an example of how you encouraged a child to talk. Explain the strategies that you used.

The importance of positive relationships in the workplace and how to contribute to them

Working in the early years sector is all about working with people. This means that you will have to learn quickly how to build positive relationships. It is essential to be able to do this when working with children, as they need to feel comfortable with you. Good relationships with parents, colleagues and other professionals are vital because information needs to be shared and this is easier to do if everyone is able to work well together.

In Unit 1 you saw how important it is to make a good impression (see pages 8–10), and earlier in this unit (page 213) you looked at why you need to show commitment. Being punctual, dressing appropriately and taking the initiative are key ways in which you can get your relationships with other adults off to a flying start.

How to contribute to positive relationships

The way in which you build positive relationships with children varies according to their age. Below are some ways in which you might work with children of different ages.

Building relationships with babies

While all children need to have a good relationship with their carers, for babies it is essential. Babies need to form an 'attachment' or special bond with you in order to cope with the absence of their parents. This means that in most day care nurseries or settings where babies are cared for, there is a key worker system. A key worker is responsible for building a constant and responsive relationship with the baby.

Understanding separation anxiety

Such is the emotional need for babies to have strong attachments that by around 8 or 9 months old, babies will cry when they are left with someone they do not know. Where babies are cared for in groups, the setting will usually have a key worker system. Key workers will spend time with the baby while the parents are there so that the baby gets to know them before the baby is left by the parents.

⇧ **The relationship a key worker has with the young babies in her care is vital to their sense of security**

Physical contact

One way to encourage strong relationships with babies is through physical contact. Simply holding and cuddling a baby can help them to feel wanted and reassured. While babies need time to play on the floor, it is important that they are not left for long periods without physical contact.

Body language

Babies quickly tune in to the human face. They recognise the adults that they enjoy being with and with whom they have a special relationship. This means that alongside physical contact, babies require eye contact and a prompt response to their needs. That means picking up and rocking a crying baby or smiling back at a baby who tries to attract your attention with babbling and smiling.

Using everyday routines

Relationships do not just happen. Babies learn about the people they enjoy being with through everyday events such as nappy changing, feeding and playing. It is therefore good practice for the same person to change the baby's nappy each day and carry out other tasks such as feeding. During care routines, the baby needs eye contact, cuddles and plenty of smiles.

Play

Babies are interested in each other from an early age but do not have the skills to play together. They need adults to play with them. Songs, rhymes and repeated actions such as peek-a-boo for older babies are ways in which babies learn about play. When you play with a baby, you are building a relationship with them.

Building relationships with children aged 1–3 years

Like babies, children under the age of 3 years old need to have a strong attachment to one person in the setting. Distress at leaving parents continues until most children are nearly 3 years old. It can be avoided if the child gets to know their key worker before being left. For children who start in a new setting during this period, it is essential that a key worker system is used so that the key worker can build up a relationship with the child.

As part of their emotional development, most children under 3 years old are unsure of strangers. They need time to get to know a new person and will show signs of distress if you 'swoop' down on them. This means that it is often best to take your time and allow children to come to you rather than go to them. It is also helpful if you do something that will attract children towards you, for example by blowing some bubbles or using a puppet. It is important to take your time and not rush in too quickly.

Physical contact

Once children feel confident about an adult, they start to need physical contact. Toddlers, for example, clearly signal that they wish to be picked up by putting up their arms. Two-year-olds may want to sit on your lap. Physical contact is important to young children and when they need physical reassurance, it is essential that they get it. Interestingly, these years are also a time when children can alternate between clinginess and independence. It is not uncommon for a child of 20 months to want one moment to be carried and the next to be put down on the floor! When this happens, remember to respect the child's desire to be free and let them go.

Responsiveness

Children of this age also need adults to be responsive to them. They may tap you on the back or point out things that they have seen. It is important that you respond or they soon learn not to bother trying to make contact. This is also an age when you need to observe children closely and think about their needs. For example, you may notice that a 2-year-old is heading off towards a sit-and-ride where there is already another child. Being aware that, at this age, most children are not able to understand the need to share means acting quickly and offering an alternative toy.

Facial expression and body language

Like babies, young children are particularly aware of faces and body language. Although they are starting to understand words, they process

Think about it

Observe how staff in the baby room work with babies. How do the key workers build relationships with the babies they are responsible for?

U6
4

visual information more easily. This means that the way adults smile, make eye contact and show genuine affection will help children to feel comfortable with them. Remember to smile and make children feel good about themselves.

Play

From about the age of 3 years, most children learn to play cooperatively. Some children are able to play earlier, but all children benefit from playing alongside an interested adult. Enjoying being with an adult is a key part of forming a relationship with them. When playing with this age group, it is important to respond to their play ideas rather than to impose your own. Remember, too, that children of this age often like repetition and so you will probably find yourself rolling a ball to a child of 18 months not once but six or seven times!

Case study

Poor relationship skills

Jenna has just started a placement in a nursery. She is working in the toddler room. She notices that the toddlers seem shy of her and when she goes up to one child he starts to cry and hides behind the legs of his key worker. Jenna feels that the children do not like her. She picks up another child, but immediately the child struggles to get away. Jenna is frustrated and starts to wonder if she really wants to work with children.

1. Why are the children not responding to Jenna?
2. What is Jenna doing that is upsetting the children?
3. Explain how Jenna should work in order to begin building a relationship.

Building relationships with children aged 3–8 years

From around 3 years, children often become more confident about being with people they do not know well. This varies according to individual children's experiences, but on the whole children find it easier to separate for brief periods from their parents. Children in this age range are also becoming more aware of other children and gain pleasure from playing with others.

Reassurance and approval

While younger children often seek physical contact with adults, older children start to look for verbal reassurance and approval. This is linked to their language development, and children coming into the setting who do not speak the language of the setting or who have some language delay may still need opportunities for physical reassurance. You might give reassurance and approval by smiling, praising a child or simply being alongside a child as they try out something new.

If you observe children at the age of 3 years, you may notice that even when they are engaged in play with other children they look around occasionally to check where the adults are. They might also be keen to show you what they have been doing or enjoy some friendly interest.

Listening to children

While babies and very young children need acknowledgement and physical reassurance, this is the age at which you need to listen to children. With their growing language skills, children begin to enjoy chatting and expressing their ideas. They may also ask questions and will want a proper response. Children are quick to sense which adults will spend the time listening properly to them, and so taking the time to relax and enjoy listening to children is important.

Being a play and language partner

From around the age of 3 years, children enjoy playing with other children but they also take pleasure in doing things with adults, especially when they feel that they are part of what is going on. A 4-year-old may, for example, enjoy helping to put up a display, while a 6-year-old will have fun learning a game of cards with an adult. Try seeing this way of working with children as being a 'partner'. For example, you may chat to children and respond to their interests and so be a language partner. At other times, if children want you to organise a game or take part in their play, you might be a play partner. Taking time to be with children in this way can strengthen relationships.

⇦ **The ability to listen to children chatting and expressing their ideas is vital when working with children aged 3–8 years**

Back to the real world

You should now know that communication skills are important and why it is essential to build positive relationships.

1. Describe two ways in which you have used verbal communication skills to work with children.

2. Describe two ways in which you have used non-verbal communication skills with adults.

3. Explain how you might build a positive relationship with a 2-year-old and a 6-year-old.

4. How would you work differently with them?

Getting ready for assessment

At the time this book was written, this unit requires that you demonstrate that you have acquired the practical and professional skills required for employment with children. There is no written assignment for this unit but you must make sure that the following items are completed by the end of your course:

Placement Summary
This is a record of the days/hours that you have worked as a student. In order to achieve this you must remember to be reliable, punctual and organised when keeping your record up-to-date.

Practice Evidence Records
These records demonstrate that you have gained the practical skills required to work with children of different ages. It is important that your placement supervisor knows about the importance of Practice Evidence Records and you remember to take them in so that they can be signed off when you have demonstrated that you are competent in the different areas. Your tutor or placement visitor can also sign the Practice Evidence Records.

Practice Evidence Diary
Your evidence diary should contain a record of the type of tasks that you have carried out in placement. You will also need to show that you are able to evaluate your strengths and weaknesses when carrying out the tasks, and provide suggestions as to how you might further your practice.

Professional Development Profiles
At the end of each placement, you need to give your placement supervisor a Professional Development Profile to complete. As with the Practice Evidence Records, it is worth reading through what is expected of you in order to achieve a pass.

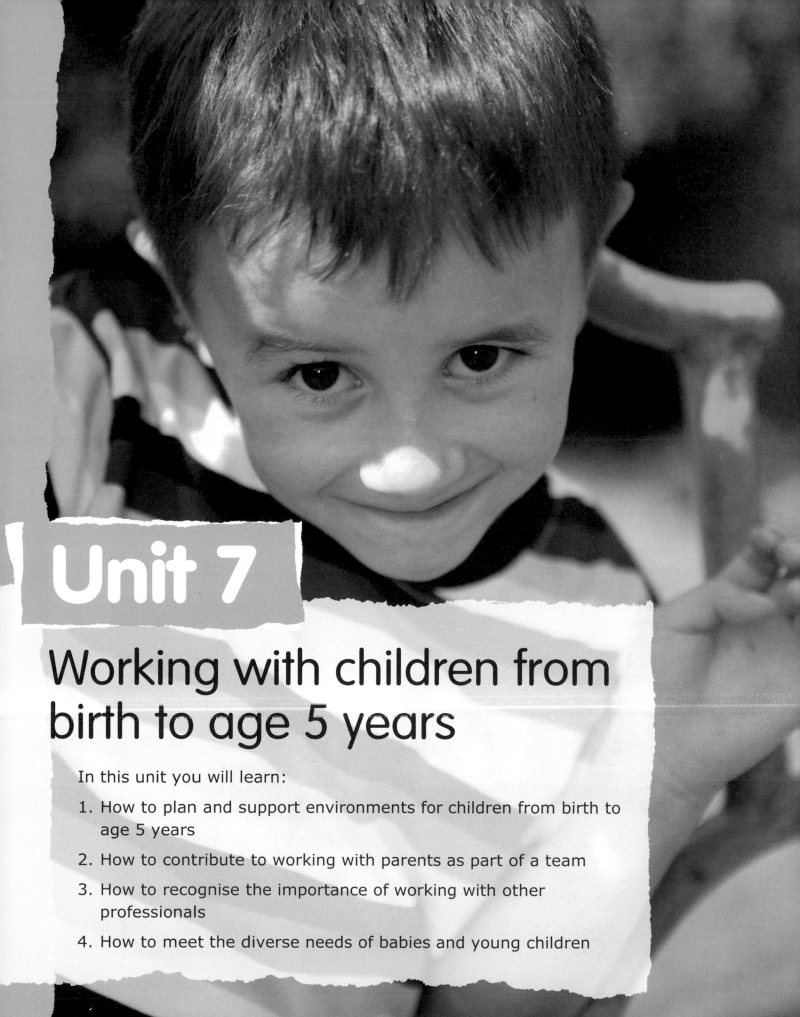

Unit 7

Working with children from birth to age 5 years

In this unit you will learn:

1. How to plan and support environments for children from birth to age 5 years

2. How to contribute to working with parents as part of a team

3. How to recognise the importance of working with other professionals

4. How to meet the diverse needs of babies and young children

Section 1

How to plan and support environments for children from birth to age 5 years

You are on placement in a nursery. The manager of the nursery is showing you around before you start. He keeps on telling you about how the nursery prides itself on its environment and the way in which they try and meet children's needs. He tells you that all learners are expected to take some responsibility for health and safety and maintaining the environment. You look enthusiastic, but are not quite sure what he means.

By the end of this section you will have a basic knowledge of how to plan and support environments for children from birth to 5 years old.

How to promote a healthy, hygienic and safe environment for children

Hygiene procedures

As part of your role as an early years practitioner, you will be expected to maintain a healthy, hygienic and safe environment for children to be in. Ensuring children's personal hygiene is one aspect of this and you may wish to refresh your memory by re-reading Unit 2, pages 81–93.

A good starting point is to be aware of the overall hygiene requirements that most settings follow. Later in this section, you will consider ways of making sure that children are kept safe. Below is a chart that outlines the general hygiene routines that need to be carried out.

Hygiene procedures

Item	Why it needs to be cleaned	Method
Toys and play equipment	These are frequently handled and may be put in the mouth.	Sterilise plastic items in solution.
Feeding equipment	Spoons, bowls and other items are put in the mouth.	Sterilise all items of feeding equipment for children under 2 years.
Tables	Children may put items that have been on the tables in their mouth.	Wipe with a clean cloth every time they are used – use a mild disinfectant.
Worktops	Food may be prepared on these surfaces.	Wipe with a clean cloth – use a mild disinfectant.
Toilets, hand basins, sinks	Toilets and areas for hand-washing are places where bacteria grow.	Clean regularly with bleach solution. Check toilets frequently during sessions.
Bins	Items such as damp paper, food and nappies will have bacteria on them.	Empty bins frequently. Place nappies in sealed bags. Wash out bins every day.
Floors	Children will put their hands on floors when playing. Food may be dropped on the floor. Toys that have been on the floor may be put in the mouth.	Clean floors regularly, using a disinfectant.

In order to provide a high standard of hygiene, you need to carry out frequent checks in the setting. During the sessions, you should wipe up any spills and areas should be kept tidy. It is the responsibility of every member of staff to report any areas or equipment that needs attention and perhaps to carry out the necessary cleaning.

Plastic gloves should be worn for protection and cloths that are used should be thoroughly rinsed after use and regularly put in a solution containing disinfectant.

Handling and disposing of waste material

When working with children, there are times when you may come into contact with body fluids such as blood, urine, faeces and vomit. Many infections, including HIV and hepatitis, can be passed on through contact with these fluids, so you must take the following precautions:

→ wear protective gloves when dealing with body fluids
→ make sure that any cuts on your hands are covered by plasters
→ wash your hands after disposing of waste materials and cleaning up.

Waste material includes tissues, cloths that have been used to mop up and nappies. In large settings, these should be placed in a separate covered bin which is then sent for incineration (burning). In the home environment this is not possible, so any waste material should be wrapped and put in an outside bin to make sure that it cannot be handled again. Never try to flush nappies down toilets, as this may block the toilet.

Food hygiene

Most early years practitioners will have a role in preparing and serving food and drinks for children, even if this is just snacks. It is important therefore to understand how to prevent food poisoning, which is often a result of poor food hygiene. Most food poisoning is caused by bacteria multiplying on food and then being eaten. Bacteria need water, food and warmth in order to grow.

There are three principles in preventing food poisoning caused by bacteria:

1. *Stop the bacteria from getting on to the food.* The kitchen area must be clean and anyone handling foods must have good personal hygiene. Remember that bacteria grow when there is warmth, water and food. This means that you must dry your hands thoroughly after washing them.

2. *Stop the bacteria already on food from spreading.* This may be done by storing foods safely. This slows the rate of growth rather than stopping it completely. Bacteria grow quickly when they are at room temperature or in a warm area such as in the sun. The 'danger zone' is between 5°C and 63°C. Between these temperatures bacteria grow rapidly. Many raw foods already contain bacteria when they come into the kitchen, for example meat, eggs and dairy produce. This is why separating raw foods from cooked foods is essential. See the chart below for the correct way to store foods.

3. *Destroy the bacteria on food.* This means heating foods to a temperature of 72°C. Foods need to remain at this temperature for several minutes to kill the bacteria. If food is only slightly warmed through, bacteria will flourish, so when reheating any food make sure that it is piping hot. When using microwaves to cook or heat food, you must follow the manufacturer's instructions as well as stirring the food to ensure that the food has reached 72°C.

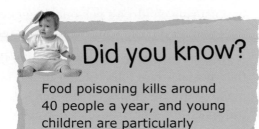

Did you know?

Food poisoning kills around 40 people a year, and young children are particularly vulnerable to its serious effects.

Food group	Examples of food	Storage
Dry foods	Rice, flour, pulses, baby milk, couscous	• Keep in airtight containers. • Do not allow to become damp – bacteria cannot grow while they are dry.
Perishables	Meat – raw and cooked; Fish; Dairy products, e.g. cheese, milk, butter, eggs	• Keep in the fridge. The fridge temperature must not be above 4°C. • Cooked foods must be covered and kept in a separate place in the fridge.
Vegetables and fruit	Root vegetables, carrots, sweet potatoes, yams, apples, plums, plantains, tomatoes, etc.	• These should be kept as cool and dry as possible and off the floor. • Root vegetables such as potatoes need to be stored in the dark. Do not eat green potatoes. • Fruit and vegetables lose their vitamin C if they are not eaten while fresh.

The spider diagram below shows the ways in which you can prevent bacteria from getting onto foods.

Make sure raw and cooked foods are stored separately

Always cover foods

Avoid handling food with hands where possible, e.g. use spatulas, spoons

WAYS TO STOP BACTERIA FROM GETTING ONTO FOODS

Regularly wipe and disinfect work surfaces and chopping boards

Keep animals out of food preparation and eating areas

Wash hands thoroughly before handling food and during preparation, e.g. after handling raw meat

Tips for good practice

Safe food storage

→ Always read manufacturers' instructions when storing food.

→ Do not eat foods that are past their sell-by date.

→ Once a tin is opened, store the contents in a covered container in the fridge.

→ Keep fridges at 1–4°C.

→ Keep freezers at minus 18–23°C.

The importance of promoting children's welfare

The term 'welfare' is often used to describe children's all-round needs. All children, regardless of their age, have certain needs that have to be met in order that they can thrive. When children's needs are met, they are more likely to be settled, happy and keen to learn. The needs include the following:

➜ *Physical needs* – Children need adults to meet some of their basic physical needs such as shelter, food, water, ventilation and warmth.
➜ *Hygiene and safety* – Children need adults to provide a hygienic and safe environment for them so that they do not fall ill or have a serious accident.
➜ *Stimulation* – Children need activities, toys and opportunities to play and explore in order that they can develop.
➜ *Love and attention* – Children need to feel that they are cared for and valued.

The provision of reassuring and secure surroundings for young children

When caring for children, you should try to create a good environment for them. This means making sure it is safe, hygienic and that the equipment and activities that are provided are suitable for the needs of the children being cared for. A caring environment, though, is more than just meeting the basic needs of children – it also involves making sure that children feel valued and that their experiences in the setting are pleasant ones. A happy environment also has a good atmosphere between staff and parents. Atmosphere is invisible but very important. To create such an environment, early years practitioners need to be able to work with parents and other team members.

The essentials of being a good early years practitioner

Some people think that a good early years practitioner is someone who gets on well with children. Unfortunately, it is not enough just to like children. There are many other roles and responsibilities that need to be considered.

A good early years practitioner has a combination of skills. These can be seen as the pieces making up a jigsaw – each is needed for the picture of a good early years practitioner to be complete.

Greeting children

Many children come into early years settings feeling nervous and afraid. They may be leaving their parents or carers for the first time or they may have had a holiday and not been in the setting for some time. As an early years practitioner, you need to be able to reassure them and make them feel settled. One of the key elements in providing a reassuring environment for children is a warm and welcoming atmosphere. (If you wish to read more about helping children to separate from their parents and carers turn to Unit 2, pages 96–105.)

Making the environment safe

One of the roles of an early years practitioner is to make sure that the environment is safe for children to be in. This means carrying out checks to make sure that there are no potential hazards, supervising children and ensuring that equipment and materials are right for their age.

Keeping the environment tidy and hygienic

Children need to be in environments that are tidy and hygienic. You need to take responsibility for tidying away equipment so that accidents are prevented and the setting is kept clean. Materials and equipment need to be put away in their correct places. Keeping the environment hygienic is also a major responsibility when working with children. Although most large early years settings employ a cleaner, it is still the duty of the early years practitioner to keep equipment clean, wipe up spills and clear surfaces. This may not always be a pleasant task, for example if a child has been sick, but it is an essential one. You also need to act as a good role model by washing your hands, wearing an apron and being tidy and clean in appearance.

Working with parents

Establishing a good relationship with parents is another major role of early years practitioners. A good relationship with parents can help children to settle in more quickly and help you to understand the needs of children. To build a good relationship with parents and carers, you need to respect their wishes and values and show that you appreciate their support and help. (Valuing and working with parents is covered in more detail in Section 2 of this unit.)

Confidentiality

While caring for children you may learn information about them and their families that is confidential. For example, you may see medical records, financial information or hear reports about children. Breaching confidentiality is considered to be serious as it means that the trust of the setting and/or the parents has been broken. If you are unsure whether information is confidential, it is a good idea to ask your supervisor.

Meeting children's needs

Being able to meet children's needs is not the same as getting on well with children. An early years practitioner needs to be able to understand which activities will help children to develop as well as being able to support children in a range of situations, for example when they feel ill, are finding it difficult to settle or are upset and angry. You also need to be able to identify children's needs, for example to recognise when they are ill as well as meet their day-to-day needs such as wanting to go to the toilet or have a go on the slide.

Being a good team member

There are many jobs that involve being able to work as part of a team. A good team creates a happy environment around it and this can be sensed by children and parents. To be a good team member you need to respect the other members and be ready to support them. This sometimes means lending a hand or putting away something that you did not use. It also means understanding the lines of responsibility within a setting, for example parents may need to be referred to a senior team member if they wish to discuss their child.

Think about it

Here is a checklist of ways in which you can make children feel welcome. Use this list to monitor your performance during one day in your workplace.

1. Do you greet children with a smile and a hello when they come into the setting or when you arrive?
2. Do you say hello to any parents that you meet?
3. Do you bend down to the children's level when you are talking to them?
4. Do you listen to what they are saying and show them that you are listening?
5. Do you respond immediately if you see a child who seems unsure or who is alone?
6. Do you sit and play with a child or group of children?
7. Do you respond quickly to children who need help, e.g. when they want to go to the toilet or need someone to fasten an apron for them?
8. Do you praise children?
9. Do you laugh and smile with children?
10. At the end of the day, do you make sure that you tell children that you are looking forward to seeing them again?

Planning environments

Planning an environment is an important part of working with children. A good environment should meet children's needs for stimulation and rest and keep them safe. Children are more likely to enjoy being in a setting if the physical environment around them is pleasant and attractive and meets their needs. It is helpful if children can be made to feel 'at home', for example being able to get out toys for themselves or being able to go to the toilet without too much help.

Making sure that the environment is comfortable

Where possible, furniture and fittings such as sinks and toilets need to be child-sized. This means that children are less likely to have accidents and are able to show independence. In purpose-built settings, toilets and other fittings will be child sized, but in home settings you may need to look at ways of making the environment more child friendly. For example, you may be able to put coat hooks at the child's height or have some drawers and cupboards where children's toys are stored and they have easy access.

⬇ **Children are more likely to enjoy being in a setting if the physical environment around them is pleasant and attractive and meets their needs**

The lighting and heating of a setting are essential aspects of a comfortable environment. You need to make sure that the room temperature is pleasant and that children are not too hot or cold. Most early years settings are kept at 18–21°C. You must also make sure that any indoor setting is adequately ventilated, for example by opening a window so that fresh, clean air can enter. This is important in preventing infections, as germs flourish in warm, stuffy rooms.

Natural light is thought to be the best for most settings, but some rooms may not have large enough windows. Good lighting helps prevent children and adults from straining their eyes which can lead to headaches.

Using layout to make an environment attractive

How a room or hall is laid out can make a difference to its attractiveness. Careful planning can make the most of the available space and ensure children's needs are met.

Tips for good practice

Points to consider when planning a layout

→ Fire exits and other access points should be kept clear.

→ There should be enough space for children to move safely from one activity to another.

→ Enough space should be allowed for the activities planned for the area.

→ Specific children's needs should be considered, for example enough room for a wheelchair.

→ Activities that require water or hand-washing should be near to the sink.

→ Good use should be made of available natural light, for example the book corner could be near a window to allow children to look at books in daylight.

→ The room should be as easy to clean as possible.

→ The room should look inviting and attractive.

→ Storage space should be used effectively and children should be able to collect equipment easily without crossing through other areas.

Layout in home settings

Most homes where children are cared for are not as large as group settings. Children can be cared for at a childminder's or in their own home. Here the layout might be affected by the other needs of a family. This means that equipment and activities are put out and then changed at different times in the day. The kitchen table may be used for a meal at lunch time and then later in the day for painting. The living room may be used for dressing up and then for a quiet time later on. You can make a home environment more child friendly by removing any objects that could be broken or that could cause an accident such as vases of flowers and ornaments. As toys and equipment can be expensive, some childminders and nannies use toy libraries as a way of borrowing new equipment for the children they care for.

Layout in a baby and toddler room

Some babies and toddlers are cared for in baby rooms within day nurseries. Most nurseries keep furniture to a minimum in these rooms to allow the children to explore safely. Babies and toddlers are able to play with toys on the floor and have plenty of space in which to crawl and walk safely. Sleeping and changing areas are often separate to this room to make sure it is a hygienic area.

Small spaces for small people!

Children often enjoy having a space in which they can tuck themselves away. This can make them feel secure. In larger early years settings, the space may need to be big enough for several children to be in it at once. This is often the home corner. In a home setting, this could be under a table draped with a cloth. Although children want to feel that they are hidden away, it is still important that they can be supervised.

👆 **Children often enjoy having a space in which they can tuck themselves away**

Quiet areas

There are often times in a day when children feel that they would like to be quiet and rest. Some children enjoy looking at books, whereas others might want to do a puzzle or quietly play with a toy. The room or hall layout may include an area that is carpeted to allow children to stretch out and relax. In a home setting, this area could be the living room where children can curl up on a sofa.

Areas for creative play

Children enjoy painting, playing with sand and water and other activities that can be messy. Most settings need an area where children can carry out these activities safely and where any mess or spills can be mopped up without causing any damage. These areas often have floors that can be wiped easily as well as sinks nearby for hand-washing and for cleaning equipment.

Outdoor areas

Many settings have outdoor areas for children. Sometimes these areas are quite small, but all children benefit from having some fresh air and being outdoors. Most settings have a paved area so that even when it has been raining, children can spend time outside. You can make these areas attractive by planting bulbs and tubs of flowers with the children. Most settings with outdoor areas use them for tricycles, slides and large play apparatus. In good weather you can put out other activities such as sand, water and paint.

Time for a change

From time to time, it can be refreshing for adults to look at the room layout and move things around. This helps create a new interest in equipment and can make the environment more interesting for everyone. Sometimes a layout may need to be changed because staff realise that one area or a piece of equipment is popular and needs more space.

Activities, equipment and materials

When children come into a room or hall, they often focus on the materials and equipment that are available. A colourful slide or an attractive home corner can sometimes make the difference between joining in the fun or staying close to an adult.

When you put out activities and equipment, you need to be aware of the amount of space that is needed and the number of children who may wish to join in. Some equipment – for example train tracks, building blocks and tricycles – need large amounts of floor space and there may not always be enough space for all of them to be put out.

At times, you may also find that you need to limit the number of children involved in an activity. A sand tray may be large enough for six children, but the risks of squabbles and accidents are likely to increase if there are eight children trying to play there.

How to adapt environments to meet the diverse needs of children

Children with a range of needs should not miss out on play and learning opportunities. Common needs include physical ones such as a child who needs to use a standing frame or wheelchair. In purpose-built settings, this is not likely to be a difficulty because doorways and ramps will probably have been planned. In other settings, it may be possible to make some simple changes that can improve access, for example moving tables. Parents and specialist workers are often the best source of advice as they tend to know what the child needs. A range of specialist equipment has been developed to allow children with special needs to play and learn alongside other children, including adjustable chairs, tables and painting easels.

As well as having additional physical needs, some children may also need the environment adapted to suit their emotional and behavioural needs. They may need quieter areas or separate trays or equipment. The key way in which you can learn about children's needs is by observing children and using the knowledge of parents and other professionals.

Meeting Kieran's needs

Kieran is 4 years old. He finds it difficult to socialise with other children and can find change very distressing. The staff at the nursery and his parents discuss ways in which they can meet his needs. It is recognised that Kieran needs to come into the nursery and find some of his favourite objects and activities in exactly the same place. This is fairly easy to manage. As Kieran also finds it hard to cope in large groups, his key worker has created a small area within the nursery where there are several small trays of things that Kieran enjoys playing with. This becomes Kieran's haven and he enjoys being there with a couple of other children who also seem to prefer quieter activities. Kieran is now much happier.

1. Why is it important to talk to parents or carers when helping children who may have diverse needs?
2. How have Kieran's needs been met?
3. Why is important that Kieran's needs are met?

The different ways to display children's work

You can use displays to make the environment more attractive for everyone. Dark corners can be transformed by bright posters or framed prints. Corridors and entrance ways can be made to look more welcoming. Visitors, new parents and children are given the impression that the people who work in the setting care about their work.

Children love to see their work on display. This could include drawings and objects that they have made as well as pieces of writing. Where possible, it is a good idea for displays to be put where parents can see them, for example in a cloakroom or an entrance. This means that even if they are not able to come into the setting – they may be in a hurry – they can still see what their child has been doing. This can make them feel both proud and reassured.

All children gain enormous benefits from seeing their work on display. It can help them to feel valued and part of the setting as well as giving them confidence. You can encourage children to look at each other's work and ask them what they like about it. This is a way of helping them to value others' efforts and achievements.

⇩ **All children gain enormous benefits from seeing their work on display. Here, children's handprints have been cut out and used to create a rainbow**

Process not perfection

You need to be careful that when children's work is displayed you do not fall into the trap of putting out only work that is perfect. Where space is limited, it is a good idea to keep a list of children's names to check that every child has some work displayed. Children need

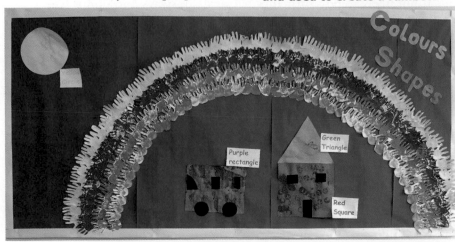

to understand that although the end product is important, the process and their effort are always what count. This is an important message for children because they can sometimes lose their confidence if they think that they have, in some way, failed.

Preparing wall displays

Wall displays can improve an environment by their visual impact. Some settings have purpose-built boards that are lined with hessian, whereas others may have simple notice boards. You can adapt areas in a setting for a display, for example using a fridge or cupboard door to show items of interest. These may include posters, photographs and charts as well as children's work.

Putting up a wall display can take time and it is not always safe to do this when there are children around, although children can be involved in making items for the display. If you are not very confident, start with a small area and keep to a simple idea.

Labelling and spelling

Labels add a finishing touch to displays. They can help children to recognise simple words and to understand that words have meanings. Children also enjoy seeing their name next to their work and will often want to show their parents and friends what they have done.

Labels need to be clear and it is good practice to use lower-case lettering, although capital letters should be used for the first letters of names. Some early years settings have particular ways of lettering, for example they may put 'tails' on some letters. Most people find it difficult to keep their lettering straight and so it can be useful to draw some pencil guidelines. Computers and templates are also useful for producing lettering.

It can be a good idea to ask someone to check your spelling, as it is easy to make a simple mistake and embarrassing to have it staring out at you on a wall! You should also check the spelling of children's names, as correct spelling shows that you value the children.

Older children can be encouraged to join in with a display by making their own labels, and where children speak more than one language, it might be possible to ask a parent to write some labels in the home language.

Mounting children's work

When children's work is mounted, it looks as if it has been framed, which makes it look more attractive. This is not difficult to do. Choose a slightly larger piece of paper and put the piece of work on top. Check that the borders are equal, and trim as necessary. Where possible, use a paper cutter, as this gives a straight edge. Otherwise a pencil and a ruler should be used to keep the edges straight.

Good effects can be achieved by using contrasting colours for the paper that makes the mount.

The Features Page:

Focus on *Displaying children's work*

Displays play an essential role in making a setting look attractive, but also in helping children to feel that their work is valued.

Ask the expert

Q I am working with babies and have been told that we have to put a display up. As the babies are not drawing or painting, I don't know what to do.

A While you are right that babies will not be painting or drawing, this does not mean that they will not enjoy seeing pictures or photos on display. Why not take a series of photographs of all the babies and then laminate them? Put them onto colourful paper at a height where the babies will be able to see them. You may be surprised at how much they enjoy looking at them. You could also ask parents if you can take some photos of them with their children, so that your display helps babies to remember their parents.

Q How often should displays be changed?

A There are no set rules, but once you see that a display is not attracting any attention it is worth changing it. A good tip is to plan displays that can be added to, so that you can keep changing them. For example, a display about shopping might include a shopping list that changes every few days.

Q I have been asked to put up a display ready for parents' evening. My supervisor says that it should be the children's work. The problem is that they are only 3 and 4 years old and their work is not good enough.

A Your supervisor is right – it should be the children's work on display. Parents do not want to see work that an adult has done, they want to see what their child can do. Children's painting and drawing develops over time and it is fascinating to see how they view the world at 3 and then 4 years of age. If you are concerned that parents will not know what the child has tried to draw, simply add a separate caption below it such as 'Jack's drawing of a dog chasing a monkey. The monkey has gone up the tree.'

Displaying children's work

Top Tips:

Setting up a display

✓ Look at other people's displays and learn from them.

✓ Simple displays are often the most effective.

✓ Use lines to keep your handwriting straight.

✓ Check your spelling carefully, especially children's names.

✓ Get the children to help you plan the display – their ideas are often the best.

My story

Joe, learning assistant

The first display I did was terrifying. The board seemed huge and I was worried that it would not be as good as some of the other displays that were in the school. It took me a huge amount of time. I kept on changing my mind about where I should put up the pictures and the whole process of mounting them was a nightmare. When it was finished, I stepped back and realised that I had mis-spelt the title and had to do it again. Eventually when it was done, I was really proud. The children were excited to see their work on the wall and I had made sure that no one was left out. It was hard work but worth it.

Spot the difference!

Can you spot the five differences between these displays?

Maintaining and changing displays

Displays need to be checked and maintained if they are to remain effective. Interest tables may need to be rearranged as children will be moving the objects around. With wall displays, items can start to fall off and young children may 'pick' at items. Once a display is no longer being noticed, it needs to be changed. Some large settings have rotas for staff members so that everyone takes it in turn to change displays.

The basic physical and health needs of children from birth to 5 years

In Unit 2 you looked at the basic physical and health needs of children and how these might be provided as part of a routine. To help you achieve this unit, you will need to re-visit pages 64–94 in addition to reading the information below.

As well as meeting children's needs for food and drink, sleep and rest, hygiene and safety, children need to wear appropriate clothing and have opportunities for physical activity.

Clothing and footwear

Dressing children can be part of an early years practitioner's role, especially if children are being cared for at home. Nannies may be responsible for choosing items of clothing from a child's wardrobe in the morning or a childminder may keep sets of children's clothes in case of an accident.

Footwear

Caring for feet is important for everyone as corns and blisters can make walking difficult and painful. Particular care needs to be taken with children as the bones in their feet are soft and still forming. Shoes need to be the right size and width for the child, otherwise permanent damage to the feet may be caused. Shoes need to be wide and long enough to allow growth but not so big that they rub and cause blisters and corns.

Socks, tights and sleep suits also need to be checked – if they are too tight, they can stop the foot from developing. Care must also be taken to cut children's toenails as these can make their feet sore.

For many families on a low income, buying correctly fitting shoes is difficult as they are expensive and young children's feet grow quickly. This means that many parents pass down shoes to younger children or buy second-hand shoes. Although understandable, this is not recommended as the shoe will have conformed to the shape of the previous child's foot.

Children's need to become independent

When caring for young children, you should always be looking at ways to help them become independent. Personal hygiene routines can be learned by children if they are encouraged to take part in them from an early age. For example, you may give toddlers the flannel so that they can wipe their face first or encourage 4-year-olds to have a go at

Tips for good practice

Selecting clothes for children

→ Clothes should be comfortable, easy to put on and washable.

→ Cotton is often chosen, as it is soft, absorbent and allows the skin to breathe.

→ Choose clothes that allow children to be active, e.g. a garment that is too big may restrict a child's mobility.

→ Choose clothes that are appropriate for the weather and the types of activity.

→ Follow parents' wishes, e.g. Muslim girls may need to wear trousers.

→ Check that clothes are clean – underwear should be changed every day.

Caring for clothes

→ Always follow manufacturers' washing instructions.

→ Sort out clothing according to colour and washing instructions.

→ Check pockets before putting items in a washing machine.

→ Check which type of washing powder is used, as some children's skin can react to certain detergents.

→ Make sure that items are properly dried before being put away.

→ Check that clothes such as jumpers and coats are labelled, if children are going into group settings.

cleaning their teeth by putting a mirror in front of them. As children become older, your role may just be that of reminding or praising them for washing their hands or supervising them at bath time. There are also many topics or themes that you can discuss with children to help them understand the importance of hygiene.

Information about health and hygiene topics can be obtained from health promotion units, health and dental clinics as well as from professional organisations.

Caring for the individual needs of children

Some children will have particular needs in relation to their physical care, which you should find out by asking their parents or carers. Common needs for children include using special toiletries because of skin conditions, or washing in a particular way to meet with religious or cultural requirements. Children with special needs may also have individual requirements, for example they might need help when going to the toilet or when dressing themselves.

Wherever possible, you should provide support but also allow children to be as independent as possible. This could mean giving children plenty of time or using particular pieces of equipment such as a standing frame.

Physical activity

Everyone needs some physical activity in order to keep the body functioning well. When considering a routine for children, you must always make sure that it contains some time for physical activity, even if this means just going out in the fresh air for a short walk. Physical exercise helps the body in many ways and as children's bodies are growing and developing, it is especially important that they are given opportunities to enjoy physical activity.

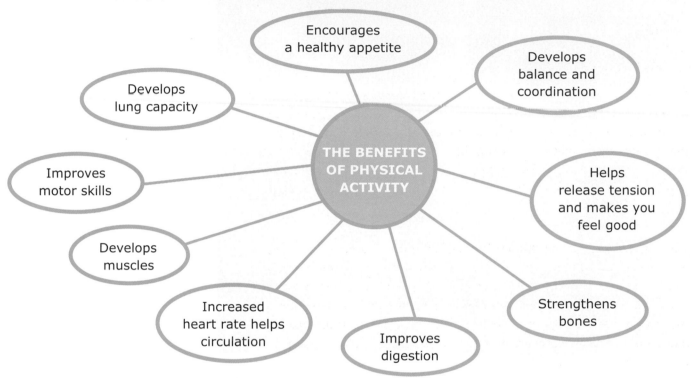

THE BENEFITS OF PHYSICAL ACTIVITY

Encourages a healthy appetite

Develops balance and coordination

Develops lung capacity

Improves motor skills

Develops muscles

Increased heart rate helps circulation

Improves digestion

Helps release tension and makes you feel good

Strengthens bones

Other benefits for children

Although physical activity can help children to develop physically, there are also many other hidden benefits. Children can gain in confidence and independence. You may hear children say 'Look at me, I can climb to the top of the slide all by myself!'

Many activities that involve physical activity also help children to socialise and work together. Older children may play organised games such as chase, while younger children may pretend that the climbing frame is a ship or a house.

The health and safety requirements when working with children from birth to age 5 years

One of the duties and responsibilities of early years practitioners is to keep children safe. Children are more vulnerable to accidents than any other age group. Whatever early years settings you work in, you have a duty to keep children safe. As young children have no sense of danger or the consequences of their actions, you need to do the thinking for them.

Think about it

Have you been in an early years setting where children have been unable to go outside and play because of bad weather? Did this affect the mood and concentration of the children? If so, how?

Health and safety legislation

The Health and Safety Act 1974 is a good starting point when looking at your duties in keeping children safe. The Act is designed to protect everyone in any early years setting. Under this Act:

→ Employees must use the safety equipment provided, for example an early years practitioner must use safety equipment provided such as disposable gloves or stairgates

→ Employees must make sure that their actions do not harm others, for example leaving a hot drink in the reach of children would endanger a child

→ Employees also have a duty to report hazards and to follow the safety policy of the early years setting.

Health and safety requirements vary from setting to setting according to the layout of the building and also the age of the children. A childminder living in a bungalow and working with older children may not need safety gates, whereas a nursery that has many babies and toddlers will probably be using them. This means that whenever you change settings, you will need to find out what the health and safety requirements are.

Promoting a safe environment

You can make sure that children's environments are safe by carrying out checks and by being generally observant. Every environment has different risks. A family home may have a kitchen that is also used as a living area, and a nursery with many children may have to ensure the entrance and exit points are kept clear. In school settings, the playground is likely to be an area that is hazardous because of the number of children at play.

The most common injuries to children are:
→ burns and scalds
→ injuries caused by falls
→ choking and suffocation
→ poisoning
→ cuts.

The chart below shows hazards that commonly cause the above types of accidents in indoor settings.

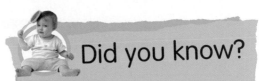

Did you know?

Each year, over two million children are taken to hospital after having an accident (Source: Child Accident Prevention Trust).

⬇ **Potential hazards in early years settings**

Type of accident	Potential hazards
Poisoning	• Medicines • Cleaning products such as bleach • Waste bins
Burns and scalds	• Matches and lighters • Radiators, gas fires, open fires • Hot drinks • Kettles • Irons • Baths • Cookers

Type of accident	Potential hazards
Electric shocks	• Plug sockets that are uncovered
Falls	• Unlocked windows • Stairs • Highchairs • Pushchairs • Climbing frames
Cuts	• Knives • Scissors • Sharp edges on furniture or corners at eye-level • Glass doors
Choking and suffocation	• Pillows for babies under 1 year • Cords and ribbons on garments or skipping ropes used during pretend play, e.g. putting around another child's neck • Plastic bags • Peanuts • Toys with loose parts • Toys without safety marks, e.g. doll's eyes falling out

The use of safety equipment

The use of safety equipment in the early years setting will help to prevent accidents from occurring. Some basic types of safety equipment and their purpose are listed in the table below.

⚷ **Safety equipment**

Equipment	Purpose
Reigns and harnesses	To prevent children from falling out of highchairs and from running into the road.
Safety gates	To stop children from climbing stairs and from going into certain rooms, such as toilets and kitchens.
Play pen	To create a safe area for children in a certain room, such as a kitchen.
Smoke alarm	To detect smoke and raise the alarm.
Fire blanket	To smother flames; they are kept in kitchens to throw over a pan that has caught fire.
Catches for windows and cupboards	To prevent children from opening windows and cupboards.
Saucepan guard	To prevent children from tipping pans on the top of cookers on to themselves.
Electric plug sockets	To prevent children from putting their fingers into sockets.
Plastic film	To cover glass and make it safer, e.g. glass windows in the home environment.
Plastic corner covers	To put on furniture with sharp edges.

Think about it

Look at these two pictures and consider how the hazards should be managed.

Checking and cleaning equipment and toys

Checking equipment and toys can prevent accidents. Equipment can become worn or unstable, so buying second-hand equipment that will be used by many children is not advisable. It is particularly important that regular checks are made on any piece of equipment that has moving parts or is taking children's weight, for example slides need to be checked for stability and tricycles for steering.

Most equipment wears out eventually. The chart below shows how the main materials used in making equipment may wear.

⬇ **Wear and tear of equipment**

Type of material	Look out for:	Examples of equipment
Plastic	• Cracking • Fading colours • Sharp edges	Chairs, sit-and-ride, seats on tricycles
Metal	• Signs of rust • Flaking paint • Metal fatigue	Climbing frames, tricycles, see-saws, pushchairs, highchairs, swings
Wood	• Rough edges • Splinters • Flaking paint	Chairs, bookcases, wooden blocks, jigsaw puzzles

Cleaning toys and equipment is another way of checking that they are safe, while at the same time preventing the spread of any bacteria. Manufacturers' instructions must be followed when washing toys and other equipment such as baby mats or rattles.

Equipment that is used for feeding needs to be cleaned each time it is used, whereas outdoor equipment can be cleaned every month. Any toys that are regularly handled, such as Duplo bricks, should be washed at least once a week. Some toys can be washed, while other equipment needs to be wiped over with a weak solution of disinfectant, which will help to kill bacteria.

Find out!

Ask your placement supervisor if you can check and clean an item of equipment.

1. Write about how you checked this item.
2. What were you looking for?
3. How did you clean this item?

Toys and play materials

Accidents can be prevented by making sure that toys and materials are suitable for the children using them. All new toys and equipment should have a safety mark on them. Toys without marks can be dangerous. They may have parts with sharp edges or they may fall apart.

 **Common safety marks found on toys: (from left to right) Lion mark, BSI kitemark, CE mark**

Accidents happen when children choke on small pieces or use equipment that is designed for older children, for example a 3-year-old trying to get on a skateboard. This is why manufacturers' instructions must be followed. By law, manufacturers must state if a product could be dangerous for younger children. If you are unsure about a toy, it is better to remove it and talk to supervisors or parents.

Case study

Avoiding a choking incident

Sonal is working as a nanny for two children aged 2 and 3 years. Their grandmother is staying with them for a few days. Sonal notices that the grandmother is about to give the children a toy with very small parts, and is worried that the younger child might swallow them.

1. Is it Sonal's responsibility to take action?
2. In pairs, consider how she should handle this situation. (You could do this as a role play.)

Supervising children

Close supervision plays an essential part in avoiding accidents. Most accidents happen very quickly. The level of supervision will vary according to the age of the children and the activity that they are involved in. Toddlers need to be supervised very carefully as their actions tend to be unpredictable, for example they may suddenly drop or throw an object. They are also unsteady in their movements and are more likely to trip over. Children under 2 years are also likely to put objects into their mouths, climb up furniture and pull things down from tables or shelves. This means that if you need to leave a room, you must take them with you, unless someone else is free to supervise.

Good supervision is a balance between allowing children to have fun and making sure that they are not doing anything dangerous. As children become older, they are more able to understand the need for rules and to be aware of dangers. You can explain to them why, for example, they must wait for their turn on the slide. Children are also influenced by the way adults act. This means that you must be a good role model – children need to see adults tidy up, use safety equipment and generally not take risks.

You can turn safety issues into learning opportunities for children by explaining why certain equipment is dangerous, for example knives have sharp blades, matches can cause fires. Other ways to make children more aware of safety include inviting fire officers to the early years setting or visiting an ambulance station.

⇧ **Toddlers need to be supervised very carefully to prevent them touching things that could be harmful**

Think about it

A group of children is having a lot of fun jumping on and off a low wall. One child starts to push the others off as part of the game.

1. What would you do and say to prevent this game from becoming dangerous?
2. How could you help the children to carry on enjoying jumping while not risking any accidents?

Providing a safe environment

When parents leave their children in your care, they need to feel that you have the skills and knowledge which will mean that their children will be happy and safe with you. A good starting point is to look at how to create a positive and safe environment for children.

In early years settings where there are many children, it is important for all the adults to keep an eye on what the children are doing. This means that even when you are working with only one or two children, you should still be aware of the other children – they may need your support or may be doing something that could cause an accident, and you will need to intervene. Some of the common signs to watch out for are described below.

→ *Loud, angry voices* – may indicate that a child is about to hit another or that an object is about to be thrown.
→ *Squeals of laughter* – may be a sign that a game is getting out of hand and that the children are seeing the possible dangers, for example jumping off equipment or daring others to do something.

→ *Silence* – could indicate that a child has found something that is very interesting for them such as a container of bleach.

How layouts can affect safety

Layouts also have a great impact on safety. A good layout means that children have space to move about safely and that toys and equipment can easily be tidied away. Most large settings separate activities into different areas for these reasons. You need to make sure that floor areas are kept tidy, clean and dry to avoid accidents, for example tripping up or slipping over. Wherever you work, you must always make sure that access points such as front doors and fire exits are kept clear in case of fire or other emergencies. In many settings certain areas, such as kitchens, are kept out of bounds by using safety gates.

Reporting hazards

There may be times when hazards need reporting to a supervisor or the person responsible for health and safety in your workplace. Where children are being cared for in their homes, it will be the parent or carer who needs to be informed. Information about dangers and hazards must be passed on promptly. Where there is an immediate danger, children should be kept away from a piece of equipment or a certain area until it is safe.

Think about it

Using a computer, design a form that could be used in an early years setting to report potential hazards. Your form should contain spaces for the following information to be entered:
→ Date
→ Area or piece of equipment
→ Potential hazard
→ Action taken so far
→ Signature of staff member.

Outdoor areas

Outdoor areas also need to be checked for safety, as described in the chart below.

⚖ **Risk assessment of outdoor areas – key questions**

Outdoor element	Questions to consider
Plants and animals	• Are any plants poisonous? • Is there a risk of any animal harming children, e.g. dogs not on leads, guinea pigs or rabbits in cages where children can put their fingers? • Is there any dog or cat faeces (poo/mess) around? (Children can pick up a disease through being in contact with dog and cat faeces.)
Access and fences	• Can children wander off? • Can strangers come into contact with children?

Outdoor element	Questions to consider
Hidden dangers	• Is there a risk of drowning because of a water hazard, e.g. pond, stream, paddling pool? • Are there any litter bins that children could reach? • Do litter bins have lids on them? • Are there any tools or items, e.g. clothes lines, that could cause accidents? • Are there any steep steps that could be unsafe for toddlers? • Is play equipment safe and clean?

Find out!

Ask your supervisor if you can check an outdoor area at your placement for safety.

1. Write down how you did this.
2. Did you spot any potential hazards?
3. How were these hazards managed?

Back to the real world

You should now know about how to plan and support environments of children from birth to age 5 years.

1. Explain why it is important to make sure that the environment is healthy, hygienic and safe for children.

2. Describe some of the ways in which hygiene is maintained.

3. Describe some of the factors involved in planning a layout.

4. How might you display children's work?

Section 2

How to contribute to working with parents as part of a team

In the real world

You are on placement. One of the parents comes to you and asks about the progress of their child. You know that working with parents is really important but are not really sure what you should say.

By the end of this section you will understand your role when working as a learner with parents and know how you might work when you are qualified.

The importance and role of parents in children's lives

Even though they might not realise it, most parents are great teachers. Through being with their parents, children learn about their own personal history and their place within the family. They learn about the culture and beliefs of their parents, which gives them a sense of belonging and stays with them for their lives.

Every family has its own traditions that are passed on to the children and make each family different and special. In some families, the children learn a language from their parents that is different from the one in their school or nursery. Families have their own ways of celebrating festivals and most families even have their own jokes. Skills and hobbies are learned from being with parents. For example, children whose parents are musical will be encouraged to make music and parents who keep animals often give their children pets to care for.

The skills, attitudes and beliefs that parents pass on to their children are just as important as those learned in educational settings and in order to work in partnership with parents, you will need to understand and respect this. It is also easy for early years practitioners to forget that by the time children come to be cared for, they have often learned many skills from their parents, for example they may know their colours and how to dress themselves.

Think about it

1. Does your family have its own jokes?
2. Do you remember learning skills or a hobby with a parent or carer?

Think about it

Sam is 3 years old and is just about to start playgroup. He has been cared for at home by his parents. He is a bright, happy child who is quite independent and confident.

→ Assuming that Sam's development is right for his age, make a list of the skills that Sam will already have learned from being brought up by his parents. For example, he will have learned to feed himself. (You may like to do this task in pairs.)

⇧ **Parents' role as the first educators of their children is critical to their children's development**

Your role in promoting and maintaining relationships with families

Every parent has different needs and each parent will relate to you differently. Parents who are leaving their children for the first time are likely to need reassurance, while parents who have used the early years setting over many years are likely to enjoy talking to their friends. Relating to parents is an important skill, as relationships need to be built up. When early years settings have good relationships with parents, difficult subjects can be brought up more easily, for example if parents are not collecting children on time.

Understanding the boundaries of passing on information

In order to relate well to parents it is important for early years practitioners to understand their exact role where parents are concerned. The key point when working in an early years setting is always to ask if you are unsure.

Confidentiality

For any good relationship to work there needs to be some trust. To trust somebody is to expect them to keep things they have seen or been told confidential. Learning how much you are allowed to repeat, and who to repeat it to, is an important part of being a professional. As an early years practitioner you will learn a lot about children's home life, their achievements, parents or carers, and so on. This information will be shared with you because you are expected to keep it confidential, discussing it only with people who are permitted to know. Years of work in building good parent relationships can be put at risk if, through thoughtlessness or temptation, an early years practitioner repeats information to inappropriate people.

As confidentiality is a complex yet important area, most early years settings have a confidentiality policy, and in some cases it may be part of your written employment contract or job description.

Being friendly is not the same as being friends

However often you see a parent, you must not confuse being friendly with being friends – you work with parents in the interests of their children. To do this you will need to show respect for parents and aim to provide them with as much support as possible. Remember – the relationship between the early years practitioner and parents is a professional one.

There may be times when you already know a parent of a child who attends the early years setting where you work. You must bear in mind that while you are in the workplace, you need to treat all the parents with equal respect and fairness. This professional approach avoids possible comments about favouritism from other staff or parents.

Finding the right balance can be difficult for nannies who live with the parents of the children they care for, because when they are 'off duty' they are sharing the family home.

Providing information for parents

How much information you should receive or give out will depend on your position in the workplace. In most early years settings there is a line of management (see chart on page 269). This means that there are rules in place to make sure that the confidentiality of either the parents or the early years setting is not broken.

The chart below outlines the roles of different people who work in early years settings. If you are unsure about your role, you should ask advice from your supervisor or tutor.

✋ The lines of reporting

Job	Role and lines of reporting
Learner	Learners are not members of staff and they must not give this impression to parents. If parents ask them for information, they must refer them to a staff member. They need to be friendly, yet understand the early years setting's code of confidentiality. They need to work under the direction of their supervisor.
New member of staff	New members of staff need to form relationships with existing parents. They need to appear confident and friendly. New members of staff need to learn quickly about the general routine of the day and to work under the direction of senior members of staff. At times, they may need to refer to other members of staff to check that the information they are giving is correct or appropriate. They must know when to refer parents to children's key workers or their supervisors, for example if parents wish to find out more about their child's progress.
Key worker	Key workers need to form close relationships with the children they are responsible for, and with their parents. They must make sure they are keeping up-to-date records and can show a good knowledge of the children when discussing them with parents. The information they keep about the children is confidential and is likely to be discussed only with parents and their manager. They need to work closely with their manager/supervisor.
Supervisor/ manager	The supervisor or manager of the early years setting needs to know all the children and their parents or carers well. Because they are responsible for all that happens in the early years setting, they need to be kept up to date with any incidents that happen during the day. This means they can talk about them with knowledge to parents if necessary, e.g. if a child is feeling unwell or has fallen over. They will also have access to all information available about the children, including emergency contact numbers.

In addition to understanding your role and who you should report to, it is important to remember at all times the importance of confidentiality. If you are ever unsure of what you can or cannot report or say, you should always ask your line manager. This is essential, as breaking confidentiality might result in you losing your post.

Think about it

Think of a time when you were approached by parents in your workplace placement and you referred them to a member of staff.

1. Write about how you addressed them and made them feel valued.
2. Why did you decide that they should be referred to a member of staff?

Make sure that when you write about this, you do not breach any confidential information.

The lines of reporting and recording to management

When you are working in a setting, there will be times when you will need to pass on information to other members of staff or the management team. In order to avoid information going astray or time being wasted, there is usually a system of reporting and recording information. As a learner, your placement supervisor is usually the first person to whom you should report. This means that if you spot a piece of equipment that is unsafe or notice something about a child, you should tell your placement supervisor. They in turn will either deal with the problem or, if it is beyond their responsibility, will pass on the information to their line manager.

While some information might be reported, occasionally you might need to write down and record information. You should be particularly careful about what you write, and think about your spelling, punctuation and grammar. If you find writing a difficult skill, do not be afraid to tell your placement supervisor or tutor so they can check your writing. Ideally, as you will need these skills for your future career, you should consider asking your tutor for extra support.

The importance of shared care between the setting, home and family

It is not many years since parents used to wait for their children by the school gates – they were not seen in the early years settings unless it was parents' evening or they had made an appointment. It is different today as it is now known that where parents and settings work together, children are more likely to fulfil their potential. In schools, for example, where children read both at home and at school, they make fast progress. This is why most schools have reading books that children can take home.

There are other benefits for children of shared care between the setting, home and family. For example, they are likely to feel more secure and will settle quicker. Information that might affect the way early years settings need to work with children is more likely to be shared with practitioners by parents if they feel comfortable with them. The term 'parents as partners' is therefore much used in the early years sector.

Open door policy

Most early years settings have an **open door policy** which means that parents are encouraged to come in at any time, with or without an appointment, and are made to feel welcome. The open door policy also means that parents and childcare practitioners can talk together, share information and build a strong relationship without waiting for the next parents' evening. They can talk informally about children's progress, mention any concerns they might have, look at their children's work and feel involved in the early years setting. This positive attitude towards

Jargon buster

Open door policy Where parents can come into the setting without an appointment parents helps children to feel more settled and secure. They can sense that all the people who care for them are working together and this helps them to talk more easily about what they have been doing.

The principles of effective communication when working with families and their children

There are some key points when it comes to effective communication with parents, as the spider diagram below shows.

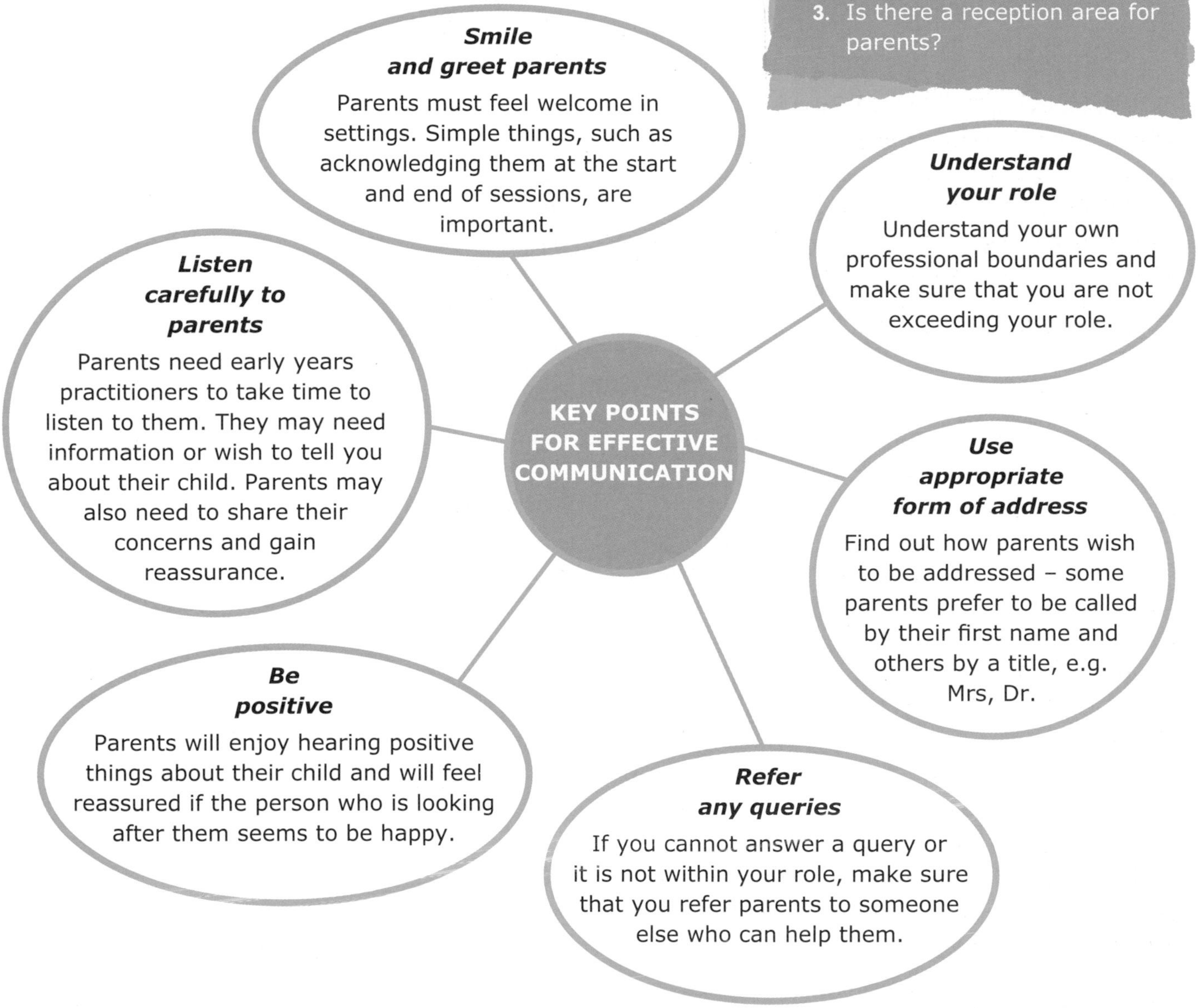

Find out!

1. Find out if your workplace or placement has an open door policy.
2. Do parents or carers often come into the early years setting?
3. Is there a reception area for parents?

KEY POINTS FOR EFFECTIVE COMMUNICATION

Smile and greet parents
Parents must feel welcome in settings. Simple things, such as acknowledging them at the start and end of sessions, are important.

Understand your role
Understand your own professional boundaries and make sure that you are not exceeding your role.

Listen carefully to parents
Parents need early years practitioners to take time to listen to them. They may need information or wish to tell you about their child. Parents may also need to share their concerns and gain reassurance.

Use appropriate form of address
Find out how parents wish to be addressed – some parents prefer to be called by their first name and others by a title, e.g. Mrs, Dr.

Be positive
Parents will enjoy hearing positive things about their child and will feel reassured if the person who is looking after them seems to be happy.

Refer any queries
If you cannot answer a query or it is not within your role, make sure that you refer parents to someone else who can help them.

For further information about ways of communicating with parents, see Unit 11 pages 410–11.

The role of the key worker

As you saw in Unit 2 (pages 98–105), a key worker is someone who takes
responsibility for the emotional well-being of a child and develops a special relationship with them. While the primary focus is towards the child, a key worker should also develop a good relationship with parents

U7
2

so that they can work well together. This benefits the child as it helps them to feel more secure and so helps them to settle in.

In addition to working with both the child and parents, the key worker will also carry out observations on the child. These observations should be used not only to help plan activities but also to check that the child is making good developmental progress. The key worker shares the information from observations with the parent and also encourages the parent to add to them. This is important as children often do things at home that they might not do in the setting. As well as sharing observations, key workers should also talk to parents about their child's interests and what the child has been doing during the session. Parents not only enjoy hearing about their child, but they need this information as well, for example a child who usually has a nap in the afternoon but has not had one is likely to be much more tired when he gets home.

While the key worker should share information about what the child has been doing in the setting, it is helpful if parents tell the key worker about what the child has been doing at home. This is only likely to happen if the parent feels at ease with their child's key worker, which is why it is important for key workers to have good communication skills. A child who is excited because her grandmother is coming to stay may want to talk about it to the key worker. Information might be of a more personal nature, too. A parent who has recently split up from their partner may share this with the key worker as this might affect the child's behaviour and mood.

Diverse family backgrounds and the importance of valuing different lifestyles

In the same way that each family is different, all parents have different ways of managing their children. Looking after children and providing them with love and care is a demanding task and parents try hard to do their best for their children. All parents have their own style of parenting which is influenced partly by their own childhood and partly by any pressures they are facing. Some parents are authoritarian in style – tending to limit and control their children – while others are permissive – preferring to allow children more freedom of expression. There are advantages and disadvantages in both approaches and, in the main, most parents fall somewhere in the middle.

The emotional bond between parent and child is often powerful, making the relationship intense. Parents can feel anger but also great love towards their children. The strong emotions that parents feel make it hard for them to be perfect all the time. Studies show that they do not need to be perfect for their children to flourish. This is the idea behind 'good enough' parenting – although most parents are not perfect, they are still the best people for children to be with.

Different types of family structure and arrangement

The way in which people live together as families has changed over the past 50 years, so you should not assume that children are living with a mother and father who are married. Some children may live in lone-parent households, while some children may grow up in communities where care is shared. There may be children who spend three days a week with one parent and four days with the other. Some children may live with family members other than parents, such as grandparents, aunts and uncles, who all help to care for them. The following chart shows some of the ways in which children may be brought up. Understanding and respecting that there are different ways of looking after children will help you to meet the needs of children and their families.

⇨ **It is important not to assume that children are living with a mother and father who are married**

Type of family	Living arrangement
Nuclear family	Mother and father, living together with their children, but separately from other family members. They may be married or cohabiting.
Extended family	Family members who live together and share the care of children.
Lone-parent family	A single parent taking care of children either through choice or other reasons, for example the death of a partner, divorce or separation.
Homosexual family	A homosexual couple taking care of children – could be gay or lesbian.
Nomadic family	Parents who do not have a permanent home and travel from place to place with their children – e.g. gypsies and travellers.
Reconstituted	Children who live with one natural parent and a step-parent. Families may also include step- and half-sisters and -brothers.
Adoptive families	Children may live with adopted or foster parents.
Communal families	Children may live with their parents in communes where other members are also involved in their care.

Think about it

Jason lives with his father for two weeks of the month and with his mother for the other two weeks. His mother has a new partner who has two children of a similar age. Jason's father has married again and so he also has a stepmother.

You are asked to make Mother's Day cards with a group of children that includes Jason. You think that it is likely that he will see both his mother and stepmother on this day.

1. Should Jason be told to make more than one card?
2. How would you handle this situation?
3. Why is it important that early years practitioners do not assume that children are living with both parents?

(You may like to do this activity in pairs.)

Parents who do not share the values of the early years setting

Every parent has his or her own set of values in terms of belief, culture and expectations of children. Some − or all − of these values may be different from the values of the early years setting and you need to appreciate that there are instances when parents have not chosen the child care arrangements, for example if there is a child protection order that requires parents to take children to a family centre or if no place is available at the parent's first choice of school. Some parents may not feel comfortable in certain educational settings because their own experience of these settings was not pleasant.

Even parents who broadly support the early years setting may not always share all of the values. They may not consider all the work that you do is important, for example making children aware of different religions or your approach to managing children's behaviour. Some parents may not understand the value of play and would prefer to see more structured activities. Early years settings can use workshops and parents' evenings to explain their approach; but remember that parents are entitled to have their own viewpoint and that good relationships are built on respect.

Meeting the needs of parents in a variety of settings

In Unit 11 you will look at ways in which some early years settings have a specialist role in supporting parents. You may therefore find it helpful to read Unit 11 alongside this one.

Parents or carers come to early years practitioners with a range of needs. Understanding parents' needs is partly the role of the manager in the setting, but individually it is also the role of the key worker. Below are some common needs of parents.

Combining work and parenthood

In many early years settings, the main need is for quality child care and education as today many people combine parenthood with working. For those parents or carers, it is essential that the setting is reliable and flexible. They need you to understand that sometimes they may be in a rush or they may forget things. Early years settings may therefore help parents by, for example, having a flexible approach to session times. Parents who work can sometimes feel guilty or afraid that they might miss out on their child's development. You can help these parents by making sure that you provide information about what their child has been doing. As parents may be short of time, this is often best done in writing.

Gaining information

Some parents gain support by using early years settings, for example settings may provide information for parents about different aspects of child development and parenting. Parents may also gain information about health, finance and employment as these services are run alongside childcare.

Gaining reassurance and confidence

A few parents may lack confidence and may have difficulties in adapting to their role as parents. Some early years settings encourage parents to be involved and through this work, parents can gain in confidence and skills. Some parents also need support in basic skills such as reading, writing or maths. Many early years settings help parents to feel more confident in gaining support and may even run learning groups within the setting.

Back to the real world

You should now know that learners will have a different role when working with parents to other members of staff.

1. Explain how you might handle a situation as a learner when a parent wants information about their child's progress.
2. Describe the role and importance of the key worker system.
3. Explain the importance of confidentiality and understanding professional boundaries.

Section 3

How to recognise the importance of working with other professionals

In the real world

You are on placement at a school and are surprised to find out that not just teachers seem to work at the school. You notice that the school has regular visits from a school nurse, a welfare officer and a liaison officer working for the police. The teacher who is acting as your placement supervisor tells you that the school works closely with other services as well.

By the end of this section you will understand why services are now working together and the importance of this for children and their families.

The key principles of legal frameworks to support working with children and children's welfare

There are some key principles behind the legislation that is in place to protect children in the United Kingdom, including that:

→ children's welfare should always be put first when decisions are being made that will affect them

→ professionals should work closely with parents and aim to support the family unit

→ professionals working with children should work closely together and share information so that children's needs can be properly met.

The Laming inquiry

In 2000 an 8-year-old girl called Victoria Climbié was killed by her primary carer. Sadly, this was not the first time that a child had died in circumstances that could have been prevented if professionals had been properly working together. As a result of her death, an enquiry was launched. This enquiry was known as the Laming inquiry and it looked at why Victoria died and how her death might have been prevented.

Every Child Matters

Many of the proposals of the inquiry were pulled together into a programme called Every Child Matters, which has been introduced into England. A key feature of Every Child Matters is the way in which professionals and services such as health and education are meant to work closely together. Every Child Matters looks at five areas that are important in children's lives. These five areas are often referred to as outcomes. All professionals working with children and their families are meant to work together to make sure that these five outcomes are met for all children:

1. Be healthy
2. Stay safe
3. Enjoy and achieve through learning
4. Make a positive contribution to society
5. Achieve economic well-being.

The Children Act 2004

In England, to make sure that Every Child Matters would work well, a new Children's Act has been passed. The 2004 Children's Act puts new duties on local authorities to ensure that all the different services that work with children and their families work more efficiently together.

Common Assessment Framework

As part of Every Child Matters, a way of looking at families' needs was drawn up. This is called the Common Assessment Framework, although you might sometimes hear professionals refer to it as 'CAF'.

Find out!

You can find out more about the Laming inquiry at the following website: www.victoria-climbie-inquiry.org.uk

Find out!

Visit the government website www.everychildmatters.gov.uk to find out more about the Every Child Matters programme, including the five outcomes and the Common Assessment Framework.

Find out!

1. Find out in what situations your placement setting uses the Common Assessment Framework.
2. Ask your placement supervisor how the Every Child Matters programme has affected the setting's work with children and their families.

The role of different professionals who may work with children and their families in a multi-agency approach

There are a number of different professionals who work with children and their families. Sometimes they may be based in the same centre as a nursery or school, although practice varies from area to area. Below is a list of some of the professionals that may be working to support children and families.

SENCO (Special Educational Needs Coordinator)

This person is responsible for coordinating the special needs policies in a setting and advising staff.

Educational psychologist

Educational psychologists consider how children learn, so are used to helping to identify learning difficulties. They visit schools and settings regularly and work alongside parents and professionals in the setting.

Physiotherapist

A physiotherapist helps to identify a child's main physical problems while working alongside other professionals and parents.

Speech and language therapist

Speech and language therapists work with children who have some difficulties with their language.

Community paediatrician

Paediatricians are mainly based in hospitals and clinics. They have specialised training in children's medicine and children are referred to them via their family doctor for diagnosis. They make regular assessments of children's progress and medical needs. They are able to refer children to other health services such as speech and language therapy and dieticians.

⇧ **Speech therapists work with children who have difficulties with their language**

Community nurse

In some areas, community nurses visit schools and settings to help provide advice and support. Integrating health and education is a major focus of the Every Child Matters programme, so some early years centres will have a community nurse based at the centre.

Family doctor (general practitioner)

The family doctor, or GP, has general training in medicine. GPs form part of the community health team and act as a base for a child's ongoing medical treatment and notes.

Child psychiatrist

Children who are showing depression or emotional difficulties may be referred to a child psychiatrist. A child psychiatrist has been trained as a doctor specialising in mental health and is able to prescribe medication as well as being able to consider the underlying issues behind a child's emotional state.

Child psychotherapist

A child psychotherapist will work with children who are showing emotional distress by talking through their experiences with them and helping the child to explore these.

Child psychologist

A child psychologist looks at a child's development and learning in a similar way to an educational psychologist. The main difference between their roles is that a child psychologist may support children in a range of different settings rather than just in the educational context.

Play therapist

A play therapist helps children to explore trauma or experiences through the medium of play.

Educational welfare officer/education social worker

The main function of these professionals is to liaise between home and families in cases where school attendance is infrequent. (It is an offence for children over 5 years old not to be in some sort of full-time educational provision.)

Special needs support teacher

These teachers travel between schools or visit children in their home or in pre-school settings. They are able to help a wide range of children and are often seen as useful sources of support and guidance.

Classroom assistant/learning support assistant

There are many variations on the title used for classroom assistants. Their main purpose is to support an individual child or group of children within a classroom under the direction of the classroom teacher.

Social worker

The majority of social workers are employed by the local authority, although some are employed by voluntary organisations. They are generally deployed in teams according to specialist areas, for example social workers may be involved in caring for older clients, adoption or fostering work. Social workers can provide guidance and advice as well as practical support for families.

Respite carers

Respite carers look after children for short periods of time so that their parents can have some time out.

Careers and benefits advisors

Some settings have career and benefits advisors as part of the team. They can help parents find employment and training courses and give them advice about claiming benefits.

Find out!

Find out what links your placement setting has with other agencies and professionals.

The protection of all children and the role of multi-agency work

The death of Victoria Climbié in England was not the first death of a child that could have been avoided. Over the past few years there have been other cases where children have died. When, afterwards, professionals were questioned about how these deaths occurred, it was discovered that the various people involved with the children and their families had different pieces of information that had rarely been shared and acted upon. It was as if each person involved with the child and the family had a different piece of a jigsaw puzzle but no one took responsibility for putting all the pieces together and realising that the child was in danger.

The focus today of child protection work is to ensure that information is passed on promptly to the right people. For you as a learner, this means that you must know what you should do if you have any concerns about a child. It also means that once you are qualified you must always follow the correct lines of reporting and recording. For more information about child protection and signs of child abuse, you should also read Unit 3 (see pages 122–6).

Lines of reporting and recording

In order to work effectively together, each organisation should have a clear strategy. You will need to need to learn about the lines of reporting and recording for any setting that you work in. You will need to find out who you would talk to if you had a concern about a child and also what you should do if you were asked for information about a child.

For professionals to work together well, it is important that everyone understands their role and the scope of their responsibility. This means you will need to know what other professionals do and what you need to do to support the child alongside them. It is also important that if you work alongside other professionals in caring for children, you are able to communicate well.

Case study

The importance of knowing your role

The staff at Tiny Tots nursery are supporting a family who have significant needs. Sandra is the key worker for one of the children in the family. She knows that as part of her role, she needs to talk to the child's parents and to gain and share information with them. She also knows that the observations which she carries out as part of her record keeping are an important source of information for other professionals. She has been told that if she has significant concerns about the child or the parents' ability to cope that she needs to report these concerns immediately to her manager. Her manager would then report these concerns to the person who is taking overall responsibility for helping this family. A meeting would then be called which would bring together everyone working with the family so that an action plan can be drawn up.

1. Why is it important that Sandra knows what she should do?
2. Explain why everyone working with the family must share information.
3. Why do children and their families benefit when different agencies work closely together?

Back to the real world

You should now have learned that multi-agency working is considered to be important in promoting the welfare of children. If you are working in England, you should also have learned about the Every Child Matters programme.

1. Can you now give some examples of other professionals that a setting may work closely with?
2. Can you describe the importance of professionals working together?

How to meet the diverse needs of babies and young children

In the real world

You have just joined a new placement. You are hoping to do an activity with a group of 4-year-olds. You explain to your placement supervisor that the aim of this activity is to make some Father's Day cards. You were quite excited about this idea, but your supervisor does not look so enthusiastic. She asks whether you studied anti-bias and discriminatory practice in your course.

By the end of this section you will understand the importance of thinking about children's diverse needs when planning activities. You should also be aware of the causes and effects of discrimination.

The rights of children and their families

It is an accepted view in society and in the early years sector that every child is special and should be given opportunities to fulfil his or her potential. This is the basis of anti-discriminatory practice in settings and is the focus of many laws today. While some laws look at the rights of children, others focus on the rights of adults, including those relating to children's families. There are two significant pieces of legislation that protect children and their families without discrimination:

1. The Human Rights Act 2000
2. The United Nations Convention on the Rights of the Child.

Human Rights Act 2000

The Human Rights Act came into force in October 2000 and has already had a huge impact on current legislation in this country. It requires courts and tribunals to make judgements using certain articles of the European Convention on Human Rights as a starting point. This Act was not designed specifically to protect children, but they are given the same rights as adults. This means that they have a right to dignity, respect and fairness in the way in which they are treated. The Human Rights Act also means that parents of children are protected.

United Nations Convention on the Rights of the Child (UNCRC)

In addition to the Human Rights Act, the UK is a signatory to the United Nations Convention on the Rights of the Child (UNCRC). The UNCRC was drawn up in 1989 and gives children and young people under the age of 18 years their own special rights. There are five main strands to the Convention which:

1. reinforces the importance of fundamental human dignity
2. highlights and defends the family's role in children's lives
3. seeks respect for children
4. endorses the principle of non-discrimination
5. establishes clear obligations for member countries to ensure that their legal framework is in line with the provisions of the Convention.

The UNCRC is divided into articles. In the table below are some of the key articles that might affect your practice with children and young people.

⚓ **Key articles from the UNCRC that affect working practice with children and young people**

Article 2	The right to be protected from all forms of **discrimination**.
Article 3	The best interests of the child to be the primary consideration in all actions concerning children.

Jargon buster

Discrimination When a person is treated differently because of their age, gender, ethnic background, culture or disability

Find out!

You can find out more about the United Nations Convention on the Rights of the Child via the following websites:

→ www.everychildmatters.gov. uk/uncrc/
→ www.unicef.org.uk/tz/rights/ convention.asp

Article 12	A child's rights to express his or her views freely. A child's view to be given due weight in keeping with the child's age or maturity.
Article 13	A child's right to freedom of expression and exchange of information regardless of frontiers.
Article 28	A child's right to education with a view to achieving this right progressively on the basis of equal opportunities.

Children Act 1989

As a result of adopting the UNCRC, new legislation was required. The 1989 Children Act, which came into affect in 1991 in England and Wales and in 1996 in Northern Ireland, attempted to bring together various pieces of legislation. It is wide-ranging and covers child protection and parental responsibility as well as the inspection of childcare settings. The 1989 Children Act is especially well-known for its stance that children's welfare is of paramount importance. The Act also made it clear that children's and young people's views had to be taken into consideration when decisions about their future were being made.

In Scotland, UNCRC legislation was brought in under the 1995 Children (Scotland) Act. This Act gave children protection from discrimination as well as ensuring that children's welfare was seen of prime importance and their views listened to.

The causes and effects of discrimination in a multi-cultural society

Discrimination is about treating groups of people unfairly. The reasons behind discrimination are complex. A good starting point in looking at the causes and effects of discrimination is to understand the role of values and attitudes.

Attitudes and values

A person is not born with a set of values and attitudes, but starts to develop them when a child. At first, a person's values come mainly from their parents. As you get older, you begin to develop your own values. Values and attitudes affect the choices people make in their lives. For example, you often choose friends who have similar values to your own and you may prefer to work among people who share your values. As people tend to get to know people 'like them', assumptions start to be made about people who are 'different'. These assumptions are known as **stereotypes**.

As an early years practitioner, it is important to consider your attitudes towards some of the issues relating to the care of children. If you have strong feelings about some issues, this could change the way you react to others.

Jargon buster

Stereotype A 'label' for a person or group of people based on assumptions made about them

Think about it

Although you may be unaware of your values and attitudes, they can be seen by other people. For example, if you are not comfortable with some people – perhaps because you disagree with what they are saying – your body language and facial expressions may show this. You might cross your arms, look away or not smile as much as you usually do. These are all signals that you do not share the same values and people will pick up these signals. It will then be difficult to establish a good relationship with them as they will sense that you feel uncomfortable.

Nobody likes the feeling of being judged or not accepted. As an early years practitioner, you must learn to make sure that you send out positive signals. By doing this you can ensure that children and their parents feel welcome and comfortable, regardless of who they are and the values and attitudes they hold. If children and parents do not feel that early years practitioners accept them as they are, there will be tensions in the relationships between them.

Children can sense values and attitudes

Children can quickly pick up the signs given out and they can sense if there is tension between adults. This means that you must ensure that your own values do not stop you from giving your best to all children and their parents. Consider the following example of a family that is not being valued.

Case study

The importance of valuing families

Kerry comes from a travelling family. The family have been in town for two weeks and Kerry is going to nursery. Staff at the nursery have not yet had a proper conversation with her parents as they know that they will not be staying for long in the area. When Kerry starts talking about her caravan, the staff do not really listen. They think that children should not be moved around by their parents all the time.

1. Why do the staff at the nursery treat Kerry's parents differently?
2. How might this affect Kerry?

Stereotypes

As you tend to work alongside and be friends with people who have similar attitudes and values to your own, you do not always learn about others. Sometimes your ideas of what other people are like are based on stereotypes. A stereotype is a fixed image of a group of people. The stereotype of a French man may be someone wearing a beret and smelling of garlic.

Stereotypes are not helpful. They can make people think that they know what a group of people – for example football supporters, blondes or teachers – are like, and this may change their attitude towards someone who belongs to a stereotyped group. Stereotypes are often learned indirectly, for example through watching the television or reading newspapers and magazines. When you meet someone from a stereotyped group, you often realise that the images are not accurate. This is why it is important to meet and get to know people before making judgements about them.

⇩ **It is important to meet and get to know people before making judgements about them**

Case study

Mrs Smith is a childminder and is going to look after a little Asian girl. She is surprised to see that the girl's mother is wearing a pair of jeans and that she speaks English. She says afterwards to her friend, 'You would never know that she was Asian, she looked so normal.'

1. What did she mean by 'normal'?
2. What stereotype image did Mrs Smith have of this child's mother?
3. If you were the child's mother and had overheard this remark, how might you feel?

Prejudice and discrimination

In an ideal society, there would be no stereotypes and people would get to know each other before making up their minds about an individual. Having a bad opinion of someone before getting to know them is called **prejudice**. People have all sorts of prejudices; for example, some people don't like men with beards, others don't like teachers! Prejudice becomes more serious when it turns into action such as refusing to talk to someone with a beard. This is called discrimination. The diagram below shows how prejudice can lead to discrimination.

At present in the UK, groups of people are being unfairly treated because of other people's prejudices. Discrimination is often based on:

→ age
→ race
→ gender
→ sexual orientation
→ health and social class.

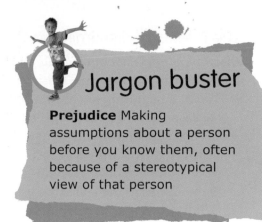

Jargon buster

Prejudice Making assumptions about a person before you know them, often because of a stereotypical view of that person

Did you know?

The charity Age Concern carried out research into ageism (prejudice and discrimination about age and ageing) in the UK in 2005. Its findings included:

→ Twenty-nine per cent of the population reported suffering age discrimination.
→ One-third of respondents said they viewed people over 70 years old as incompetent and incapable.

(Source: www.ageconcern.org.uk)

Find out!

Visit the website of the Commission for Equality and Human Rights (www.cehr.org.uk) that has been set up to promote equality and challenge many types of discrimination.

⇦ **Every day in the UK, older people face prejudice and discrimination simply because of their age**

U7

4

287

The effects of discrimination

Discrimination is not only unfair for the individual, it is also damaging for society for the following reasons:

→ The best people do not always do the jobs they are capable of because talented people can go unrecognised.

→ Groups of people may feel that they are not part of the society in which they live. They may feel that nobody who understands their value is in power. For example, there are not many black judges or many Asians in the police force.

→ Children can also be discriminated against. This is particularly unfair as they need to feel valued in order to fulfil their potential and eventually take their place in society.

→ In some communities a pattern of low achievement is formed because children do not have good role models to follow. For example, black children may not see black teachers or doctors. Because of this, they may start to believe that black people cannot do these types of professions.

Children and discrimination

The children you care for will be the next generation of adults, and by teaching them to value and respect each other you may be able to make society fairer. There are many reasons why some children may not feel valued.

Ethnicity and culture
Children may be made to feel awkward because they wear different clothing or speak other languages.

Disability
Children in wheelchairs may not be able to get into some public places.

REASONS WHY CHILDREN MAY FEEL UNDERVALUED

Poverty
Children may miss out on classes, such as ballet, piano or swimming, because their parents cannot afford to pay for them.

Gender
Children may be treated in different ways because of their gender, e.g. girls may be seen as being poor at science.

Size
Other children may make fun of fat, thin or small children.

Equality of opportunity

Equality of opportunity means making sure that children in your care are seen as being individual and special. This does not mean treating all children the same. Some children may need more adult help or special equipment to carry out an activity. Equality of opportunity means making sure that children are equally valued and are given the same opportunities to fulfil their potential.

Think about it

Edward is 4 years old and has a visual impairment. For this reason he is given more adult support during sessions, for example he often sits near an adult at story time and the adult often stays alongside him when he plays outside. One of the other parents feels that this is unfair to the other children as they do not receive the same treatment. He has come to complain about this.

In pairs, act out a role play of the conversation between the father and the early years practitioner. The practitioner will need to:

1. Explain why Edward needs more adult help.
2. Explain why it is not possible for every child to get this amount of extra care.

Strategies to promote and meet the needs of individual children and their families

A key strategy in meeting children and their families is to think about how welcome you can make them feel. When you go anywhere for the first time, you can pick up a feeling about the place and the people – it is as if there are hidden messages. Children and their families need to feel that they are not just accepted, but actively welcomed and seen as part of the community.

Hidden messages are signals that are often negative and can put off children and their families from participating. An example of this might be the types of signs that are displayed on a noticeboard. Signs that are positive such as 'Welcome' or 'Thank you for your help' are positive, but ones such as 'Don't bring pushchairs inside' may send out a different signal especially if the noticeboard is full of other 'Don'ts'. Hidden messages can also be more subtle. Families who use a different home language to that of the setting may not feel included if there is no acknowledgement of their language. This might send out a signal that their language is not valued.

Being aware of children's and families' needs

A key way in which you can provide a supportive and participative environment is to be good at communicating with parents and meeting their needs and those of their children. It requires staff to adopt a 'can do' approach. This means actively looking for ways of removing possible barriers, for example a parent who needs to drop off their child ten minutes after the session time has started or a child who may need additional support in order to access the sand tray.

Providing information

Some families may find it hard to access information that will make a difference. A family new to an area may not be aware of free story sessions at the local library, while a family who are struggling financially may not be aware of all the benefits they can claim. This means that many early years settings now provide booklets or leaflets, or tell parents information that they think will help them.

The identification of, and how to support children with, additional needs

Many children at some time in their lives will have some additional needs. These needs may be temporary or they may be permanent. The term **additional needs** is a wide-ranging one. It can cover children who need a little more emotional support, as they may, for example, be coping with the separation of their parents, as well as children who may have learning difficulties.

Identifying children with needs

Ways to recognise a child with additional needs are:

➜ *Observation* – Through observing children you may notice a developmental delay or behaviour that is not typical of the child or stage of development.
➜ *Parents* – Parents are often the first people to provide early years practitioners with information about their child's needs. They may have concerns about their child's development or they may have background information about what is happening in their child's life.
➜ *Behaviour* – When a child has an unmet need, it is generally clear from their behaviour. Most unwanted behaviour is a response to an unmet need. For example, a child may show aggressive behaviour because they want more adult attention or because they are frustrated.

Supporting children with additional needs

The way that you support children with additional needs will depend on what their needs are. Some children may need extra time and attention, while others may require specialist activities or equipment. When supporting children with additional needs, it is essential not to stereotype or make assumptions about what they need, but to listen to parents or carers, other professionals and even to the children themselves. This is because children are individual and will have different interests, strengths and ways of coping. Hence, support tends to be of a very individual nature, even when children may appear to have similar needs, as the case study below shows.

Case study

Supporting children's additional needs

Mehmet and Sara are 7 years old and attend the after-school club. They both have asthma.

Mehmet enjoys playing football, and occasionally needs his inhaler if he overexerts himself and feels breathless. His key worker makes sure that Mehmet knows where the inhaler is and checks from time to time that he is not feeling breathless. Mehmet is fairly relaxed about using the inhaler in front of his friends and talks to them about why he needs it.

Sara also needs to have access to an inhaler, but it is much harder to predict when she will need it. When she does, it is important to reassure her and to take her to a quiet place away from others. Her key worker knows this and is able to keep her calm.

1. Explain how the after-school club supports these children.
2. Why do these children have different needs?
3. Why is it important not to assume that children will have the same needs?

The role of the adult in supporting an anti-discriminatory and anti-bias environment

As an early years practitioner, you have a duty to make sure that children are valued and not discriminated against either by adults or other children. In order to promote equal opportunities it is important to think about what this actually means when working with children.

Indirect discrimination – looking at resources

Challenging all forms of discrimination often means looking hard at the resources and images in the setting. You need to decide if any of them are sending out hidden messages that might reinforce stereotypes and prejudices.

Books, posters and wall displays

→ Check books for stereotypes. Images of people should be positive. For example, a book that has an image of black children not wearing any shoes is negative and children may think that all black children are poor.

→ Are children able to see positive images of people around them, especially children with disabilities?

→ Do wall displays show that you live in a multicultural country?

Activities and equipment

→ Are activities planned that actively promote an awareness of other cultures and beliefs?

→ Are a variety of religious festivals acknowledged, particularly ones that reflect children's backgrounds, for example Diwali, Eid ul-Fitr, Easter?

→ Do materials and equipment such as jigsaw puzzles and board games show a range of positive images?

Promoting a positive environment for children

Children benefit from an environment that is positive and encouraging. This means making sure that it provides for children with special needs as well as being multicultural and respecting other languages. From a positive environment, children:

→ learn that everyone is different and special
→ see a wider view of life, for example that there is more then one way to prepare food, talk or pray
→ gain learning opportunities through different tastes, ways of painting and through hearing different types of music − this helps them to be more creative
→ learn to respect different life styles and values − this will prepare them to form relationships with others.

There are three main ways in which you can create an environment that promotes equal opportunities:

1. Value all children and their families.
2. Act as a good role model.
3. Provide varied play activities, resources and images.

Valuing children and their families

Involve parents, carers and families in the setting

Parents and carers may wish to help in the early years setting or may be able to provide information, resources and books that can help you, for example, objects for the home corner, dressing-up clothes. Where families speak more than one language, they may be able to lend books or music, and even come in to teach the children the words of some songs.

Display positive images of groups of people who are often discriminated against

Children who wear glasses need to see that other children also wear glasses, and that they are not the odd ones out. A range of books, posters and other images is important. All children need to feel proud of who they are, so providing positive images is essential where children are likely to feel different, for example children who have asthma, live in a caravan or have particular beliefs.

Good role models

Children need to see good role models − they learn from how they see you behave and how you act towards others.

Tips for good practice

Promoting an anti-discriminatory environment by being a good role model

→ Avoid using language that is prejudiced, for example don't say things like 'I don't expect girls to behave like that'.

→ Children need to see you, as an adult, cooperating and being pleasant with everyone you come into contact with, whether parents, other professionals or visitors. This also means that you must be careful not to make assumptions, for example Tiffany's mother may not be a Mrs, or the person who has come to collect Tom may not be his grandad but his dad.

→ Children need to see adults being open-minded and interested in the world around them. This might involve showing children interesting or beautiful objects from different countries or clothes that are worn by people in other cultures.

⇩ **Children need to see adults being open-minded and interested in the world around them**

Obtaining information and resources

There are many organisations that provide information, ideas and resources to promote equality of opportunity. Often local organisations are happy to send out information or even provide a speaker, for example children's charities, local churches, synagogues, and so on. Public libraries, the local phone book and the Internet are often useful sources of contact numbers for these organisations.

Back to the real world

You should now understand the importance of thinking about children's diverse needs when planning activities. You should also be aware of the causes and effects of discrimination.

1. Can you now explain the causes and effects of discrimination?

2. Suggest practical ways in which you might promote an anti-discriminatory and anti-bias environment for children and young people.

Getting ready for assessment

In order to prepare for your assessment, you may like to see if you can answer the following questions:

1. Outline some of the factors that have to be taken into consideration when planning a layout in an early years setting.

2. Explain the benefits to children of displaying their work.

3. Describe the role of the keyworker when working with young children.

4. Explain the importance and role of parents in children's lives.

5. Identify three professionals who may be involved in a multi-agency team.

Unit 8

Play activity for children from birth to age 16 years

In this unit you will learn:

1. How to meet the diverse play needs of children

2. How to support a range of play opportunities for children

3. The role of the adult in providing play activity for children

Section 1

How to meet the diverse play needs of children

In the real world

The school where you are on placement has an after-school club and this is part of your placement experience. The play leader talks to you about the values of playwork and the importance of involving and consulting children in the play environment.

By the end of this section you will understand what playwork principles are and know about the interests and play needs of children.

The stages of play

The importance of play

In other units, you have looked at the importance of play in terms of helping a child's all-round development. In this unit you will look at the importance of play for its own sake and as something that children want and need to do. Play needs to be seen as something that children and young people have as a right. A good starting point, therefore, for anyone working with children is to look at the playwork principles.

Assumptions and values of playwork principles

1. All children and young people need to play. The impulse to play is innate. Play is a biological, psychological and social necessity, and is fundamental to the healthy development and well-being of individuals and communities.

2. Play is a process that is freely chosen, personally-directed and intrinsically motivated. That is, children and young people determine and control the content and intent of their play by following their own instincts, ideas and interests, in their own way for their own reasons.

3. The prime focus and essence of playwork is to support and facilitate the play process and this should inform the development of play policy, strategy, training and education.

4. For playworkers, the play process takes precedence and playworkers act as advocates for play when engaging with adult-led agendas.

5. The role of the playworker is to support all children and young people in the creation of a space in which they can play.

6. The playworker's response to children and young people playing is based on a sound up-to-date knowledge of the play process and reflective practice.

7. Playworkers recognise their own impact on the play space and the impact of children and young people's play on the playworker.

8. Playworkers choose an intervention style that enables children and young people to extend their play. All playworker intervention must balance risk with the developmental benefit and well-being of children.

(Source: www.skillsactive.com/playwork/principles)

Understanding the stages of play

The way that children play changes as they develop. This means that a baby will not have the same play interests as a 15-year-old. In Unit 4, you looked at Piaget's stages of play and the social stages of play; it will be important for this unit to re-visit pages 153–4. The chart below gives some general points about how children of different ages may play.

Think about it

Do you remember playing as a child and 'losing yourself' in your play?

⚓ **How children of different ages may play**

Age	Description
From birth to 1 year	Babies enjoy playing with adults as well as exploring toys and the environment for themselves.
1–3 years	Toddlers enjoy watching other toddlers play and are often interested in watching older children play. They begin to enjoy imaginative play and start to take roles.
3–5 years	Pre-school children try to play cooperatively at times. They start to develop friendship and play preferences. Children often enjoy a wide range of play types.
5–11 years	Play is often more cooperative and can become increasingly elaborate. Children may pick up play that they started earlier and resume it, for example at playtime in a school, children will re-group and carry on with play that was started earlier.
11–16 years	Young people may develop a preference for a certain type of activity. Friendships and activities with others is important, although young people may also enjoy doing activities by themselves.

The interests of children from birth to 16 years

Babies, children and young people will have varied and often changing interests, so you will need to provide a wide range of materials and play opportunities to cater for their interests. It is important not to stereotype or make assumptions about what children will or will not be interested in doing, as sometimes children will choose to play in ways that at first sight look too difficult or simple for them. Interestingly, children are very adept at creating their own challenges or, on the other hand, making play work for them. This means that a pair of 5-year-olds playing a traditional game of Monopoly may start to devise their own rules rather than keep to the existing ones that might not be working for them.

Schema theory

One of the main ways in which you can meet the play needs of babies and young children is to observe them and consider what is holding their attention and fascinating them. Some people believe that babies and young children will have times when they are exploring through play concepts or **schemas** and this will mean that there are identifiable themes within their play.

The spider diagram below shows some schemas and ways which they might show as themes within play. Thinking about play schemas that children are using can be helpful as you can work out what is of interest to children and then plan play opportunities based on their interests.

Types of play

In addition to schema theory, playworkers have identified different types of play that children and young people may engage in. These can be helpful when identifying the variety of ways in which children may choose to play. Examples of these are shown in the table below. (Different types of play are also described in Unit 4, pages 157–70.)

Find out!

Observe three children of different ages as they play.

1. What do you notice about their play?
2. Are they playing with anyone else?

Jargon buster

Schema A pattern of thought or action

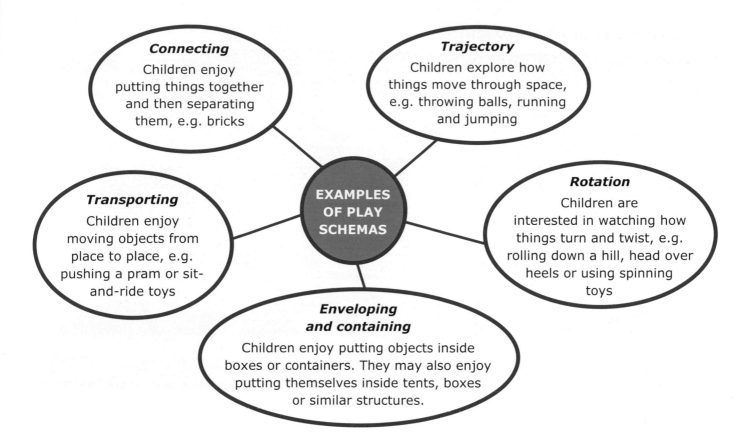

Connecting
Children enjoy putting things together and then separating them, e.g. bricks

Trajectory
Children explore how things move through space, e.g. throwing balls, running and jumping

EXAMPLES OF PLAY SCHEMAS

Transporting
Children enjoy moving objects from place to place, e.g. pushing a pram or sit-and-ride toys

Rotation
Children are interested in watching how things turn and twist, e.g. rolling down a hill, head over heels or using spinning toys

Enveloping and containing
Children enjoy putting objects inside boxes or containers. They may also enjoy putting themselves inside tents, boxes or similar structures.

👆 **Examples of play types that might be used by playworkers**

Type of play	Example in practice
Symbolic	Children use objects in their play to represent other objects, e.g. a stick is used to stand for a magic wand.
Rough and tumble	Playful fighting where children do not harm each other.
Discovery	Play where children can explore and discover new materials.
Socio-dramatic	Play where children can act out personal experiences.
Loco-motor	Children enjoy movement and physical activity.
Creative	Children use and enjoy materials and tools to enjoy creating new products.

It is important for babies, children and young people to have access to varied resources and the freedom to explore these fully. Adults should encourage children to choose and develop their play. This means making sure that there are varied resources and they are easily available to the children. It is good practice for children to help themselves to toys, equipment and resources that that they would like to use. This approach helps children to gain confidence and learn the skills of independence.

Jargon buster

Loco-motor play Play that involves physical activity and large physical movements

299

The importance of consulting with children about their play environments

Whatever setting you work in, it is important to think about how you involve the children in the planning and layout of play spaces. Children need to feel comfortable and have ownership of the play environment if they are to benefit from all that play can offer them. When adults organise the play environment themselves, they have to 'second guess' what they think a child will want and may often underestimate what children can do. This can lead to an over-structured environment.

Consulting children should be an ongoing process. At the start of and during a session, you should encourage children to think about what they want to do, the equipment or props they will need as well as how the space might be organised. It is important to listen carefully to what is being suggested and to avoid 'taking over' the conversation or directing it so that children are not really being involved.

⇧ **Children need to feel comfortable and have ownership of the play environment if they are to benefit from all that play can offer them**

When working with older children, you will need to ensure that everyone within the group has a 'voice' and that a discussion is not dominated by any one particular child or group. Children can be asked at the start of a discussion for their ideas on how everyone will be able to have a 'voice'. As well as group discussion, children and young people might prefer to come to you in small groups or as individual in order to talk about what they would like in their play environment.

With very young children or with children who may have difficulty in communicating using language, you may need to observe their play in order to think about what they need in the environment. For example, a toddler may be fascinated with pressing buttons, so you might look at providing toys and resources that have buttons on them.

Changing resources and environments

As well as consulting with children during sessions, there will be times when new equipment may need to be ordered or when an environment is going to be enlarged or changed. It is essential at these moments to consult with children in order to find out what they would like. It can also be useful to think about the things that children try to do in their play but may be prevented from doing because of health and safety considerations. Looking at what children want to do in their play is often a good starting point as it tells you the types of opportunities they may require.

Listening to children's ideas

The Jolly Roger pre-school had been given a large sum of money to improve their outdoor play area. From the outset, the staff decided to involve the children aged 2–5 years in the design. They spent time showing children photos of other outdoor areas, encouraged parents to visit local playgrounds with their children and observed the children as they were playing in the current space. They listened as the children expressed their ideas of what they liked doing in a play area and also what they disliked. One child, for example, said that she liked hiding in bushes but was often told by adults to come out, while another child said how he wanted to be able to 'dig for gold'.

When the outdoor area was redesigned, everyone was delighted with it and staff realised that if they had not spent time listening to the children, the area would have been sterile and potentially boring. The children's contributions meant that there were places for them to climb, bushes to hide in and places where they could dig in the mud and play with water!

1. What did the children gain by being involved in the design of the new play area?
2. What did the adults gain by involving children in the design?
3. Explain why children may see things from a different point of view to adults.

How to recognise the individual play needs of children

One of the greatest skills when working with children is to recognise when they want to play and what they might want to play with. While older children may often say what they want to do, you may need to carefully observe younger children. The term **play cues** has been adopted by playworkers to describe the way that you might observe the play behaviour of a child and then become aware of their needs. You should recognise that children's needs will vary considerably and will also change during a play session. For example, a child may give subtle signals that they want to play alone but later show by approaching an adult or another child that they wish to play with someone else. The examples below show how adults have recognised the play needs of children.

Jargon buster

Play cues Signs that children show to indicate their preference as to how to play

U8
1

Recognising the play cues of children

Example 1

Katie is on the floor with Anna, who is 8 months old. Anna reaches across and picks up a scrap of fabric. She tries to pull it over her head. She then pulls it away and grins. Anna then leans over Katie and tries to drape the fabric over Katie's head. Katie realises that Anna wants to play peek-a-boo. Katie says 'peek-a-boo' and pulls the fabric away. Anna chuckles.

Example 2

Joel is watching two 4-year-olds in the outdoor space in a nursery. He sees that they are picking up sticks and pushing them through the chain link fence. They are enjoying themselves but are running out of things to use. He discreetly puts out some strips of plastic, ribbons and other materials so they can use them if they wish.

Example 3

Arti is sitting on a bench. An 8-year-old with a ball makes eye contact and then kicks the ball towards her. She gets up and kicks it back to him. The child kicks it back to her again. They begin to play a game of football.

Example 4

A small group of 10-year-old girls get the prop box out. One of them notices a sparkly dress while another gets out a feather boa. They start pretending they are pop stars. Tumi, who has been watching them, gets out the karaoke machine. The girls arrange a space and they decide to have a talent competition.

Think about it

Look at the four examples of how the practitioner has observed children's play cues.

1. Why is it important that children have a chance to play without being told how by adults?
2. How did the adults in each of these examples respond to the children's play cues?
3. Can you think of how you have supported a child's play?

How to review resources and opportunities for individual children when planning

All children should have access to play opportunities, which means that you might have to adapt play resources to meet the needs of individual children. There are many reasons why you may need to do this:

→ Children might see something that they want to play with but not have the physical strength or developmental skills to do so. By adapting the resource, children can then play with it. For example, a child may want to play with a watering can which is too large and heavy when full; the early years practitioner might look for another watering can that is slightly smaller.

→ Children may have particular needs as a result of a disability or a medical condition. The manner in which you adapt resources may depend on what the child needs; sometimes you will need to take other professionals' or parents' advice on how best to do this. A good example of this might be the way in which a game could be adapted so that a child who has difficulty in breathing can still take part.

→ Children themselves may know how they want a play resource changed. In this case you should check the manufacturer's instructions as some resources may become unsafe if modified.

Case study

Ensuring access to play opportunities

Jenna wants to join the other 8-year-olds in a game of rounders. She knows that she will find it hard to hit the ball with the rounders bat as she will have difficulty in seeing the ball. The early years practitioner suggests that the game could be played with a soft yellow ball and a slightly larger bat. The children agree that this would be fair and are also keen to try the new resources themselves.

1. Why is it important that Jenna join in?
2. How has the early years practitioner found a way of adapting the resources?
3. Why might it be helpful to involve the other children as well?

 Back to the real world

You should now understand that play is a right for all children and that it is also important for its own sake. You should also understand that children should be consulted about the play environment.

1. Give some examples of the different ways in which children might play at different ages.
2. Explain the importance of children being consulted about their play environment.
3. Describe ways in which early years practitioners might find out more about the play needs of individual children.

U8
1

Section 2

How to support a range of play opportunities for children

In the real world

You have come into a busy play setting. There are children aged 4 to 14 years. You are surprised to see how many different things are going on. The children are happily playing. Your placement supervisor tells you that it is important to create the right environment to support play. She says that it is important that children have opportunities to find their own ways of playing. You are not sure what she means by this.

By the end of this section you will know about different types of play and how they might be provided for in a play setting.

Suitable activities to facilitate inclusive play for children from birth to age 16 years

In Unit 4 (pages 157–70) and in the first section of this unit (pages 298–9), you saw that play can be categorised into different types. The way that play is categorised will vary according to the aims and purpose of the setting. While the names of different types of play can vary, the key point is to understand that children will want to play in different ways according to their age, mood and who they are with. The chart below looks at some of the equipment and activities that might be used to support children's play.

⇩ **Equipment and activities to support the different types of children's play**

Type of play	Examples of equipment and activities
Discovery play	• Treasure basket and heuristic play for children under 3 years old • Sand, water and other sensory materials • Loose part play
Pretend play	• 'Small world' play • Dressing-up clothes • Home corner • Dens, playhouses
Creative play	• Collage materials • Paint and mark-making materials • Junk modelling • Musical instruments • Puppets
Physical play (sometimes known as loco-motor play)	• Sit-and-ride toys, ball pools, soft play • Wheeled toys and equipment, e.g. bicycles, skateboards, wheelbarrows and tricycles • Slides and climbing frames • Trampolines • Hide and seek • Chase games
Construction play (some parts of this play may also be referred to as **mastery** or manipulative play)	• Wooden bricks • Duplo and Lego • Making dens and structures • Building dams to block water

Jargon buster

Mastery play Play that gives children feelings of control

Find out!

Look at the setting in which you are working.

1. How is play categorised?
2. What type of toys, activities and equipment are available for children?

How to use music, movement, rhythm and games to promote play

Some children love making sounds and responding to sounds. This can be an important way for some children to express themselves. Ideally, adults should introduce children to music at a very young age, but then over time the focus should be for adults to encourage children to explore sounds for themselves. A level of skill is needed to master some musical instruments so there is often a role for adults to share their expertise with children, although in terms of a play environment this should not be too directed.

Children aged 0–3 years

Babies and children under 3 years old enjoy rhymes and songs, rattles, shakers and making sounds with objects. At this stage, adults play an important role in helping children to learn about music. This means that you should try to sing songs and say rhymes to children from an early age.

⇩ **Children enjoy making sounds from a young age**

Children aged 3–5 years

Children of this age love playing simple percussion instruments and finding out what sounds they can make with them. They enjoy learning new songs and games that involve music. This is an ideal period for children to be exposed to a range of different types of music, so some settings will put on music for children to play alongside. Children may also choose to join in with a singing or rhyme session.

Children aged 5–11 years

This is an ideal age for children to learn to play an instrument if they are interested, and many children receive tuition either at home or school. Play settings should provide musical instruments that children can explore and use if they wish. Early years practitioners can also support children's interest in dance, musical games and sounds.

Children aged 11–16 years

Young people start to have definite preferences for music, and for some music can become a major part of their life. You can help young people to enjoy their music by providing support for those wanting to practise or play instruments, as well as opportunities for them to listen to music or dance to it. Young people may, for example, want to organise karaoke sessions, discos or dance competitions.

The opportunities for drama and pretend play

In Unit 4 you looked at imaginative play and considered its many developmental benefits. You saw also that there are different forms of imaginative play. To complete this unit you will need to re-read pages 160–3.

Nearly all children enjoy imaginative play; for older children this may lead eventually to drama and performances. Imaginative play has many different forms and it is important to provide opportunities for each type. This means providing sufficient props and materials. Examples of different props are given on pages 161–2; below are some further ways of supporting drama and imaginative play.

'Small world' play

'Small world' play is used by younger children but is often enjoyed by children in their primary years. Small world play includes farm animals, racing cars, train tracks as well as play people. Children enjoy small world play more if there are sufficient items that are of a high quality. As children become older, they are often interested in more intricate small world play such as making a spaceship using technical Lego.

Small world play is sometimes seen as something just for indoors, but children will enjoy taking it outdoors too, although some negotiation is needed to ensure parts will not disappear. Children often enjoy small world play when it can be combined with sensory materials, for example they may take the play pirates outdoors and pretend there is treasure buried in the pile of sand.

⇨ **As part of drama and imaginative play, children enjoy dressing up and taking on different roles**

Dens, tree houses and other structures

Many children will enjoy creating a structure in which their imaginative play can take place. While this can be provided by adults, for example a home corner, as children become older they may find their play more enjoyable if they create the space themselves. To support them in this you will need to make sure that there are materials such as boxes, fabrics, wood, tubing, tents and beach shelters available.

Puppets

Older children can begin to master using puppets, while younger children enjoy watching puppets. Look for good quality puppets that are inspiring for children. Ideally, they need to fit children's hand sizes; if a puppet is too large, it is much harder for a child to manipulate. While it is possible to buy a puppet theatre, it is not always necessary as children can create their own and have the fun of designing it.

Supporting drama

As they become older, some children enjoy working on a piece of drama for performance. They may decide on a script or improvise and rehearse scenes. You can support this by helping them to create a stage or a space that they can use. It is important that when children are exploring drama adults do not take over – ownership of the play should remain with the children, as the case study below shows.

Case study

Putting on a play

A group of four children aged 8 years decide to put on a play. They have been influenced by a drama workshop they have been to at school. While the workshop at school was led by a teacher, now the children want to do the play on their own. They spend time practising different parts and scenes. Occasionally they disagree, but always manage to resolve their differences. They decide that they need to work out a stage space. They ask the adult what they can use and look with the adult for somewhere suitable. The adult asks them if they will want an audience and the children say they would like just the other children and the adults to watch and that maybe later their parents. The children spend several sessions working on their project and make or borrow the props they need.

1. Why is it important that children can spend the amount of time that they wish on their play?
2. What have the children gained from having ownership of their drama?
3. Why is it important that adults do not take over children's play?

Ways to support children to express their creativity

Creativity is a wide-ranging term. It is about self-expression, exploring textures, new ideas and concepts, and problem solving. Children and young people are almost instinctively creative and so, in theory, encouraging children to be creative should be an easy task. The reality is that some children have experienced situations where their creativity is not viewed positively or is even discouraged. This, in turn, causes some children to lose confidence in their ability to do things themselves. To encourage children to express their creativity, you first need to ensure that you provide them with the right conditions.

Giving children choices

Choice is essential when it comes to creativity. Being able to choose what to do and being given some freedom as to how to do things can foster creativity. Activities that are not creative tend to have been organised by adults in such a way that children are no more than factory workers following instructions! Activities that support creativity will have significant elements of choice such as a range of paint colours, brush sizes and papers at a painting activity.

Choice in terms of play opportunities is also important, so children should be able to choose which materials to play with and, as far as is safely possible, how they might play with them. Babies and toddlers, for example, benefit from treasure basket and heuristic play as these activities encourage children to choose and explore.

Encouraging children to experiment

You will need to encourage children to experiment with materials. For example, water and sand play can encourage them to experiment if a good selection of materials is put out alongside the sand and water and adults let children find their own way of using them. While traditionally water and sand play have been used with younger children, older children enjoy them too.

You can also encourage children by showing that you are ready to experiment, for example 'I am not sure what will happen but it will be interesting to find out.' Experimentation is part of creativity, but it is also part of children's play as they often try out new roles and games and may not always know how their play is going to turn out.

Avoiding a focus on end products

Creativity is often associated with products such as a painting to take home or a dance performance to show others. While some creative play and activities may result in an end product, it is important for you not to focus on this as it might lead children to think that they cannot experiment. Some children may even lose their confidence as they unfavourably compare their finished product to another child's. This can be off-putting, so it is important that you focus on the enjoyment that children are having 'doing' the activity rather than producing a product.

Providing children with a range of materials, equipment and resources

Children are more likely to be creative if they have access to materials, equipment and resources which they can explore and experiment with. You will need to look for materials that will interest children and help them to feel inspired. This does not necessarily mean buying expensive equipment and materials! Children will, for example, enjoy using materials from the local scrap project. These are organisations that collect spare paper, card and other materials from factories and businesses.

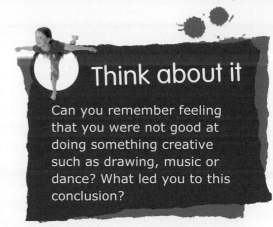

Think about it

Can you remember feeling that you were not good at doing something creative such as drawing, music or dance? What led you to this conclusion?

Find out!

Ask your placement supervisor if there is a scrap project in your area.

Case study

Making puppets

Danielle is a learner on placement at an after-school club. At the end of the previous session, some children asked whether they might be able to do some collage and make things. Danielle was given the task of getting an area ready for the children. When they came in, she showed them a cardboard puppet that she had made the night before. She had also cut out the shapes needed to reproduce the puppet and started to tell the children how to make it. One of the children said that they wanted to do something else. Danielle said that this was not possible and if the children used this area, they would have to make a puppet like the one she had made. Several children left the area. Danielle felt cross that all her hard work had not been appreciated by the children.

1. Explain how Danielle was preventing the children from being creative.
2. How had children lost ownership of the activity?
3. What should Danielle have done to prepare for the activity?

The role of the adult in supporting physical play opportunities

In Unit 4 you looked at the importance of physical play for children's overall development and the types of equipment that could be used to support this type of play with different ages (see pages 163–6). You will need to revisit this learning in order to complete this unit. In this section, you will look at how adults might support physical play.

While physical play can build children's overall development, it is also something that children enjoy doing for their own sake. Older children, for example, like playing chase and hiding games while younger children love the freedom of using wheeled toys. Physical play is therefore something that adults need to recognise as being important in children's lives. There are many different ways of supporting it.

Providing equipment

A key way to support physical play is to provide varied equipment for children to use. While the chart on page 305 shows some equipment that is often found in settings, you will probably notice that many play environments also contain materials that have not necessarily been designed for children, such as rubber tyres and plastic bottle crates. Items from the 'real world' must be risk assessed, but they generally provide children with plenty of scope to develop their creativity and help them to learn to explore, for example two 8-year-olds building a bridge using two rubber tyres and a plank of wood.

Suggesting games

While there should be plenty of opportunities for children to devise their own games, there are times when children will want an adult to organise or show them a new game. It is important here to note that in a play environment, these games should be voluntary so that children only come if they wish to. For example, you could show children how to play traditional games such as hopscotch and skipping games, as well as provide obstacle courses; older children enjoy games that have rules such as five-a-side mini-hockey.

Space

Space and time are essential elements for children to be able to engage in physical play. The play environment must be interesting enough for children to want to run, hide and use wheeled toys and other materials.

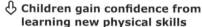
⬇ **Children gain confidence from learning new physical skills**

You may need to look at the space and consider whether it has places where children can hide, slopes where children can roll down and areas where children may climb, balance and throw. It is important to think about how the space is being used and whether it is sufficiently interesting.

Confidence

Some children can quickly lose confidence in their physical skills. This means that there must be equipment that will cater for children's different abilities and skills, for example both tricycles and bicycles. There may be times when you will help a child to gain or practise new skills such as throwing or dribbling a ball. You must also encourage children to try out new

Starting points for play

Many settings will create areas for play, particularly when they are working with young children. These can act as starting points for play so that a child can begin by using materials that are out and then, if they wish, go on to find other things that will support their play. A good example of this is the dressing-up box and a home corner in a nursery. These will act as a starting point for play, but a group of children may move on to play outdoors wearing dressing-up clothes. With older children and young people, some settings encourage discussion at the end of the previous session or at the start of the new session and the ideas given then are used to provide further opportunities for play.

⇧ **This home corner in a nursery provides various starting points for children's role play**

Indoor areas

There are no rules as to what an indoor play environment should look like, although for all ages of children it should not be the same week after week. This is because children will need variety and interest in order to enjoy their play. Many settings divide the space to accommodate different play types and to ensure that all children are able to follow their own interests. As children get older, you may also need to make sure that there are areas where they can chat and relax. This is especially important in after-school clubs, where children may need this time because they might be tired.

Tips for good practice

Key questions to consider when assessing an indoor play area

→ Do children have sufficient space in order to play?

→ Are children able to get out play equipment and resources themselves?

→ Are starting points for play provided if needed?

→ Does the environment look interesting and inspiring?

→ Are there areas where children can sit and chat to each other?

Outdoor areas

In some ways, the same principles apply to outdoor areas as to those indoors. Children should feel that the space is interesting and they should be able to see immediately some possibilities that they can choose to use in their play. Again, you might plan some starting points for play, for example items that can be put together to create an obstacle course. It is also important outdoors to observe children and notice what they especially enjoy doing. This might help you to provide further materials and equipment that will enrich the children's play experiences.

Think about it

1. What will children see when they come into your placement setting?
2. How is a play environment created?

Back to the real world

You should now know how to create a play environment and how adults might work to encourage children to play.

1. Can you explain how some opportunities and activities can support different types of play?
2. Can you describe ways in which the adult can support physical play?

U8
2

Section 3

The role of the adult in providing play activity for children

In the real world

This is your first placement in an after-school club for children aged 5–11 years. Today, you have been asked to observe how the club works. You are interested to see that the children seem to take control of the play and you notice that sometimes the adults tend to observe rather than intervene. This is a different approach to what you have seen when you have been working in the school.

By the end of this section you will understand the ways in which adults might support play with children of different ages.

The health and safety requirements in the country in which you live

There is a balance between keeping children safe and making sure that their play is worthwhile, satisfying and challenging for them. It is essential that you understand the health and safety requirements for your setting when providing a play environment for children. Requirements for **adult to child** ratios vary enormously as they depend on the age of the child and the type of activity that is being undertaken.

The starting point for understanding the health and safety requirements in your setting will be your placement or work supervisor, as he or she will have the overall responsibility to maintain the health and safety of children in the setting. You can also find out about the general requirements for the type of setting that you work in by contacting the organisation in your country responsible for setting standards, for example in England you can visit the website of Ofsted (www.oftsted.gov.uk). In addition, there are many organisations that provide advice about heath and safety such as the Child Accident Prevention Trust and the Health and Safety Executive.

The policies and procedures of a range of settings

Every setting will have its own health and safety policy together with procedures that help inform staff of what they should do in different situations. Some settings may, for example, have a policy about letting children play outdoors unsupervised, while others may have a policy about games such as wrestling and play fighting. Policies and their procedures have to be followed by everyone in the setting in order to minimise the risk of accidents and ensure that children are not given mixed messages.

Most settings involved in providing play activities recognise that it is impossible and not even desirable to create a totally hazard-free environment. The idea is always to look for ways of reducing the risk and to balance the risk against the benefits for children. Where settings are over-cautious and the play environment is dull and sterile, there is often a danger that children's behaviour changes, and this in itself can create a risk, as the case study below shows.

The importance of children's rights and making choices in play

In the first section of this unit, you looked at the playwork values and assumptions (see page 297). Children's right to play is a key part of these. This means that when you are thinking about how you should work with children, you must consider how to provide play opportunities in a way that meets their needs and rights.

Jargon buster

Adult to child ratio The legal requirement as to how many children an adult can supervise

Find out!

What are the recommended adult to child ratios for children aged 0–8 years in the country where you live?

Find out!

Visit the Child Prevention Trust website at www.capt.org.uk. What advice does it give about children's play?

U8
3

Case study

An over-cautious reaction

Two 8-year-olds are enjoying playing a game outdoors. One of them is standing on a low wall while the other throws a ball at him. The aim of the game is to dodge the ball. An adult looks at what is happening and worries that if the child falls off the wall, he might hurt himself. She intervenes and stops the game. The children now have nothing to do and are not interested in the other things that are available. After a few minutes, they put an empty can on a window ledge and start kicking a ball to see if they can knock the can off the window ledge. The ball keeps hitting the window.

1. Why is it important for adults to carefully assess risks rather than immediately assume that an activity is not safe?
2. Why is the children's new play activity more dangerous than the previous one?

Play can be **empowering** for children. It can help them to feel strong and confident about themselves. For play to be empowering, children must be allowed to take control of their own play rather than follow what an adult wants them to do. This means that when you are providing play opportunities, you need to think about how children can genuinely be encouraged to choose how they want to play and what they want to play with. To do this means ensuring that children are able to get out their own choice of equipment and toys and that they are aware of what is available.

Jargon buster

Empower To give children a sense of power and confidence

How to encourage children to direct their own play

You have seen that it is important for children to have plenty of opportunities to choose what they want to play with and to decide how they want to play. The role of the adult in play is to act as a **facilitator** – that is, someone who helps children to play rather than directs, takes over or shapes the way that they play. How you encourage children to direct their own play will depend largely on their age and the situation.

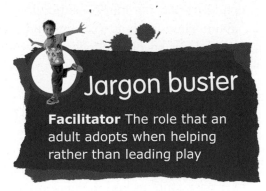

Jargon buster

Facilitator The role that an adult adopts when helping rather than leading play

Babies

Babies often want to play with adults. Although you may need to initiate the play, you should observe the baby carefully to see what they are enjoying. By around 7 or 8 months, by which time babies are often mobile, they will show you what they are interested in playing with and they will clearly signal when they have had enough of a play activity and need something else. It is important to play with babies, but also to introduce heuristic play, as this type of play is particularly led by the child.

Toddlers

Toddlers still need adults to support their play and will often want an adult to play with them or to watch them as they play. Toddlers are beginning to understand that adults can be useful tools when it comes to play. A toddler may, for example, give an adult something to hold or make the adult pretend to drink a cup of tea. Toddlers will also start to indicate that they need an adult to do something for them such as open a box or get something from a high shelf. From time to time, toddlers will need an adult to initiate play but may then want to take over.

The Features Page:

Focus on *Treasure basket and heuristic play*

Treasure basket and heuristic play are opportunities for very young children to organise their own play and to explore without the help of an adult. This makes it very empowering for them. It is also interesting to watch because it can help practitioners realise that even babies and toddlers are not helpless and are capable of concentration and perseverance.

My story

Katie, baby room leader

We introduced treasure basket play this year into the baby room. It is amazing to see how young babies who are only just sitting up enjoy taking things out of the basket and exploring them. It is also interesting to see what they are most fascinated with. I put a bristle brush into the basket the other day and it was a huge success. When we are observing the babies, we note down when they first start to explore objects with their hands and eyes rather than immediately with their mouth. We make videos of the babies when they are playing and parents have been amazed to see how their children can concentrate and for how long they continue at this activity.

Top Tips:

Treasure basket play

✓ After play, wipe or wash the objects.

✓ Vary some of the items so that babies do not get bored.

✓ Use the time to observe the babies' interests and skills.

✓ When choosing objects, check that they are not choking hazards.

Ask the expert

Q What is the difference between treasure basket and heuristic play?

A Treasure basket play is usually used with babies and all the objects in the basket are made of natural rather than synthetic materials. This means that no plastic objects are put in the basket.

Q We don't have any baskets. Can we still do treasure basket play?

A While the ideal is a basket, it is still possible to provide treasure basket play using other containers such as a box. The main thing is to ensure that the baby can reach into the container and help themselves to the objects.

Q I tried using heuristic play with toddlers, but a parent complained that the children were playing with junk.

A While it is annoying that a complaint was made, it is important to learn from this. It is often a good idea to let parents know about any changes to practice or new ideas that you are trying to introduce. When parents understand the benefits of heuristic play, they are more likely to accept that their child is playing with a plastic bottle or a plastic hair curler!

Word search

Can you find examples of objects that might be used in treasure basket play in the grid below? The missing words are:

- Brush
- Coconut
- Cone
- Leather purse
- Lemon
- Metal scoop
- Shell
- Sponge
- Teaspoon
- Wooden spoon

W	E	N	O	C	H	N	J	A	L	I	Y	M
V	M	S	U	S	N	O	M	E	L	P	K	E
K	G	W	R	U	O	K	L	D	E	S	E	T
A	A	O	L	U	O	I	I	O	H	P	T	A
G	H	S	F	D	P	R	R	C	S	X	M	L
T	X	L	Z	L	S	R	P	K	E	W	E	S
U	U	O	F	I	N	R	E	H	J	L	O	C
H	J	N	Z	A	E	I	P	H	G	G	W	O
S	T	G	O	A	D	Z	S	Q	T	Y	K	O
U	M	E	M	C	O	M	E	R	Y	A	O	P
R	D	B	N	O	O	P	S	A	E	T	E	I
B	B	I	G	W	W	C	K	L	Z	X	C	L

Pre-school children

By 3 years, children are able to play independently of adults and start to enjoy playing together. From this age, children begin to have friendship preferences as well as play preferences. They will need you to make equipment and play materials available and to introduce them to new possibilities in terms of skills. At times, children are also likely to come to you for support, for example if they cannot make something work or if they are finding it difficult to play together.

Case study

Playing shop

Ashleigh, Jo and Ayse are playing in the role-play area. They help themselves to props and pretend to go shopping. Another child comes into their game and starts to take things. Jo tells the other child not to take things away. The adult comes along and asks whether they need a shopkeeper. The adult involves the other child in being the shopkeeper. The play resumes and after a few minutes, the adult discreetly leaves the children to play.

1. Why might pre-school children sometimes need an adult to help them with the social aspects of play?
2. Why is it important that the adult does not change the type of play?
3. How did the adult ensure that children still had ownership of the play?

Children aged 5–11 years

Children in this age group are generally extremely independent and have clear ideas of what they would like to do and whom they would like to be with. The role of the adult is often to keep an eye on play and to assess the risk. Children will need to know what is available and that adults are there to support the play.

Case study

Dancing party

A group of 8-year-olds want to organise a dance party. They work out the food and equipment they require and when it is to be held. They share their ideas with the adult, who suggests that they write a few things down so that she can get what they need. The adult tells the children that she has some fabric which they can use either to decorate or make outfits if they wish. The adult says that she is happy to show anyone how to use the sewing machine. Two of the children decide that they would like to have a go. They quickly master how to use the machine and sew strips of fabric together to make a banner. The dance party takes the children a few days to organise, but is a great success.

1. How did the adult act as a facilitator?
2. Why was it important that the adult made suggestions and gave offers of help rather than insist on children doing things?
3. How did the adult ensure that children still have ownership of their idea?

Children aged 11 years plus

Most young people are able to direct their own play and will have clear ideas about what they would like to do and how best to organise their play. Again, the role of the adult is to act as a facilitator and to help young people to assess and minimise any risks. They are likely to have a range of different interests, so it will be important that varied resources are available for them to use.

Case study

Snooker league

A group of 14-year-old friends enjoy snooker and spend a lot of their free time playing the game. One of the members of the group thinks it would be fun to have a snooker league and has put this idea to the group. The rules of the competition are hammered out in the group and one friend suggests that it would be possible to create a chart on the computer showing each round of the competition. The adult is asked about prizes and whether the youth club could provide a prize. The adult asks the group to think about the value of the prize, the type of prize and whether a prize might make the competition less friendly. The group talk and exchange viewpoints about how competitive the snooker league should get. They finally decide that a cup would be the best idea and that there should also be some novelty prizes for fun.

1. What have the young people gained by organising a league?
2. How did the adult work to help them think about some of the issues?
3. How did the adult ensure that the young people had the ownership of the activity?

How to support children according to their age, needs and abilities

There are many ways in which you can support children in their play, as described below. However, it is important to think about children's individual needs and to be aware that the way you support children should change as they develop. For example, you may spend a lot of time playing directly with a baby, but as the child gets older they will often prefer to play with children of a similar age.

Providing resources and equipment

A key role of adults is to ensure that there is a variety of materials that will appeal to children which are appropriate for their age/stage of development. Some children with additional needs may need the adult to source specialist playthings, for example sensory and light toys.

Supervising

Play needs to be supervised, although the level of supervision should be appropriate to the activity and the age/stage of the children. Babies and toddlers will need constant supervision in order to maintain their safety, while older children will need adults to be around but not necessarily standing over them!

Giving children time to end their play

Sometimes, adults will need to end a session of play. It might be home time or there might be organisational reasons why the play needs to end, for example another group is waiting for the space. The best way to conclude a play session is to give children sufficient advance warning. They can then use the remaining time to 'finish' their play in a way that suits them. The amount of warning required for children will depend on their awareness of time. Older children who have watches and a feeling for time may be told at the start of their play how much time they have, with just a simple reminder 15 minutes or so before the session has to end. With toddlers, who have less understanding of time, you might tell them just a few minutes before it is time to end and maybe play alongside them.

Wherever possible, children should be given the option of leaving out the materials and resources so that later on they can choose to return to what they were doing. Where play cannot be resumed until another day, it may be possible to store the materials or encourage the children to think of a way in which they might preserve their play so that if they wish to return to it at another time, they can.

Reviewing play

Some settings like play sessions to end with a review time so that children can talk about what they have been doing and make plans for future play. This can work well, although if the amount of time for children to play is very limited, it might be argued that it would be better if children spent this time in playing rather than talking about it.

Tidying away

Tidying away helps children to take responsibility for their play environment and can encourage a group feeling. It is important that tidying away is not seen as a chore but as an act of responsibility. This means that you should avoid directing children, but instead help children to take on the responsibility themselves. This can be done by asking children what they would like to tidy away and by joining in with children rather than supervising or directing them.

Young children will need help to tidy away fully and may easily get distracted. You can help young children by praising them and by talking to them as the tidying takes place. Similarly, older children still enjoy having some recognition that they have done a good job in tidying the play environment.

Ending a play session

→ Aim to give children plenty of time to play.

→ Give children sufficient warning that they will need to end their play.

→ Look for ways of helping children to store props, materials or things that they have constructed for their play.

Case study

A bad ending to play

Kieran and Jaleem have spent most of the afternoon creating a complicated track system that they can use with cars. They have played very well together and have been totally absorbed in their play. The adult tells them that they must tidy up immediately and that they should make sure that everything is put away properly. Kieran and Jaleem feel angry and frustrated. They try to argue, but the adult does not listen to their point of view. Kieran becomes so upset that he kicks one of the plastic storage boxes.

1. Why are Kieran and Jaleem upset?
2. What mistakes has the adult made?
3. Explain how the adult should have ended the play session.

U8
3

 **Back to the real world**

You should now understand the role of adults in the play environment.

1. Which health and safety requirements apply to your placement setting?
2. Explain why adults may need to work in different ways according to children's age and stage of development.
3. Describe how best to end a play session with children.

Getting ready for assessment

In order to prepare for your assessment, you may like to see if you can answer the following questions:

1. Identify the different social stages of play.

2. Why is it important to recognise children's individual play needs?

3. Outline how an adult might help children to explore and investigate through play.

4. Explain the importance of children making choices in their play.

5. Describe four ways to support children during their play.

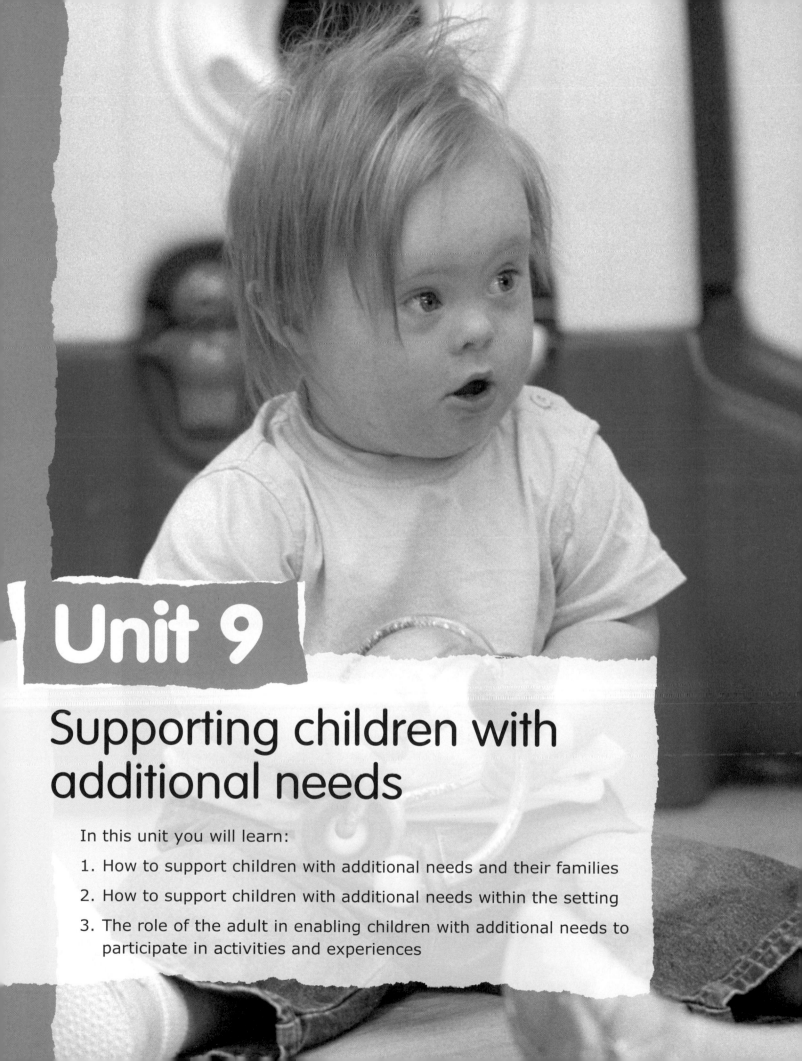

Unit 9

Supporting children with additional needs

In this unit you will learn:

1. How to support children with additional needs and their families

2. How to support children with additional needs within the setting

3. The role of the adult in enabling children with additional needs to participate in activities and experiences

How to support children with additional needs and their families

In the real world

You are working in a placement and your supervisor proudly tells you that one of the aims for the setting is that it is inclusive. You are not sure what this means. The supervisor then shows you some specialist equipment and talks to you about changes at the setting so that it can take children with additional needs.

By the end of this section you will understand what the term inclusive means and how settings must meet the additional needs of children.

Introduction

Understanding the term additional needs

Many children at one time or another will have needs that are slightly or very different to those of other children. They may have a medical condition, a disability, learning difficulties or simply be in need of extra emotional support. The term **additional needs** is now being used alongside the more traditional term of **special educational needs** (SEN), which was devised as a way of identifying children who needed extra support in order to have access to education. The term SEN is still in use although not everyone likes it as it is sometimes seen as a way of labelling children (see pages 343–4). The term additional needs is much broader; it recognises that every child is unique and from time to time may have their own special needs.

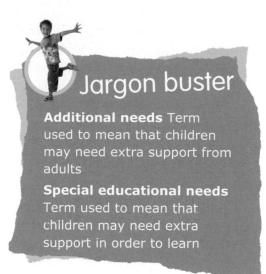

Jargon buster

Additional needs Term used to mean that children may need extra support from adults

Special educational needs Term used to mean that children may need extra support in order to learn

The importance of inclusion and how this should work in a range of settings

Inclusion involves ensuring that all children, regardless of their gender, lifestyle or needs, are given the same opportunities as other children to fulfil their potential and, crucially, that their needs wherever possible are met alongside those of other children. Previously, children who had disabilities, medical conditions or a learning difficulty would often be educated separately. While this worked well for some children whose needs were particularly complex, it was an inappropriate solution for many others. It often resulted in children who had a disability or special need underachieving and being labelled. Once a child was labelled as finding learning difficult, there was a danger that teachers would not expect the child to do that well.

Jargon buster

Inclusion Term used to describe the importance of including all children in education settings

Today, there is still specialist provision for children who have very complex needs, but the idea of inclusion is to ensure that schools and early years settings make the necessary adaptations so that children with additional needs can attend (see also Section 2, page 348). The term **mainstream** is used to describe educational settings that are not special schools.

Jargon buster

Mainstream Educational settings that are not special schools

U9
1

The advantages and disadvantages to the child of inclusion

The concept of inclusion in care and education is still relatively new. While for some children, specialist provision will better meet their needs, most children prefer to be with other children of the same age (and their parents want this too).

Inclusion has many benefits for children:
→ Firstly, they can feel part of a group and of society. A frequent criticism of the traditional way of meeting children's needs is that they were segregated and made to feel like outsiders.

Think about it

Have there ever been times in your life when you have needed extra support from adults?

→ Secondly, it encourages children to have higher levels of confidence and self-esteem. This is important in many ways, as confidence is needed in order to become independent and achieve.

→ Thirdly, inclusion gives children more opportunities to learn and gain qualifications. Previously, people had quite low expectations of what children with additional needs might be able to achieve. By having access to the mainstream curriculum, the idea is that children will have more opportunities.

Recently, however, the inclusion policy has been criticised. There are claims that some children's needs are not being met properly and that in some cases, children with additional needs have prevented other children from learning. The reality is a little different. What has often happened is that children who have additional needs have not been properly supported. This in some cases is because settings have not understood how to meet the child's needs or there has been insufficient money to pay for extra staff or resources.

The legal requirements in the country in which you live

Laws and policies reflect society's views and attitudes. As a result of campaigning by organisations, the rights of children who have disabilities or special educational needs have been strengthened. Below are some of the key components of legislation that will affect your work with children. The aim of the legislation is to ensure that all children and adults are treated fairly and that they have the same opportunities to achieve as others.

Disability Discrimination Act 1995

The Disability Discrimination Act is an important piece of legislation which covers all countries within the UK. It gives disabled people new rights in the following areas:

→ Employment
→ Education
→ Goods and services, including transport
→ Buying/renting property.

The Act is designed to prevent **discrimination** against disabled people.

Special Education Needs and Disability Act (SENDA) 2001

This Act is divided into two sections:

1. Part one strengthens the rights of parents and children to access mainstream education.
2. Part two extends the Disability Discrimination Act to educational settings.

Both England and Wales have codes of practice that reinforce this Act (see below). If you work in England or Wales, you will need to follow the code of practice for your country.

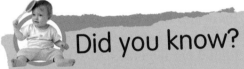

Did you know?

While this unit uses the term additional needs, you will probably find that legislation in your country refers to special educational needs or disability, although in Scotland 'additional needs' is increasingly being used.

Jargon buster

Discrimination When a person is treated differently because of their age, gender, ethnic background, culture or disability

The codes of practice and how these affect provision across the voluntary, private and public sectors

Codes of practice are legally binding documents that outline the duties and responsibilities of settings and services. The latest code of practice in England is the SEN Code of Practice 2001. If you work in Wales, you should use the Special Educational Needs Code of Practice for Wales. These codes of practice do not use the term additional needs but instead refer to special educational needs.

Codes of practice are changed every few years in order to reflect the latest thinking or legislation. The current codes in England and Wales are based on the idea that all practitioners will aim to meet the needs of all children through their daily practice and will, for example, change layouts, differentiate activities or use a variety of resources. The codes then look at what settings and services should do for those children who require extra support beyond this.

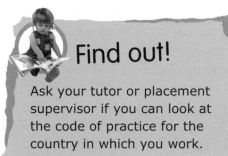

Find out!

Ask your tutor or placement supervisor if you can look at the code of practice for the country in which you work.

Key principles

Four principles are reflected in the codes of practice or legislation:

1. The right to mainstream education

The right to mainstream education is about children being able to attend the school of their choice. Mainstream schools have to make physical adaptations to their buildings such as putting in ramps, widening doors, and so on. They must also look at how their teaching ensures that children can learn. For children with complex needs, specialist provision is likely to continue, although the trend is to provide classes for these children which are situated within a school complex.

U9
1

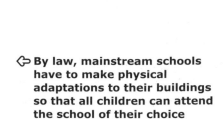

⇦ **By law, mainstream schools have to make physical adaptations to their buildings so that all children can attend the school of their choice**

2. Support for children in the early years

All four countries in the UK recognise the need for early identification and support for children in the early years. This is important as there are many benefits to the child when help and support is given early on. In some cases, such as when children experience difficulties with speech, hearing or vision, early identification can prevent the child from having difficulties in other areas such as behaviour and concentration.

3. Support and rights for parents and carers

Current legislation and proposals for new legislation in each of the countries strengthens parents' and carers' rights. Parents and carers have to be kept informed of what is happening and their views and ideas must be taken seriously. To help parents and carers gain information and to act as **mediators**, special services are being set up. In England and Wales, these are called Parent Partnership services.

4. Empowerment of children

Children's thoughts about their education should be taken into consideration. In England and Wales, under the Code of Practice, adults are expected to take into account children's interests and views when drawing up plans for them. This approach is also echoed by legislation in Scotland and Northern Ireland.

Jargon buster

Mediator Someone who acts as a go-between where there is conflict between a setting and parents or carers

The range of local and national support available for children and their families

There are many sources of support for children and their families and for those working with them. Support is sometimes in the form of practical help or advice, but just gaining information can sometimes be of great assistance.

Local support groups are often organised by parents who find it helpful to meet with others and share experiences, information and advice. You will probably be able to find out about what is available in your local area from the library, education department or (more easily) from parents.

National organisations such as Contact a Family (www.caf.org.uk) provide a range of services. They not only provide support for children and their families but also offer information to the general public. Some organisations provide helplines, leaflets and organise training for professionals. Many organisations also aim to raise public awareness and may campaign for better services and rights for children. Many national organisations will have a website where you can access information.

Find out!

Choose one of the following national organisations and visit their website:

→ Asthma UK (www.asthma.org.uk)
→ Sickle Cell Society (www.sicklecellsociety.org)
→ Scope (www.scope.org.uk)

1. What support do they offer children and their families?
2. Do they arrange any support locally?

Other sources of support and information

Early years services

Advice and support can also be obtained from early years services, although the way in which they are organised will depend on the area and the country in which you live. In many areas, early years teams are connected to the education department. These teams usually employ experienced practitioners who in many cases will visit and advise settings.

Health professionals

Health professionals may support some of the children in your setting, and may be able to give you additional information, strategies or advice to help you work more effectively. In some cases, they may also need you to assist them by working in particular ways with children. Health professionals are bound by a strict code of confidentiality. This means that you need to ask parents for permission before approaching them. The chart below outlines the roles of some of the principal services that are usually available.

⇧ **Recognising children's need for support at an early stage is beneficial**

⇩ **The range of services offered by health professionals**

Health professionals	Type of service they provide
Speech and language team	This team will include therapists, who assess, diagnose and work out a programme of exercises to help children's communication and speech.
Sensory impairment team	Many education services have a team dedicated to helping children with a visual or hearing impairment. They may visit homes and settings to advise on how best to help the child and use any equipment effectively.
Health visiting service	Health visitors are trained to promote health across all age ranges in the local community. Health visitors can provide advice for parents about care and development.
Occupational therapy service	Occupational therapists work to maximise physical movements and development. In many areas, there are specialised occupational therapists to work with children. They usually work closely with families but may advise how best to make a setting accessible.
Physiotherapists	Physiotherapists are usually provided by the health service. They work directly with children and their parents to provide exercises and movements that will help the child to strengthen an area of the body or to reduce the impact of a medical condition.
Educational psychologists	These are professionals who have been trained to assess children's development and learning. They are able to identify children's needs and help parents and professionals meet them. Educational psychologists often watch a child in the setting in order to build a picture of how the child is coping as well as seeing the child separately. They are then able to give advice and suggest a programme to assist the child.

Social Services

Social Services provides funding and support to meet children's needs and their families. Children who are defined as 'in need' because their needs are complex and severe are likely to have a social worker assigned. Respite care, a service which allows parents some time off, is usually organised by Social Services.

How to access available information to support children and their families

You have seen that there are many sources of support and information available, but remember that you have a duty of confidentiality towards children and their families. This means that you should not talk about a child or their family to others outside of the setting, unless you have their permission to do so. In addition, you must always follow the procedures of the setting.

The spider diagram below shows ways in which you might access available information to support children and their families.

WAYS OF ACCESSING INFORMATION TO SUPPORT CHILDREN AND THEIR FAMILIES

Directory of children's services
This should be available in the setting where you work and should list the phone numbers of the teams in your area.

Internet
This can sometimes be a good source of information. A search on the Internet can help you find out about support organisations available as well as additional information on the child's needs. (Note: information pasted on the web may not be accurate.)

Networking
The term networking is used to describe how you might meet one professional who, in turn, may introduce you to or help you learn about another professional. By going to meetings and training, you are likely to make contacts in this way. This can help you to learn about the professionals who are involved locally in helping children and their families.

Libraries
Many public libraries have information about local networks and groups. They may also have a noticeboard.

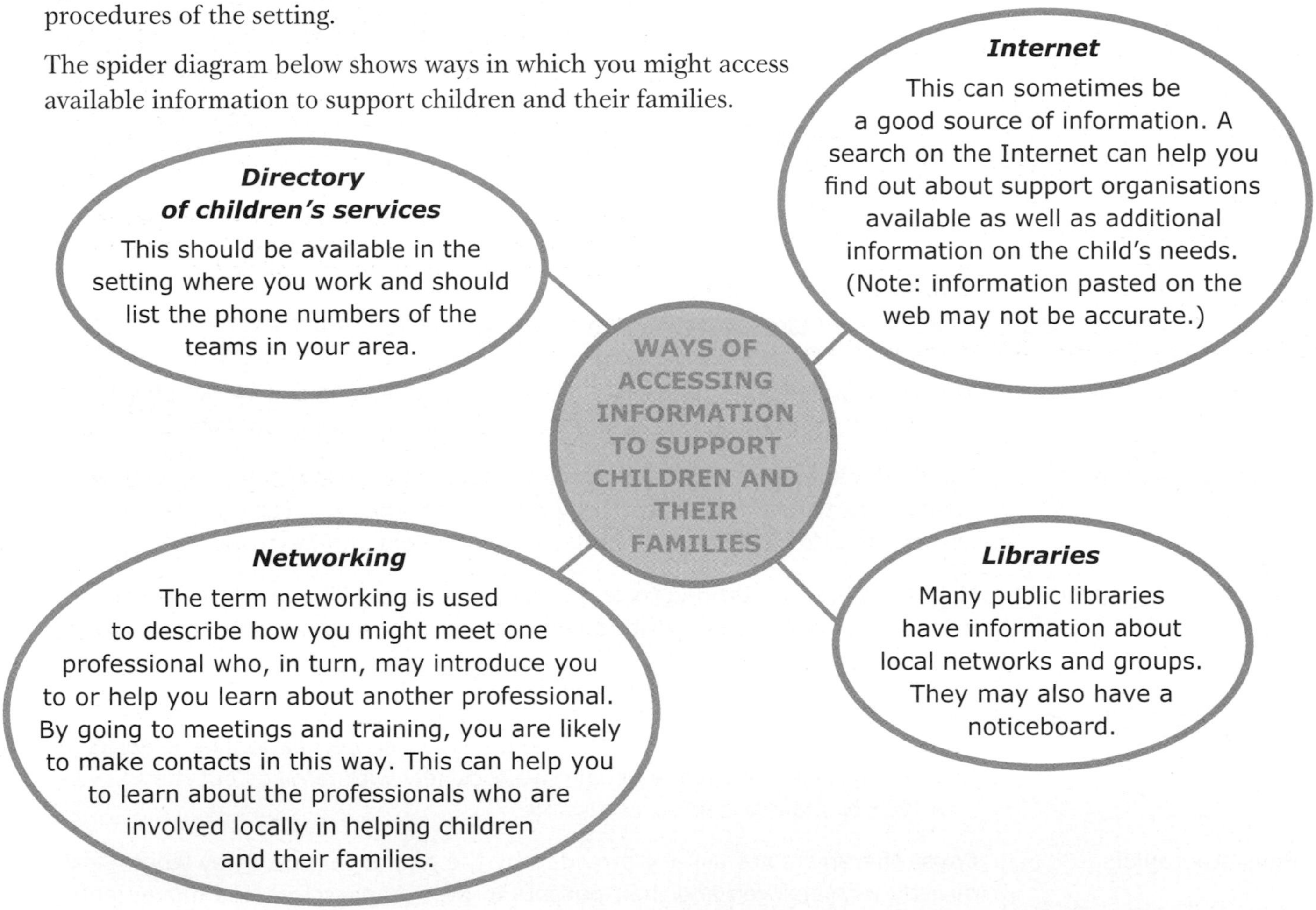

Establishing and maintaining partnerships with parents and families, according to the procedures of the setting

Parents and carers know their children well – they will be aware of their child's interests, strengths and needs. Parents have usually learned how best to help their child and will have developed strategies that

336

support him or her. Many parents will also have researched extensively in order to work out how to help their child, especially where the child has a medical or physical disability. For example, they may have contacted support organisations, seen other professionals and met other families.

All children benefit when the people who care for and educate them work well with their parents. This is particularly true for children who have additional needs. There are many ways in which you can build a partnership with parents.

Seven key principles when working with parents and carers

The SEN Code of Practice 2001, which is used in England (see page 333), outlines seven key principles when working with children and their parents. These principles are based on good practice and are worth reading even if you do not work in England (see chart below). As a learner, you will have a slightly different role with parents – you must always follow the procedures of your placement setting as well as the advice of your placement supervisor.

⇧ **When working with children with additional needs, it is vital to acknowledge and support the role that parents and carers play in their child's life**

⬇ **Seven key principles when working with parents and carers**

Principle	What it means
1. *Acknowledge and draw on parental knowledge and expertise in relation to their child.*	This principle is a reminder that parents will usually be able to share some valuable advice, thoughts and strategies with you.
2. *Focus on the children's strengths as well as areas of additional need.*	This principle should help you to remember that children are 'whole people', not problems that need curing or sorting out. Think about the language you are using and about how it might sound if it was said to you.
3. *Recognise the personal and emotional investment of parents and be aware of their feelings.*	Parents love their children unconditionally and see them as valuable. If you focus only on the child's areas of need, parents will feel that you do not really know their child.
4. *Ensure that parents understand procedures, are aware of how to access support in preparing their contribution and are given documents to be discussed well in advance of the meeting.*	Meeting with parents and working through individual education plans (see pages 352–3) is an essential part of supporting children, so this principle emphasises the need to make parents feel at ease. It is also about ensuring that parents can properly contribute.
5. *Respect the validity of differing perspectives and seek constructive ways of reconciling different viewpoints.*	You will need to understand that parents will have and are entitled to their own opinions about what is best for their child.

Principle	What it means
6. Respect the differing needs that parents themselves may have, such as a disability or communication and linguistic barriers.	Some parents may have particular needs which prevent them from contributing. Inclusion means thinking about parents' needs and looking for ways of meeting them. This might mean translating documents, encouraging parents to bring along a friend or setting up a travel cot so that a baby can be brought along.
7. Recognise the need for flexibility in the timing and structure of meetings.	This principle is a reminder that parents may have jobs, difficulty with transport arrangements or other commitments. Partnership with parents means that you should look for times which everyone finds convenient, not just you!

Tips for good practice

Establishing and maintaining partnerships with parents and families

→ Think about the limitations of your role if you are a learner.

→ Make sure that parents and carers are always welcomed and acknowledged.

→ Notice parents' and carers' body language – what is it telling you?

→ Think about whether the information or conversation needs to take place in a calmer environment.

→ Always look for something positive to say about the child.

→ If there is sensitive information to pass on, always look for a quiet area and take your time.

→ Listen carefully to parents' views and take time to think about them.

→ Look for ways of helping parents to join in activities or to provide feedback about their child at home.

→ Recognise that parents know their child well and will often be experts about his or her needs.

Providing support for children and families to include effective communication

There are many ways in which children and families might be supported. Where a child has a recognised disability, the local authority is required to carry out an assessment of needs for both the child and the family. The type of support then provided varies enormously and will reflect what the child and family require. Parents may be offered a place at a nursery or holiday club as well as practical items that will make caring for the child easier such as a car, hoist or washing machine.

Practitioners should also be looking for ways of making families' lives easier and this is achieved by listening to parents and finding out more about their child's interests and how you can help them. Parents also need information from you about their child and so finding ways to communicate effectively with them is important. For some parents, this might mean regular chats when they come into the setting, but where a child is brought in by taxi or by another carer, you need to communicate using a home-setting book that can be exchanged each day.

The impact on families

All parents find that having children can be a roller-coaster ride. There are moments that are stressful, fun, challenging, loving, as well as tiring. Parents who have children with disabilities or additional needs are no different, but they may have some extra challenges. The impact of having a disabled child or a child with additional needs is hard to judge, as families are all so different, but a list of common difficulties that parents sometimes mention is given below. Remember, though, that what one family feels will not be the same for another.

Isolation

Some families find that they are lonely. They may not receive social invitations for a variety of reasons. They may not have transport or the place where they are going might not be equipped for their child. Some parents also find that other people are not able to accept and cope with their child. This can be extremely hurtful for them.

Worry

All parents worry about their children. For some parents, their worries are financial ones or concerns about the next steps for their children. Other parents try not to look too far into the future and take each day as it comes.

Time

Time can be the hardest thing for some parents. While most children are demanding in terms of time when they are small, they gradually become independent. For some parents, supervising their child and meeting their needs can be constant. This means that they may not have time to talk, play and simply relax with their other children or partner.

Back to the real world

You should now understand the concept of inclusion and the way that it benefits children and their families. You should also have knowledge of the legislation that links to this practice.

1. Explain which legislation affects current practice.

2. What is meant by the term inclusion?

3. Describe why meeting children's additional needs in an inclusive way is important.

How to support children with additional needs within the setting

In the real world

You have just started work in a new setting. You have been working with a child for a short while and notice that she does not always seem to answer questions or follow instructions. You wonder whether the child is hearing you properly but are not sure if you should say something about it to someone.

By the end of this section you will know why it is important to recognise individual needs and how you might do so. You will also know about the importance of meeting children's individual needs.

How to recognise and plan for individual needs and learning opportunities

Children who have unmet needs will not thrive and develop. It is therefore essential that everyone working with children must be able to recognise when a child may have additional needs. Sometimes these needs will be temporary and the child may simply require a little extra time and support with an adult, while other needs will be more complex and may require professional advice and support.

How to recognise individual needs

There are many ways in which you might recognise that a child has individual needs.

Parents

Parents know their children and are sometimes the first people to recognise that their child is not developing as expected or requires extra support. A parent may, for example, tell you that a child has not been sleeping well because they are worried about moving home. In the same way, a parent may ask you to keep an eye on a child because the parent has noticed that the child seems to sit very close to the television. Listening carefully to parents and talking with them is therefore a major part of working with all children.

Observations

Regularly observing children is now considered to be good practice. This means that you will be asked to observe the children that you work with regularly. The aim of these observations is to build up a picture of the child. Observations should help you to identify and notice when a child is not making progress or when a child's development is significantly different to that of other children. In order to make sure that you can use observations to recognise children's needs, you must have a good knowledge of the milestones and sequences of development (see also Unit 2, pages 31–47).

As well as observing children's skills and abilities, you should also notice children's emotional well-being. For example, through observation you might see that a child does not seem to smile very much or rarely makes eye contact with others.

Behaviour

A common way in which it is discovered that children have additional needs is through their behaviour. Children often show unwanted behaviours that are not appropriate for their age because they have a hidden or underlying need. For example, a child whose speech is delayed may find it hard to join in role play with other children and instead try to play with them in more physical ways; the other children might complain that this child is spoiling their game. Also, a child who is not feeling settled may be extremely clingy and attention-seeking. While

342

it is of course important to respond to unwanted behaviour, it is more important to think about what the causes of the behaviour might be.

Case study

Observing challenging behaviour

Jason is 4 years old. He finds it difficult to sit down to activities and spends quite a lot of the session running around or disrupting other children's play. He often spends only a few minutes in any place and cannot sit and join the other children at snack and story time. His key worker carries out a series of observations. She notices that he seems to respond better when there are sensory materials available.

1. Why is it important to observe children to understand their behaviour?
2. Suggest ways in which sensory materials might be used to help Jason cope with snack time.

What you should do if you have concerns about a child

As a learner, you are unlikely to be working directly with parents. If you notice any additional needs, you should talk to the child's key worker or the placement supervisor – always remember the need for confidentiality and do not talk about this to anyone else.

As a qualified member of staff, what you do will still depend on your role. If you are not the child's key worker, the usual course of action is to talk to the child's key worker as he or she should have responsibility for liaising with the parents. The key worker should also be the person who spends the most time with the child and should know the child well.

If you are the child's key worker, you must discuss your thoughts with the parents. While some parents may immediately agree and share concerns, remember that children can sometimes behave differently at home and show different skills. Thus, a child who does not talk much in the setting might be a chatterbox at home. Sharing information with parents is therefore important. Where the concerns involve development, the next step is usually to gain some further professional advice. This may mean that the parents will need to see the health visitor or the child's family doctor so that the child can be referred to the relevant specialist team. The SEN Code of Practice in England makes it clear that you should not refer a child without a parent's consent.

The importance of avoiding labelling and stereotyping

In Unit 7 you looked at discrimination and the way in which stereotyping children can lead to discrimination (see pages 286–8). It is important, therefore, when recognising that a child may have additional needs to avoid making assumptions or stereotyping the child. This is essential when it comes to children's behaviour. Some children get a reputation in a setting of being 'difficult', so when a child changes group or class the new adult starts to 'look' for instances of his or her difficult behaviour.

While it is important to recognise that a child has additional needs, it is essential that the child is not known because of these needs, for example 'Tommy, he's the deaf one' or 'Jemma, the little girl with Down's'. When this happens, children can lose out because the focus is put on the 'needs' rather than on the child.

Seeing children as individuals

In terms of children with additional needs, you need to view each child as an individual. Two children may have similar additional needs, but quite often the way you have to meet them is different. This is because children will have different strengths, interests and personalities. It is very dangerous just to read about a medical condition, disability or special educational need and assume that any strategy or idea will work for all children.

A good way of preventing stereotyping of children is to listen to children themselves and to their parents. You also need to be very careful in the way that you talk about children and the language you use.

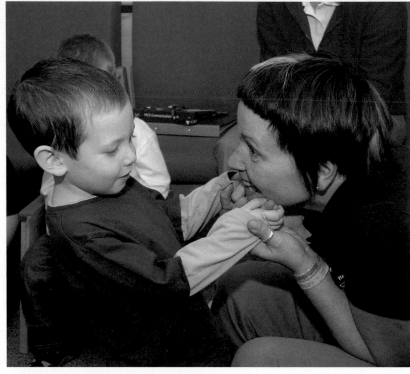

⇧ **In terms of children with additional needs, it is vital that you view each child as an individual**

Tips for good practice

Focusing on the child as an individual and avoiding stereotyping

→ Remember that children should not be labelled or known only for their disability or need.

→ Avoid drawing attention to the child's disability, difference or condition unless it is relevant.

→ Ask the child or their parents about their preferences in terms of language.

→ Listen carefully to the language that they use.

→ Check out with support organisations the terms that are currently being used.

The importance of realistic expectations of children's development

You have seen that a child's additional needs should be identified. While you should not label or make assumptions of children, it is important to make sure that you have fair expectations of them.

Behaviour

One of the key ways in which you might have noticed that a child has additional needs is through their behaviour. This is because difficult or unwanted behaviour is often a result of an unmet need. A good example of this is aggressive behaviour, which is quite common in children who have a language delay or need extra emotional support. This means that it is important when working with children to make sure that your expectations of them are fair and realistic. A 4-year-old whose additional needs mean that they show the behaviours of a 2-year-old will require you to adapt the way you may normally work.

Independence

While you may need to adjust the way you work in terms of a child's behaviour, you will still need to encourage children to become independent. Some types of additional needs mean that children require considerable physical and personal care. Despite this, you should look for ways of giving children as much responsibility and choice as possible. The danger is that sometimes adults can 'take over' and forget to encourage the child to do as much as he or she can. Being as independent as possible is one way in which children can gain in confidence and self-esteem.

Case study

Promoting independence

Jack is 5 years old. He needs help at mealtimes and his key worker feeds him. While Jack communicates quite well, he uses body language rather than speech. Today, his key worker is absent and a new member of staff is working with him. Although there is a choice of meals, the staff member does not ask Jack what he would like. As she is feeding him, she does not let him choose what to eat first. When he turns his head away to show that he has had enough, she still tries to carry on feeding him. Jack shows that he is not happy by wriggling and pushing away. A beaker of drink is spilt. The member of staff comments that Jack is being difficult.

1. Describe how Jack might have been feeling and explain how this showed in his behaviour.
2. How could the member of staff have worked differently?
3. Why is it important to look for ways of allowing children to be independent?

The Features Page:

Focus on *Seeing children as individuals*

It is very easy for children with additional needs to be seen as 'the child with the hearing impairment' or 'the child with epilepsy'. However, the medical condition, learning need or disability is not the whole child, and it is important to see each child as an individual.

Q I recently went on a course about autism. While it was interesting, it has not really made the child I work with better.

A Many practitioners attend training and courses about additional needs secretly hoping for a cure that will magically change a child and 'solve' a problem. While training can often help you to learn more about different needs and even give ideas about strategies, remember that every child is different so what works well for one child might not be so effective with another. The key is often to keep trying new approaches and to accept the children for who they are. It is also worth talking to parents as quite often they will have found ways to help their child.

Q Have you got any ideas of how I can help a child who dislikes reading?

A Reading is a skill that requires practice and some effort. Sadly, children can easily be put off learning to read, especially when they notice that other children are reading more fluently. As with any activity, the starting point should be to think how you can make reading fun and give a child confidence. Begin by looking at the book that the child is meant to be reading. Is it too difficult? Is the book interesting? You can also make books with children or take it in turns to read. Remember, children need plenty of praise and encouragement so they can start to believe they are capable of reading. Encouraging a child to enjoy reading requires a little effort and may take a few weeks, so keep sessions short and stop while you are both having fun.

Q A child with hearing loss is coming to our nursery next term. She wears a hearing aid. Is there anything that we should do?

A Begin by talking to the child's parents to find out more about how her hearing loss affects her and how you can support her. You also need to know how to check the hearing aid and, if necessary, change the battery. It is worth being aware that many children with hearing aids need adults to remember that they may not fully hear in all situations. This means that it may be a good idea to speak clearly but not shout and to make sure that you have the child's attention before talking. Some children with hearing aids also find loud background noise very difficult to cope with, so you may need to find ways of minimising some sounds, for example by placing activities on carpeted surfaces or by considering how a large room is being used.

Ask the expert

346

Seeing children as individuals

Janet, mother of Sophie

We knew that Sophie was not developing like other children by the time she was 18 months old. She was not trying to walk and still only babbled. However, it took us a while to accept that she had a learning difficulty which meant that she would always be very different from other children. For a while I kept thinking about what she ought to be doing rather than enjoying what she was doing. Now, we take life one day at a time and focus very much on what she is interested in. While other parents might be delighted that their children can read, we are delighted when Sophie is dry through the night. Fortunately most practitioners have been very good, though there was a practitioner who only told us what Sophie was not doing and seemed unable to change her approach and see that Sophie had different needs. The staff where Sophie is at the moment are brilliant – Sophie is very happy and the staff make us feel that she is special.

Top Tips:

Working with children with additional needs

- ✓ Remember that children are always special to their parents.
- ✓ Focus on what child can do rather than what he or she cannot do.
- ✓ Talk to parents, who tend to know what their child likes doing.
- ✓ Accept each child for who he or she is – try to work with him or her rather than to change the child.

Word puzzle

Can you unscramble the following titles of professionals who support children with additional needs? The first title has unscrambled for you, to start you off

- **TIME GUN LACY MEAT**
  Multi-agency team

- **ODECANTULIA CHISTOLOGYSP**

- **THEAHL RIVISTO**

- **PACCOTUNALIO RATEHSTIP**

- **HISOPYTRAESTHIP**

- **CHEEPS DAN GUALANGE PITSHETAR**

How inclusion works within the setting

You saw earlier that inclusion involves finding ways of helping children who would traditionally have been excluded from settings or activities. This way of thinking has had an enormous impact on the way early years practitioners work with children. Instead of expecting children to fit in with what you are doing, inclusive practice involves adapting activities, changing routines and even sometimes the layout of the setting so that children can participate (see also barriers to participation below).

How to use specific methods of communication

Some children need particular help in order to communicate and interact. Speech alone may be difficult for them and they may require special methods of communication. There are several of these and usually advice will be given by a speech therapist in consultation with parents as to which one to use and how to use it. Over the past few years, the range of methods has increased and technology is increasingly being used. Voice simulation has, for example, meant that children can press a picture or type in a computer or handheld device and have 'their voices' heard. In the same way, for children who find it hard to write, voice recognition can put their words into writing. Below are some examples of the methods that might be used.

Visual systems

Some children need visual cues in order to make sense of language. If the child you are working with uses a system of visual communication, you will need to spend time learning how to use it quickly and fluently.

Picture representations

Some children benefit from using pictures to supplement communication. You may show a child a picture of an apron and at the same time say the word so that the child knows that they need to get their apron.

Picture exchange system

This system, based on pictures, not only helps children to understand the meaning of words but also helps them to learn about the way in which communication is a shared and a two-way process. The child takes and receives pictures and so learns how to interact.

Sign representations

Some children's cognitive development is the reason why they find it hard to talk and communicate. At first, babies learn about language through seeing the object that the adult is talking about at the same time as hearing the word. For example, an adult may point to a cat and say 'cat'. The child then remembers the word and so eventually does not need the cat to be around to know what the word means. For some children, sounds alone are not enough and they need to have their language supported by signs. A common sign system is Makaton. It helps children link the word to an action or object and so is easier for them to understand. Makaton is not a language in itself but a tool to help language. It is important not to confuse Makaton with British sign language (see below), which is not used for the same purpose.

Scissors (to cut)

Drink (cup)

Ball

⇧ **Some common Makaton signs**

British sign language

British sign language is an alternative form of communication. It is a complete language and is used instead of speech. Users of sign language do not have learning difficulties. Most users have significant hearing loss and so need a different way of communicating.

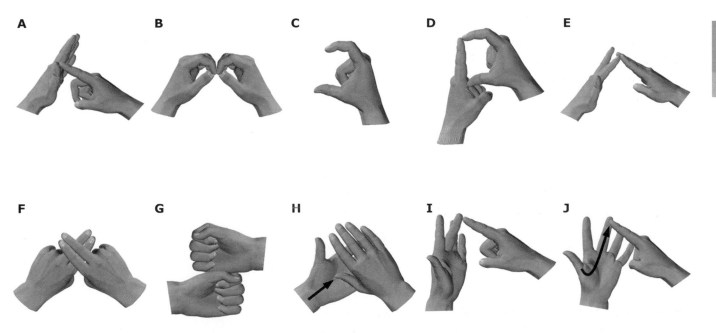

⇧ **Letters a–j from the British finger spelling alphabet**
   (*Source:* The National Deaf Children's Society, www.ncds.org.uk)

Back to the real world

You should now know how you can best help the child that you have been working with. You should also have some understanding of how not to stereotype children and ways in which you might work with them.

1. Explain what you might do if you recognise that a child might have additional needs.

2. Explain why it is important not to label children.

3. Describe why inclusion is important for children.

Section 3

The role of the adult in enabling children with additional needs to participate in activities and experiences

In the real world

You have been asked to plan an activity for a group of children. You know that some of the children have additional needs, but are not quite sure what you should do about this when planning the activity.

By the end of this section you will have an understanding of how to plan activities and how to adapt them to suit the needs of children.

Introduction

Planning for individual needs

When planning for all children, the key thing is to make sure that you think carefully about individual children. As we saw in Unit 8, it is always important to think about children's interests, strengths and stage of activity. For children who have additional needs, you might also think about activities or experiences that will help them make progress in some way. Assuming all children will be able to cope with exactly the same activity is not a good approach to take. One activity may suit one child, but it may not be of interest to another. In the same way, an activity might be at the right level for one child but not be challenging enough for another.

Using observations when planning

You saw in Unit 2 that observations are a vital tool in helping practitioners to work with children. Observing and keeping records will also be essential in helping children with additional needs. As well as monitoring children's progress, observations should be used to work out how best to adapt what you do to help children. You might, for example, notice that a child is interested in a particular toy. This information can then be used to help you plan other activities which will help the child, using the toy as a starting point.

Individual education plans or programmes.

It is important to plan to meet all children's needs. As you have seen, sometimes this planning may be done informally, but for children with significant needs, a separate plan of action might be needed. In England and Wales, an individual education plan (IEP) or programme is used. This looks at a child's current needs and at ways of supporting the child. It is almost like a plan of action and helps everyone working with the child focus on ways to help him or her.

Case study

The importance of reading children's individual plans

Liam is 4 years old. His individual education plan for this term focuses on building his hand–eye coordination. Maria is new to the setting. A small group of children are playing in the sand tray. She notices that Liam is spilling quite a lot of the sand. She tells him that he will have to stop playing if he carries on making such a mess.

1. Why is it important for adults to find out about children's individual needs?
2. How might Maria have worked differently with Liam if she had read his IEP?
3. What are the benefits to the child if staff understand their additional needs?

An individual education plan is drawn up in consultation with parents in recognition that parents know their child's strengths, interests and developmental needs. If you are working with a group of children or an individual child, you will need to consider what is on their IEP. As a learner, you may not necessarily be given the IEP to read as it is a confidential document, but your placement supervisor may give you advice as to how best to work with the child.

The barriers to participation for children and families

The aim of inclusion is to ensure that all children can take part in activities and experiences. An important part of the adult's role is to work out what might prevent a child or children with additional needs from joining in. These can be thought of as barriers to participation.

The spider diagram below shows some common barriers that might prevent children from being able to join in, unless you plan carefully or adapt what you are doing.

Attitudes and expectations
Some of the biggest barriers are adults in settings. Adults who are not ready to change their routines or approaches may make children and their families feel unwelcome.

Communication
Some children may need support in order to communicate or understand what is being said. This may prevent them from joining in and making friends with other

BARRIERS TO PARTICIPATION

Physical
Some barriers are physical ones such as layout, height of tables, obstacles such as steps and lighting.

Routines and structures
Sometimes the routines and structure of a setting may act as a barrier. A child might need additional snacks or to come in later than other children.

How to review activities and experiences to ensure an inclusive approach

The spider diagram above shows some examples of common barriers that might prevent some children from joining in. The skill in working with children is to think of ways in which you can adapt practice to make sure that these children can now join in. The flow diagram below gives some examples of ways in which you might adapt activities to meet children's needs and so remove some of the barriers. As well as using your own ideas for adapting activities and experiences, remember that parents, support groups and other professionals will also have experience and therefore some ideas. Sometimes, children themselves will be able to help you think about how to remove possible barriers.

Communication

A child might not be able to hear instructions or what other children are saying

Physical

A child might not be able to stand up to do an activity or may not have the coordination skills to play a game

Behaviour

A child might find it hard to play with a group of children

↓

- Write down instructions or show pictures to help children understand what is happening.
- Encourage other children to face the child so that it is easier for them to hear.
- Use pictures or signs to help children to communicate with each other.
- Plan games in which action is more important than hearing or talk.

↓

- Plan games which do not involve standing up or games where children can sit down.
- Put some activities onto tables so that children do not need to stand.
- Put out a range of toys and equipment so that children with different skill levels can use them.

↓

- Plan activities and experiences where children can be together in small groups or pairs.
- Ensure a child has an adult to support and help them in a group situation.

⇧ **How to ensure an inclusive approach**

Think about it

Look at the following situations. See if you can think of practical ways of adapting the activity or experience to suit each child.

1. Mustafa is 5 years old. He wants to play football, but the ball that is being used is too small and hard for him to kick.
2. Annabel is 4 years old. She wants to do a jigsaw puzzle, but the ones that are on the table have too many pieces and she is becoming frustrated
3. Zaynab is 3 years old. She enjoys playing in the sand tray, but finds it hard to share with others.

Jack is finding it hard to finish a jigsaw puzzle. When he puts a piece in, the whole jigsaw puzzle often slips away from him. His coordination is such that he cannot put one hand down to act as a stabiliser. The supervisor recognises the difficulty that Jack is having and comes up with the idea of putting the jigsaw onto a sheet of rubber matting. This allows Jack to finish the puzzle without further adult help.

1. Explain why this type of adult support is preferable to helping Jack finish the puzzle.
2. Why is it important to look for ways of allowing children to be independent?

Specialist aids and equipment

There are many aids and pieces of equipment that are used to support children with additional needs, as the spider diagram below shows. Some types of equipment help children with their mobility or their dexterity. In addition, some children may have aids and equipment that will help them with a sensory impairment such as hearing or sight. They may wear a hearing aid or glasses.

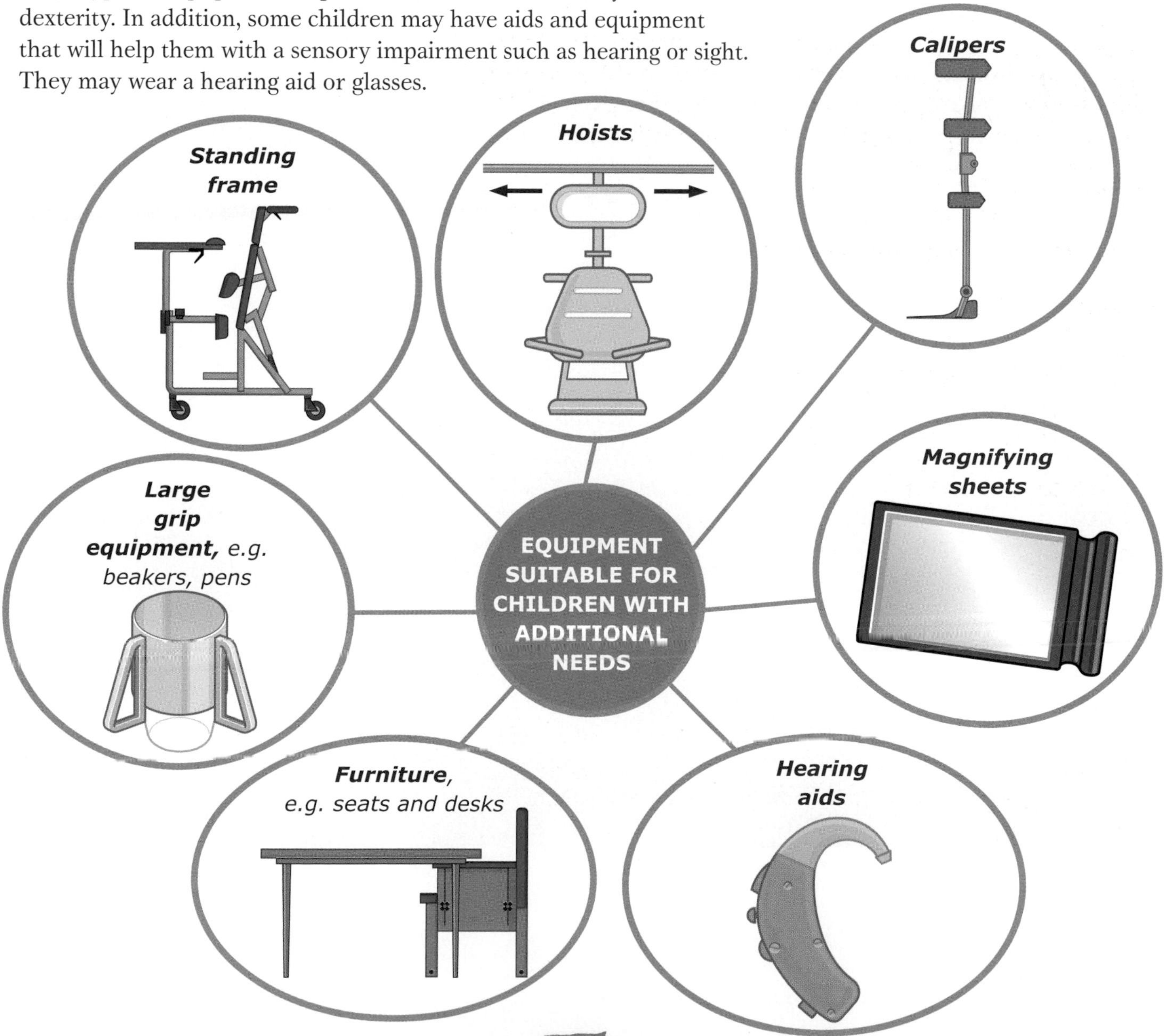

Standing frame

Hoists

Calipers

Large grip equipment, e.g. beakers, pens

EQUIPMENT SUITABLE FOR CHILDREN WITH ADDITIONAL NEEDS

Magnifying sheets

Furniture, e.g. seats and desks

Hearing aids

U9
3

As well as equipment that supports the child, you could find out about toys that are designed to support children with additional needs. You can get advice and often borrow these toys from local authority teams or from your local toy library.

The safe use of specialist aids and equipment

Aids and equipment that some children might use are vital for them. A child who is not wearing glasses may not see the pictures during a game, while a child whose hearing aid requires a new battery may not hear the other children talk. This means that it is essential to learn what each piece of equipment does and when and how to use it.

Equipment and aids are usually recommended or provided by the services that are supporting the child and the family. In some cases, the professionals that support these children will teach you how to use the equipment. You may find that parents, colleagues and even children themselves know about them.

You may also be taught how to adjust the equipment and how to check whether it is working correctly. You must follow instructions carefully and carry out any routine maintenance procedures given, particularly for equipment which supports children's mobility or takes their weight, for example a hoist that is not being used properly may cause injury.

Find out!

Visit the website of the National Association of Toy and Leisure Libraries (www.natll.org.uk) and find out where your nearest toy library is.

Case study

The importance of specialist aids and equipment

Christina is 2 years old. She has recently been fitted with two hearing aids. The difference in her behaviour is incredible and she is now keen to try to talk. To support Christina further, a member of the sensory support team has come in to explain to staff how the hearing aid works, and how best to help Christina. He explains that the hearing aid does not 'cure' a hearing loss, but that it makes a considerable difference to the wearer's hearing. He stresses the importance of checking that the batteries are working and shows the staff how to change the battery. He leaves some spare batteries for the setting.

A few weeks later, a member of staff notices that Christina is not joining in during a game of picture lotto. She realises that Christina is not hearing but does not feel like going to get the new batteries. She decides to wait to the end of the day before telling Christina's mother that maybe the hearing aid is not working properly. Christina's mother is quite cross about this.

1. Explain why the staff member should have changed the battery immediately.
2. Why might Christina's mother have felt angry?
3. How might the delay in changing the batteries have affected Christina?

Back to the real world

You should now know how to plan for children's individual needs and how to adapt activities to help meet children's needs.

1. Explain why it is important to find out if a child has an individual learning plan or programme.

2. Explain another way of finding out more about a child's needs.

Getting ready for assessment

In order to prepare for your assessment, you may like to see if you can answer the following questions:

1. Give one example of how a piece of legislation might affect a child's rights.

2. Identify two organisations that support children and their families.

3. Describe ways in which the policy of inclusion might benefit a child.

4. Explain why it is important not to label children.

5. Give one example of a specialist aid and how it may be used to support a child.

U9

3

Unit 10

Introduction to children's learning

In this unit you will learn:

1. The different frameworks for learning for children from birth to age 16 years

2. The principles of how children learn

3. The role of the adult in supporting children's learning from birth to age 16 years

The different frameworks for learning for children from birth to age 16 years

In the real world

It is your first week in placement. Your placement supervisor has been showing you the planning system. She has asked you to prepare an activity for the following week that links to the framework that the setting is using. You look a little puzzled and so she tells you that they are using the Early Years Foundation Stage and that you ought to get a copy of it.

By the end of this section you will know about the framework that is being used in your country for early years and in schools and the different approaches to working with children.

The different frameworks for learning available for children from birth to 16 years in the country in which you live

In order to plan effectively for children's learning you will need to know about the frameworks that are being used in your country. In the UK, each country has developed its own approach towards the early years. For example, in England there is a framework that looks at children's care and learning that covers the age range 0–5 years. It is called the Early Years Foundation Stage and has taken over from two separate frameworks, Birth to Three Matters and the Foundation Stage.

When you have found out which framework is being used in the setting in which you work (see below), you will need to check if it is recommended or statutory. A statutory framework means that it has to be used by law if a setting receives government money (see also Unit 1, page 3).

It is also helpful to know about the frameworks for older children. In England, there is a National Curriculum. This is statutory and so all schools in England that are government funded must follow it. (The National Curriculum of each country is discussed below.)

Keeping up to date

You will need to learn about the current frameworks that are being used in your country, but remember that frameworks are often updated. At the time of writing, Wales is introducing a Foundation Stage that will include their current Key Stage 1, while Scotland is in the process of changing its curriculum for 5–14-year-olds. Scotland has also introduced a framework for children under 3 years old. There are many ways in which you can keep up to date – by looking at the education website for your country or reading educational magazines and newspapers.

The structure and content of different learning frameworks

An overview of the frameworks for England, Wales, Scotland and Northern Ireland is given below. You will need to find out about the structure of the different frameworks that are used in the settings in which you work.

England

There are five separate stages in education – they all have a statutory curriculum:

→ 0–5 years   Early Years Foundation Stage
→ 5–7 years   Key Stage 1
→ 7–11 years   Key Stage 2
→ 11–14 years   Key Stage 3
→ 14–16 years   Key Stage 4

Early Years Foundation Stage

From 2008, all settings that receive government funding will follow the Early Years Foundation Stage framework, which consists of the following six areas, known as 'areas of learning and development'.

EYFS Six Areas of Learning and Development
1. Personal, social and emotional
2. Problem solving, reasoning and numeracy
3. Communication, language and literacy
4. Knowledge and understanding of the world
5. Physical development
6. Creative development.

Each area of learning is subdivided into separate aspects. Each aspect of learning has a series of targets that children are likely to meet by the end of their Reception year. These are known as 'Early Learning Goals'. For each aspect of learning, age bands are given to help practitioners think about what activities and experiences they might plan for children.

National Curriculum

The National Curriculum is divided into four key stages, as described above. At the end of Key Stage 4, most pupils will take GCSEs or equivalent level qualifications. The chart below shows the subjects that children will study in each of the key stages.

👆 **The key stages of the English National Curriculum**

Key Stage 1	Key Stage 2	Key Stage 3	Key Stage 4
Mathematics	Mathematics	Mathematics	Mathematics
English	English	English	English
Science	Science	Science	Science
Design and Technology	Design and Technology	Design and Technology	Citizenship
Information Communication and Technology	Information Communication and Technology	Information Communication and Technology	Information Communication and Technology
History	History	History	Young people will also opt to study other subjects including vocational subjects such as Business Studies or Health and Social Care.
Geography	Geography	Geography	
Art and Design	Art and Design	Art and Design	
Music	Music	Music	
Physical Education	Physical Education	Physical Education	
Religious Education	Religious Education	Religious Education	
		Modern Foreign Language	
		Citizenship	

Other frameworks used in England

→ *Primary framework for literacy and mathematics.* This is a further document that gives guidance about how reading, writing and mathematics should be taught in primary schools.

→ *Social and emotional aspects of learning.* This is a curriculum produced by the Department of Education and Skills and is designed for primary schools.

Although neither of the above primary frameworks is compulsory, most primary schools follow them.

Wales

In Wales, the Foundation Phase is replacing 'Desirable Outcomes'. The Foundation Phase covers children aged 3–7 years and covers seven areas of learning.

Foundation Phase Seven Areas of Learning:

1. Personal and social development and well-being
2. Language, literacy and communication skills
3. Mathematical development
4. Bilingualism and multi-cultural understanding
5. Knowledge and understanding of the world
6. Physical development
7. Creative development.

National Curriculum

Key Stage 2 (7–11 years)

At Key Stage 2, primary schools must by law teach the Welsh National Curriculum and the basic curriculum which consists of religious education and personal and social education. All children are expected to learn Welsh as either a first or a second language.

The National Curriculum consists of the following:

→ *Core subjects* – English, Welsh, mathematics and science

→ *Non-core subjects* – Welsh second language, design and technology, information technology, history, geography, art, music, physical education and religious education.

Key Stage 3 (11–13 years)

From 11 years, children continue to follow the National Curriculum, which comprises:

→ *Core subjects* – English and Welsh, mathematics and science

→ *Non-core subjects* – Welsh second language, modern foreign languages, design and technology, information technology, history, geography, art, music, physical education and religious education.

Key Stage 4 (14–16 years)

From the age of 14 years, only five National Curriculum subjects are compulsory and many students will take GCSEs or equivent level

Find out!

You can find out more about curriculum provision in England via the following websites:

→ Early Years Foundation Stage – www.standards. dfes.gov.uk/eyfs

→ National Curriculum online – www.nc.uk.net

qualifications at the age of 16 years. The compulsory subjects are:

→ English
→ Welsh or Welsh second language
→ mathematics
→ science
→ physical education.

Scotland

Birth to Three

Scotland has developed a framework called Birth to Three to support adults who work with babies and toddlers. The material is designed to support practitioners and improve the quality of care and education for babies and toddlers. Unlike the English Early Years Foundation Stage, the framework is not compulsory for settings.

A Curriculum Framework for Children aged 3 to 5 years

This document sets out guidance for pre-schools, nurseries and childminders working with children aged 3–5 years. As with the other early years curricula in the UK, areas of learning are identified, including:

→ Emotional, personal and social development
→ Communication and language
→ Knowledge and understanding of the world
→ Expressive and aesthetic development
→ Physical development and movement.

5–14 years

At present, Scottish schools follow the 5–14 curriculum, which runs through until the second year of secondary schooling. Schools work with their local authority to determine the structure and content of the curriculum, although some guidance is given on the amount of time that should be spent on different curriculum subjects:

→ Language – 20 per cent
→ Mathematics – 15 per cent
→ Environmental studies – 15 per cent
→ Expressive arts – 15 per cent
→ Religious and moral education – 15 per cent
→ Flexible time to use on any of the main curriculum areas – 20 per cent.

Standard Grades

Young people aged 15–16 take Standard Grades; most will take seven or eight subjects including English and maths.

New developments

In order to provide more flexibility, the Scottish Executive is in the process of launching Curriculum for Excellence, which will run from 3 to 18 years. The aim is to make learning more personalised. Young people will be able to take exams when they are ready rather than according to the number of years spent in school.

Find out!

You can find out more about curriculum provision in Wales via the following website:

http://new.wales.gov.uk/topics/educationandskills

Find out!

You can find out more about curriculum provision in Scotland via the website Learning and Teaching Scotland (www.ltscotland.org.uk)

Education in Northern Ireland is complex as it had been devolved to the Northern Ireland assembly. Owing to political developments, when the Assembly was suspended (in October 2002), reforms to the structure of the curriculum were postponed. At the time of writing, devolved government is again in place and it is likely that changes to the curriculum will follow. If you work in Northern Ireland, you will need to be aware of any developments.

The curriculum is the responsibility of the Northern Ireland Council for the Curriculum, Examinations and Assessment.

There are four key stages in the education system:

→ 4–8 years   Key Stage 1
→ 8–11 years   Key Stage 2
→ 11–14 years   Key Stage 3
→ 14–16 years   Key Stage 4

Find out!

→ You can find out more about curriculum provision in Northern Ireland via the website of the Northern Ireland Council for the Curriculum, Examinations and Assessment (www.ccea.org.uk).
→ For information about early years, you will need to contact NIPPA – the early years organisation (www.nippa.org), although at the time of writing there is not a specific framework for use in nurseries and pre-schools.

The principles and approaches of competing frameworks for learning

A good starting point when looking at a framework is to consider its principles. You would normally find these in the introductory pages of the framework document. Principles provide an outline of the way in which the curriculum or framework should be delivered, for example the Early Years Foundation Stage in England has four principles (see box below).

Early Years Foundation Stage

This framework is due to replace the Birth to Three Matters and Foundation Stage curricula in September 2008. You will need to use this framework if you are working in England with children from birth to the end of the reception year. The framework consists of four principles:

1. A unique child
2. Positive relationships
3. Enabling environments
4. Learning and development.

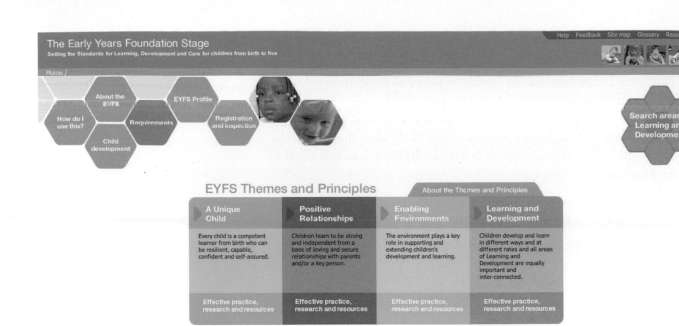

⇧ The DfES website for the Early Years Foundation Stage (EYFS) curriculum clearly states its themes and principles

Your role in supporting different approaches to learning

Every nursery, pre-school and school has its own feel and even smell! This means that while you might find that two schools or nurseries are using exactly the same framework, the way that they interpret and use it may be different. This is why it is useful to have placements or visit a range of different settings. By being in different settings, you will probably find that each setting uses its strengths in order to deliver the framework, thus a pre-school with a large outdoor area may plan many learning activities that involve the children being outdoors.

In order to support different approaches to learning, you will need to develop confidence in planning and using the framework in a setting. It is therefore a good idea to ask if you might look at planning and to be interested in the activities that are planned. You should also try to plan an activity or play opportunity using the framework and then review its success. Ideas for activities can often be found in early years and teaching magazines and newspapers.

You will find it helpful to know what resources and equipment are available in the setting. Many settings have a resources room and this can be a good way of looking to see what is on offer.

Find out!

Read about each of the principles on page 9 of the Early Years Foundation Stage framework. You can either download this from www. standards.dfes.gov.uk/eyfs or obtain a free order copy from the order line 0845 60 222 60.

Think about it

How might the principles of the Early Years Foundation Stage framework affect the way in which adults work with children?

Find out!

Visit two settings in your area that work with the same age range.

1. What do you notice about the differences between the settings?
2. How do they plan for children's learning?

(*Note:* If you are unable to visit two settings, you could ask another learner about their placement.)

Back to the real world

You should now have a copy of the relevant framework for the country in which you work and understand its structure. You should also know about different approaches in the way that settings work with children.

1. Explain the principles of the early years framework used in your setting.

2. Describe two different approaches to the way settings might work with children.

Section 2

The principles of how children learn

In the real world

You are on placement in a nursery attached to a school. You have noticed that while the older children can often look at a number of objects and immediately say how many there are, the younger ones seem to need to touch them and count them one by one. Your placement supervisor tells you that this is linked to their cognitive development. You are not sure what this means.

By the end of this section you will know about the stages of cognitive development and some of the factors that affect it. You will also understand why play is important in supporting children's learning.

Introduction

What is learning?

The term learning is used a lot when working with children. It is a complicated and not fully understood process by which the brain takes in new information and uses it in some way. There are many process involved in learning, including the ability to concentrate and use memory. While it is not completely understood how learning takes place, children are known to learn from the moment of birth.

Theories of learning

There are two main theories of learning that are used by practitioners when helping children to learn:

1. Social cognitive theory
2. Behaviourist theories.

Social cognitive theory

This is also known as social learning theory or learning through observation. It is an interesting theory as it also explains some aspects of children's behaviour. It was first put forward by Albert Bandura (b. 1925) and is still being developed.

The idea behind the theory is that children are able to learn various skills and behaviours by watching other people. This means that a young child might watch you write on a piece of paper and later try to do the same thing. This theory has been shown to be quite a powerful one.

⇩ **In Bandura's experiment, the adult modelled attacking the Bobo doll and the children then copied her behaviour**

The Bobo doll experiment

To prove the theory, Bandura carried out an experiment (1963) in which he showed three groups of children a short film about an adult hitting an inflatable doll. Each group saw one of these endings to the film:

1. The adult was praised and given sweets.
2. Nothing was said to the adult.
3. The adult was smacked and told off.

Bandura then looked to see how children behaved when they were left alone with the same doll. He found that children who saw endings 1 and 2 were more aggressive with the doll than the children who saw ending 3. He came to the conclusion that the children who had seen endings 1 and 2 were more aggressive towards the doll because they had learned from watching the adult that it was acceptable to hit the doll.

Implications for practice

Albert Bandura's work shows that children are quick to copy. This means that practitioners have to think about what they do and say when children are present, as children may copy aspects of unwanted behaviour. As well as behaviour, Bandura's theory can also help practitioners to plan for children's learning. If you know that children are able to copy adults, this means that they may be able to learn some skills and pick up positive attitudes from you. A good example of this is the way that a young child might notice the way that you are counting out beakers and then try and do the same.

The flow diagram below shows the steps early years practitioners can take with children in light of Bandura's social cognitive theory.

Social cognitive theory Children learn from watching and copying other adults and children	→	*The role of the early years practitioner* • Encourage children to learn from each other • Allow children time to imitate what they have seen • Remember that you are a role model • If children see you doing something, for example painting, they are more likely to want to try it themselves

Behaviourist theories

There is a group of psychologists, known as behaviourists, who believe that learning is shaped by people's direct experiences. One of the most famous behaviourist theories was put forward by Burrhus F. Skinner (1904–94). In simple terms, it states that people repeat experiences that are enjoyable and avoid experiences that they have not enjoyed. In this way, people learn skills and types of behaviour. For example, if a child is given praise or has enjoyed doing a puzzle, he or she is likely to do the puzzle again.

Skinner called things that would make people repeat an activity, **positive reinforcements**. There are many different types of positive reinforcement – food, praise and money are common positive reinforcements for all of us!

This theory is the idea behind trial and error learning. You might try something out and if it is successful, you will learn from this and repeat the experience. For example, a baby shakes a rattle and hears a noise. She is pleased with the noise and so shakes the rattle again. The baby has learned that rattles can make noises. A 10-year-old enjoys making an electric circuit and seeing a light bulb switch on. The child decides to try making some other circuits.

Find out!

Observe children in the setting and see if you can identify examples of this theory at work for yourself.

Jargon buster

Positive reinforcement
Offering a desirable effect for a behaviour to increase the chance of that behaviour being repeated in the future.

Behaviourist theory Children will repeat an activity if they have had positive reinforcement	→	*The role of the early years practitioner* • Praise children when they are playing and learning • Learning must be fun and pleasurable • Make sure that children can manage the activities and equipment that are provided for them

The behaviourist theory is widely accepted by early years practitioners, not only as a theory of how children learn but also as a way of managing children's behaviour. This is why you might praise children when they show wanted behaviour.

The stages and sequence of cognitive development

Cognitive development is sometimes referred to as intellectual development. It is about the way in which children's ability to use logic, think and plan changes over time. Watching children learn and develop is extremely interesting. While all children are unique, there still seems to be a pattern when it comes to learning. Some theorists have tried to explain this process. For example, Piaget believed that children need to have direct experiences of the world but that there are also stages of development that children pass through (see below).

In Unit 2 you looked at some of the probable stages and sequences that you might see in children's cognitive development (see page 40). You will need to revisit this material again in order to complete your learning for this unit.

When looking at children's cognitive development, a key point to remember is the way in which children are gradually able to think abstractly. Below are some examples that will help you to understand this:

➔ Annie is 18 months old. When she sees a cat, she says 'cat'. She needs to see a cat or a picture of a cat in order to think about cats.

➔ Frankie is 4 years old. He is interested in animals. He tells his key worker that his favourite animal is a cat. He can think about cats without needing to see one.

➔ Joseph is 13 years old. He can talk about and imagine what it might be like to be a cat even though he knows that he is not an animal.

Piaget's theory

This theory suggests that learning and cognitive development is a process and children need to pass through different stages. The most famous psychologist who worked with this theory is Jean Piaget (1896–1980), a Swiss biologist. He was working on intelligence tests when he became interested in finding out why children's logic was different from that of adults.

Piaget's main idea was that children develop logic based on their experiences and try to draw conclusions from these experiences. Sometimes these conclusions – or **schemas** as Piaget called them – are wrong, but the errors children make are understandable. For example, many young children think that all women must be 'mummies'. Their own experience is often that women are mothers and so they develop this schema. Eventually, they learn that some women are not mothers and then they have to adapt their schema. (For more about schema theory, see Unit 8 pages 298–9.)

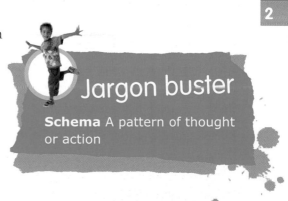

Jargon buster

Schema A pattern of thought or action

U10
2

From studying children carefully, Piaget concluded that there were stages of learning broadly linked to children's ages, and children were unable to move from one stage of learning to another until they were ready. The chart below outlines Piaget's stages of learning from birth to 16 years.

Piaget's stages of learning from birth to 16 years

Age	Stage of learning
0–2 years	 *Sensory motor* Babies are starting to find out about things around them and discovering what these things can be made to do.
2–7 years	 *Pre-operational* Thought processes are developing. Children are starting to use symbols in their play, although children often need to see things and feel them to learn about them. For example, 5-year-olds find it hard to add up in their head but can manage with counters.
7–11 years	 *Concrete operations* Children can think more logically. They can follow rules of games. They can use and understand symbols, such as letters and numbers.
12–18 years	 *Formal operations* Young people are increasingly able to plan, predict and speculate.

Although Piaget's work has been criticised because often children do things earlier than he suggested, the idea that children need to learn at their own pace has been accepted.

Piaget suggested that children's direct experiences help them to form their ideas.

The critical periods for learning

In recent years, neuroscientists who study the development and function of the brain have learned more about the structure of the brain and the way in which it grows. They are excited by what they have learned so far although they know that there is plenty more to discover. Their work is already influencing early years work with children, and frameworks such as the Early Years Foundation Stage are based on the certain knowledge that babies and young children need good stimulation in order for their brain to develop.

To understand the importance of early stimulation, you need to look at the way in which the brain grows and develops.

Making connections

The brain is a complex organ, which essentially is made up of cells called neurons. In the first months of life, a major task is for these cells to find ways of connecting with each other so that they can pass information across. These connections are vital in the developing brain. Babies who are in stimulating environments are able to make these connections easily and so their brains develop healthily. Where a baby's brain is not being stimulated, fewer connections are made and this may result in the brain not being able to process information so easily later. It would seem that early care and stimulation in a baby's life will play an important role later on.

Periods of brain growth

As well as the brain making some key connections early on, the brain also has other periods in which it grows rapidly. This may explain why children seem to make significant leaps in their cognitive development.

➜ *6–8 years* – This growth spurt results in better physical coordination, particularly fine motor and hand–eye coordination.
➜ *10–12 years* – The next growth spurt affects the frontal lobes of the brain (in the forehead). Brain activity in the frontal lobes is linked to the ability to think and so this growth results in better logic and planning.
➜ *13–15 years* – This growth spurt seems to be linked to increased spatial perception, physical coordination and the ability to think in an abstract way.

The role of active learning and the importance of play

Most research shows that children use play as a way of learning. They also learn more easily when they are doing and exploring rather than sitting down and being taught. It would seem that by doing something for themselves, children are able to learn more effectively than just being told about it. This is probably because the brain finds it easier to process information that is multi-sensory (using more than one sense). Hence a young child is likely to find it easier to learn about cooking by doing some rather than simply being told about it.

The importance of active learning and play means that settings working with children will plan many games and activities so that children can learn through play. The spider diagram below shows some of the skills that children might learn as they make a play den out of cardboard boxes and fabric.

Organising and planning

Textures

Patience and perseverance

SKILLS THAT CHILDREN MIGHT LEARN WHILE MAKING A PLAY DEN

Gravity and weight

Learning to share and take turns

Shapes and size

Design and creativity

Case study

Name games

Matthew works in a nursery. He thinks that three children in his group would be ready to recognise their names. He decides to plan some activities that will draw the children's attention to their names. These are three of his ideas:

→ A treasure hunt. Matthew wraps up some toys and labels them so that each package has an individual child's name on it. He hides them in the garden. He shows the children a card with their names on it. He asks the children if they can find the toys that have their names on them. The children start looking for their names. They ask if they can wrap up the toys and play the game again for themselves.

→ Water boats. Matthew laminates the children's names and, for each child, sticks a name on the bottom of a boat in the water tray. The children are excited to find that the boats have names on them. They start to look for their names.

→ Stickers. Matthew puts the children's names onto stickers. He leaves the stickers on the writing table. The children find their stickers and love playing with them. They ask if they can write on the stickers too.

1. Explain why children might enjoy these activities.
2. Do you think that the children might notice their name?

The factors that can affect the child's ability to learn

There are many factors that can affect children's learning, as described below. It is important not only to understand the factors that affect children's learning but also to think about ways in which you might be able to support children.

Diet

Research seems to show that children need to eat a healthy and balanced diet in order for their brain to develop well. This is because the brain requires certain chemicals, fats and minerals in order to function properly. Children whose diet is poor may find it harder to concentrate and learn. This means that everyone involved in looking after children must think about the type of foods that they provide. As water is important too, it is essential that children drink sufficiently during the day.

Sleep

Most people know that they cannot remember things or concentrate well when they are tired. Children are the same, and it would seem that repeated lack of sleep affects children's concentration, memory and ability to think. It also makes a significant difference to their behaviour. It is thought that babies and young children need more sleep in order that their brains can process information and develop. Adults must therefore ensure that young children get enough sleep, including making nap times available for children who need them.

Stimulation

Children's ability to learn is affected by the amount of stimulation that they receive. As you have seen, this is linked to the environment as well as to the people they are with. Babies and children who are frequently bored will find it harder to learn. This is why it is important to think about activities that will be of interest and to observe children to check that you are providing sufficient stimulation.

Emotional well-being

The way a person is feeling can affect their mood and their ability to concentrate and learn. This means that babies and children who are not feeling settled, happy or relaxed will find it hard to concentrate and take in information. Children who are confident and feel good about themselves find it easier to learn. You will therefore need to think about your relationships with children and notice when children do not seem to be happy and secure.

Health

Children need a level of good health in order to be able to learn. Feeling poorly can impair their concentration and lower their ability to learn.

Find out!

Does your placement have a policy on providing food and drinks for children?

Think about it

How does lack of sleep affect your behaviour, mood and ability to think?

U10
2

Some children have a medical condition which might make them tired, while appointments or illness can mean that some children miss lessons or sessions. In addition, some medicines can affect children's levels of concentration since they cause drowsiness. You will need to take into account a child's health or pattern of attendance when planning activities. For example, you might need to change the pace of an activity or remember that a child was absent when a particular skill was taught.

⇦ **Children need a level of good health in order to be able to learn**

Learning disabilities

Some children have learning disabilities, which means that they find it difficult to concentrate and process or store information. The speed at which they learn may be different to that of other children or you might need to change the way in which they need to be helped to learn.

The effective types of environments that encourage learning

You have seen that children need play opportunities and learn best when they are active in their learning. You have also looked at the factors that affect learning. Both of these will have an impact on the environments that you provide for children to meet their learning needs. Below are some of the key elements of an effective learning environment.

Resources, toys and equipment

A good environment offers a range of toys, resources and equipment that will inspire children to play and explore. Some resources will not be specifically designed for children but will be of great interest to them. For example, a 4-year-old might enjoy rolling a ball down the inside of a drainpipe, while a 6-year-old might try to create a house from cardboard boxes and fabric. Toys, resources and equipment will need to be challenging, interesting and varied because, as you saw in Unit 4, children can learn from different types of play. In most early years environments, children spend time in and out of doors, so there should be plenty of different types of activities, resources and experiences available for them.

Indoor and outdoor space

Babies and children need plenty of space so they can develop their physical skills and 'spread' out as they play and explore. Children need different types of spaces according to their age and play needs. Children who want to play large-scale games, such as hide and seek, will need some open areas, while those wanting to engage in role play may want somewhere cosy.

Children enjoy playing and being active from different heights. A baby might get pleasure from being in a swing, while a 7-year-old might like playing on top of a climbing frame.

The early years practitioner's role within the play environment

As an early years practitioner you will be extremely important in creating a play environment, ensuring that you help children gain in confidence, planning activities and supporting children during their play and exploration. You will also have a role in helping children to understand what they have been learning. There are a variety of ways to do this, including asking children questions, listening to their thoughts and encouraging them to share ideas. You will be responsible for meeting children needs, such as naps, food and drink, and providing children with emotional support.

How to encourage concentration and attention in children

The starting point for learning is attention and concentration. Children need to notice something in order to then concentrate on it. To help children concentrate, you need to make sure that an activity, equipment or experience is sufficiently interesting. Below are some key points to help you plan activities and experiences that help children to concentrate.

Timing

Everyone has various points in the day when they find it easier to concentrate than others. The same is true for children so you must consider the timing of activities and experiences – some will require greater levels of concentration than others and will need to be done when children are not tired. Babies and toddlers find it easier to concentrate after they have slept and when they are not hungry. In older children, concentration levels are often better first thing in the morning.

Think about it

Look at the following three activities. Which one of these will require greater levels of concentration from children?

1. Listening to a story
2. Finding hidden toys in the sand tray
3. Riding on the tricycles

Sensory activities

Activities and experiences that are **sensory** help concentration. This is particularly important to remember when planning activities for children under the age of 8 years. Babies' and toddlers' concentration improves when they can explore things using their mouth and hands. You could put out safe objects made of natural materials such as wood, metal and fabric, as these 'feel' good for children. This type of sensory activity is often known as heuristic play (see Unit 4, page 170).

For children aged 3 years onwards, water, sand, paint or other materials will ensure that their hands experience a variety of sensations. This is why children will often play for long periods in the sand tray. When planning activities, therefore, you should think about the feeling of materials. A 3-year-old will prefer to paint on a large piece of paper rather than write in pencil on a very small sheet just because it will feel better to make the larger movements.

⇧ **Activities and experiences that are sensory will help children to concentrate**

Jargon buster

Sensory Activities and experiences using materials such as sand, water and dough that stimulate the hands

Participation

Babies and children find it easier to learn when they are doing rather than watching or just listening. This is not only because they are likely to be using their hands (see sensory activities above) but also because they are physically likely to be more active. Activity helps children to keep alert, so you should avoid working in ways where children are sitting and listening. Interestingly, children will show you through their behaviour that they cannot concentrate in this way.

Interest and motivation

It is easier to concentrate when you are enjoying something and this is usually linked to how interesting you are finding it. Babies and children will show that they have preferences for particular toys, books and types of play activity. They will spend longer looking at or playing with something that they are interested in. On the other hand, they quickly lose interest in something that they do not enjoying doing. Finding out what babies, children and young people like doing is not difficult – you can observe them, put out choices and, of course, ask them!

Think about it

Do you find learning more enjoyable when you are doing something, such as group discussions and practical tasks, rather than just listening?

The skills children need to learn effectively

As children get older, they need to be able to take control of their learning. This is a process, but the way early years practitioners work with children and young people can make a difference.

Determination

In order to be able to learn effectively, you have to learn how to persevere. Young children learn this by choosing activities that challenge them slightly but are still enjoyable. This is why so much play in the early years is chosen by children themselves. The way that you praise and support children can also help them learn to persevere.

Tips for good practice

Helping children to persevere

→ Give children plenty of praise when they are persevering.

→ Offer to provide some advice or practical support, but do not take over the task.

→ For complex tasks, show the child how it can be broken down into smaller steps.

Reflection and evaluation

It is important to be able to evaluate what you have learned and, if you have experienced difficulties, to consider why this might be. Children can learn to evaluate what they have been doing if adults sensitively take an interest in what they are doing. This is why some early years approaches encourage a 'review' session with children at the end of sessions. It is also important that children are given support when their play is not working out as they had hoped or are encountering difficulties. You can then help children by exploring with them the cause of any difficulties, as the case study below shows.

Case study

Learning to feel independent

Harry is 6 years old. He is keen to make an electric circuit with a kit that he has been given. He wants to do it by himself, but his nanny realises that he is becoming frustrated. She asks him about the problem. Together they talk about what he had hoped to do and he shows her which parts he is struggling with. She suggests that they take a look at the instructions. They agree that the instructions are not clear and that the kit is designed for slightly older children. They jointly work out the solution to the problem and the nanny is careful to make sure that Harry is the one who finishes it off. Harry is pleased with himself.

1. Why was it important for the nanny to guide Harry rather than do the kit for him?
2. Why was it important for Harry to finish the kit?
3. What skills has Harry learned?

The Features Page:

Focus on *Learning using sensory materials*

Sand, water and dough are found in nearly every early years setting. They are useful materials to use with children because they can provide plenty of learning. So why are they so popular and what exactly can you do with them?

Q I want to put water into the sand tray, but my placement supervisor says that it will smell after a while.

A Your placement supervisor is right – wet sand takes an age to dry if it is in a sand tray and can become very smelly. However, wet sand also provides many new opportunities for children. Fortunately, there is a way of solving this problem. You can put sand into smaller containers so that when water is added, it will dry out more quickly. This also means that you can take the sand outside for children to play with. A good activity is to allow the children to put the water into the trays – ideally, make sure each child has their own tray so they can see what happens as they add water. Put out small teaspoons and beakers so that children can make sandcastles.

Q The children at my setting seem to be bored with the sand and water.

A Sand and water are exciting materials, but if the same toys and equipment are put out with them, they can lose their fascination. It may therefore be a good idea to think about new items to put in the sand or water tray and to make sure that you rotate your existing toys. This is especially important for the older children in the setting, who may have spent many hours in the sand or water tray. Interestingly, children quite like finding unusual things in the sand or water tray. Try filling some rubber gloves with water and freezing them so that 'ice hands' can then be put into the water

Q There is one child in my nursery who does not like the feel of sand or dough. What can I do to help him?

A Some children don't like 'messy' activities. It is worth remembering that children do have more sensitive hands than adults and this can make sensory activities an uncomfortable experience for some children. You can help them by putting the sand or dough into clear plastic bags. This means that they get some of the feel of the material and their hands can get used to it. Gradually, you can reduce the thickness of the plastic bag. You can also provide water bowls or wipes so that children know they can wipe their hands when they want to.

Ask the expert

Learning using sensory materials

My story

Nick, nursery nurse

At our nursery we make sure that there are at least eight different sensory materials out for the children. We have found that it makes a fantastic difference as the children seem to concentrate for longer. We rotate what is out so that when children come in there are some old favourites as well as some new materials. One thing that really works is to put out some small world toys such as farm animals with the sensory material. I think our best activity so far was to put a piece of turf with the toy dinosaurs. The children had great fun watering the turf and even cutting it with scissors.

Top Tips:

Ideas for sensory materials

- ✓ Shredded paper
- ✓ Hay or straw (not suitable if dusty)
- ✓ Turf
- ✓ Dough
- ✓ Fish gravel
- ✓ Bark chippings
- ✓ Shaving foam
- ✓ Cornflour and water (gloop)
- ✓ Soap flakes and warm water
- ✓ Jelly (use vegetarian jelly)

Word search

Can you find the 10 items that could be hidden in a sand tray in the word search below?
The missing words are:

- Bottles
- Buttons
- Cars
- Coins
- Dinosaurs
- Magnets
- Ribbons
- Shells
- Teaspoons
- Pine cones

B	N	S	N	O	B	B	I	R	D	M	A	P
J	U	Y	R	P	O	E	W	H	F	S	I	M
R	Q	F	D	U	G	I	D	U	F	N	H	T
S	T	E	N	G	A	M	W	E	E	L	K	G
A	S	T	Y	Z	X	S	J	C	O	I	N	S
S	N	O	T	T	U	B	O	S	T	Y	P	H
E	R	T	S	Q	W	N	P	N	K	E	K	E
L	E	H	F	A	E	E	P	O	I	A	R	L
T	U	D	L	S	L	W	U	H	J	D	W	L
Q	G	M	S	J	R	I	T	F	D	S	Q	S
O	X	D	G	T	E	A	S	P	O	O	N	S
B	F	B	V	R	I	O	C	Y	U	O	M	I

Making connections and using memory

In order to learn effectively, it is important to link new information to existing information. This skill develops with age but requires that children have had plenty of opportunities to learn how to make connections. The way that activities are organised and the way in which you work with children can help this.

The conversation below shows how an early years practitioner helps a young child to make a connection between a new piece of information and a piece of information that the child already has.

> *Child:* Look at that cat. There. That's a black cat!
>
> *Adult:* Yes, that's a lovely black cat. He looks a little like your cat at home, doesn't he?
>
> *Child:* Yes, like Sammy. Sammy's black, too!

Back to the real world

You should now understand ways in which children learn and how children's thinking changes as they develop. You should also know why it is important that children play and how this supports their cognitive development.

1. Explain why a 4-year-old might need to touch objects in order to add them up, but an older child can do number sums in their head.

2. Describe some of the factors that will influence cognitive development.

3. Explain what is meant by active learning and why this is important.

Section 3

The role of the adult in supporting children's learning from birth to age 16 years

In the real world

You have just started placement in a pre-school. The pre-school leader talks about the importance of the learning environment and mentions that they provide a balance between adult-directed and child-initiated activities. You are not sure what she means by this.

By the end of this section you will understand the role of the adult in supporting children's learning.

How to provide an environment that supports and encourages children's learning

In Unit 7 you looked at the importance of creating an environment which is comfortable and attractive and in which children feel safe (see pages 248–50). In order to complete your learning for this unit, you will need to re read these pages. In this section you will look at some of the key elements of a learning environment for children.

A good learning environment should be attractive and have varied elements. In most settings with young children, this will include an indoor area as well as an outdoor space. Many settings organise their layouts so that different play and activities can take place, to allow children to gain different opportunities and types of learning through play. Below are some examples of the type of areas that you are likely to see.

Writing, mark making and drawing

Most settings will encourage children to draw, write and paint. Many settings will have areas and tables for this, although children may draw and write in other places, too. Look out for whiteboards, blackboards and chalks as well as painting easels.

Literacy areas

To encourage children to enjoy reading, many settings will have areas where there are books, story tapes or story sacks. Some settings also have outdoor story telling areas where children can gather to tell stories or listen to them.

Science and technology

Many settings will have toys and equipment that will encourage children to learn about computer or remote-controlled toys as well as about their environment. In some settings, specific activities will be put out for children to explore, for example a wind box or a rain box.

Role play and 'small world' area

Role play and 'small world' toys such as trains help children not only to use language but also to practice their social skills. Most settings will encourage this imaginative play by making sure that children have access to a role play area, dressing-up props and 'small world' toys.

Sensory materials

Sensory materials are in some ways the backbone in early years. Children learn from experimenting with their textures and properties. Many sensory materials are found both in and out of doors. Look out for sand, water, mud and dough play. Many settings will plan activities based on these and other materials.

Construction areas

Children enjoy making things and working out how things fit together. A good learning environment will provide opportunities for children to use bricks, Lego and other equipment to construct large and small models, shapes and structures.

Physical areas

It is well known that physical exercise is important to children's health, but physical movement is also important to their learning. A good learning environment should be planned to give children space in which to run about and make a range of movements. In many settings, this will be provided outdoors, and settings are likely to have a range of equipment such as a climbing frame, tricycles and balancing beams and small equipment, for example balls, hoops and even everyday materials such as cardboard boxes.

⇧ **This soft play area in a setting provides children with the space to try out a range of movements**

Creating the right emotional environment

While the physical layout, resources and environment are important, so, too, is the emotional environment. This is about the way in which children feel confident enough to explore, try out new things and use their initiative. A good environment is therefore one in which children do not feel constrained or worried about making a mess or getting things wrong. This is essential as children need to feel relaxed in order to learn effectively. They must also feel that adults are giving them permission to try out different things. The case study below shows what might happen if children do not feel this.

Case study

Taking over an activity

A new member of staff has noticed that the 4-year-olds are not very good at playing creatively. She decides to plan an activity that should help them learn to make decisions and explore new materials. In the outdoor area, she puts out some cardboard boxes and fabric and asks the children if they would like to make a den or house. The children start to get quite excited and begin to use the things. Another member of staff comes over and tells the children that they are being too noisy. She also tells them that they are making a mess and starts to show them exactly how to build a den. The children look a little discouraged and gradually just stand and watch her.

1. Why would it have been best for the children to make the den by themselves?
2. Why might the children learn to stand back rather than to take the initiative?
3. Why is it important for children to be given opportunities to explore and do things for themselves?

The different learning opportunities in everyday situations and daily routines

While the environment can play a significant part in children's learning, so, too, can everyday situations and daily routines. You will need to recognise the importance of these and think about how you can best use them to help children learn. The spider diagram below gives some everyday opportunities for learning.

The chart below shows how everyday situations such as getting dressed or helping to tidy away may help children's overall development.

☝ **How everyday situations and routines encourage children's development**

Development	How development is encouraged
Physical	Many everyday situations and routines require physical skills. Getting dressed, feeding and tidying up will all encourage children to develop physical skills.
Cognitive	Some everyday situations can help children explore concepts such as number, weight or size. A pre-school child might be encouraged to count the buttons on a coat as each one is done up, while an older child might have to read instructions in order to prepare a simple snack. Babies, too, can learn from everyday situations as they may, for example, start to recognise when it is meal time or when it is time for a nappy change.
Language	Many everyday situations and routines involve an adult in some way. This time can be spent in chatting to children and developing their vocabulary. An adult might talk to an older child about how they are getting on at school while waiting for some pasta to cook.

Development	How development is encouraged
Emotional	By being involved and encouraged to help out, children gain confidence and a sense of independence. This can make them feel competent. In young children this can avoid feelings of powerlessness and frustration.
Social	Many everyday situations require children to work together or with an adult. This can help children to learn the skills of cooperation.

Below is an example of how an everyday situation can be a learning experience for children of different ages.

👇 **How meal and snack times can be a learning experience for children of different ages**

Development	How development is encouraged
Babies	Babies enjoy being fed and learn language as well as social skills from the extra attention that their key worker should be giving them. Babies are also stimulated by being given a range of different foods and this can help them learn about textures and tastes.
Toddlers	Toddlers may learn fine motor skills by trying to feed themselves with a spoon and then a spoon and fork together.
Pre-school children	Pre-school children can use their developing fine motor skills to feed themselves using a knife and fork or other equipment such as chopsticks. You should also be looking at ways to help them enjoy the company of others at meal times. It is good practice to encourage children to pour their own drinks and serve themselves. You can also integrate meal and snack times with cooking activities so that children learn about how food is cooked and prepared.
Older children	Snack and meal times can be used to explore a wide variety of foods and the concept of healthy eating. Adults should involve older children in the preparation and choice of foods. Meal and snack times are good opportunities for older children to socialise.

Learning through role modelling

In the previous section, you saw that children can learn by observing an adult's actions and then attempting to imitate them. This means that children of all ages will be able to learn from you during everyday situations. A baby, for example, may try to imitate the way in which you use the spoon to feed them, while a 8-year-old may notice and copy the way in which you encourage others to take turns.

Some key ways in which children will learn by being alongside adults are:

→ *Practical skills* – Children are able to learn by watching adults modelling practical skills. They may also become motivated to try out some of the skills they have seen adults perform.

→ *Attitudes* – Children learn about people's attitudes by watching adults. They may, for example, notice how the pencil is held when adults write or how they turn pages as they read. Young people also learn about attitudes and values by watching adults' reactions in different situations.

Behaviours towards others

Children also learn about codes of behaviour from adults. They may notice when you show patience in a situation, you greet someone or are respectful towards others. With older children, you may explain your action alongside role modelling behaviours.

The different types of activities that meet the diverse needs of children from birth to 16 years

In England, settings working with children from birth to 5 years must make sure that they are delivering the Early Years Foundation Stage curriculum and that children are working towards the Early Learning Goals that are set out in the document. In order to support learning, most settings will plan activities or provide materials for children to explore. The terms adult-directed, child-initiated, structured and spontaneous are often used when planning activities. You will need to have an understanding of what these different terms mean.

Adult-directed activities

Some activities are adult-directed, which means that the adult will take the lead and literally 'direct' the children as they learn. Adult-directed activities can be very useful in helping children to acquire skills or knowledge. A good example of an adult-directed activity might be where an adult does a cooking activity with a pair of 4-year-olds. The adult might show the children how to cut cheese with a knife or how to wash salad and use the salad spinner.

For adult-directed activities to work, it is important that children's interests are thought about and that the activity closely links to their stage and age of development. Many adult-directed activities are also short and quite focused. They may be used as a starting point so that children can learn a skill and then use it in their own way, as the case study below shows.

Think about it

Think of an everyday situation or part of a routine. Make a list of the benefits for children of their being involved in this

⇦ **A cooking activity is a good example of an adult-directed activity**

Planning an activity based on an interest

Jessica is interested in writing her name. She has already started to make some of the shapes in her name, but her key worker notices that she is getting into the habit of incorrectly forming the letter 'a'. She decides to plan an activity so that Jessica can learn to form the letter 'a'. The activity involves using a teddy bear because Jessica is very fond of teddies and cuddly animals. The key worker asks Jessica if she could come and look at what teddy is doing today. She explains that teddy is playing a painting game and that he is trying to make the letter 'a' shape. She shows Jessica how to make a letter 'a' using a large paintbrush on a sheet of paper. Jessica asks if she can have a go as well. Jessica loves making the 'a' shape and asks if she can carry on doing it by herself with teddy.

1. Why was it important for the key worker to think about Jessica's interests?
2. Would Jessica learn how to form the 'a' shape without the adult's support?
3. Why is it important that Jessica is given time to practise by herself?

Limitations of adult-directed activities

While adult-directed activities are valuable, it is important to recognise that they have limitations if not used properly.

Children may become bored and frustrated

Some adult-directed activities can be frustrating and boring for children if the adult does not encourage children to be active or the activity is not participative. This means that activities where children just watch or listen to an adult tend not be very effective.

Children may not concentrate

Adult activities only work well if they are pitched at the right level for children. If the adult chooses an activity that it is not challenging or is too difficult, children will quickly lose concentration. Where children choose play opportunities or learning experiences for themselves, they are more likely to persevere and concentrate. This means that if you are planning an adult directed activity, you will need to be sure that the activity is interesting and think about how children can be active during it.

Children may not develop thinking skills

Adult-directed activities, if not carefully thought out, can prevent children from developing confidence in their own abilities and thinking skills. This is because the adult may have done all the 'thinking' beforehand so that the child just has to follow instructions, as the case study below shows.

U10
3

389

Case study

When an adult-directed activity goes wrong

Michael has planned a card-making session with the children. He has cut out the shapes and worked out the design for the cards. He tells the children to come and sit down. He explains what they have to do to make the card. The children are told what to use. One of the children starts to do something a little differently. Michael takes the card off them and tells the child that they must do it properly. Another child is finding it hard to colour in the shapes and asks Michael to do it. Some of the children start to become bored and two of them ask if they can leave the activity. Michael complains afterwards to his placement supervisor that the children do not know how to concentrate and listen.

1. Why is this adult-directed activity not working?
2. Make suggestions as to how the activity could have been improved.
3. Why are the children not concentrating on this activity?

Child-initiated activities

Child-initiated activities, sometimes known as **free play**, are those where children choose what to play with. These activities have many benefits for children's learning. Firstly, children tend to concentrate and persevere for long periods when they are 'in control' of their learning. Their levels of motivation are higher because they have chosen something that appeals to them.

Opportunities for child-initiated play can vary according to the setting and the age of children. In some settings, children choose the equipment, games and toys to take out and so are actually planning their play. In other settings, adults may have already put things out for children to play with so that there are some starting points for children's play. For example, children may go into the outdoor space and see that there are some tricycles, shopping baskets and dressing-up clothes and these help them to think about the type of game that they want to play.

The role of the adult

In child-initiated activities, the children should be taking the lead with the adult in some ways acting as a follower! This means that a baby or toddler may show you that you are to be a play partner, while a 7-year-old may ask if you can fix something to the wall for them. The adult therefore has to be quite skilled at learning when to intervene and when to step back and observe the children and their play.

Limitations of child-initiated play

As with adult-directed activities, child-initiated play has some limitations, although this can depend on how it is being provided.

Jargon buster

Free play Opportunities for children to choose their own play

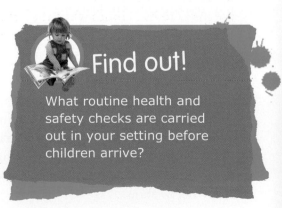

Find out!

What routine health and safety checks are carried out in your setting before children arrive?

Some skills such as learning to read, writing their name or counting require some adult input. Through child-initiated play alone, children may not choose to do activities that will help them gain these skills. Some children may also constantly stay with one type of play activity and never try another, such as only playing in the sand tray and never choosing to paint and draw. This would mean that they would gain limited skills or understanding, although in reality this scenario is quite rare.

Structured play and activities

As well as looking at the role of adults in activities, there can be a difference in the types of play and activities themselves. Some play and activities are likely to be more structured. This means that there is a clear way of doing or using them. A good example of this might be where children are playing a game of picture lotto. As this game has rules, it is a structured type of play activity. Children may choose to leave the game, but the play itself has a clear structure to it.

Spontaneous play and activities

The term spontaneous is used to describe play, activities and learning that are unplanned. A child might accidentally drop a table-tennis ball and discover that it bounces. This might become the start of a new game. In the same way, an adult might be reading a story when it suddenly starts to hail. The children are fascinated by the sound of the hailstones and the adult decides to take the children outdoors so that they can touch and feel them. The adult encourages the children to feel how hard they are and helps them to realise that they are small balls of ice.

The importance of providing a balanced of activities

You have seen that each type of activity has both advantages and disadvantages. This means that most settings try to organise a balance of different activities and styles. Children are likely to have times when they are being shown or led in an activity by an adult; at other times they will be free to design their own activities and play in their own way.

⇨ **It is vital that practitioners allow for spontaneous play and activities**

The principles of effective communication when supporting children's learning

Adults working with children need effective communication skills. In Unit 5, pages 181–4, you saw some of the components of effective communication, including listening, body language and facial expression. In order to complete this unit, you will need to re-read these pages, as well as look at the specific ways below in which you might use communication to support children's learning.

Running commentary

Babies and young children learn language by hearing adults talk and comment about things. An adult might talk to a baby about the food on the plate while the baby is being fed. **Running commentary** is very important when caring for babies and toddlers as it helps them to hear the sounds and expressions in a language. Running commentary is usually punctuated by smiles and pointing out things to the child. In the conversation below, the adult is giving the baby a running commentary as they put the baby into a highchair.

Adult: Right, its time to get your bib on, isn't it? It's your favourite bib today! Look, here's Peter Rabbit coming to find you. Let's get you into your highchair. One leg, now the other. Good boy! That's you in now. Let's find that strap. We need to get that strap on you so that you don't fall out. We don't want you falling out, do we?

Using questions

One of the ways in which you can support children's learning is by using questions effectively. With a baby or toddler, you may draw their attention to something by using a question such as 'What's this?' This helps the baby or toddler to notice something and learn the word for it. As a child's language develops, you are likely to need to name the item, as the conversation below shows.

Adult: Look what I can see (pointing to a toy rabbit on a shelf). What's that?

Toddler: Rabbeee

Adult: That's right. It's your rabbit.

Toddler: Rabbeee

Adult: Shall we get rabbit down to see you?

With an older child, the style of questions changes as children need to be encouraged to think and reflect. Questions are often a good way to help children break a task down so that they can complete it by themselves but with some help. The conversation below shows how an adult helps a 5-year-old to work out a mathematical problem. Look at how the adult is helping the child to structure the task.

Think about it

You are working with 4-year-olds. Which of these activities is likely to be adult-directed?

→ Playing in the sand tray
→ Playing a game of snap
→ Making fruit salad
→ Playing in the role play area
→ Sharing a book

Jargon buster

Running commentary
When an adult talks aloud, describing his or her actions and thoughts so that a baby hears language

Adult:	What do you need to do first of all here?
Child:	I need to count how many carrots there are.
Adult:	That's right. Start off by counting how many carrots there are.
Child:	1, 2 … 15, 16. Sixteen!
Adult:	What can you do so that you don't forget that there are 16?
Child:	I can write that number down.
Adult:	That's right. Can you see a space on the sheet to write it down?
Child:	Here. I am going to put 16 here.
Adult:	So what do you find out next?
Child:	I need to know how many rabbits there are.
Adult:	How could you do that?

Discussion

As children's language skills develop, adults should increasingly use discussion as a way of supporting their learning. You may, for example, encourage children to explain their thinking or give their opinions. It is important that you listen and encourage the child, so you should be careful not to do all the talking! Some children need time in order to think through their ideas – don't rush them. In group situations, all children should get a chance to express their ideas.

The importance of consulting the child when supporting children's learning from birth to 16 years

Learning is an active skill. Wherever possible, you will need to think about ways of helping children to be involved in their learning. One of the key ways is to listen to them and, with young children, to observe them. By consulting children you are more likely to provide activities and equipment that they are interested in and this will help their concentration. In some situations, children may be asked to do something they are not confident about or dislike, for example maths, but by talking to them you may be able to work out ways of making it more interesting. For example, you could turn the work into a quiz or a game.

With babies or children who do not yet have language, observation will be important. You will be able to learn about their interests from the way that they smile or are motivated to play, while with toddlers you will need to use a combination of observation and talking with them.

Case study

Involving a child in learning

Callum's school encourages the children to take home a book each night to help with their reading. Callum's childminder knows that Callum is finding reading a little difficult and is reluctant to spend time reading. She asks Callum about what kind of books he enjoys looking at. He tells her that he likes books with animals in them and that make him laugh. The childminder has a word with the teacher and at the end of the day, they show Callum a range of books. Callum chooses a book with a large, smiling monkey on the front cover. He is quite excited and as soon as they are home, he asks if they can look at it. Normally, they look at books at the kitchen table, but today the childminder asks Callum where he would like to sit. He says that he wants to look at the book on the sofa. Together, they look at the book and agree that they will take it in turns to read a page. Later on that afternoon, Callum picks up the book again and reads it aloud to himself.

1. How did the childminder find ways to consult Callum?
2. How has involving Callum helped his motivation to read?
3. Explain the importance of consulting with children.

How to support the development of skills for children to become effective learners

In the previous section you looked at some of the skills that would help children become effective learners. In this section you will look at ways in which adults can support children in their learning. The spider diagram below shows some of the skills that will help children become independent and effective learners.

Self-reliance and independence

Children need to be able to do things by themselves and learn how to organise themselves. You can help children become self-reliant by planning activities that help them to make choices and that they can achieve by themselves. Encouraging children to take responsibility for tasks such as dressing, feeding and tidying up can also develop self-reliance. It is important for children to have plenty of opportunities to choose their own play opportunities as this means that they have to think about what to use and how to organise their play.

Motivation

Children have to want to learn. You will therefore need to encourage children to be motivated. Role modelling plays an important part here. Children will, for example, be more interested in learning to read if they see adults reading. Sometimes adults might think about doing an activity so that children become interested in it.

You can also motivate children through praise and tangible rewards such as stickers, although it is always better that children are motivated because they themselves want to do an activity.

Confidence

Children need to have enough confidence to try out new activities. Some children are so concerned that they may not succeed or are not sure that they will be 'good' enough, that they do not actually take part. Confidence is something that develops over time and is usually boosted when children have had a lot of experience of success. This means that young children need to have experienced plenty of activities where they feel good about themselves and where they have succeeded.

As you saw in the previous section, it is useful for adults to talk to children about why they are finding an activity difficult and to help the child learn to reflect and evaluate their performance or the difficulty of the activity. This can prevent a child from simply deciding that 'I'm no good at it'.

Determination

In the previous section you saw that determination plays an important role in helping children to complete tasks. You can support children's determination by praising their efforts and making sure that when you offer help that you do not take the responsibility for the activity away from the child. For example, a child asks an adult to help them with a jigsaw. The adult does not finish the jigsaw puzzle, but instead talks the child through finding the right pieces so that it is the child in the end who completes the puzzle.

Find out!

Try sitting in your placement setting and doing an activity by yourself, for example drawing, filling in a form or playing cards. See how long it takes before a child comes over to you and shows an interest in what you are doing.

U10
3

Metacognition skills

Metacognition is a term used to describe the way in which you actively use your brain. To be an effective learner, you need to know how to use your brain to best effect, for example 'forcing' yourself to concentrate a little more on something that you know will be difficult. In the previous section you looked at the way in which children need to make connections between new and existing pieces of information. This is a metacognition skill. It is thought that adults can help children learn how to 'use' their brains by sharing their thinking processes with them.

Think about it

Look at the two sample conversations below

Conversation 1

Child: I've finished painting now.

Adult: Great! I've just got to think about where to put your painting to dry. I don't think that I can leave it here, because other children will want to paint. I was thinking about putting it on the table, but it might get splashed as it is a little close to the water tray. I know! I'll put it here on this table. It will dry quite quickly because it's close to the radiator.

Conversation 2

Child: I've finished painting now.

Adult: Great! I will just find somewhere to put it.

1. Which conversation will help the child's metacognition skills?

2. Explain what the child might learn as a result of this conversation?

3. Why is it important to 'think aloud' when working with young children?

Back to the real world

You should now understand what is meant by an adult-directed activity and some of the resources that might be included in a learning environment. You should also understand the role of the adult in helping children to learn.

1. Explain the difference between an adult-directed and a child-initiated activity.

2. Describe the importance of adults consulting with children.

3. Suggest ways in which an adult might encourage a child to become an independent learner.

In order to prepare for your assessment, you may like to see if you can answer the following questions:

1. Identify the frameworks that are used to support children under five years in the area where you live.

2. Outline the stages and sequence of children's cognitive development from 0–8 years.

3. Describe three factors that might affect a child's ability to learn.

4. Explain two ways that you can encourage a child to concentrate.

5. Describe the benefits of child-initiated activities.

Unit 11

Supporting children and families

In this unit you will learn:

1. The range of support available for children and families

2. How to build positive relationships with children and their families

3. The role of the adult when supporting children and their families in a social care setting

Section 1

The range of support available for children and families

In the real world

Your tutor has arranged a placement for you at a Children's Centre. You are not really sure what a Children's Centre does. Your tutor tells you that it is a jointly-funded centre.

By the end of this section you will know about the types of support that are available for children and their families.

The range of social care settings that provide support

Some children and their families will need extra support and services. All local authorities are legally obliged to compile a list of 'children in need' and to support them.

At the time of writing, the government is trying to make it easier for families to gain access to more support, as it is recognised that it is better to help families when their children are young rather than to wait. This means that the government has invested heavily in providing support for children under 5 years and their families. There are a range of different initiatives throughout the UK and you will need to know what is available in your area. The table below gives examples of support that are found in most areas. This support may be organised in different ways according to the area in which you live.

⊕ **The range of social care settings**

Setting	Support
Day care, crèches, after-school care and holiday clubs	Many areas will have care provided for families that need additional support. Early education can help young children reach their potential and can also support children with special educational needs and disabilities.
Respite care	Some families will need time away from their children in order to cope. For example, a family with a child with severe disabilities who requires round-the-clock care will need a weekend off. Respite care is sometimes offered by other families, but may also be residential.
Counselling	Some children and families need counselling in order to come to terms with things that have happened to them, for example domestic violence, persecution in another country and crime.
Parenting groups	Some parents find it difficult to cope with the role of being a parent. Parenting groups help them to work out how to manage their children's behaviour and support their education.
Supervised contact	Some parents may not be allowed to be alone with their children unless they are being supervised. This is often a condition of a court. Settings such as family centres will provide supervised contact.
Health services	Children and their families may need additional support such as speech and language therapy and advice about health conditions.

Places where support may take place

Family centres

Family centres work with families who need additional support. Most families will be referred to these centres by social workers, family doctors or other professionals.

Children's Centres

Children's Centres are the result of a government initiative known as Sure Start, which has been introduced in England. The idea is that children and their families can find a range of services coordinated in one place. Many Children's Centres provide day care as well as services such as parenting groups and health services. While many Children's Centres are placed in areas where there is some poverty, most of their services are open to all families in a local area.

The national and local support that is available for children and families

The type of service that is available varies from area to area. While the government passes laws about supporting families, it passes on the responsibility for how this is to be done to local authorities. This means that local authorities will look to see what is needed in each town and area. An area that has many families that do not speak English will therefore have some centres that will help the families to settle and learn English.

One criticism of the local approach is that it can be hard for families to know what is available. Some services can only be accessed through a family doctor's referral, while others are self-referred, which means that a family can seek help directly. The spider diagram below shows the different ways in which families might be able to gain support.

GP referral
The family's doctor might make a referral for support.

Drop in
Families might simply be able to arrive for a session.

Self-referral
Families might phone and make an appointment.

Social Services
A family's social worker might make a referral.

THE DIFFERENT WAYS IN WHICH FAMILIES MIGHT BE ABLE TO GAIN SUPPORT

School referral
A school might make a referral for a family.

Find out!

To find out what is available in your area, contact your local Children's Information Service. You can find out how to contact them by typing your local authority's name into an Internet search engine and then visiting their website.

1. Where is your nearest Children's Centre?
2. Is there a family centre in your area?

The range of statutory, private and voluntary organisations that support children and their families

Statutory settings

These are services that by law have to be provided for children and families. The role of the government is either directly to provide statutory services or to supervise them through government departments. Each government department is headed by a secretary of state who is responsible to Parliament. The prime minister chooses the secretaries of state from the members of parliament (MPs); they are normally in his or her political party. Secretaries of state are responsible for making sure that the statutory services are provided. They often do this by supervising the work of local authorities, health authorities and other organisations. Parliament can ask a secretary of state to explain if services are not provided, either by asking questions during parliamentary question time or by asking the secretary of state to appear in front of a selected committee.

The main services that families use are health, education and social services. Services and support are provided either directly through central government, for example social security is directly under government control, or through local authorities.

Education is a good example of a statutory service. By law, schools have to be provided for all children, although their size and the age range they cover is decided by local authorities.

Voluntary settings

Voluntary organisations have become more complex to understand. Originally, they were often charities which depended entirely on donations from the public in order to carry out their work. Traditionally, voluntary organisations were staffed predominately by volunteers. Today, the situation is more complex as many local authorities and other government-funded organisations will 'buy' their services. For example, the children's charity NCH is a registered charity whose aim is to prevent child abuse; as well as receiving funds from members and donors it also works for and receives funds from local authorities. The key point about voluntary settings is that they are not profit-making and any surplus income is used to further their activities.

 Find out!

Find out about the work of the following voluntary organisations:

➜ NCH, the children's charity (www.nch.org.uk)
➜ SCOPE (www.scope.org.uk)
➜ Home Start (www.home-start.org.uk)

The case study below describes a centre that is public funded but run by a voluntary organisation.

Case study

Providing respite care

Greenwood is a respite residential centre for children aged 3–19 years. Most of the children who attend the centre have complex learning difficulties and physical needs. Parents are referred to Greenwood via their social worker. Children who attend the centre are considered to be 'children in need'. Some children stay just for the day, others for a night or two and others for a couple of weeks. The amount of respite care is decided according to the needs of the children and their families. Families often use this time to rest, relax and do things that otherwise would be difficult for them. For some families, this means going shopping, swimming or having a meal out. Staff who work in the centre are fully qualified and understand their important role in supporting parents. The centre is funded by the local authority but run by a voluntary organisation.

1. Why might parents need some time away from their children?
2. Why is it important that respite care is arranged directly with families?
3. Do you know of similar centres in your area?

The range of challenges experienced by children and their families

There are many reasons why children and their families may need extra support. It is important here to recognise that not all families will want their circumstances to be known and so you may find that frequently you are not told about why a family is attending a centre. The table below shows some of the challenges that children and families may be experiencing.

⚓ Challenges faced by some children and their families

Cause	Affect on parents
Alcohol and substance misuse	Some parents may find it difficult to look after their children because they are addicted to alcohol or drugs.
Bereavement	Some families may be coping with a bereavement that means they need extra support and counselling.
Child protection issues	A family may be gaining support in order to prevent child abuse. Some family centres are responsible for providing a safe environment for supervised visits. Supervised visits means that a child can have contact with a parent, but with an adult present to ensure the child's safety.
Domestic violence	Some children and their families may be seeking support because of incidents of domestic violence. Some children and their parents may be living in a refuge.

Cause	Affect on parents
Preparation for adoption	Some children may be moving out of social care and into an adoptive family. The new parents may be gaining support and learning about their adopted child in a supportive atmosphere.
Mental illness	Some parents may not find their parenting role easy as they may be living with depression or have a mental illness that is affecting their ability to cope.
Learning or sensory disability affecting parenting	Some parents may have a learning disability or a sensory disability that means they or their children will need extra support.
Child's disability	Some children may have a disability that means the parents need extra support in order to cope or to help stimulate their child.

Back to the real world

You should now understand that some children and their families may need additional support. You should be aware of the role of Children's Centres and family centres.

1. Give three reasons why a family may need extra support.

2. Explain what the difference is between a statutory and a voluntary organisation.

3. Give an example of a social care setting in your area.

Section 2

How to build positive relationships with children and their families

In the real world

You are on placement at a family centre and you know that some of the parents are there because they have neglected or abused their children. You are not sure what you should say to them. You have been told that children sometimes show extreme behaviours because of their circumstances. You are feeling nervous.

By the end of this section you will understand the importance of building positive relationships with parents and children.

How to interact with and respond to children and their families

Working in settings where some children and families may have difficulties requires a very sensitive approach. While some parents are voluntarily attending the setting and are happy to receive support, in some situations, especially in a family centre, the parent may be there as a result of a court order. This means that you will need to be very professional in manner. You will be able to learn a great deal about how to interact with children and families by noticing how other members of staff work with them. You must also be ready to accept and ask for help from experienced members of staff.

Interacting with children

Some children may not always respond in the way that you would expect for a child of their age. It is important, therefore, to be ready to change your style and be flexible. Some children can be friendly and seek reassurance, while others may be more reserved and will need longer periods to settle in and get to know you. Many professionals find it helpful to use a puppet with children who are cautious as this can act as a way of breaking down potential barriers. When interacting with children, it is important that you understand the **child protection procedures** in the setting, especially regarding physical contact. Until you are qualified at Level 3, you should not be left alone with a child.

Interacting with parents

Parents will need to feel comfortable in a setting as this will help them to gain the support that they need. You should always acknowledge and greet parents and be ready to listen and help them. In some family centres you will need to find out how and when you should interact with parents as there are likely to be policies and reporting procedures in place.

Jargon buster

Child protection procedures Procedures that inform staff or volunteers what they should do in order to protect children from abuse or if they suspect that a child is being abused

How to allow children to express themselves to enable a supportive framework

All children need opportunities to express themselves. This is particularly important for children who, for a variety of reasons, may be frustrated, angry or frightened.

Play seems to be a key way to help children. You have seen in Units 4, 8 and 10 that play can provide a number of benefits for children. In settings that support families in need, play is often used to 'heal' children, and some settings provide a trained play therapist who will help children to talk about and literally 'play out' their feelings. Play seems to help children as they can re-enact what has happened to them in a safe environment. It can also act as a trigger for children to express their experiences. While your role is not to act as a play therapist, you can support children by making sure that there is a range of materials available to help them play.

The following materials seem to help children to express themselves so should be made available at the setting.

Paint and drawing materials

Some children find it helpful to show their anger, frustration or to recall what has happened to them by drawing and painting. In some settings, you might be asked to date and keep all samples of children's work so that their state of mind can be assessed.

Role play

Many children enjoy role play, but those who are in difficult situations may be helped to make sense of the world through role play. It can be disturbing to watch as some children will act out what they have seen or what has happened to them. You may sometimes be asked to observe and record this.

⇧ **Play therapists can help children to 'play out' and come to terms with difficult feelings**

It is important that there is a mixture of role-play opportunities so that children can take on realistic roles as well as superhero and fantasy roles. It is usual for settings to provide a home corner so that children can play out domestic scenes. Some children will also enjoy being in confined spaces as this can help them to feel secure.

Musical instruments

Singing and playing musical instruments can help children to express feelings of joy, frustration and anger. Some children may move between these states within a few minutes of each other. Music can also be used to help children feel at peace and part of a group.

'Small world' play

'Small world' play gives children the opportunity to create their own worlds and can empower them. This is important for children who need to think about what has happened to them or who wish to create a better world.

Sensory materials

Sensory materials such as sand, water and dough can help children to feel calm. Children often use these materials to build things up then later destroy them. The act of destruction can help children to feel more powerful, which is important if children have been victimised.

Physical play

Some children need to express their emotions by using their whole body. They may kick or throw a ball or want to punch a punch bag. It will be important to make sure that children can play quite vigorously to let out some violent emotions.

The importance of recognising and valuing the role of families in building relationships with children and families

One of the reasons why so much support is provided to children and their families is that all the research shows that children who grow up within their family do better than those growing up in residential or foster care. Taking children away from their family is therefore considered a last resort. This has meant that government policy looks at ways of helping children to stay with their family by supporting families in different ways.

Why are families so important?

Families give children their identity and emotional stability. Few, if any, families are 'perfect', but despite this, children are usually better off staying with family members. Remember that even parents who are not coping with their role or who are living with illness or addiction care about their children and love them. This love or 'attachment' (see Unit 2, page 96) is so powerful that it has a protective effect on children. Parents are also likely to be around throughout their child's life.

As well as parents, children benefit from staying with their siblings as these relationships are also likely to be life-long. In addition, families often consist of other relatives such as grandparents, aunts and uncles. Other family members can be important in giving a child a sense of identity and they usually have a strong attachment or interest in the child. In recognition of this, grandparents now have more rights to see their grandchildren, even if parents have split up.

Think about it

Can you remember a family member who was important to you as a child? Why did you enjoy being with him or her?

⇧ **There are many benefits to children living with their family**

How to share information when requested, in line with procedures

Parents will not only share information with you but may sometimes want it from you as well. The information you are able to provide will depend very much on your role within a setting. At the start of your placement or work in a setting, you should therefore make sure that you know what your role is. This means that you should always check with a member of staff or refer parents to a staff member unless the information required is fairly general and readily known. (For the lines of responsibility in most settings, see the chart in Unit 7, page 269.)

Where you work with families who are facing challenges, it is especially important to know what information you can and cannot provide. You may find that, as a learner, you are not told very much about the family's need in order to protect their confidentiality, in which case you will need to refer parents to a supervisor. In some situations, as the case study below shows, even information that seems quite ordinary can actually be very sensitive. If you do pass on information to parents in sensitive situations, you should always tell your supervisor what you have said.

Case study

The importance of maintaining confidentiality

Sarah and her mother are in a refuge for women. They are there because Sarah's father has repeatedly beaten her mother and has threatened to kill them both. Sarah's father has been allowed by the court to see her once a month on supervised visits to a family centre. Today, the father casually asks a junior member of staff if she knows which school Sarah will be going to next term so that he can buy her school uniform. She tells him the name of the school that Sarah will be attending. The father smiles.

1. How have Sarah and her mother been put in danger?
2. Why should the member of staff tell her supervisor about Sarah's father's question and her reply?
3. How could this situation have been avoided?

How to communicate with children and their families

The principles of how to communicate with children and their families remain the same as in other settings. You looked at these in depth in Unit 5, and you will therefore need to re-read pages 181–7 to refresh your memory.

While the principles remain the same, you may find some differences in the way that children and their families respond in situations where there has been a family trauma. For example, a child may take much more time to become comfortable and talk, while an adult may be reserved. On the other hand, the opposite may be true and a child might be desperate for reassurance and attention and a parent might have quite strong and angry feelings.

Most settings working with families experiencing challenges will provide training to help you communicate effectively and to learn how to respond in difficult situations. It will be important for you to observe experienced members of staff and consider how they are communicating effectively.

How to treat adults with courtesy and respect to enable positive relationships

All adults in a setting, regardless of their abilities as a parent, should be treated with the respect and courtesy to which everyone is entitled. Parents should be supported without feeling judged. The success of helping them is often linked to the relationships that they have with staff members. Showing respect and courtesy can help parents to trust staff and to value their help.

Showing respect and courtesy is about making sure that you do some simple things, as the spider diagram below shows.

Acknowledging
If you are not near enough to say hello when a parent arrives, make sure that you acknowledge them by smiling or nodding your head.

Using an appropriate tone of voice
The way that you talk to someone can show respect, so speak with some warmth to a parent.

Greeting
Say hello and goodbye to parents as they arrive and leave.

SHOWING COURTESY AND RESPECT

Making eye contact
Eye contact shows that you are listening to a person and recognising that they exist. To show respect, always make eye contact with a person as they are talking to you.

Listening properly
Show that you are listening to a parent by using some of the active listening skills that were covered in Unit 5 (see pages 181–3).

Saying please and thank you
These are traditional ways of showing respect. You should make sure that you use them when asking anything of or from a parent and in situations where you are given anything, e.g. 'Thank you for bringing the form in.'

411

Planning activities and experiences to meet the needs of individuals and their families

Depending on the different needs of families, a range of activities and experiences will be planned. Each service and setting is likely to have its own specialisms when working with families. This might mean that some settings work with children and parents together, for example arranging sessions when parents are encouraged to do activities with their children such as baking cakes. The aim of these type of sessions might be to give parents confidence in their parenting skills and to help them realise how important their role is, while it might also be about helping a parent and child to build a stronger relationship. Other settings might provide time for parents to be away from their child so that parents can explore their own feelings and needs.

As a member of staff, it is important to know what the purpose of activities and experiences are so that you can make sure that you adjust your role accordingly. For example, during supervised visits a staff member is likely to almost be an 'invisible' presence so that the child and their absent parent can spend time together.

Back to the real world

You should now understand the importance of building positive relationships and how it is important to be non-judgemental. You should know how you might help children to express their anger and feelings.

1. Give two ways in which children might be helped to express themselves.
2. Describe why it is important to treat adults with respect.
3. Explain why it is important for families to be given support.

The role of the adult when supporting children and their families in a social care setting

In the real world

You have just started working in a family centre in the nursery. A parent says that she would like the phone number of another parent so that their children can play together. You are not sure about whether you can provide this. You also know that there is team meeting planned for after the session. You are not sure who will attend.

By the end of this section you should understand the importance of confidentiality and know which other professionals may be involved in supporting children and their families.

The importance of working in a team and providing feedback to colleagues

In most social care settings, you will find that you are working alongside a range of different professionals. This is because many settings offer a wide range of services and may also need to support families in different ways.

The chart below shows some of the activities that one family centre offers. Referral to this family centre is via Social Services.

Example of services offered by a family centre

Service	Characteristics	Professionals who may be involved
Welfare rights advice	Provides information about benefits advice. Some centres will also give career advice and further training.	• Benfits counsellor • Careers adviser • Basic skills tutor
Parents' groups	Provides support for parents. Topics may include managing children's behaviour, communicating and playing with children.	• Family worker
Children's groups	Provides support for children from 5 years. Children are encouraged to share feelings and experiences as a group and gain support, e.g. a young carer's group for children who look after a disabled parent.	• Psychologist • Family worker • Social worker
Nursery	Provides a safe environment for children to play and learn.	• Nursery manager • Nursery assistants
After-school activities	Provides a safe environment for children to play after school.	• Play worker
Holiday play schemes	Provides a safe environment for children during holidays.	• Play worker
Work with individual children	Provides support for children who may have experienced trauma or who have other individual needs.	• Play therapist • Educational psychologist • Child psychiatrist
Individual work in the home	Provides support for families in their own home.	• Family worker
Family support sessions	Provides support for the family unit.	• Social worker • Child psychiatrist
Assessment	Provides assessment of a parent's ability to cope with their children. Assessment is also used for families seeking to adopt a child.	• Social worker

From the chart above, you can see that a wide range of professionals may be working in or come into the family centre to support children and their families. It is therefore essential that you have the skills necessary to work effectively in a team. Unit 6 looked at the importance of working in a team, and you will need to re-read pages 211–12 in order to complete your learning for this unit.

◁ As an early years practitioner, it is vital that you develop the skills necessary for effective team work

The importance of good communication skills

You will also require strong communication skills if you are to work well within a team. There are three elements to communicating:

1. *Courtesy and politeness* act as the oil in day-to-day situations. Always remember to say please and thank you, even if you are in a rush. Small things such as holding doors open and offering to carry things if someone is overloaded make the working environment more pleasant.

2. *Recognition* of what other people think or do is essential. No one in a team can manage alone, and recognising other people's contributions and expertise helps build good relationships. You should thank a member of the team who has helped you. Always listen to other people's points of view and respect them, even if you cannot share them.

3. *Explaining* your actions or your thoughts is part of day-to-day communication. You will receive more help from colleagues if you explain why you need equipment or why you disagree with an idea. Staff who do not take the time to explain tend to be thought of as arrogant or abrupt, although quite often this is not the case.

Following instructions

Experienced members of staff understand that one of their duties is to follow instructions. Sometimes they may disagree with them or may not like the task they have been given, but as long as it is a fair and reasonable request they will do it willingly. Staff who moan and try to get out of tasks will quickly find they are not considered for promotion. They will also find that other team members become irritated with them, especially if they have left a task unfinished.

U11
3

When you are given a task, make sure that you understand exactly what you need to do and when the task needs to be completed. If you are unsure about whether you are capable of carrying it out, you should voice your concerns straight away to your placement supervisor.

Gaining feedback

As a new member of staff, you will need to listen carefully to any feedback that you are given from other members of staff or your line manager. This is important because, in this way, you will be able to fit into the team more easily and carry out your role more effectively. Most people find that each setting has its own way of carrying out certain tasks, for example a setting might have a rota for washing staff mugs, while another might ask that staff wash their own. It is often through feedback from other staff that you will find out how to carry out some of these tasks and, by showing a willingness to listen and learn, you will fit into the team more smoothly.

Providing feedback to colleagues

In order to help children and their families, you will need to provide feedback to colleagues. This will help them to assess children's and families' progress and needs and they will use this information to plan. To do this effectively means that you will need to find out what type of feedback your colleagues want. In many settings, a team meeting is held after a session has finished or at the end of a week. Staff will then share information. Remember that all information shared between staff is confidential (see also page 420). Examples of feedback that you might pass on are shown in the spider diagram below.

Find out!

What type of feedback is shared between colleagues in your work placement or setting?

Comments that the child has made

The type of play activity that the child has chosen

A child's level of anxiety

A child's participation in activities

Observations that have been carried out on the child

FEEDBACK TO SHARE WITH COLLEAGUES

A child's progress in areas of development or particular skills

Drawings and paintings that the child has done

Incidents of unwanted behaviour and the situation that occurred

The importance of maintaining confidentiality

You have seen elsewhere that confidentiality is important when working with children and their families. During your work in a setting you are likely to learn a lot about children, families and the personal lives of staff members. This information is confidential. Breaching confidentiality is a serious issue – if you do this, you might be asked to leave your placement or even your work. Confidentiality means remembering that the information which you gain in a setting is not passed on to others unless there is a professional and important reason for doing so.

Outside of the setting

You should be extremely careful when you talk about your work or placement to friends, family members or other learners. Most of what you have learned in placement is likely to be confidential, so think before you speak! Some settings work in such a sensitive way that their address and phone number are confidential, so you should not reveal these. Remember that friends and family members may repeat something that you have said to someone else, not realising how sensitive the information is.

To parents in the setting

You should not pass on information to parents unless you are the child's key worker or you have checked first with your supervisor. You should be careful not to pass on any information about other children or families.

To staff in setting

Information about a child is generally shared with the child's key worker and the manager alone. This means that you should not talk about children and their families to other colleagues unless there is a particular reason why they should know. As a learner, you should always check first that you are able to pass on information.

To other professionals

No information about children and their families should be passed on to other professionals without your placement supervisor's or manager's authority. You must always check first before passing on any information.

Your role in supporting the individual needs of the child

When working with families in social care settings, it is important to understand that each family will have their own particular history. Also, families will often have very different needs and requirements in a setting. Staff working in social care settings therefore need to be flexible in their approach and to see each child and family as unique. You should not imagine that you 'know' about a family's needs because you have read about domestic violence, disability or adoption. While reading about the types of challenges that families face will provide you with some knowledge, you must not make assumptions about what these challenges will feel like or what the child and family personally will need.

Your personal role and responsibilities within the setting

If you are on placement or working in a social care setting, you are likely to find that you have your own role and responsibilities within the setting. For example, the chart at the start of this section (see page 414) showed how in one family centre, many professionals were working in their own ways with children and families.

Each practitioner is expected to keep up to date in their professional area and attend training courses, and will also have a clear area of responsibility. As a learner or a new member of staff working with children, you are likely to have a more experienced member of staff directing you. Therefore you will need to find out from him or her what your role is within the centre or area. You must also be careful not to exceed the level of your responsibility or to become involved in other people's areas of expertise, unless asked to do so. It is also essential that you learn to manage your time effectively.

Time management

A skill that you will need to learn is how to use your time effectively. It is easy to fall into the trap of blaming lack of time for tasks not being completed. In settings where everyone has a unique role, there may not be anyone else to fall back on.

When you have several tasks to do, try to consider which ones are absolutely essential and concentrate on those. Many people write lists so that when they have some free time they can do one of the tasks. It is also a good way of making sure that you focus on the time that you have. Ten minutes is not long but may be enough to complete a small task such as finding a particular piece of artwork that a child's social worker has asked to see.

Some people set themselves goals, for example 'By the end of today I will have finished the display and written three reports'. Goal setting can be useful because it divides the work into manageable tasks. Employees who find it difficult to use their time effectively are often wasting time by thinking, 'There's no point in starting this, as I won't be able to finish it.'

Find out!

Who works in your setting? How do they support children and their families? How does their role differ from yours?

How to deal with sensitive situations in a positive way

In some situations, parents may become confrontational or express anger, or other feelings such as distress. It is important that you know how to handle these situations with sensitivity. Most settings will offer some training for new staff as they will be aware of the type of situations that might occur in their setting. Below are some general points about dealing with sensitive situations, but if you are interested in working in a social care setting it will be worth seeking additional training about conflict management and assertiveness.

Anger

There are many reasons why a person may show anger. It is sometimes the result of stress and anxiety, particularly in situations where a person is feeling powerless and frustrated. Anger is sometimes a learned response as a person has used it before and found that being angry works.

If you find yourself in a situation where someone is angry, it is essential that you remain absolutely calm and show this in your body language and the way that you are communicating. You should keep your body relaxed and not raise your voice in response to theirs as this will only create more tension and will not help the situation. Sometimes anger can be diffused by reassuring the person that you are listening to what they are saying, especially if you recognise that the reason behind the anger is linked to the person feeling that they are not being taken seriously or respected. If a person feels that they are being listened to properly, the anger can often melt away. As a learner or a new member of staff, it is not your place to resolve an issue with the person and so it is essential that you are able to calmly say that you will need to refer them to someone else.

⇧ **As an early years practitioner, you will need to know how to deal with parents who feel angry or upset**

The Features Page:

Focus on *Confidentiality*

Confidentiality is one of those topics that keeps coming up. Knowing what you can say or write and to whom can be a bit of a minefield, so let's look at why confidentiality is so important and how you can be sure that you are getting it right.

Ask the expert

Q As a learner on placement, I find that parents often want to talk to me about what their child has been doing. It doesn't feel right to say that I can't talk about it.

A Your first step is to make sure that parents know that you are a learner and not in charge. If a parent asks you about what their child has been doing during the day, you can tell the parents about the type of activities that have been put out for all of the children as this is not top secret information. But what you should avoid doing is talking specifically about the child's progress. Try saying things such as 'Well, we have had the sand, water and tricycles outside, but as I am not Euan's key worker I am not sure exactly what he's been up to. Sarah will know. Would you like to talk to her?'

Q My mum and friends are interested in my work. What can I tell them about my day?

A It is really important to watch carefully what you say to friends, relatives and people that you meet. While they may not have a direct connection to any children or their families in a setting, the danger is that they in turn may talk to someone who does. This means that you need to talk only in general terms about what you have been doing and not be tempted to talk about specific children by name or in a way that might identify them. This means that is fine to say things such as 'My activity with the soap flakes went really well. The children were really excited, although it did get a little messy', but you would be breaching confidentiality if you were to say 'I did this one activity, but this boy, Marvin, kept on ruining it by throwing soap flakes on the floor.'

Q I am a key worker to five children. What am I allowed to say about the children to a learner who is coming on placement?

A The phrase 'need to know' is often used in relation to confidentiality. Obviously, the learner needs to know the children's names and ages, but not necessarily their exact birth dates and surnames. If a child has a particular need, you may also tell the learner about this if it will affect how the learner works with the child, but again avoid going into unnecessary details. For example, instead of saying 'Tom's behaving like this because his father has left his mother and she now has a new partner', you might say 'Tom is finding it difficult to adjust to some significant changes in his family.' The key is to remember that parents sometimes provide quite personal information assuming that it will stay confidential.

Maintaining confidentiality

Kerry, Nursery Nurse in a family centre

The children and their families we work with often have quite complex needs. With some children there are child protection issues, so you have to be really sensitive about what you say and to whom. We regularly have meetings as a team and everything that is discussed is always confidential. After a while, you quickly get a sense of how important it is that nothing is said outside of work. Sometimes if I have had a difficult day, my partner asks me about it, but I am really careful not to go into any details.

True or false?

Enter a tick or a cross in the boxes below to show whether you agree or disagree with the following statements about maintaining confidentiality.

True (✓) or False (✗)?

1. Learners can say hello to parents. ☐

2. Learners can tell their friends about individual children in the setting. ☐

3. Learners cannot give any information about individual children to the manager of the setting. ☐

4. Learners cannot tell their friends where they are working. ☐

Distress

In some situations you may find that stress and anxiety cause a person to become distressed. As with anger, you should stay calm in such situations. You will need to listen to a person who is distressed, but remember that as a learner or new member of staff you should aim as quickly as possible to refer them to a more experienced member of staff. However much you wish to help someone who is distressed, it is important not to give them false hope by promising something that is not possible.

Meeting someone again after a sensitive situation

You are often likely to meet someone again after they have shown anger or distress. This can be hard for both of you. By remaining friendly towards them you will show that you are a professional, and if they make an apology you should accept it and let them know that you are pleased that they are feeling better.

Case study

Dealing with anger

Darren is angry. He has been told to come to the family centre at 2pm to see his son. He has had to leave work early and has lost some pay to do so, and money is very tight. He arrives and is told that his son has chicken pox and that he cannot come to the centre. Darren is frustrated because he has been looking forward to this visit and he has not seen his son for nearly two months. He had bought some presents to give his son and has been thinking about this moment for a week. He is also cross because no one had rung him to let him know that the visit had been cancelled. He shouts at the member of staff who has told him that his son is not there.

The member of staff listens carefully to what Darren says and asks permission to write down his complaint so that it can be dealt with. The staff member also asks if Darren would like to meet with the centre manager. When Darren realises that he is being listened to, he starts to calm down, although he is still irritated. He apologises for his outburst and says that all he wants is to see his son. The staff member says that he understands and suggests that Darren sees the centre manager so that another visit can be arranged.

1. Why is Darren showing such anger?
2. Why is it important for the staff member to remain calm?
3. How has the staff member shown respect for Darren?

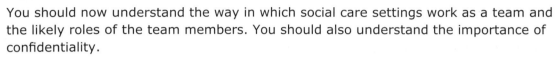
Back to the real world

You should now understand the way in which social care settings work as a team and the likely roles of the team members. You should also understand the importance of confidentiality.

1. Give an example of a piece of information that would be confidential.
2. List some of the other professionals that might be involved in supporting a family.

Getting ready for assessment

In order to prepare for your assessment, you may like to see if you can answer the following questions:

1. Identify three different types of provision that might support children and their families.
2. Outline some of the challenges that some families may face.
3. Describe two activities that help children to express their feelings.
4. Outline three strategies or skills that might be used to communicate with children and their families.
5. Explain the importance of maintaining confidentiality.

U11

3

Index

linking to ages and stages of development 45–8, 131–2

managing 13, 132, 134, 135, 137–9

supporting positive 129, 142

theories of 133, 136–8

unwanted behaviour 139, 140

behaviourist theories of learning 136, 370–1

bibliographies 25

biting behaviour 134

Bobo doll experiment 369

body language 37, 183–5, 236, 237–8

bottle feeding 74–7

boundaries, setting 137–8

bowel and bladder actions, babies 91

Bowlby, John 96

brain growth 372–3

breastfeeding 74

British sign language 349

bullying 141

C

car safety 119

care needs of children 64–5

food and drink 66–81

personal hygiene 81–8

sleep and rest 65–6

toileting 88–91

see also health and safety

career progression 202–5

changes experienced by children 99

effects on behaviour 130

helping children cope with 105

see also transitions

child-centred learning 149

child-initiated activities 177, 390

child protection

abuse, identifying and dealing with 123–6

and confidentiality 122

legal frameworks 277–8

policies and procedures 12–13, 122, 407

role of multi-agency work 280–1

safe working practices 117–18

childcare settings 3–4

Children Act (1989) 122, 284

Children Act (2004) 277

Children's Centres 401–2

children's development, factors influencing 59–62

cleanliness see hygiene

clothing

for babies 92–3

for children 256, 257

for work 8–9, 213

codes of practice 333–4

coeliac disease 72, 80

cognitive development 39–41

and brain growth 372–3

stages and sequence of 371–2

see also learning

comfort objects 97–8, 99

commitment, showing 214

Common Assessment Framework 277–8

communication skills 181

building positive relationships 235–9

children learning 36–7

and confidentiality 188–9

in difficult situations 410–11

and learning 392–3

listening skills 181–2

non-judgemental approach 187–8

non-verbal communication 183–6

with other professionals 188

with parents 271

paying attention 182–3

special methods of communicating 348–9

in team working 415

using sensitive questioning 186–7

written information 185–6

concentration, ways of encouraging 377–8

confidence

aiding learning 395

in physical skills 311–12

confidentiality 16, 188–9, 247, 268, 417, 420–1

and child abuse 122

sharing information with families 268–9, 410

when observing children 52, 219, 222

conflict management, strategies for 138–9

consistency, importance of 136, 138

coordination and balance 32

cot deaths, preventing 66

courtesy, showing 411

creative play 157–60

cross-infection 81–2

cultural differences

child rearing 61–2

dietary customs 72–3

in toileting 91

valuing 292

D

destructive behaviour, dealing with 140

determination 379, 395

diet

balanced diet 67, 69

and brain development 375

of different cultures 72–3

special diets 80

see also food and drink

Moving on to Level 3?

Get the next book to take you all the way!

- Taking you through **all** mandatory and a **range** of popular optional units at Level 3, this Student Book provides you with complete support for the new CACHE Level 3 Child Care and Education qualification.

- The easy-to-use textbook has an eye-catching page layout designed for maximum ease of use and an extensive, user-friendly index help you find just what you're looking for.

- Case studies, activities and photos help you to apply your learning, develop professional skills and become a reflective practitioner.

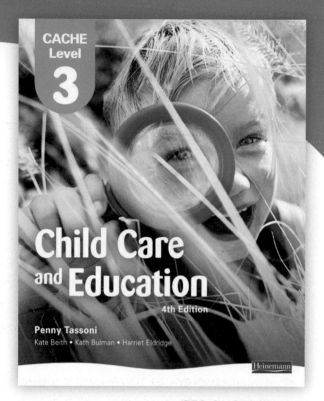

CACHE Level 3

Child Care and Education
4th Edition

Penny Tassoni
Kate Beith • Kath Bulman • Harriet Eldridge

Heinemann

978 0 435987 42 8

Get your copy today from your local bookshop, or order direct from Heinemann using the contact details below.

www.heinemann.co.uk/childcare

Simply contact our Customer Services Department for more details:

 (t) 01865 888118   (f) 01865 314029   (e) myorders@pearson.com   (w) www.heinemann.co.uk

 Heinemann

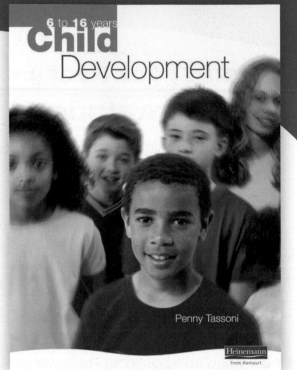

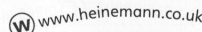

N025

Professional Development Series

new!

Books to last you a lifetime!

From your first year of studying, through placements and right on into the workplace, this series of handbooks provides you with in-depth information on key areas of childcare and education that will get you through your assignments and support you in your career.

Inclusion, Equality and Diversity in new! working with children

- Explains, in a sensitive and easy-to-follow way, how to turn good intentions into effective anti-discriminatory practice when working with children of all ages.

  978 0 435402 40 2

Understanding Early Years Theory in Practice

- Features all the major theorists and theories covered in early years courses, with tips on where to find out more.

  978 0 435402 13 6

Working with Babies & Children under Three

- Links the theory and practice of working with children under three years to help you be more professional.

  978 0 435987 31 2

Planning Play and the Early Years, 2nd edition

- This popular best-seller is ideal for gaining deeper understanding of children's play and helps you plan successful, curriculum-based activities.

  978 0 435401 19 1

How to Observe Children

- Gives practical guidance on the different techniques for effective child observation and helps you evaluate your observations.

  978 0 435401 86 3

Protecting Children

- Informs on the latest legislation and guidelines in child protection and explains the Assessment Framework and child protection procedures.

  978 0 435456 79 5

Managing Children's Behaviour

- Covers the theory and practice of behaviour support from birth to adolescence and provides strategies for empowering children using Individual Educational Plans.

  978 0 435455 32 3

Supporting Special Needs

- A comprehensive guide to policies and best practice in the area of special needs.

  978 0 435401 62 7

Planning for the Foundation Stage

- Packed with ready-made ideas showing how to plan a curriculum successfully, including advice on how to differentiate activities to meet the individual needs of children.

  978 0 435401 67 2

Baby and Child Health

- Practical advice on promoting and maintaining health in babies and young children.

  978 0 435401 51 1

Research Methods in Health, Care and Early Years

- Presents in-depth information on research methods for all early years and care courses.

  978 0 435401 68 9